"[LINDSAY] CAN DO IT ALL—
cat-and-mouse plotting, deliciously nasty Bureau by-play, sharp domestic vignettes, dozens of sparkling anecdotes—with as much panache as his beleaguered, irresistible hero."
                    —*Kirkus Reviews* (starred review)

"Devlin entered the fiction scene in Lindsay's superb first novel, *Witness to the Truth*. That novel was very good. GENTKILL is even better."
                    —Associated Press

"Lindsay keeps you guessing right to the end of this first-rate thriller."
                    —*The Providence Sunday Journal*

"Paul Lindsay writes like a house afire!"
                    —DAVID MAMET

"Because this novel's author spent twenty years as an FBI agent in Detroit, there's a ring of authenticity to his writing."
                    —*Wilmington Sunday News Journal*

"Entertaining . . . Paul Lindsay makes his material ring utterly true."
                    —*Booklist*

By Paul Lindsay
Published by Fawcett Books:

WITNESS TO THE TRUTH
CODE NAME: GENTKILL

CODE NAME: GENTKILL

A NOVEL OF THE FBI

Paul Lindsay

FAWCETT GOLD MEDAL • NEW YORK

A Fawcett Gold Medal Book
Published by Ballantine Books
Copyright © 1995 by Paul Lindsay
Excerpt from *Witness to the Truth* copyright © 1992 by Paul Lindsay

http://www.randomhouse.com

Library of Congress Catalog Card Number: 95-96172

ISBN 0-449-14902-1

This edition published by arrangement with Villard Books, a division of Random House, Inc. Villard Books is a registered trademark of Random House, Inc.

Manufactured in the United States of America

First Ballantine Books Edition: August 1996

10 9 8 7 6 5 4 3 2

*In memory of my mother, Shirley,
and my father-in-law, Frank Capodice*

There is no such thing as justice—in or out of court.
—CLARENCE DARROW

III CHAPTER 1 III

Although the idea was contrary to everything he believed his life stood for, John Lawson, thinking of his family, disregarded the pride he had carefully gathered over his forty-two years and begged for his life. "Don't do this to my wife and kids." Even the looming bully of death could not make him plead for himself, because unscheduled death had been a lingering consideration for the last fifteen years; it was part of what an FBI agent was paid for.

Through the openings that had once been windows and doors, hot summer sunlight gushed violently into the forgotten Detroit factory, interrupting the darkness with angled passages of blazing light, reducing the agent's taut, graceful face to black and white planes more handsome than that of a silent-film star. He looked back beyond the muzzle of the gun pointed at the middle of his face, and into the irrevocable eyes of the man who condemned him. "You are only the first," the answer came methodically. Lawson recognized the meter of the voice: There would be no commutation of his sentence.

Water dripped somewhere, eternally, desperately touching Lawson with an illogical hope for survival. But as he timed its coded message, the cadence seemed to slow like the last tentative grains in a foreboding hourglass. Unexpectedly, he thought of his twelve-year-old son, two days before, hitting baseballs, disrespectfully pounding his father's best curveballs over the two-hundred-foot sign that hung indignantly at the

1

limit of the fence. Once your son is able to hit a curveball, he
reasoned, there is not much you can change in him.

Then he thought of the other FBI agents this sociopath was
promising to kill, and once again felt the anger that injustice's
thriving course had always caused in him. But the only thing
he could dictate now were the terms of his own death. His life
would be taken, but not his dignity. He charged the gunman.

The weapon roared its terrible dirge twice. John Thomas
Lawson—husband, father, FBI agent—never heard the second
shot.

It was supposed to have been perfect. The plan, the target, the
money. The money, $5 million, was literally a drop in Sea-
card's corporate bucket. But, as the extortionist was about to
discover, perfection was frequently humbled by chance.

A small bomb, the formal pronouncement of the extortion,
was scheduled to detonate at midnight, a time chosen to maxi-
mize its chaotic effect. Sitting on the roof of the Seacard Hospital for Children in Ann Arbor, Michigan, the bomb would
explode primarily in an upward cone, causing only enough
damage to illustrate the extortionist's capability and commitment. Because of the children, there would be an emotional
overreaction. The extortionist was counting on it.

As a practical matter, the bomb maker had appended a small
booby-trap mechanism, known as a mousetrap, to the under-
side of the device. If lifted one inch or more, the bomb would
explode prematurely, destroying any and all evidence.

Once a month, the afternoon janitor dutifully inspected the
roof of the hospital as part of his maintenance checklist. If he
found anything wrong, he wrote up a work order and left it for
the day crew. Until that night, being the afternoon janitor had
always been a "good deal."

The bomb's size was less than a cubic foot. Its construction
reflected the maker's annoyance with imperfection. The walls
were three-quarter-inch marine plywood, which were held together with large brass wood screws. The precisely mitered

corners, along with all other seams, were glued together to ensure weatherproofing. Finally, it had been painted with two coats of flat black latex to diminish its noticeability.

But the afternoon janitor did notice the device and thought he heard a small metallic snap as he picked it up.

The Ghost Riders' clubhouse stood surrounded by an intentional starkness that served as a warning to the uninvited. The structure had been redesigned to keep law enforcement out and the bikers' secrets in. All the windows had been bricked up, and the rear door, with complete disregard for the municipal fire code, had been welded shut. The front door, a thick steel device with the impenetrability of a bank vault, completed the perimeter. The members thought of its interior as foreign soil, impervious to the laws of the United States. Two signs were bolted to the wall outside. One displayed the gang's colors, a skeleton in a dark robe and hood. The other hung at eye level and served as a final warning:

> IF YOU ARE FOUND HERE TONIGHT
> YOU WILL BE FOUND HERE IN THE MORNING

The Detroit Police Department had an unwritten but strictly observed policy not to enter the clubhouse unless it was absolutely necessary, and then, with no less than a SWAT team. A year earlier, a badly beaten body had been found behind the building. When the membership was interviewed by Homicide they offered two defenses: "The blacks dumped the body there to make the club look bad" and, when that failed, "Fuck you." Although the case would never go to trial, the investigators determined that the victim had diverted some of the club's drug profits to his own pockets. In addition to a fairly successful narcotics operation, the gang financed themselves by providing muscle for loan sharks and bookies. They felt their "victimless" choice of commerce would keep them out of the overburdened eye of the police. But three days earlier, one of them had, without permission, broken new ground: Member Daniel Ricci had robbed a bank.

It was a warm night, and because the Ghost Riders were not committing any of Detroit's prosecutable felonies at the moment, the front door to the unventilated clubhouse stood open. About twenty members were inside, standing at the bar or shooting pool. They gulped Jack Daniel's straight out of the bottle, and empty beer cans were everywhere.

Mike Devlin slipped in the door and remained unnoticed for a few seconds. The blasting acid-rock music from the jukebox deflected off the bare, gritty walls with a grating intensity. The air was blue with smoke and stank of stale beer, marijuana, and urine. Devlin scanned the group and spotted Ricci, who looked older than his mug shot. Bikers did not age well. Their glazed eyes looked out from behind sagging, gray faces, like sated birds of prey who were no longer aroused by anything but an opportunity to attack.

One of them wore a dirty, brown T-shirt that had YOUR HOLE IS MY GOAL printed across the front. As he raised a bottle of whiskey to his mouth, he saw Devlin. "What the fuck do you want?"

Sardonically, Devlin said, "Is this where the Mensa Society meets?"

"The what?"

Heads started turning. Someone turned off the music. The evening's entertainment had arrived. "Actually, I'm looking for a Daniel Ricci." So as not to reveal his identity, no one looked at Ricci. The Ghost Riders were well practiced in group lying. Devlin smiled at the foolishness of his next question. "Anyone know him?"

A second biker, with the authority of a sergeant at arms, stepped up to within a foot of Devlin. He was heavyset, with a beef-red face that was half hidden by a mutinous black beard. He wore a black T-shirt with a perfect four-inch circle cut out of the right chest. It exposed a nipple that was pierced with a brass ring. Devlin looked at it and said, "I'll bet you have an unnatural fear of merry-go-rounds."

The biker ignored Devlin's remark and smiled slowly. His face reflected impending pleasure, as though he not only wanted to inflict pain but, with a little luck, would be the recipient of some. He snarled, "Don't fuckin' know no fuckin' Ricci."

Devlin's tone was now one of academic aloofness. "You'll have to excuse me. I don't really know you but I believe you have grammatically misused the double-fucking negative."

"Who the fuck are you?"

"Come on—the suit, the tie. You Girl Scouts know exactly who I am."

Someone in the crowd said, "I thought I smelled federal pig." They laughed and started to gather around Devlin.

"Let's be honest. The only thing you freaks are capable of smelling is bicycle seats."

The laughter stopped, and the sergeant at arms moved his nose within an inch of Devlin's. He spoke slowly, as if trying to grind each word into the agent's face. "Motherfucker, it's a long way to that door." He looked at some bikers standing behind Devlin and smiled. "How you planning on getting out of here?"

Devlin smiled back. "I was going to call someone."

"Who you going to call, asshole?"

"The proper question is: 'Who ya gonna call?' "

"Okay, asshole, who ya gonna call?"

Devlin nodded his satisfaction with the biker's perfect question. He looked at his watch and held up a finger, signaling the group to wait. After a few seconds, he pointed at the door as some throbbing music started playing over the loudspeaker that every Bureau car was equipped with.

> There's something strange
> in the neighborhood.
> Who ya gonna call?
> Ghostbusters!

Just as the song yelled "Ghostbusters," Bill Shanahan jumped through the doorway wearing a World War II flamethrower on his back, holding the control nozzle with both hands. He walked toward the bikers, and although the device weighed seventy pounds, he bounced lightly to the music.

One of the bikers said, "What the fuck is that?"

Shanahan sang along with the next chorus.

> There's something weird
> And it don't look good.
> Who ya gonna call?
> Ghostbusters!

Timing it to coincide with "Ghostbusters," Shanahan, holding the control nozzle like a guitar, struck the igniter and squeezed the stream control at the same time. A forty-foot flame hit the pool table, and it caught fire like cardboard. He swung around and, while keeping the beat, pointed his muzzle at the wide-eyed bikers.

They started running toward the door, but Devlin managed to clothesline Ricci, take him to the floor, and handcuff him.

Another chorus was ending, and as the last biker got to the doorway, Shanahan, on the "Ghostbusters" command, fired a stream of flaming gasoline out the door. He then walked over and stood in its burning flame. Devlin heard engines start in a panic and then: "Ghostbusters!"

Another flaming whoosh was followed by screaming voices. Shanahan walked back in, and Devlin asked, "Any luck?"

"No, they all got away, but one guy's van is going to need repainting."

Devlin looked at Ricci. "Danny, we've got a bank robbery warrant for you."

The words did not seem to register with the biker. In a voice that was a mixture of bewilderment and respect, he said, "You guys are crazy."

Devlin smiled. "It seems to be the only way we can keep our sanity." As Devlin started toward the door with the prisoner, he detected a familiar distraction in his partner's eyes. "Bill, let's go."

"Just one more," Shanahan pleaded.

Devlin spoke with a schoolteacher's tone: "William! The bell has rung and it's time to put the toys away."

Shanahan smiled in resignation and looked around. "Well, here's another one of my cases I suppose they won't be featuring on *FBI: The Untold Stories.*"

An hour later, after dropping their prisoner at the Wayne County Jail, Shanahan drove Devlin to his undercover car. "Come on, Mike, just one. You know how thirsty I get after a napalming."

Devlin got in his car and rolled down the window. "Don't start. I broke enough rules going with you on this little stunt tonight. You know I'm not supposed to be working the street."

As Devlin pulled away slowly, Shanahan held up his index finger pleadingly, attempting to sell the biggest lie in law enforcement: that the night's celebration of justice's rare visit would end after *one* beer.

Devlin stopped in the federal building basement and used the men's room to change into his undercover clothes. He drove to a deteriorating neighborhood on West Warren Boulevard and parked. Out of the trunk, he took a large black canvas shoulder bag and walked two blocks to a building that appeared deserted. He put a key in an oversized lock that secured a heavy, rusted steel gate. Then he unlocked the door inside and started up the stairs. The building, a two-story frame storefront, was completely boarded up except for the doors.

The second floor had the damp, sour smell of abandonment. It was an empty apartment that had not been occupied in ten years. Peeling layers of paint cratered the sagging walls. He walked into a small bedroom that contained only one piece of furniture, an overstuffed chair of medieval vintage that had retained only three of its original four legs. Uncomfortably, it canted to the left front.

Out of his bag, he took a twelve-gauge shotgun with a collapsible stock and loaded it with alternating rounds of double-aught buckshot and deer slugs. He jacked a round into the chamber and clicked the safety off. He stood the shotgun in the corner, half an arm's length from the chair.

Then he pulled out a long, heavily knotted rope and tied it around an exposed pipe near the front window. He pushed against the plywood that covered the glassless frame, confident that he could kick it out if the building should catch fire. In that area, fires of suspicious origin were common, and he knew how fast the old building would incinerate. With his full weight, Devlin tested the tied end of the rope and was satisfied with his fire escape.

In the bedroom, a thick lock and hasp guarded a closet door. He opened it, and on newly built shelves sat three television monitors. They were for the video cameras hidden in the walls on the first floor of the building, which the FBI's technical people had converted into a fairly luxurious gambling casino.

The "project" was designed to engulf anyone, from degenerate gamblers to tribute-demanding mafiosi to cops offering protection. But the undercover agents had been too obvious, offering better odds than logic would dictate, having equipment that was too good, and—always a fatal flaw for the Bureau—being too courteous and too well organized. The only people who had come to the casino since its opening were FBI informants. Armed with FBI dollars, they were to give the impression of fast action, which was the narcotic of the compulsive gambler. The undercover project's lack of success was becoming evident, and its end was in sight.

Devlin inserted new tapes into the video recorders. The monitors revealed that the first floor was still unoccupied. Taking out a brown paper bag containing a sandwich, he slumped heavily into the unstable chair, which bowed joylessly to the southwest.

Once again, Mike Devlin's Irish charm had landed him a prestigious assignment.

The last of the inexhaustible gamblers left the Warren casino at 6 A.M. looking for another game. Devlin removed the video-tapes from the recorders, dated and initialed them, and finished the surveillance log. He packed everything into his bag and headed for the office. The early-morning sky was filled with clouds that were thick and overstated, as if they had been applied by an artist who had used a palette knife rather than a brush. Traffic was starting to build for the morning race to the center of the city.

Because his car had neither a Bureau nor a commercial radio, Devlin had no idea of the events that had taken place during his casino shift. His first indication was when he drove into the garage and noticed that three television-station crews were camped outside in their trucks. Because of the growing number of groups protesting against the government, that was not unusual, but he thought the hour was. Generally, demonstrators were a civilized bunch, never getting angry before 10 A.M.

As soon as he walked through the employee door he knew something was wrong. Usually unpopulated at that hour, the office swarmed with agents who lacked the grooming and business attire that would be normal at the start of their work-day. Devlin grabbed an agent. "What's going on?"

"John Lawson was murdered last night." The agent hurried away, leaving Devlin stunned. Every time he heard an agent had been killed, he was sure it was a lie. Agents were not supposed to get killed. The FBI, unlike the police, had the luxury of safely planning every aspect of their work. Back in a narrowing tunnel of time, when Devlin was a new agent, he remembered the feeling of invincibility, of youth whose only consideration was hasty victory. Death was only a rumored consequence. But now, another agent had died, and unfortunately, it was not a lie.

Devlin knew John Lawson casually. They had never worked

on the same squad, but Devlin was aware of Lawson's reputation for convicting organized-crime members, which took a patience that Devlin could only admire. Lawson was thought of as a "good agent"—high praise from peers who normally found flaws much more quickly than virtue. But now that good agent was lying on the Wayne County medical examiner's stainless-steel table unable to protest its chilling indifference.

Devlin was pulled along in the direction that most of the grim agents seemed to be going. He found himself in a crowded C-4 area that was filled with small groups of serious voices, all oblivious to one another, each designing their own solutions to Lawson's death.

Criminal Squad Four investigated the Assaulting a Federal Officer Statute. Also contained in that law was the more serious provision for Killing a Federal Officer. C-4 was Devlin's squad before his "assignment" to the casino project.

At the front of the room stood a huge pad of coarse white paper on an easel. Written on it, for report-writing purposes, was the title of the case.

>   UNSUB(S)
>   SA JOHN T. LAWSON (DECEASED)—VICTIM
>   KFO

UNSUB(S) was the only word that interested Devlin: One or more UNKNOWN SUBJECTS was now the object of his seething intentions.

Jim Harrison, the C-4 supervisor, stood next to the easel and asked for everybody's attention. The group, with somber quickness, complied. "By now you all know that John Lawson was shot to death yesterday, sometime in the late afternoon or early evening, by a person or persons unknown. We have no idea who or why. The last thing we know about his movements is that he received a call around three o'clock yesterday afternoon and told the squad secretary he had to meet an unnamed person at the old Bridgeline glove factory on West Fenkell.

The caller was supposed to provide some information on an old organized-crime case. Around eight last night, John's wife, Sandy, called the office to see if he was working late. When he hadn't shown up by ten, we went out to the factory and found him." Harrison closed his eyes in a slow, tranquilizing blink and fought something back. Devlin guessed he had been the one who found the body. Harrison then continued with a forged aloofness. "He was hit twice in the face. The entry wounds looked to be thirty-eights. There was only one exit wound, but it was large. My guess would be hollowpoints. We don't know if both rounds exited through the same wound. We couldn't find any slugs in the dark last night, but the building has been sealed off, and there are people from the lab in the air right now. They'll laser the entire building, along with John's car, which was parked in the factory lot. Also, they will search for the slugs and any other . . ." The supervisor's voice dissolved into the noisy anger that was rushing through Devlin's head. Someone had invaded the sanctity of their ranks and destroyed a life—one of their own. In response, something stirred within Devlin, something that would be necessary to regain justice's difficult balance. He let the beast rise within him and memorized its promising violence.

A harder edge now ribboned through Harrison's voice, recapturing Devlin's attention. "Our number one best guess is an organized-crime hit. John had a trial starting in another month. Paulie Gerrardi and Rhino Scarpa were looking at a lot of time. C-Nine is out looking for them right now. We're putting twenty-four-hour surveillance on them. Before I start assigning leads, are there any questions?"

A new agent in the back asked, "Could it have been a robbery?"

The fatigue was becoming evident on Harrison's face. "Not likely. In this town, robberies are more accidental than planned. Whoever lured him to that factory had a plan. And"— Harrison scanned the agents' faces to emphasize what he was about to say—"I don't want this leaving the office: The only thing taken was his badge. God knows why. He kept it on his belt on one of those leather backings. PD style."

"Is Behavioral Science going to do a profile?" another agent asked.

"They're also on the way out here. As soon as they give us something, you'll have it."

"What about the media? I saw them circling this morning when I came in."

"They're not going to give us any room. Every station has had a crew at the Bridgeline factory all night. No one talks to them, on *or* off the record. This case is going to be tough enough to solve without the media getting to our suspects before us. If they ask you any questions, refer them to the media rep. If they try to follow you out of the garage—and don't laugh, they've done it before—lose them. As a general rule of thumb, if your face is seen on TV, you'll be in the front office explaining why. Fortunately, the nationals haven't picked it up yet. Anything else?"

There were no other questions, so Harrison started assigning leads. They were logical. Interview Lawson's wife for enemies, especially any outside the Bureau. Conduct a neighborhood investigation around the glove factory in hopes of finding witnesses. And four agents familiar with organized-crime cases would review all of Lawson's files, open and closed, for the last ten years. All names in those files would be interviewed and, if deemed appropriate, would be asked to take a polygraph examination. As tried and true as those types of leads had proven over the years, Devlin's straining beast failed to be aroused by them.

"Two final things," Harrison said. "Evidence—if you find some, whether it's a handgun or an innocuous piece of paper, protect it. Make sure when it gets to the lab it doesn't have your fingerprints or crumbs from your lunch all over it. We have boxes of plastic gloves and different-size evidence containers up here on the table. Everyone take an adequate supply of both. All physical evidence that needs examining will be hand-carried back to the lab. If it is found to be contaminated in any way, you'll be standing in line with the unwilling television stars rehearsing your clemency plea for the SAC. And speaking of the SAC, he has ordered that, until this is solved, no one is to work the street alone. *No one.*" Devlin looked around for the Special Agent in Charge and, with a mixture of curiosity and relief, realized he was not there.

As everyone started pairing up, Harrison unceremoniously lumbered into his office, the weight of the case obvious in his gait. Devlin followed him and watched as he picked up a framed photograph of his family and stared at it for a moment before putting it down. He did not notice Devlin until he sat down behind his desk. "Mike" was his simple greeting as his eyes fastened onto Devlin cautiously. Harrison knew why he was there.

"Jim," Devlin answered. "Where do you want me?"

Harrison looked down and shook his head. "Goddamnit, Mike, there's nobody I'd rather have on this, but"—he nodded at Devlin's clothes—"you're still doing hard time."

"Come on, Jim. You can fix that. An *agent's* been killed."

"Oh, no! For the most part I like my job. When it comes to you, there is no fix." Harrison saw something rising in Devlin. "Christ, Mike, you don't embarrass—no, *humiliate*—the SAC in front of the director of the FBI and then expect business as usual."

"There's no proof that I had anything to do with that."

"Okay, let's review the *non*evidence. Because the director was coming to visit, the SAC ordered all the clerks to come in on Saturday to clean the office. Because he wouldn't authorize overtime for them, they asked you to speak to him on their behalf—which, with their best interests in mind, you did. And then when he refused to discuss it, you told him he was trying to kiss the director's ass at the expense of the clerks." Harrison looked carefully at Devlin, trying to find some admission of guilt in his stony face. "Now it's Monday. The SAC rolls out the red carpet. Limousine at the airport. A dozen roses for the director's wife. Lights and siren to the office. Agents waiting at every door with radios. The director, who—being a regular guy—prefers to be called Bob, and his wife get to the elevator. It opens. And what's inside? A life-size photo of a naked male from behind, bent over, mooning the director and his wife. On each cheek of his ass is a large letter B. And between the straddled legs someone has skillfully masked in the SAC's face, complete with a speech balloon at the corner of his mouth that says: I DON'T HAVE TO KISS DIRECTOR BOB'S ASS BECAUSE WHEN I BEND OVER I'VE GOT HIS NAME TATTOOED ON MINE. And sure enough, there's the two B's with the missing vowel in between." Harrison shook his head. "How do you guys come up with this shit?" Devlin continued his silence, so Harrison asked, "Now, Mike, you're an investigator. Who would you say that points to?"

"Very circumstantial."

"When you work for Sudder, circumstantial is as good as overwhelming."

"The project is almost over. I've done my time."

Harrison's voice changed. Its intent was no longer to justify, but to dismiss. "You're not getting it. There is no end to your time; Charles Manson will be paroled before you. The SAC isn't the head of some corporation that has checks and balances. When it comes to employees, he has the authority of a warlord, able to do or have done whatever he pleases. An agent, especially Mike Devlin, doesn't piss him off and then skate away. As long as he's here, you have a serious problem. I was there when he decided to send you on the casino project. He said, 'Since he loves those clerks so much, maybe if he has to work and dress like one of them he'll develop their humility.' "

"Maybe someone should teach him the difference between humility and dignity."

Harrison looked into Devlin's unyielding eyes and watched as treasonous sparks danced through them. "Jesus Christ, Mike, don't even think about it. Try to remember, if you could have been a little more compromising with Sudder, you would be out there right now looking for John's killer. But instead, you're this very proud *shit shoveler*."

Devlin got up to leave. A smile of inevitability settled on his face. "Jim, there's an old Irish proverb that says it is far better to shovel a ton of shit than to swallow one grain of it."

Devlin sat at his desk. His mind raced through familiar, forbidden turns. It was probably better this way, he thought. Although he would have to be careful not to let the wrong people know what he was doing, he could choose the course of his own investigation while the authorized agents would be at the mercy of whatever leads were assigned to them.

The phone rang. "Mike?" Although Devlin had heard his wife pronounce his name thousands of times, the single syllable had never sounded so desperate. A splinter of light shot through him: She had heard about Lawson's murder. "I didn't know where you were. I've been calling everywhere trying to find you."

"Knox, I'm sorry. I should have called you but I just found out about John myself."

She didn't seem to hear him. "When I got here this morning, Father Richter told me he heard on the news that an FBI agent had been killed, but they couldn't give a name. I must have called a dozen wives before I found out it wasn't you." Her voice began to fill with emotion. "I didn't know where you were."

With an intentional calmness, he said, "Everything's fine. In fact, I'm through for the day. Can I stop over there before I go home?"

"Sure, but you don't have to. I'm okay now."

Devlin knew she wasn't. "About half an hour."

"Okay."

Knox had never been a wife who involved herself in Bureau business, but an agent had been killed, and, as always, the families wanted to know what had gone wrong, what preventable error the victim had made—an error they were certain their spouses would never make. Within the FBI, denial was a precious drug.

Devlin went to the garage and changed into a suit he had started keeping in his Bureau car when he was assigned to the casino project. He hoped when Knox saw him in it, rather than undercover clothes, she would sense a return to the security of the everyday grind and not ask too many questions about his intended involvement in the murder investigation.

As he pulled out of the building, he turned north into the Cass Corridor. Two generations of drug addicts, and the terrorism that always accompanied them, had stripped the life from the once-vibrant area. He drove past a few hookers, who stood guard over their corners and with little enthusiasm tried to flag down johns on the way home from night-shift jobs. Listless junkies lined the street, patiently waiting for the only motivation left in their lives—withdrawal.

Devlin parked in front of St. Barnabas. The ancient mansion had somehow survived. The last owner had tried to sell the building for three years before taking the tax write-off by donating it to the Catholic Church. When the diocese could find no immediate use for the three-story structure, Father Karl Richter stepped in and started using it as temporary housing for children afflicted with cancer. The hospice's proximity to the Henry Ford Hospital made it a natural for out-state kids who would travel to Detroit for treatment at the cancer center. Many of the families could not afford to stay in hotels, so Father Richter charged them five dollars a night. More times than not, the money went uncollected. Ignoring the Church's pay-your-own-way fiscal policy, he seemed to take pleasure in St. Barney's indebtedness. "If we weren't operating at a loss, we wouldn't be providing much of a service." Because he had taken an oath of poverty, the priest claimed that wallowing in red ink was his religious duty; it kept him in God's good graces. But he also liked to, as he called it, *go begging*. He would fiercely cajole contributions anywhere he saw somebody's generosity left unguarded. Whether the contribution was a thousand-dollar check from a black-tie affair or a beer-soaked five-dollar bill won in a saloon arm-wrestling contest, he accepted it with unqualified appreciation.

Because he was also one of the Detroit Police Department's chaplains, he involved not only the cops but the FBI in his work. His children loved rides in the police helicopter or tours of the Bureau office, which always ended with the gift of an FBI baseball cap to cover their temporary baldness.

One night at a fund-raiser, Devlin introduced Knox to Father Richter's charm, after which she became a regular volunteer at St. Barney's. She would do anything from driving kids to the hospital to cooking meals to—what she seemed best at—just talking to the young patients about what they were going to do once the cancer was banished from their bodies.

Devlin rang the bell. Father Richter opened the door with a smile and a handshake. His hands were enormously strong yet soft, the perfect touch for someone whose main industry was reassurance.

"Michael, how are you?"

"Just fine, Father," Devlin answered and stepped inside.

The priest's expression became sober. "I'm sorry about the agent who was killed." Devlin nodded his appreciation. "One minute, I'm on the phone with one of our creditors." Devlin sensed that *one minute* meant Richter wanted to talk to him before he saw Knox. Both men moved into the comfort of the dark red, mahogany-lined study that served as Richter's office. There were books everywhere. Devlin moved a half dozen of them off a chair and sat down. Father Richter sat down behind a hand-carved desk and picked up the waiting phone. "Yes, Mr. Kramer, I'm back. Where were we? . . . Yes . . . I understand. I don't suppose you're Catholic . . . You're Jewish. Let me explain how important the Church's service to the community is . . . I know we owe you thirty-eight hundred dollars . . . You're sorry you don't understand the Catholic religion! Well, goddamnit, you should—one of your people started it!" In a single flowing movement, the priest slammed the phone down and snapped his eyes upward. "Sorry," he whispered in a reverent tone and then just as quickly looked back at Devlin. It was an efficient apology that had apparently been streamlined by sheer repetition. Richter's voice was now warm and involved. "Mike, I just wanted to give you the heads-up before you talk to Knox. During the year that she's been coming here, I've seen her handle everything from telling a family their child was dying to wrestling down some poor kid who was having a chemically induced fit. She has always been unshakable—until this morning. It scared the hell out of me. She was absolutely panicked. I just wanted to be sure you knew, because I think she intends to downplay all this with you."

"Thanks, Father, it was pretty obvious when she called me, but I appreciate your concern."

The priest gave Devlin his safe-harbor smile. "I've been told I give good concern."

Devlin laughed as the phone rang. Before Richter answered, he said, "She's upstairs, Mike." As Devlin started to the second floor, he could hear the priest, "St. Barnabas . . . Yes, Mr. Kramer . . . Thirty days? That's very gracious of you, but sixty days would be much more, shall we say, Judeo-Christian . . . Okay, okay, thirty days."

Devlin found Knox in one of the second-floor bedrooms putting clean sheets on a bed. "Hey, here we are at the best bed-and-breakfast in the Cass Corridor. And your mother was afraid once we got married, you'd never get to travel."

Knox turned around and did her best to smile confidently: Her lips obeyed, but her eyes refused to give up their fear. She put her arms around his waist and settled against him. He could feel an invisible trembling within her. For a long time, neither of them spoke. Finally, she said, "It's so awful, so sudden."

"Knox, everyone's in shock."

"Not everyone has had their husband shot and his partner killed."

"You had every right to worry, but it *wasn't* me. Everything is fine."

Her eyes became paralyzed with the memory. "I'll never forget that call. I don't ever want to get another one."

"Do you know how many agents in the history of the FBI have been shot twice?" Devlin had no idea himself, but quickly answered, "None. It's like the chicken pox and I've been vaccinated."

"So, you're telling me I should feel good that you've already been shot."

"Well, not good, maybe—relieved?"

"You've never been on a debating team, have you?"

He laughed. "Just this one."

Her face remained rigid. "Do they know who did it?"

"They're taking a hard look at some organized-crime people."

"Thank God you never worked that."

"Evidently, John was about to put a couple of guys in prison who have a reputation within the mob for being pretty bad."

"Those people are crazy. Do they know how it happened?"

Devlin noticed that Knox was now referring to the FBI in the third person, excluding him from the investigation. "Not yet. And don't worry about me. I was told today that I couldn't be spared from my present assignment."

The restriction of Devlin's freedom finally seemed to reassure her. "In other words, they won't let you out of your punishment." She smiled.

"You know, a good wife allows her husband to lie a little to retain some of his dignity."

"I'll be a good wife, just don't get shot again."

"That seems like a reasonable request to me." He pulled her back into his arms. The trembling was gone. "Besides, these things never stay unsolved for very long. This guy'll shoot his mouth off and somebody will call us."

"Thanks for coming by. It was terrible when I didn't know who it was."

He kissed her softly. Now was not the time to tell her what he was going to do. But he would have to soon; Knox Devlin was not someone who could be distracted for long.

* * *

As soon as Devlin started his car, he keyed his microphone. "DE Four-one to Four-five."

"Go ahead, Four-one."

"Can you meet me somewhere downtown?"

"In front of Tiger Stadium in ten minutes."

Devlin waited for Bill Shanahan at the corner of Michigan and Trumbull. The ballpark's marquee announced that the Red Sox were in town for a three-game series. Devlin promised himself he would take Knox to a game as soon as John Lawson's killer was found. He would teach her how to keep score and make her eat lots of junk food. And make her laugh. Especially make her laugh.

Shanahan's car pulled up behind Devlin's and both men got out. Shanahan spoke through a smile wilted with exhaustion. "Nice to see you driving a real FBI car."

"You look like you've been up all night."

"Yeah, I was in the first wave. Harrison called me out about an hour after I dropped you off."

"Did you see the body?"

"Unfortunately. Two head shots, at least one was through-and-through."

"What about the exit wound?"

"Tennis ball size. Probably high-velocity hollowpoints—thirty-eights." The two men looked at each other, neither wanting to say what they were both thinking.

Finally, Devlin asked, "Was John having problems with anyone in the office?"

"I didn't know him that well. I never heard anything, but I'll ask around." After a moment, Shanahan spoke again as if answering Devlin's unasked question. "I know Hydra-Shok hollowpoints are standard Bureau issue, but they *are* available to people outside the FBI. Besides, I think whoever blipped him enjoyed doing it."

"Why?"

"We can't be sure until the M.E. confirms it, but it looks like the first shot hit him high in the forehead and angled down. That, coupled with the pattern of his footprints in the dried silt on the floor, indicated that he probably put his head down and charged the guy." Devlin felt a shudder of admiration for Lawson's courage, and then hatred for the person who had extinguished it forever. "That shot had to kill him instantly. Probably spun him over in the air and caused him to land on his back. Based on the lead tattooing, the second shot looked like it was fired from directly above, at close range. I'd guess less than a foot away. Dead center through the bridge of the nose. It was completely unnecessary, so I think the guy must have liked doing it."

"Where was John's gun?"

"About fifteen feet from where he started his charge. The guy probably surprised him and had him toss it."

"Anything besides his badge missing?"

"Nothing. It was weird, because his credentials were in his inside suit pocket. Why take his badge and not his creds?"

"If it wasn't a robbery, what was it?"

"As clean as it was, it could have been a pro, but those guys usually don't do hits by themselves. Aside from John's, there was only one other set of footprints in the factory."

"Who does that leave?" Devlin asked.

"I don't know. A wacko? Maybe BSU can figure it out." Shanahan looked at his watch. "They should have landed a half hour ago." The Behavioral Science Unit was located at the FBI Academy in Quantico, Virginia. They were world famous for developing criminal profiling. From the circumstances of the crime, they could make accurate assessments about the characteristics of the person responsible. When that person became involved in a pattern of similar acts, they could provide astonishingly specific parameters for that individual. But Devlin knew no matter how brilliant their analyses were, if the investigators did not exhaust the leads that BSU provided, their chances for success were severely limited.

"Let me know what they say."

"Where are you going to be?"

"Serving the rest of my casino sentence."

Because Devlin was wearing a suit and driving his Bureau car, Shanahan had assumed he had been reassigned to investigate the murder. "Wait a minute. If you're not working on this, why all the questions?"

"Just curious," Devlin answered. Shanahan studied his friend's face. Back behind Devlin's eyes, like a nocturnal animal avoiding sunlight, he saw something hiding. Only for a moment, and then it was gone.

A clever smile bubbled to the surface of Shanahan's face. "You sonofabitch. You're going after this guy on your own."

Devlin smiled conspiratorially. "Every man needs a hobby."

"That's fine, Michael. Just don't get me involved this time."

"If I didn't, you'd never forgive me."

"Please give me the opportunity to prove you wrong."

"I just need you to keep me up-to-date on what's happening, officially."

Officially reminded Shanahan where Devlin was heading. With a halfhearted challenge, Shanahan asked, "And if I don't?"

Devlin smiled confidently. "I know whose moon that really was in the elevator—*BOB!*"

III CHAPTER 2 III

Intentionally, the world headquarters of the Seacard Corporation sat on a remote edge of Washtenaw County in the town of Grayton, Michigan. In contrast to its rural, farm-ringed neighbors, it was secure, urbane, and, by any standards, middle-class. The chemical and manufacturing giant provided a tax base that allowed the luxuries of a contemporary life in the midst of pastoral midwestern values and pace. It was a community of quiet sidewalks and busy shops, with tree-lined streets that summer had turned into cool, dark green tunnels. Its inhabitants filled their days with work and family, never questioning the permanence of their tranquillity. For them, crime was a distant and vague land. When the lethal bomb had exploded on the roof of their children's hospital, it had served its plotted purpose: Door-locking fear had come to Camelot.

At ten o'clock the next morning, seven men from two different worlds sat gathered in the Seacard boardroom to resolve that fear. Three of them were FBI agents. They sat across from three of the corporation's executives. At the head of the table was James Pendleton, a Seacard executive vice president. He spoke to Malcolm Sudder, the Special Agent in Charge of the FBI for the state of Michigan, who sat between his two agents. "I appreciate you taking the time to oversee this investigation. I know you must be busy right now. We heard about the agent being killed last night. You have our deepest sympathies."

"Well, sir, I appreciate that. I have every available agent working on the case, but when I heard some lunatic was setting

off bombs around sick children"—Sudder cleared his throat—
"I felt it was equally worthy of my time." He cleared his throat
again. It was an irritating habit that everyone in the room was
aware of but him.

Pendleton guessed that allergies were causing the SAC's si-
nuses to drain constantly, but the pattern of the throat clearing
was more of an interest to him. Because it was used more often
during conversation, Pendleton suspected that it was not only
physically relieving but emotionally soothing. Pendleton had
become a student of such psychological indicators. A nervous
laugh, an anxiously bouncing knee, or a lack of eye contact
were the more obvious forms of the body's giving away the
mind's secrets. When these devices were properly examined,
they could reveal anything from stress to insecurity to an out-
and-out lie. "On behalf of everyone at the hospital, we thank
you for your personal involvement."

"It's what we get paid for. I'm just glad we can help." Sudder cleared his throat and Pendleton studied the other two FBI
agents. Both sat impassively, almost disrespectful of their
boss's noble words, as if they had heard his distracting rhetoric
once too often. For Pendleton, this extortion was placing a
great deal at risk and he wanted to know the strength of those
who were tasked with defeating it.

Sudder said, "I know he's demanding five million dollars.
Does the hospital have that much in available assets?"

"Closer to six million," Pendleton answered.

"Who would be aware of that figure?"

"Anyone who took the time to read the hospital's financial
report." Pendleton pushed a sheet of paper he had been holding
across the table to Sudder. Instead of reaching for it, the SAC
let the agent between them pick it up and hand it to him dutifully. "That was faxed to our billing office shortly after midnight."

Sudder read it out loud. "You have five days until the next
bomb explodes. The cost to prevent it is five million dollars.
You will receive instructions in the interim. Cops will only

shorten the five days." He passed the demand note to the agent to his right and said, "That's a good sign. He's not looking for the FBI to be involved. Should give us a leg up on him." The SAC noticed that Pendleton was watching the agent who was examining the note. "This is Jack Tarver. He's our most experienced extortion agent. That's why I've assigned this case to him. You're in good hands." He turned to Tarver and cleared his throat. "What do you think, Jack?"

Tarver looked up at the three men across from him. "Did anyone try to find out where the originating number on the fax was at?"

Neal Ferguson, the head of corporate security, said, "The only thing we know for sure is that it's an Ann Arbor exchange."

Sudder was leaning slightly toward Tarver, trying to see the number, when he noticed Pendleton watching him. He straightened, cleared his throat, and said, "Let's call the phone company right now and find out."

Ferguson had Tarver follow him down the hall to his office, where he could make the call in private. An older woman walked into the boardroom with a tray of coffee and cups. While the others got up to serve themselves, Sudder and Pendleton remained seated at the table. The vice president smiled pleasantly and said, "I'm a little surprised that you would come all the way out from Detroit. Usually any contact we have had with the FBI is with your branch office in Ann Arbor."

Sudder sensed that Pendleton's question had a deeper purpose than small talk. He watched the unreadable mask that the executive vice president presented for a moment before answering. "This is a serious violation of the law, and since I am ultimately responsible for all cases within the state of Michigan, I thought I should take a hands-on approach." Then he smiled mischievously, as though admitting the tiniest sin. "Besides, you wouldn't believe what a madhouse it is in Detroit with this agent's murder. Headquarters calling every five minutes. And the media—they never stop." The other agent walked up and set a cup of coffee in front of the SAC. Pendleton found it interesting that Sudder failed to even look at the agent, but instead continued, "Sometimes I'm tempted to just go ahead and retire."

Again, Sudder sensed Pendleton studying him, and although he did not understand the purpose of the scrutiny, he felt its vague threat.

Sudder knew his type. Pendleton was athletically handsome, intelligent, and his voice had that deep, creamy authority to it. People thought of him as a person who knew how to get things done, and quickly looked to him in a time of crisis. But every man has inadequacies and Sudder had taught himself how to find them. During twenty-five years of promotion in the Bureau, he had witnessed the careers of such men, and Pendleton's flaw was obvious: He was too young to be an executive vice president of such a large corporation. Deep down inside, men like him always possessed some aching incompleteness that secretly drove them to early success. But sooner or later, the speed of their career would no longer satisfy that addictive beast, and they would step out of bounds to feed it. The same inextinguishable void that compelled them to gain so much would eventually overwhelm them and take back everything it had given and, almost certainly, more.

A smug smile caught one corner of Sudder's mouth. It was always the same. He remembered the enemies of his youth— the good-looking kids, the athletes, the in crowd. But where were they now that one of the most powerful corporations in the world was being paralyzed by this deadly extortionist?

Tarver and Ferguson came back in, and everyone sat down. "It comes back to a building at the University of Michigan."

Sudder said, "We'll take care of that. Jack, why don't you brief everyone on what we'll be doing."

"Okay. I'll start by explaining some of the dynamics of an extortion. Of course, we would never put this information out to the general public, because it would be equivalent to giving the extortionists a how-to book. The most important thing to remember is that extortions are never successful. We may not identify and arrest every individual who uses this crime to demand money, simply because many of them lose their nerve halfway through. But those that do follow through never get away with the money. I'll explain why in a minute. Nine times out of ten, these people are nuts. If they think of themselves as criminals, they are *intellectual* criminals. But many of them do not consider what they are doing illegal. Somewhere in their twisted reasoning, they think that the mighty corporation needs to be taught a lesson because of some imagined unethical conduct, such as pollution, monopoly, huge profits at the little people's expense, et cetera. They see themselves as modern-day Robin Hoods and that helps them rationalize what they are doing. See, they need that excuse, because they are not career criminals. In fact, very few of them have been involved in any type of unlawful activity before. Which is to our advantage, because they are not aware of the techniques we use in dealing with this kind of crime. And that brings us to how we catch them. Am I clear so far?"

The Seacard executives sat quietly engrossed in Tarver's lecture. He noticed it and felt a small pinprick of pride. Handling high-profile crimes became so routine that agents tended to forget the public's fascination with their work.

Neal Ferguson asked, "Do these people actually give the money to whoever they feel was wronged?"

Tarver smiled. "Like I said, they never have the money long enough to do anything with it, but when we do get a confession from them, that's usually the part of their plan that doesn't seem to be as well developed as the rest of it." Everyone laughed. "Now as far as catching them, you have to understand that this type of criminal lacks the resolve to pull off a face-to-face crime, such as bank robbery or kidnapping; so, because they are dreamers, they see themselves as intellectuals, capable of winning this psychological war. They believe, to be successful, they need only their wits and the victim's fear. The extortionist thinks of it as a perfect crime, because it is something he orchestrates at a distance. If he can successfully intimidate his target, the money will be left for him wherever he wants. And that's his downfall, because no matter how distant he is, no matter how badly he has scared his victim, he has to pick up the money."

"And that's when you catch him," Pendleton said.

"That's right. That's how we catch them all. No matter how ingenious the extortionist thinks his plan is, he has to come to the drop site. And when this guy comes, we'll be waiting for him."

Although Tarver's words were encouraging, Pendleton was not about to underestimate the extortionist by accepting the FBI's casual assurances. He turned and looked directly at Sudder. "How often does one of these people explode a bomb or use a fax machine? Or, for that matter, ask for five million dollars?"

Pendleton's tone was becoming demanding and set off a reluctance in Sudder that had served him well for twenty-five years. He patted the table in front of Tarver. "Jack."

The case agent hesitated and then said, "Actually, I've never heard of any of these before."

Tarver's answer, unlike his explanation of the extortion process, was guarded and indicated to Pendleton that there was more risk involved than the FBI wanted to admit. "Then, how would you rate this extortionist?"

Tarver sensed this question needed diplomacy rather than substance, and since he did not want to give an inappropriate answer and then be held responsible by the SAC, he said, "That's hard to say, sir. How would you rate him, boss?"

Caught off-guard, Sudder cleared his throat slowly. "He seems to be well organized."

In a tone devoid of charity, Pendleton asked, "Which means . . . ?"

"That means, he appears to be a legitimate threat."

"In other words, he could blow up the hospital?"

Tarver saw that Sudder did not have an answer and said, "Boss, if I may? Mr. Pendleton, this man's purpose is to extort five million dollars from your corporation, not blow up your hospital. The threat is against the children's hospital, because that is where the corporation is most vulnerable. He wants one thing—money. And we're not going to let him walk away with a dime of it."

"You're sure?"

"Don't worry. We always get them at the drop." Pendleton thought the answer sounded practiced, like a salesman using the trustworthiness of his company's slogan to close a shaky deal.

Sudder said, "That's right. My men will wrap this up before any more harm can be done."

"I assume you won't need the entire five million dollars to catch him," Pendleton said.

Tarver smiled. "Oh, no, sir. Just a couple of hundred dollars to make it a felony. We'll make up dummy bundles. You probably won't receive instructions for a couple of days, but when you do, please call us immediately. We'll take it from there."

The agents were trying to sound confident, but Pendleton knew the difference between the hard, tempered ring of authority and the hollow echo of bravado.

Although the sun was warm outside, Devlin felt a draining chill inside the bottomless damp shadows that lined the cavernous glove factory. Bridgeline was another of those Detroit businesses that had been in existence for fifty years before finally succumbing to the group of diseases known as *urban America*. When its owner finally gave up, he sent a letter to the mayor and warned that Detroit would be the first city ever to be taken off the map of the United States.

Devlin stood back and watched the Bureau evidence technicians work in front of their obtrusive portable lights. With slow-motion thoroughness, they combed the musty floor and walls for evasive clues. Earlier, they had found one slug that had passed through John Lawson's skull. The tech said it was in "good" condition, which meant the lab would be able to match it with its originating weapon. At about the same time, the crackling Bureau radio had informed the agents at the scene that the Wayne County medical examiner had X-rayed the deceased's skull and was about to extract the second slug from the tissue of his brain.

One of the technicians called to Devlin, "We're going to turn the lights off and work the lasers. If you want to see anything, you'd better put on goggles."

Devlin strapped the filtering devices over his eyes as the lights went out. Immediately, the laser's water-cooled fan started its hum. Red beams dipped and soared on the walls like the exploratory flights of spring butterflies.

For an hour, with torturous patience, they searched every vertical surface in the building, looking for the residue of human touch—latent fingerprints. Finally, a tech said, "Nothing." Devlin swore. Physical evidence, especially good physical evidence like fingerprints, provided hope. It was a signal from the god of all major cases to the investigator: *Go ahead and work this: It's solvable.* Without it, the investigator and the criminal disappeared into the distance like railroad tracks. They seemed as though they would intersect, but they never really did. The agent just kept chasing the horizon.

"Stand behind us. We're going to do the floor." Again, the techs plodded along. Almost half an hour later, without warning, they stopped, their beams steady. Devlin looked over their shoulders and saw what appeared to be crushed pearls glowing in the silt that covered the floor.

"What's that?" Devlin asked.

With scientific detachment, one of the techs said, "Bone fragments, from the skull. They fluoresce under this light." As they started packaging the fragments, Devlin ripped off his goggles and walked toward the light that was coming from the doorway. He had had enough.

He stood in the doorway and for the first time noticed the

sound of water dripping somewhere in the factory. He thought about its perfect rhythm being the last thing John Lawson heard before his skull was shattered. That sound had witnessed abandonment, vandalization, and murder, and still it maintained its eternal precision. It reminded Devlin of the power of persistence. Maybe those railroad tracks would cross—just beyond the next rise.

As they usually did, the news teams being held at bay by a long yellow-and-black plastic streamer had attracted a crowd of the idly curious. They wanted to know what was going on. What—in a city where evidence streamers were such a familiar part of the landscape—could possibly attract such media attention? They crowded in behind the camera crews and watched the activity in and around the abandoned factory. Men and women wore blue nylon jackets with FBI printed across them and searched the grounds outside the factory, occasionally picking up something and putting it in a container.

Spotting the jackets, one newly arrived woman asked, "FBI? Somebody rob a bank?"

The man standing next to her said, "No, it was on the news this morning. In there's where they killed an FBI agent."

"Somebody killed an FBI agent?"

There was awe in the woman's voice causing the man behind her to smile. That's right, he thought, someone killed one of those invincible FBI men, someone better than him.

The woman asked, "Do they know who did it?"

"Don't know," someone in the crowd answered.

The man behind her smiled again and told himself, No, they don't know. He put his hand in his pocket and let his thumb trace the raised letters of John Lawson's badge. He found the confusion intoxicating, especially the bewildered faces of the agents and evidence techs who wandered aimlessly around and through the old factory, looking for evidence that was not there. All the king's horses and all the king's men.

He had come to watch how the FBI would gather evidence, *for future reference,* he thought with amusement. But because he had left none, they were being forced to search haphazardly, to waste hundreds of what he supposed the elitist bastards called *agent-hours*. Wasting agent-hours was something else he would keep in mind for the future.

He watched as an agent walked into the factory using the same door that Lawson had used. He closed his eyes and remembered the surprise on *Agent* Lawson's face when he saw the gun. Funny how he knew he was going to die. He put his head down and charged. As he did, he yelled insanely, trying to panic the shot, his contorted face slowly coming at the gun's front sight. The killer heard the two shots again.

His eyes opened slowly, and as his mind struggled to gain clarity against the dizzying memory, Mike Devlin walked out of the factory. He placed his hands on the hood of his Bureau car and let the midmorning sun warm away the factory's chilling secrets.

One of the reporters at the barrier yelled, "Hey, Mike, can you tell us what's going on in there?"

The killer heard the question and moved up behind the newsman to hear the response. Before he could see who the question was directed at, Devlin spotted the TV cameras and turned his back on them.

The cameraman positioned himself to shoot some footage of Devlin's back and asked, "Who's that?"

The reporter said, "Don't bother. That's Mike Devlin."

"FBI?"

"Yeah. Remember the Puget Sound murders?"

"Out in Seattle, but the killer was shot to death here."

"That's the one. There were a lot of people taking bows for that case, but Devlin's the guy who actually solved it."

"Then he's probably in charge of this case. Shouldn't I get some footage of him?"

The reporter laughed. "They'll never let Devlin be in charge of anything. He works alone and usually against orders. The way he turned his back to us, I'm going to guess that he's not even supposed to be out here."

The killer stood up on his tiptoes and looked at the back of the man they were talking about, trying to memorize his height, weight, sandy blond hair, and even his blue pinstripe suit, for future reference.

Without turning around, Devlin got in his car and drove in the opposite direction.

The killer looked back at the building and closed his eyes, trying to regain the luxurious images of the day before. But as hard as he tried, the only thing he could see was a man's back covered in blue pinstripes.

Before he pulled out of the lot, Devlin looked back at the old factory with all of its broken-out windows and gaping doorways—an old toothless face whose dilated eyes no longer blinked at death.

But it had once been the benefactor of scores of people, providing them with not only wages, but purpose. Like all businesses, most of its employees had been assets, but there were always a few who were liabilities. One, Devlin thought, may have lured John Lawson to his death; it had been his experience that killers used familiar surroundings.

Devlin drove to the nearest phone booth and dialed the office. A female voice answered, "C-Five. This is Temper Hanlon."

"Temper. Mike Devlin."

"Oh, sure, now that I'm married *and* pregnant you call."

"You're pregnant? There goes another one of my fantasies."

"You're such a pig. What kind of fantasy?"

"Like most fantasies, its pleasures will be lost if brought to light."

"Ooooo, that good, huh?"

Special Agent Temper Hanlon had been with the Bureau for seven years. While in new agents' training, she had incurred the wrath of her sister agents by openly admitting that her primary purpose in becoming a special agent of the Federal Bureau of Investigation was to find a man. But because of her uncommon good looks and mischievous sense of humor, no one could imagine that being her real purpose. She had a physical attractiveness that was not contemporary. It was unembellished by cosmetics or accentuating styles. It took a reordering of the beholder's eye, a translation, to understand the graceful subtlety of her unflawed face. And, as men developed that awareness one by one, they felt the sweetness that comes from believing they alone had discovered the secret. Still, she had remained single, and when she was occasionally asked why, she would claim to be a victim of unfortunate timing: "All the great guys are either married or have had an orgasm within the last fifteen minutes."

But a year earlier, her timing had finally improved. She bought a house in the suburbs and decided to put a deck on. The carpenter she hired to help her fell hopelessly in love when he saw her long, flashing strokes with a hammer. But his construction pals were skeptical. They warned him about getting involved with any woman who carried a briefcase. He defended her by saying she was the only woman he had ever known who carried a briefcase *and* drove a pickup truck. His friends were not convinced, until one night she demonstrated her ability to slam beers with the best of them. Men always found a way to fall in love with Temper Hanlon. Six months later, the carpenter and his apprentice were married.

Whenever her mother was asked why she had named her only child Temper, she swore that after the delivering doctor spanked her daughter into life, she yelled at him and swung back. What else could a mother have named her? Temper always claimed it had been self-defense. She had grown up in a little town just outside of Pittsburgh. Her mother and her steelworker father had endowed her with the common sense and work ethic that seemed so prevalent in that part of the country. Even though she was "just passing through" the Bureau, she was a capable and hardworking agent. She had dark red hair, green eyes, and described herself as being "lucky enough to have my father's long legs and my mother's high-beam headlights." Temper Hanlon always had a good time.

"I need a favor," Devlin said.

"I told you, I'm married now. I don't do *favors* anymore."

Devlin laughed. "No, this is a business favor. Are you still handling Assumed Names?"

"Yes, I still get to stand in line at the city-county building waiting for those manikins they call employees to process my requests. I really shouldn't complain. What they lack in speed they more than make up for with enthusiastic snottiness. What's the name?"

"Bridgeline Glove."

"Oh-ho, no! I may be young, good-looking, and heavily armed, but they taught us in training school about helping Mike Devlin. They called it 'career suicide.'"

"You know, Hanlon, it's a medical fact that pregnant women sometimes overreact."

"Overreact. I've got two words for you: *Bob* and *casino*. And Bob is spelled with the *big* O."

"You don't miss much."

"Something tells me I'm going to wish I had missed this call."

"So you will check it for me?"

She hesitated, her voice sincere. "Hey, Mike, I liked John Lawson a lot. I'll do anything I can to help, even if it gets Mike Devlin–expensive. Do you need anything besides the owner's name and address?"

"I wanted to get a list of the employees; but that's just between you and me."

"Oh, you mean I can't run and tell Sudder?" Devlin laughed, and then she said, "Would it help if I got ahold of the owner to see if he'll give me the list?"

"You're the best."

Temper's voice again became amusingly sarcastic. "You'll never know now."

"Congratulations on being pregnant."

"Funny, my mother had a different reaction when I was in high school."

"How'd it happen this time?"

"Christ, Devlin. No wonder you never called me."

While agents assigned to the Seacard case sat in the office cutting up enough typing paper to briefly fool the extortionist, Jack Tarver drove to Ann Arbor. Although he had been designated the case agent, the SAC had announced that he was personally taking charge of the investigation. He had ordered Tarver to drive to the University of Michigan and find out where the demand note had been faxed from. Then maybe the extortionist could be identified and arrested before the FBI had to go through the tedious one-act play at the drop site.

The case worried Tarver. He had worked enough extortions to know this one was going to be trouble. Pendleton had been right: The extortionist was unusual in his demands and methods. Using a bomb to demonstrate his authority had been not only unprecedented, but effectively terrifying. At this point, the extortionist was unquestionably in command.

Before he realized it, Tarver had driven past the building he was looking for. He stopped, backed up, and parked. He had to be careful not to be made. Like he had told Pendleton, the whole investigative thrust was to catch the criminal at the drop site. But the SAC had insisted that Tarver check the building. He argued with Sudder that if they scared the subject away, it would be twice as hard to catch him the next time. As Tarver had expected, his cautions were disregarded by the SAC.

He got out of his car and walked to the building's entrance. Michigan Bell had determined that the phone was located on the third floor west. He climbed the stairs and walked to the west end of the building. There was a series of small, unmarked offices that appeared not to be in use. Tarver tried two doors and found them locked. Thinking any further investigation would increase his chances of being discovered, he decided to discontinue his search.

Instead of taking the elevator, he took the stairs again to avoid any chance encounters with the extortionist, in case he happened to routinely be in the building. As he walked to his car, a pair of eyes, hidden in the darkness of a fourth-floor window, followed him. Their owner smiled, glad that such an obvious man had been sent to stop him. So far the Bureau had lived up to its predictability.

Devlin drove up Gratiot Avenue, out of Detroit and into Macomb County. Because its residents were predominantly white and blue-collar, it was considered a bookie's paradise. Many of the local Mafia bookmakers lived and thrived there.

He pulled his car off the street and parked in front of a dilapidated gray two-story building that had been selected by its occupants for its anonymity. The first floor was a storefront with window signs that defied the keenest problem solver to determine what business was being conducted inside. BRAND NAME PARTS read one. BUY, RENT OR LEASE explained another. And the one that made Devlin smile, FAMILY OWNED. The store was never open.

Next to the store was a black windowless steel door with a fisheye peephole. The door looked newly installed and led to a second-floor apartment. Devlin rang the bell, and from a speaker just above it came a friendly "Yeah?"

"Nicky, it's Mike Devlin."

"Hey, Mikey," came the response. An electronic buzz unlocked the door, and Devlin went up the stairs. When he walked in, Nick Trampelli stood and greeted Devlin with a handshake as he continued to talk on a small telephone operator's headset. He shrugged sheepishly and smiled, acknowledging that he had been caught at his trade. As a bookie, he was part of an illegal gambling operation that brought millions of dollars annually to the head of the Detroit organized-crime family. The apartment, which was moved every six months or so, was his latest hole.

Four years earlier, the organized-crime squad had borrowed some agents to conduct a dozen simultaneous gambling raids on Christmas Eve. Devlin was assigned to a crew that was to raid a high-stakes poker game. After the initial entry, all of the gamblers were put on the wall in the customary search position. Devlin was sent to the back room to search for stray cardplayers. The only person he found was Trampelli. When Devlin patted him down, he found $1,000 in one of his socks. The gambling laws allowed the seizure of all money found on the premises. Trampelli looked at him and said, "It's Christmas present money. For my family. Take the deuce in my pocket. It's for the game." One of the preraid instructions was to try to recruit informants. Gambling raids had always presented an excellent opportunity to "deputize" the aimless players, so Devlin took out his business card and, without a word, stuck it in the middle of the $1,000 and pushed it back into Trampelli's sock. The gambler's disarming smile told Devlin he would get a call. When organized-crime agents needed some information, Devlin would call his source. But this time Devlin was not there for gambling intelligence.

Trampelli hung up. Immediately, the phone rang. "Sorry, Mike, the Tigers are playing Boston in fifteen minutes and Clemens is pitching. Everybody thinks it's a lock." Trampelli answered the phone, "Yeah!" A second phone rang. On the third ring, Trampelli looked at Devlin and waved his index finger at the phone pleadingly. Devlin tried to remember if there were any gambling wiretaps in progress at the office, but because he had been out on the casino project for so long, he could not be certain. As a safeguard, he lowered his voice, beyond recognition he hoped, and answered "Yeah!"

"Nick?"

"Can you hold on?"

"No, that's all right. This is D.D. Just tell me what ya got on the Boston game."

Devlin looked over at Trampelli and asked, "Boston?"

Trampelli interrupted his call, "Red Sox, one and a half."

Devlin repeated the favorite and the spread into the phone. The caller said, "Give me a nickel on Boston."

After D.D. hung up, Devlin looked over at Trampelli, who

was taking another call. Devlin mouthed "Boston" while holding up his spread fingers indicating the five-hundred-dollar bet. Trampelli motioned with his hand for Devlin to write it down on one of the betting slips that were stacked in front of him. Devlin's phone rang again.

For the next ten minutes Devlin answered the furious phone and recorded the wagers. At 1:35 P.M. the phones suddenly stopped. The game had started, and the gamblers knew no more bets would be taken.

Trampelli walked over to Devlin's table and shuffled through the betting slips. "Not bad. Could give you a part-time job. Need a little extra cash, Mikey?"

"Just enough for a defense attorney."

Trampelli laughed like an innocent child. "Well, this obviously isn't a raid, so what can I do for you?"

"Ever heard of an agent named John Lawson?"

"Yeah, I think so. Isn't he the guy who did Paulie Gerrardi and Rhino Scarpa?"

"That's why I'm here. Lawson was murdered last night."

"You're shittin' me! Man, I'm sorry. I know how it is when you lose one of your own."

Devlin nodded appreciatively and then said, "Nick, I need to know if it came from your side."

"If I find out something for you, I'm not going to hear about it, am I?"

Devlin did not answer, but stared at Trampelli long enough to make him reconsider his question.

"I'm sorry, Mike. I know you'd never front me, but this ain't me puking up some little gambling thing. This is all day. And both these punks got people at the top of your charts. You know what I'm saying?"

"If the questions were easy, I'd be at the library looking up the answers."

"Okay, okay. I'll ask around—gently."

"I'd expect no less from a gentle guy like you."

"Seriously, Mike, I've known these two since they were

born. They've had it easy their whole life. I don't think they got the stones to zipper a fed."

His informant was probably right. Gerrardi and Scarpa were nouveau mob and, as such, had never faced the criminal hardships that their fathers and grandfathers had. They had not developed the toughness that came from a reliance on code, tradition, and courage. They knew how to look and sound like gangsters, but when it came time to act, they lacked the dangerousness that was so necessary to enforce the everyday schemes of organized crime. Devlin doubted that the young mafiosi he had encountered had the equipment to cold-bloodedly execute an FBI agent, knowing they would then have to withstand the resulting onslaught. But Devlin did not know Paulie Gerrardi and Rhino Scarpa—yet. "Well, as soon as you tell me where they are, we're going to find out."

Effortlessly, Paulie Gerrardi's black Fleetwood cruised along the eastbound I-94 expressway at eighty miles an hour. His passenger was Peter "The Rhino" Scarpa.

As a young boy, Scarpa had been given the nickname "The Rhino" by his classmates who were busily discovering cruelty as a preadolescent form of expression. They laughed at his fat, clumsy body and the evil nose that started at the top of his eyebrows between dark, dull eyes and ended with a blunt upturned tip. But by the time he turned twelve, the fat had been displaced by thick sheaths of dense muscle and Peter Scarpa was teaching his critics that cruelty begets cruelty, in spades. After that, "Rhino" was carefully whispered only behind Scarpa's expansive back.

Eventually, he came to rely on the intimidation that the nickname and his menacing physique provided. When he was eighteen, his father, a local underboss, decided to start him out at the bottom and gave him a job collecting illegal debts. He was extremely successful—one warning from the ominous Rhino brought quick compliance with the Mafia's payment schedules. He was so feared that, in the four years he had collected for his father, he never once had to "tune a guy up," leaving the lesser leg-breakers green with envy.

Paul Gerrardi was a year older than the brooding Scarpa and felt, because of the blood oath between such men, it was his duty to pass down the unwritten but death-protected *codice* of the Mafia. " 'Nother thing, you always gotta lie to cops and women."

The subtleties of generations of Sicilian *codice* had their usual effect on Peter Scarpa. "Hey, Paulie, turn up the air, will ya? I'm sweatin' my balls off."

Gerrardi shook his head in resignation and smiled. "Man, the way you sweat, you should have a doctor check your fucking thermostat or something." He leaned over and turned up the air-conditioning slightly. As he did, he glanced in the rearview mirror. "Fuck!"

"What?"

"Someone's tagging us."

The Rhino knew it was futile to try to turn around in the constrictive front seat, so he bobbed and weaved like a boxer, trying to watch the road behind him in the side-view mirror. "You sure?"

"I'm doing eighty. One car behind us is doing eighty. He's way back but he's on us."

"You carrying anything?" Scarpa asked.

"No. I'm clean."

"Then fuck 'em. Let 'em follow us all day. We ain't doin' nothin'."

"Pete, where's your sense of humor? We got a chance to fuck with the FBI. Remember these are the cocksuckers that are trying to schedule us for a federal vacation."

Sullenly, Scarpa leaned back in an attempt to get comfortable and said, "Fuckin' do what you want."

Gerrardi was in the far left lane and carefully took the big Cadillac up to eighty-five miles an hour. He adjusted the rearview mirror and watched the tiny blue car at the edge of his vision increase its speed equally. Then he took it to ninety. The blue car responded. Finally, Gerrardi saw what he was looking for. There was a seam in the traffic in the middle and right lanes with an exit coming up. He pulled hard to the right, across both lanes, and slammed on his brakes. His car found the right-hand shoulder just short of the exit. As soon as his car stopped, he jumped out and waved to the blue car as it screamed by the exit. He watched as two more speeding, nondescript cars flashed by, trying to get to the right-hand lane while remaining inconspicuous. Gerrardi got back in his car and laughed. "Let's go do something illegal."

Scarpa's only response was "Let's go eat."

"Perfect! The way you eat *is* illegal."

Gerrardi found a hamburger joint. The exterior was covered with large white tile panels. Inside there were no tables, just a few stools bolted to the floor along the counter. As far as a block away, the restaurant's best advertisement was the overwhelming smell of its grilled onions. Scarpa loved the "bite-size" burgers in those places and usually ate a dozen at a sitting.

Gerrardi pulled around the back of the isolated building and nosed the car within a foot of the wall, in case the FBI was searching the area in an attempt to reestablish their surveillance.

As soon as he put the car into park, the two men felt a thud from behind. This time, Rhino managed to turn around and saw that another car had pinned them in.

The surveillance squad had been unaware that Devlin also was following the two men. He had spotted the C-9 cars and, because he hung back behind them, was able to anticipate the Cadillac's reckless exit from the expressway. Devlin got out of his car and walked up to Gerrardi's window, showing his credentials. "Paulie, nice move on the expressway."

Gerrardi shook his head slowly with disdain. "Why don't you fucking college boys get a fucking life?"

"Right now, girls, you are my life."

Gerrardi started to say something, but Scarpa put a hand on

his arm and leaned over so Devlin could see his dangerous face. "Hey, asshole, why don't you shit in your hat and wear it?" Scarpa nodded to Gerrardi, who smiled as his window rolled up with an expensive whir. "We'll just sit here until the motherfucker goes away." Defiantly, Scarpa turned up the radio so Devlin could hear it through the closed window. Then he turned up the air-conditioning and smiled at Devlin, who stood in the warming sun.

Devlin walked slowly back to his car and got in. He took something out of the glove compartment. Both men tried not to notice him walking to the front of the Cadillac. Below their line of sight, he sprayed a full can of Mace through the car's grille and into its air-conditioning system.

Devlin decided it would be a test to decide which of the two men was most committed to his anger. He stood in front of the car and watched through the windshield as their expressions changed from smugness to confusion to panic. Gerrardi caved in almost immediately. He threw his door open so hard it sprang back and knocked him to the ground as he blindly lunged out of his seat.

Scarpa held his ground a moment longer. He glared at Devlin through screaming eyes and then tunneled his way through the front seat toward the sweet air that beckoned him from outside the driver's door. He tripped and fell across Gerrardi. Both men were on their hands and knees, gasping for air.

The tear-gas test indicated to Devlin that if either of these men had killed John Lawson, it was probably Scarpa. Devlin stepped across Gerrardi and pulled Scarpa up by the front of his shirt. He could feel the armorlike muscle underneath and knew he would have to work fast. Devlin leaned him against the car and slapped him hard. "I'm sorry, Rhino. Did you say something about my hat?"

Scarpa tried to focus his threatening eyes on Devlin, but they still burned too much. Devlin slapped him again, harder. "I didn't think so, bitch." Devlin heard Gerrardi trying to stand up behind him. Turning around, he kicked one of Gerrardi's feet from under him. Gerrardi landed on his back. Slowly, Devlin bent over him and gave him a couple of light slaps on the cheek. "How about you, stupid? Do you have something to say?" As Devlin was about to slap Gerrardi again, Scarpa's eyes began to clear. Because Devlin was bent over, his jacket had ridden up over his stainless-steel Magnum. All in one motion, Scarpa jerked the gun out of Devlin's holster and pushed him on top of Gerrardi.

Scarpa had the gun pointed at the middle of Devlin's face. He helped his partner to his feet and smiled at Devlin nervously. "Who's the bitch now?"

Devlin stood up comfortably and said, "I thought they called you Rhino because of your size, but being this close, I guess it's because of that horn you call a nose."

"I ought to ace you right here, you motherfucker."

"Ought to? Pretty iffy for a tough guy like you. Maybe what the boys say is true: You *don't* have the stones, Rhino."

"Don't call me Rhino, you motherfucker!"

"I know what's bothering you, but don't worry. Even someone as ugly as you will find love in the joint."

Scarpa was starting to fear Devlin's sureness. He did not know why, but either this agent was crazy or he knew something Scarpa didn't.

"Christ, Pete, you can't whack a fed and walk away from it. Let it go," Gerrardi said.

Scarpa asked Devlin, "What do you want from us?"

"I just wanted to see if you'd kill me."

The two men looked at each other incredulously and then back at Devlin, who suddenly had a snubnose in his hand pointed at Scarpa. He waited a moment for them to react, and then Scarpa set Devlin's Magnum on the ground and both men put their hands in the air. Devlin picked up his revolver, reholstered it, and walked to his car. As he started to get in, Scarpa, with unintended respect, asked, "How'd ya know I wouldn't shoot?"

Devlin opened the car door and threw the snubnose on the

passenger's seat. Quickly, he drew his Magnum and pointed it at the Rhino's chest. He pulled the trigger, and both men winced as they heard the hollow click. Devlin smiled. "Because I had the only loaded gun."

||| CHAPTER 3 |||

He had chosen his crime carefully. After extensive research, most of which had been done at the University of Michigan's accommodating library, he decided on extortion. It was an exquisitely unsuccessful undertaking. No one ever really got away with it. He feared that was what appealed to him the most—its unconquerability. He had to constantly remind himself that his ego, if left untethered, would prove to be a greater adversary than the lawmen he was about to take on.

Because the FBI had been so successful preventing extortions, they would use the same tried-and-true procedures they always had. And why not? They had a 100 percent success rate. But he felt that their inflexibility, along with their complacency, would be the cause of his success. He had designed an intellectual Trojan horse.

His research, almost entirely from after-the-fact newspaper accounts, exposed one irrefutable warning: Everyone was caught at the drop site. As remote as extortionists tried to be, retrieving the money always brought them within arm's length of the law. No matter how ingenious the plan was, the Bureau's massive manpower seemed to overwhelm it. Manpower had always been their strength, but their dependency upon it would become their Achilles' heel.

Consequently, he decided, the Bureau had to be divided to be conquered. After long hours of planning and rereading his research, he decided his scheme must be devised to, above all, keep the FBI disorganized and off-balance.

* * *

Although Jack Tarver had told Seacard's executive vice president that experience had shown that the instructions for the delivery of the money would not be sent for a couple of days, the FBI agent did not immediately understand the significance of their early arrival. When he received a radio message that the extortionist's demands had arrived before his prediction, he hurried back to the office, only remotely aware of his discomfort at being kept off-balance.

The moment Tarver walked into the SAC's office, Sudder handed him two large clear plastic envelopes. "These arrived at Seacard two hours ago by Federal Express." One evidence jacket contained the billing slip and the other a typed note.

$5,000,000 (50 and 100 dollar bills) in two large suitcases. Ship on Greyhound Bus leaving Detroit 6 AM tomorrow to Miami, Florida, under name Robert Johnson. No interference.

"Shit!" Tarver said.

"What?"

"Do you know how many agents it will take to cover this? That's at least twenty-four hours' driving time plus at least a half-dozen stops."

"I don't care," said Sudder. "You just tell me what you need."

"But everyone's working John's murder."

"A couple of agents aren't going to be missed for a day or two. I just got another call from the director, and I'll tell you what I told him. We've got two hundred agents working on the murder; we'll get whoever killed Lawson. But this guy is threatening to kill innocent children. We can't ignore him; he's already killed one person. Now, how about the name and address on the billing slip? Is there anything we can do with that?"

"Robert Johnson" was also listed as the sender. He gave an

address on Dix Road in Dearborn, Michigan. Years of checking names had taught Tarver that Robert Johnson was an almost perfect alias. Johnson was one of the most common names in America; Robert only added to its anonymity. And, unlike some names, it was impossible to guess the racial or ethnic background of Mr. Johnson. Without other identifying data, such as a date of birth or Social Security number, an eternity could be wasted trying to identify all of the Robert Johnsons that would result from standard computer inquiries. A wave of uneasiness flooded Tarver. How had the extortionist picked such a flawless nonidentity?

The address promised similar resistance. Dearborn, a large suburb just to the southwest of Detroit, was the home of the Ford Motor Company, and the south end of Henry Ford's community, where Dix Road was located, was home to the world's largest concentration of Arabs outside the Middle East. Any law-enforcement inquiries in the area were usually greeted with a sudden, unexplainable loss of the ability to speak English. Tarver suspected the address would be as useless as the name.

He told the SAC about the calculated unidentifiability of the name and address. Sudder said, "Check it out anyway."

"I intend to. I'll also go by the Federal Express office and see if they remember who sent it."

"Good. What about the phone number in Ann Arbor?"

Tarver decided to lie. "When I found the room the call came from, there were a lot of people there. I remembered that you told Pendleton we had an advantage, because this guy was unaware that the Bureau was involved, so I decided not to go bigfooting through there and left without telling anyone who I was."

Like Tarver, the SAC was starting to feel the vague, shapeless confusion caused by the extortionist's ingenuity. "After you cover those leads in Dearborn, you better get packed for Miami."

* * *

When Devlin got home, Knox had not returned from St. Barney's yet. He checked his watch and guessed that she was on her way to pick up their children, Kathleen and Patrick, from one activity or another. Upstairs, he fell into bed, and as if it were a trailing parachute, sleep collapsed over him with a billowing softness.

Four hours later, Devlin's alarm went off. He sat on the bed, staring through eyes that were thick with sleep's delicious opiates, and tried to remember if any of the events of the last twenty-four hours were real or just part of slumber's nightly magic show. He picked up the phone and called Bill Shanahan.

"Mike. I was just hanging out the do-not-disturb sign."

"Anything happening?"

"They had C-Nine on Gerrardi and Scarpa, but they made the surveillance and lost them."

"Something tells me we should be looking somewhere else."

"You're probably right. I don't think they're smart enough to pull off something like this," said Shanahan.

"Did the evidence techs find anything else at the factory?"

"Nothing."

"What about John's car?"

"The only latents were his. He just had it washed that afternoon. Not another print anywhere."

"What about Behavioral Science?"

"Do you know Bill Hagstrom from the unit?"

"Only by reputation."

"He flew in but could stay only about three hours. There's another hostage crisis. Somewhere out west. Let me dig out my notes." After a minute, Shanahan came back on the phone. "Let's see. He said he's a male, probably white. No guess on the age. The organized type of killer. He based that on the fact that he was disciplined enough to lure John to the factory. Intelligent, because he was able to fabricate a story with enough insight about how the Bureau works to get John to meet him alone. Hagstrom also felt the kill was efficient, controlled, and economical."

"If it was economical, why the second shot when he was already dead?"

"That's what I asked. He said it was economical from the killer's viewpoint. Time-wise and within a space that offered no risk for him. The second shot had nothing to do with the economy of the kill. It had a purpose, but Hagstrom wanted to give it some more thought before venturing a guess. When I hear, I'll let you know."

"What about the slugs?"

"They *were* Federal Hydra-Shok." Anticipating Devlin's next question, Shanahan said, "*And*, I asked around. Everyone said he was a family man first. I confirmed this with one of my reliable sources. So it's unlikely he was fooling around with another agent's wife."

"Not that I don't trust everyone from South Boston, but define *reliable*."

"Reliable is a lusty young thing that made him an offer he evidently *could* refuse last month at the office bowling party. Do you want me to define *lusty*?"

"Go to bed, William."

"There is one other thing. You know they're reviewing John's old cases and they found one that was interesting. Do you know who Watusi Sims is?"

Devlin had heard the name years ago at Detroit Homicide. "A narcotics hit man?"

"That's the guy. About five years ago, he gets tangled up with the Sicilian Mafia which John had a case on, and he makes Sims on a heroin importation case. He catches twenty years, but they can't make a case on any of the Sicilians. But the Watusi man isn't your typical dope dealer; he won't roll over on anyone, not because he's ethical but because he hates everybody. So the Italians get some high-octane law firm to get him out on appeal. He got out two weeks ago. Remember the caller said he wanted to talk to John about an old organized-crime case? And this guy is supposed to be an ice-cold hitter. Harrison wants us to concentrate on him, but we can't find him. If I were him, I wouldn't want anyone knowing where I was, either, especially the Sicilians."

"Do you like him?"

"The timing's right. Just out of the joint. And he's making himself scarce. I'll know better if I can get him in and talk to him. That's my job tomorrow."

"Any idea where he's at?"

"You're the one with the contacts. Hell, I didn't even know who he was."

"But I'll be at the casino for the next twelve hours."

"Mike, save that bullshit for the suits. I know you. I could blow that building up tonight and you wouldn't be close enough to hear the bang."

"I might be able to make a call for you."

Shanahan laughed. "I'd appreciate it." Both men hung up.

Devlin considered Watusi Sims. He had a few checkmarks in the right columns, but some things just didn't fit. As cold-blooded as he was, Sims knew that John Lawson was just "taking care of business." Lawson had sent him to prison straight up. He had not lied, cheated, or falsified. As twisted as a criminal's mind becomes, *business* is a universally accepted reason for not seeking revenge. Then there were the hollowpoints. It would have been a hell of a coincidence that Sims would have randomly selected ammunition that was issued to FBI agents. But Devlin had found the word *coincidence* was unexpectedly common during murder investigations.

He dialed Temper Hanlon's home number. "Any luck with those stiffs down at Assumed Names?"

"That's a frightening thought."

"What?"

"Getting lucky at Assumed Names. I guess if you were ever charged with necrophilia, that would be the perfect defense: I didn't know they were dead. I just thought I was having sex with a civil servant."

"Let me ask you a different way: Did you find out who owned Bridgeline Glove?"

"Yeah. Are you ready for this? Amos Codswallor. With a name like that you'd think he would be either the bare-knuckles champion of the universe or a serial murderer. But I tracked him down and he's cooperative. He's putting together what he has, but the bulk of his records are stored up north in a barn at his summer place. I told him it was urgent, so he's doing it right now. I'm supposed to pick up the list tonight at ten. He lives in West Bloomfield. Where are you going to be tonight between ten-thirty and eleven?"

Devlin thought for a second. "I should be down at Homicide by eleven."

"Very romantic, Devlin."

Devlin dressed, and when he came downstairs he found a note on the stove.

Hope we didn't wake you. Took Katie with me to Pat's game. He's supposed to pitch tonight. Dinner's in the oven.

We miss you,
K

He did not like missing any of his children's activities. He had played baseball all the way through high school and his father had never come to a game. It was something Devlin never understood, because when he was there watching the two of them, his life, as dark and confusing as it could sometimes get, made perfect sense. Especially at this age—Pat was nine and Katie would soon be twelve. They were discovering who they were, which, while occasionally frustrating, was a fascinating passage to witness. He folded the note and put it in his pocket. Somewhere in the loneliness of the night, he would read it again.

Devlin parked half a block from the casino and walked quickly to the building. He had decided to fake the video monitoring.

He was assigned the 10 P.M. to 10 A.M. shift, but usually everyone was gone by dawn, leaving him plenty of time to complete the paperwork before his shift ended. His sole responsibility was to witness, for testimony in court, the videotaping of the activities of the casino. It was a menial task that required very little work, so Devlin was going to start the video cameras at ten, leave to work on the murder, and then return to review the tapes on fast-forward while creating the corresponding log of events. In reality, there had not been, and probably would not be, a single federal law broken at the casino, but what Devlin was about to do was a blatant violation of the wiretap statute. Ironic, he thought, that he could be the only one charged with a felony during the entire project. He turned on the monitors and started recording. It was just before ten and the casino was still empty. He headed for his car.

At the Detroit Police Department headquarters building, he took the elevator to the fifth floor and walked into the Homicide Unit. The sergeant working the desk waved him through. Inspector Jerome Wicks's office was open, and his suit coat hung on the back of his chair. A detective walked in and placed a report on Wicks's desk. "Where's Jerry?" Devlin asked.

"He's interviewing the guy we got in on those hooker strangulations." Nine black prostitutes had been found bound and strangled in the last six months along Woodward Avenue, the busy Detroit street that separated the city's east and west sides.

Devlin walked into a small room that was adjacent to the interview room. Two young black detectives, both wearing suspenders and floral-print ties, sat on the edge of a long wooden table. They peered through the one-way mirror, and watched intently as if Jerome Wicks were performing a secret surgical procedure unknown to the rest of the world. With mock snobbery, the two detectives nodded at Devlin's casino clothes. He smiled and sat down next to them on the table.

Wicks had just finished advising the prisoner of his rights and handed him a felt-tip pen. The suspect signed the waiver form, indicating that he understood his rights. The thick inky signature dominated the typed warnings above it, as if it were itself a confession.

As soon as the suspect finished signing, the detective next to Devlin started the timer on his wristwatch. Devlin noticed that Wicks, the first black inspector in charge of Homicide, was also wearing suspenders and a floral-print tie.

The head of Homicide started in a low, defined voice that gave promise, like the distant rumble of thunder, that an awful authority was heading that way. "Now let me ask you something, Antonio. There are one million people in this city, and out of that million you're the one guy we have in here talking about these murders. Do you think that's an accident, or do you think we've got some reason to believe that you're our man?"

The confidence in Wicks's voice made Antonio fold his arms across his chest defensively as he considered his answer. Then his face changed as if some serious decision had been reached. "Man, I don't even like girls. You see"—a small, clever smile rockered his lips—"I'm a male prostitute." He looked into Wicks's restless eyes to see if his irrefutable defense had registered and then uncrossed his arms and thrust his hands into his pockets buoyantly.

People who knew Wicks would have detected the slightest change in his expression. It was one of advantage, as if an opponent had chosen the wrong opening square in a chess match.

Stoically, Wicks sat and let Antonio ramble on about his experiences as a prostitute and about the lover he lived with. For five long minutes Wicks listened attentively while both detectives looked at each other, questioning their boss's lack of interviewing control.

Then suddenly, as if an alarm had gone off, Wicks shot to his feet and, through clenched teeth, hissed, "Shut the fuck up! I'm not listening to any more of your lies. Do you understand?" Antonio turned away. "I said, do you understand?" The prisoner seemed frozen. "Look at me!" Wicks ordered, but Antonio could not. Wicks's voice was now evil. "Look at me, goddamnit!" Antonio's eyes surrendered. Again Wicks said, "Do you understand? No more lies."

Antonio's glance dropped to the floor; an embarrassed "yes" was his only answer.

"Stand up!" Wicks ordered, and Antonio stood up. "Take off your shirt." The suspect obeyed, exposing his taut brown skin, graffitied with pale scratches and bite marks.

"Where'd you get those?"

"Some of my dates get pretty rough."

Wicks's voice rose again. "Look at me!" Reluctantly, Antonio's eyes found Wicks's. "I told you, no more lies. Take off your pants."

With increasing resignation, Antonio slowly stripped off his pants and stood embarrassed in his red bikini shorts. His legs were relatively free of marks. "Sit down."

"Can I put my clothes on?"

"No," Wicks answered quickly. The two detectives sitting beside Devlin shook their heads in appreciation of Wicks's ingenious method of taking control of the suspect. Antonio folded his arms across his chest, signaling his vulnerability. Wicks continued, "It's not normal for a man to have sex with another man for money. There's something wrong with your head, and until we get that figured out, we can't even begin to understand this other shit."

Antonio looked genuinely curious about what Wicks was saying. "Can I call my mother? I need to talk to her." In tandem, the two detectives leaned closer to the glass, sensing a change in the direction of the interview.

Wicks, realizing he had found that vulnerable nerve that all interrogators search for, pressed his attack. "Why would a male prostitute want to talk to his mama?"

Antonio stiffened with anger. "I love my mother."

"What about your father?"

"He left when I was born."

"So your mother raised you?"

"Yeah, I guess so."

"Doesn't sound like she did."

"Well, she did! When she could."

"When she could?"

"When she wasn't in prison." Now Devlin leaned closer. He knew it was not uncommon for serial murderers to have mothers who had spent time in prison.

Wicks pressed on. "Who did you live with when she was gone?"

Antonio looked down at his long, powerful hands. "Foster homes and the orphanage," he said, his voice trying to find some pride in the survival of his childhood.

"How old were you when you were first molested?"

Wicks asked the question matter-of-factly, but it slapped Antonio across the face. "I ain't never been molested!"

"I'm trying to understand what happened to you so I can help you, but I'm not going to tell you again—don't lie to me! I've never seen anyone yet who's put in time in an orphanage that wasn't molested. It isn't anything to be ashamed of— Christ, you were just a kid. Now, how old were you?"

Silently Antonio struggled with the question. His eyes darted around the room but could find no escape. He grabbed the seat of his chair with both hands and rocked back and forth nervously. Understanding Antonio's body language, the detective who was timing Wicks looked at his watch. In a straining whisper, Antonio answered, "Seven."

Wicks hesitated so Antonio could become comfortable with his admission and then asked, "What is your first recollection of your mother?"

Antonio thought for a second before answering. "I guess I was about five. My mother would dress up my brother and me and take us with her."

"Take you where?"

Again his eyes sank to his hands. "On her dates."

"And what would you do during her dates?"

"We would sit in the backseat of the car."

"Your mother's car?"

"Her date's car."

"And where was your mother?"

Antonio was frozen, as if he were standing at the edge of a hundred-story building. Calmly Wicks asked the question again. "Where was your mother, Antonio?"

With equal calm Antonio answered, "In the front seat."

Although Wicks knew the answer, he patiently asked the next question. "What was she doing in the front seat, Antonio?"

The prisoner's shoulders began to shake, his hands knotted hatefully. He looked up at the inspector. "She was fuckin' him. The bitch was fuckin' him. Right in front of me and my little brother."

Wicks put a reassuring hand on Antonio's shoulder. "Anyone in their right mind could see why you hate prostitutes." Antonio was nodding now. "It's not like they deserve to live." He continued to nod. "Now I understand why you killed them."

Antonio stared at Wicks hopefully, as though the inspector had the power to absolve him of his guilt. "I'm glad you got me. I had to tell someone about it. Thank God, I won't be able to kill any more of them." Wicks lit a cigarette for Antonio and told him to get his clothes on. He closed the door as he left and opened the door to the room that Devlin and the detectives were in.

As he walked in, the detective with the watch said, "I think that's a new record, boss." Both detectives applauded slowly.

Wicks said, "Knock that shit off. Go in there and take the confessions. He killed at least nine women, so I want at least nine confessions. Confessions filled with detail. Details that will keep us off of his attorney's Christmas card list. Do you understand?"

"Yes, sir," both detectives responded in unison. As they got up, they watched as Antonio stood and walked over to a clean spot on the graffiti-covered walls. With Wicks's felt-tip pen, he wrote carefully: BELIEVE IN THE LORD AND HE SHALL DE-LIVER. He then sat down and contemplated the words.

Wicks led the detectives back into the room and introduced them to Antonio. As he was leaving, he picked up his pen and wrote under Antonio's words: DON'T CONFUSE GOD WITH DOMINO'S.

Wicks came back into the room with Devlin and watched his detectives to make certain Antonio was going to talk to them. Then he nodded for Devlin to follow him to his office.

The two men shook hands. Wicks seemed amused by his friend's clothes. Devlin started to explain, but Wicks held up his hand. "I don't even want to know."

"You'll listen to Antonio's lies, but not mine."

"I get paid to listen to his. Yours have a habit of making my life more difficult."

"Speaking of making your life more difficult—Watusi Sims."

"Yeah, I heard he was out."

"We need to talk to him."

"On the Lawson killing?"

"Have you heard something?" asked Devlin.

"I heard you weren't going to be working it. I tried to get some money down, but no one in your office wanted to bet on you following orders."

"A disloyal bunch."

"Is Sims supposed to be tied in?"

"I don't know. You know him. Has he still got the heart?"

"Oh, he's got the heart. Back when I was a sergeant on Squad Six during the heroin wars, we pulled out the Ouija board and figured him for lighting up at least twenty-five of the drug culture's entrepreneurs. Just last year in Marion, he used an acetylene torch to warm up a guy's head past the melting point. Needless to say, there were no more late dope payments in that prison."

"Lawson's the guy who put him in Marion."

"I made that scene. Didn't feel like Sims. He likes to shoot them more than twice. But who knows? You do learn to be more economical in prison."

Economical was the word Bill Hagstrom from BSU had used to describe the killing. That was the second coincidence that had Sims's name attached. "How hard are your people working this?" Devlin asked.

"Your ASAC asked us to lay back. Said that they would like to handle it themselves. He was decent about it, and we certainly have enough to do. But we still have an open case."

"Can you find out where Sims is?"

"Dinner at the restaurant of my choice?"

"Dinner at the restaurant of *my* choice. I've had enough chili dogs to last me the rest of this millennium."

"But the way you're dressed *screams* chili dog." Wicks picked up the phone and dialed one of his informants. When he hung up, he handed Devlin a piece of paper with a Detroit address on it. "He's supposed to be there all night."

One of the detectives interviewing Antonio knocked on the door. "Inspector, he just gave us number ten. Says she hasn't been found yet."

"Did he give you the location of the body?"

"Not yet."

"Go in there and get it. It'll prove beyond any doubt that we've got the right man. I'll be right there." He turned to Devlin. "Sorry, Mike, I'd like to stay and help you get into some more trouble, but . . ."

Devlin held up the slip of paper. "Thanks, Jerry. I'm sure you've done enough already." They shook hands again, and Devlin watched him walk away. Some called Wicks the world's greatest salesman. It was probably true, because at Homicide there was only one product to sell—a life sentence.

Devlin went out to the desk. The duty sergeant sat across from Temper Hanlon, playing liar's poker. From the relative size of the stacks of dollar bills in front of each of them, she appeared to be beating his brains out. But, like everyone who encountered Temper, the sergeant was enjoying himself.

Devlin looked at his watch. "You came early."

"You don't know how many times I've made that exact

same complaint to my husband." She turned and, with the flair of a Las Vegas croupier, swept her stack of dollar bills off the desk and said to the weathered sergeant, "Want some advice?" The sergeant, knowing the answer was unstoppable, just smiled his surrender. "Don't cheat on your wife. The way you lie, she'll murder you in divorce court." The sergeant smiled a little harder and slowly shook his head.

Temper and Devlin started down the hall. She said, "He wouldn't let me go back and find you."

"So you were going to take all his money?"

"It was going to be a bribe. But I got the feeling I wouldn't have gotten in anyway."

"Count yourself lucky. It's probably the best place in Detroit to be barred from."

She pulled out a large tan envelope. "Here's some of the Bridgeline employees. These are the ones that were working there when the place closed."

"What about the rest?"

"In a week or so. Codswallor has to go out of town on business."

"Sounds good."

"What are you going to do with them?" she asked.

"Nothing right now. When we get the complete list, we'll cross-check them against any names that come up. If there are any matches, then we'll have somebody to look at. Thanks for running these down."

"Thanks? That's it? You make me a coconspirator and all I get is *thanks*! Come on, Devlin, you're at Homicide for a reason."

Devlin tried not to look into her irrepressible eyes, but once he did he felt his defenses crumble. He told her about Watusi Sims being a suspect and about getting his address from Wicks.

"Well, let's go," Temper demanded.

"Whoa. I thought you were pregnant."

"Just a little. About a month."

"I can't take you with. This isn't beach volleyball. This guy is in the *Guinness Book of Records* under 'Lowest Heart Rate During a Homicide.' "

"Let me explain something to you, Devlin. And listen good, because I don't like to whine about the same thing twice. In another month or two, when I'm good and pregnant, I'm going to kiss this mutha good-bye." Devlin looked at her, surprised she was thinking of quitting the Bureau. "That's right, I'm going to leave the Big Crime Club and spend the next ten years with the carpenter having spectacular babies. For the last seven years, they've tried to turn me into Little Miss Muffet by having me work those god-awful Medicare-Medicaid fraud cases. I'd like to have some memories of helping on at least one decent case, and I can't think of a better one than this."

Devlin felt himself slipping into her quickening eyes. "And what do I tell your husband if something goes wrong?"

Her eyes smiled. "Tell him he lost the best trim he'll ever have."

The address Wicks had given Devlin was on the northwest side of the city. It was a little after midnight when he and Temper pulled to the curb a block away. Devlin did not like working the street at that time of the night. It seemed that at midnight no one in Detroit was asleep.

"Wait here," he ordered, and was out of the car before the debate could begin. Temper watched him disappear into the navy-blue shadows that lined the sidewalks. Uncharacteristically, she dug through the layers of normal handbag items until her graceful fingers found the hard, reassuring edges of her revolver. She opened the cylinder to ensure it was loaded. She never unloaded it; the act was simply to offset the fear she was feeling after being set adrift so abruptly amid the anarchy of Detroit's night.

Ten minutes later, Devlin reappeared and got into the car. "He's in there."

"Whatta we do?" Devlin detected a slight adrenaline-induced staccato to her speech, indicating that she understood the volatility of the situation.

"They're in there right now whackin' and sackin'." Temper looked at him for an explanation. "They're cutting and packaging dope for street sale. They had the curtains drawn, but the window was open a crack, probably to keep the air clear. I could hear them discussing how much cut to put on it. I even heard them working the grinder."

"Can we call Narcotics?"

"There isn't time. These dealers know how long it takes to get a search warrant, so they do the entire process in a couple of hours. They bring in the dope and all the equipment, package it, and it's gone before anyone can do anything about it. They know that narcotic-enforcement crews are rarely scheduled after midnight, so if you wanted a search warrant you'd have to scramble them out of their homes or, more likely, out of whatever saloon they had taken over for the night. Then you have to type the warrant, drive to some judge's home, and get him out of bed to sign it. Then hit the house. Minimum three to four hours. By then, half of that dope will be in their customers' veins."

"Didn't Wicks's source say Sims would be there all night?"

"You have to remember: Drug informants are some of the most unreliable. There's no national review board for their information. They can tell us whatever they want, exaggerate it, shade it, or just be honestly wrong. Sources are a great tool, especially Wicks's, but even the best tools have built houses that have slid into the ocean. Besides, these dope dealers are unpredictable. If Sims finishes packaging and leaves, there's a good chance he won't be back here tonight. He doesn't know *why* the Sicilians got him out of prison, but he's smart enough not to want to find out. From now on, he probably won't stay more than one night anywhere."

"Do we forget about it?"

"No, but if we took his dope away, he'd have no reason to leave, and Shanahan could round him up in the morning."

"Hey, Mike, I know I said I wanted a little adventure in my life, but I was thinking about something relatively safe, like skydiving with Dr. Kevorkian packing my chute, not sticking up dope pads."

Devlin smiled artfully.

Watusi Sims stood back from the Formica-top table that the three men were using to cut and package his heroin. They had finished mixing it with the cutting agent and a large powdery cone sat in front of each of them. All three men working at the table wore commercial sanding masks for the same reason Sims stood away from the table: to avoid inhaling the addictive dust that floated up into the immediate air. The angry black handle of Sims's large-frame automatic stuck out of the waistband of his pants, reminding the three men of his reputation. Carefully, each kept his particular hill of poison visible at all times. To skim Watusi Sims's dope was one of Detroit's quickest methods of suicide.

Suddenly there was a loud, hard pounding on the front door. The four men froze. Then came the words that panic the most hardened dope dealers: "Police! Open up! We have a search warrant!"

All four men broke for the back door. Now there was pounding at the back door as well. Sims called out instantly, "Flush it!"

As each of the three men took his portion of heroin to the available sinks and toilets, the banging and yelling outside intensified. In the kitchen, Sims took a large bowl and started filling it with water. He peeked out the back window. A female narcotics officer was banging on the back door with a black metal flashlight in one hand and a gun in the other. He remembered the gun he always carried in his belt and threw it into the freezer. In less than two minutes, all the heroin was flushed down the dope-house drains. Sims took the bowl of water from the sink and with short, well-aimed splashes rinsed the narcotic residue off the table. It soaked deep into the thick shag carpeting from which it would never be recovered.

Sims told the three men to sit down in the living room and relax as he went to the front door.

Devlin and Temper stood at the door, smiling equally. Temper stepped forward and looked into Sims's flinty eyes. "Hey, you're black. I'm sorry. We must have the wrong house."

Devlin found a phone and called Shanahan at home. He gave him the address where he would find Watusi Sims in the morning.

III CHAPTER 4 III

Jack Tarver was definitely off-balance. He was on I-75, one hour south of Toledo, Ohio, in a Bureau car that would in all likelihood be his home for the next twenty-four hours. He had not gotten to bed until one in the morning, but because he was the case agent for the extortion, he felt it was necessary to be up at four to double-check all the arrangements for leading the six-man team to Miami.

Two of the agents, under the guise of travelers, would ride on the bus. Tarver and the other three men would drive two Bureau cars trailing the relentless Greyhound. Two suitcases, containing the cut typing paper, were stored in the belly of the diesel-driven beast.

Tarver urged his mind to search for different ploys that the extortionist might use to retrieve the suitcases. He and his crew had discussed the obvious ones, such as trying to rob the bus at gunpoint during one of its stops or simply getting some dupe to pick up the bags in Miami. The dupe theory had gotten the most votes during the previous night's briefing. But now the soothing hum of FBI tires on the Ohio interstate was releasing a wonderfully warm fatigue into Tarver's brain, and in reprisal his mind refused to create any new contingencies.

He had spent the previous afternoon in Dearborn trying to identify Robert Johnson both at the sender's address and at the FedEx office where the instructions had been mailed.

Before he went to Dearborn, he had pondered the trail the extortionist was leaving. Was he doing it purposely? Was he watching the Federal Express office to see if Seacard had alerted the FBI? Tarver contacted the surveillance squad and requested that they cover his visit to Dearborn and photograph any worthy targets. The only information Tarver's investigation had developed was that Robert Johnson's home address was fictitious and that the man who had sent the letter was in his twenties or thirties and appeared to be an Arab. The clerk remembered him because she knew that the name Robert Johnson, whatever it might be, was not Arabic.

Tarver rolled down the Bureau car window and dumped out the cold coffee he had been carrying the last sixty miles. His eyes closed heavily, and just as he was about to drift off, he reminded himself that he had more important things to do. He could sleep after he captured and personally strangled the extortionist.

He pulled out the photos of the twenty-three men that the surveillance squad had taken the day before. Each member of his team had an identical set of photos. He studied the faces of the young Arab males, hoping that one of them would simply show up at the next stop and ask for the suitcases. For a moment he let his concentration wander as he thought about transferring to white-collar crime, civilized violations of the law that occur, *and are investigated*, between 9 A.M. and 5 P.M.

The night before, after leaving Temper at her Bureau car outside DPD headquarters, Devlin drove to the Bridgeline glove factory. He knew that an extensive "neighborhood" had been done by an army of agents the day after the murder, contacting residents for six blocks in every direction. It was not unusual in Detroit that a single factory would be the only industrial property in a residential neighborhood. The city contained hundreds of such factories. Before World War II, many of the people in the industrial Midwest had jobs they were able to walk to.

Devlin also knew that at one o'clock in the morning, different people were in those houses than had been there during the day. The difficulty was in getting them to answer the door after dark. Realizing he could not canvass every house for six blocks in every direction, he drove slowly through the streets surrounding the factory and studied a map for routes to and from the expressways. Years of investigating bank robberies had taught him that quickly accessible expressways were always a major consideration in planning a crime. He narrowed it down to four one-block stretches. The task would be tedious and frustrating, and chances for any success were unlikely, but, historically, reinvestigating leads was responsible for the solution of a surprising number of difficult cases. Devlin took out Knox's note and reread it slowly. He drew a deep breath of resolve and knocked on the first door.

By 7 A.M. he had completed the neighborhood investigation. Of the dozens of people he had interviewed, not one would admit seeing anything. He hated that type of investigation; it was something he knew would be unproductive, but the haystack always had to be searched for the possibility of a needle. He drove to the casino and for the next two and a half hours reviewed videotapes of the gambling activity and counterfeited the corresponding logs. When he arrived at the office, he dropped off the "evidence" with the Electronic Surveillance clerk and went looking for Shanahan. On the twenty-sixth floor, he found him in an interview room. He was interrogating Watusi Sims. When Devlin stuck his head in the door, Sims glared at him, remembering his face as that of one of the people who had caused the dope dealer to flush enough heroin to rate a middle-class tax bracket.

Shanahan stepped out into the hallway with Devlin and shut the door.

"Well?" Devlin asked with a mixture of exhaustion and blind hope.

"I'm afraid we got off on the wrong foot. When we rolled up on the house this morning, he was leaving. I gave him a pat and he was carrying the biggest forty-five automatic I've ever seen. He knows he's going back to the slam for the piece, so he *ain't* real friendly. I also think he's into transcendental meditation. Keeps chanting the same mantra—'Wantmymuthafuckinlawyer, WANTMYMUTHAFUCKINLAWYER.' "

"Did you ask him about John?"

"When I asked him the name, he says he doesn't know him. When I told him about the murder, he smiled and said he wished he had hit him."

"What do you think?"

"I can't get a read on him at all. Thought about asking him to take a polygraph, but I'm sure I'd get better vital signs in a frozen meat locker. Meanwhile, they're over at the United States Attorney's office getting search warrants for his house and car."

"Is there anything I can do?"

"How about taking a run at him?"

Devlin laughed. "Did you see the look he gave me?"

"Mike, these animals love you. The worse they are, the more they're drawn to you." Shanahan smiled. "You have a gift."

Devlin shook his head slowly. "*I* have a gift?" He walked into the interview room and sat down in a chair in front of Watusi Sims.

Sims looked at Devlin with lifeless eyes. He knew what was coming. It was always the same with cops: They had to punish you. Even if they couldn't get you to confess, they were going to torture you with their self-righteousness. Whether they were playing the bad cop or the good cop, they had to look down on you. Devlin said, "I guess you'll have to go back to prison." His voice was unexpectedly soft, with an odd mixture of empathy and resignation.

The boredom left Sims's eyes and he looked at Devlin differently, sensing something genuine in the agent's words. "What's your name, man?"

"Mike Devlin."

"How come you didn't bust me last night while we was packaging?"

"Come on, you know how long it takes to get paper in the

middle of the night. Besides, I've always been a big supporter of the small businessman."

Sims smiled. "Anyway, I appreciate it. Woulda cost me a lot in legal fees for my people, plus now they're gonna flop me only on the gun. If you got me with all that, boy, I'd been lookin' at a lot more time. Maybe even all day."

"We just needed to know where to get ahold of you this morning."

"Pretty slick."

"How about returning the favor."

"The agent?"

"Yeah. I know you're not going to give yourself up, but if you can prove to us that you didn't do it, we can get off of you and look somewhere else." Sims nodded. Devlin said, "Okay, I'm *not* going to give you your rights, so whatever you say is inadmissible."

"You *are* slick."

"Did you know John Lawson?"

"You know I took a cop on the heroin charges so I never went to trial. That's when you get to hate the guy who's trying to put you inside. If he's the guy who cracked me, I never paid much attention."

"So you're telling me you had no beef with anyone in the FBI."

"Only a fool would go after whoever locks him up. When you're in that cell, all you think about is getting out and staying out. Besides, I ain't crazy enough to fuck with you people."

"You're not?" Devlin said with half a smile, reminding Sims of his reputation.

"Whatever I did in the past, I meant to. You know, to protect my business. But killing a cop, especially a fed, is extremely bad for business. When did it happen?"

"Day before yesterday. Late afternoon, early evening."

"I can't even remember where I was."

The two men sat in silence. They both knew that nothing

could be proved or disproved in this room unless Sims confessed, and they both knew that was not going to happen.

"I guess we're not going to figure this out today."

"If you're going to keep looking at me, you ain't never going to figure it out. It's simple—I don't do cops."

"Do you know anyone who does?"

Sims hesitated. He was making a decision. "I'm forty-seven years old. I've been in prison almost half of my life. I'm tired. I know I gotta go back; I ain't asking for nothing. You probably checked and know I never gave nobody up. And I'm not giving them up now because I don't know for sure." Sims hesitated again. Devlin gazed at him patiently. "My lawyer told me something about the Sicilians."

Sims stopped. He wanted to be prodded into continuing, to be relieved of informer status. Devlin understood. "What about the Sicilians?"

"Do you know anything about them?"

"I know they take business very seriously."

"You ain't bullshittin'. I've survived a lot of shit during thirty years of dealing. The reason I have is because I know the moves. I'm pretty sure they got me out so they could kill me. Like you say, they don't leave business unfinished. And *I'm* unfinished business. But when my lawyer met with the federal prosecutor to deal, the Sicilian who was indicted with me had his lawyer there too. That fucking prosecutor was smart. He knew he had a bullshit case on the Sicilian, so he gets my lawyer in there and starts talking about cutting me a deal so the Sicilians will think I'm going to roll over on everybody. But my lawyer knows what the fuck is what, so he insists the prosecutor makes my deal with the government in front of the Sicilian lawyer so they'd know I wasn't going to testify. Then, after all that is worked out, the prosecutor asks if the Sicilian wants to cop a plea. The lawyer just smiles and says he'll see him in court. The prosecutor smiles and says the FBI has their best man on the case and it's only a matter of time. The Sicilian lawyer then asked for the guy's name."

"Did the U.S. Attorney give it to him?"

"I don't know, but when my attorney was telling me about it, he was saying what a stupid move it was because the agent's name was on most of the papers. You know, from the wiretap and search warrants."

"Did your lawyer think they were going to do something about the agent?"

"Alls I know is that he told me the story because he thought they might see me as a loose end too."

"We're going to need to talk to your lawyer."

"Stanley Katz. In the Buhl Building. You can tell him it's from me."

Devlin nodded his appreciation. He stepped out into the hallway and gave Shanahan the details of the interview. "Thanks, Mike. We'll talk to the United States Attorney and Katz."

"And the Sicilians?"

"We'll do the best we can." A certain degree of surrender sounded in Shanahan's voice. It was a natural reaction when an agent was called on to investigate the Sicilian Mafia. The Americanization of the traditional Mafia was irreversibly disintegrating its infrastructure. Lost forever were its strengths—code and brotherhood. They were being replaced by greed and the Witness Protection Program. Unlike its American cousin, the Sicilian Mafia remained perfectly ruthless. Its allegiances remained with the underworld bosses in Sicily. Their crime was usually the importation of drugs, primarily heroin. While the Sicilians were excellent smugglers, they had no "marketers" in America and looked to established outlets to sell their product. They used large-scale heroin dealers, usually the LCN, but occasionally they would employ others who had good reputations, such as Watusi Sims. Known for their "business is everything" attitude, they took no prisoners. Their justice system was simple. All violations had only one penalty—sudden, unconditional death. In the United States they were all related by blood or marriage and kept low profiles by working regular jobs.

Many of them spoke very little English, which deepened their
bond and strengthened their impenetrability.

"Where are you going?" Shanahan asked Devlin.

"To bed."

Reluctantly, Knox Devlin had come to the distasteful conclusion that she had wanted her husband to deceive her. Believing
his little fable about not being allowed to investigate John
Lawson's murder was the easiest way for her to deal with a renewed fear of losing him.

Before, she had always, as he joked, "supported his wander-
ings into the night," but after he had been wounded in a
shootout with a serial murderer, she no longer found his meta-
phorical "night" amusing. For the first time since he had joined
the Bureau, she found herself involuntarily asking less-than-
encouraging questions about his assignments; and he, sensing
her apprehension, slowly offered guarded and understated,
if not misleading, responses. Paradoxically, their concern
for each other was the cause of a growing lack of communication.

He had tried to create a safety net between what he was doing and what she was exposed to. And she returned the favor
by developing night blindness. Why else would she accept his
denial about the Lawson case? His not getting involved was
contrary to everything he stood for, everything that caused her
daily to fall in love with him.

She did love his recklessness, his refusal to let fear constrain
justice, his unwillingness to concede to any outrage, no matter
how difficult the weight of its repair. But now, because of the
stakes, she hated it too.

That afternoon she had been listening to the news when the
anchorwoman said, "Agent Lawson apparently had gone to
meet an unknown person alone." *Alone!* It was the way her
husband preferred to work—especially when excluded from a
case of such personal importance.

She looked at the clock. He was due home soon. She knew

that if she confronted him, he would tell her the truth no matter how unhappy it made her. She was determined to find out and, already knowing the answer, to try and stop him. She sat down at a desk in the kitchen and busied herself paying bills.

As soon as Devlin walked into the kitchen, he recognized the combative alignment of his wife's eyes and mouth. Hoping for the best, he casually asked, "How are you?"

"You know, I was sitting here this afternoon listening to the news about John's murder, and this wonderfully warm feeling came over me because I knew my husband wasn't looking for this lunatic. But then this strange voice asked me, 'Are you stupid? We're talking about Mike Devlin.' Am I being stupid, Mike?"

"I told you. I was ordered not to get involved."

"That's what was bothering me. When someone tells you not to do something, the only thing you hear is the starter's pistol. Just tell me you're not *going* to work on it and I'll tell that little voice to mind its own business." Since he knew he could not lie to her, he said nothing. Her tone became hard, sardonic. "For once, let the other ten thousand agents handle it."

"I'm sorry, Knox. You know it doesn't work that way for me."

"That's right . . . for *you!*"

"It's just another case. Nothing more."

"No, this time it's some maniac who thinks nothing of murdering an FBI agent!"

"That's exactly why I can't walk away."

"No, you can't walk away because you're selfish. That's why you will only work alone. You don't want to share that fire inside of you, because if you do, somehow it might go out. You're afraid to let anyone else inside, because it might throw the great Mike Devlin's need to set the world straight into some sort of proper perspective and somehow make him an average agent—or worse, an average person."

"I'm sorry" was his only justification.

To Knox, his sentence seemed unfinished, lacking some explanation for his actions, but then, he never defended himself. "That's another thing. That damn silence." She looked into his steady gaze and realized she was not going to provoke an answer from him. She turned her attention back to the bills.

Devlin went upstairs to bed, trying not to remember Knox's words. But the ones he denied the most followed him into his sleep.

As his father came through the door, nine-year-old Mike Devlin snapped a glance at his face. Drunk! Unconsciously, the boy began backing up, anticipating the worst. Thomas Devlin, an infamous barroom brawler, staggered toward his son, sensing his fear. "C'mere!" he barked. "Say something, goddamn you!" The boy said nothing and took another short step backward. It triggered his father's right hand, which started for the boy's face. He fell away from the punch instinctively. It grazed his left cheekbone, knocking him to a sitting position on the hard floor.

Before his father could square his body, the boy was on his feet and out the door, running.

The running would distance him not only from his father, but from his anger. His white canvas gym shoes silently carried him through the west-side Chicago streets, the silence as healing as the running.

An hour later, when he arrived in front of the house, he could not remember where he had been. Two twelve-year-old boys from the neighborhood were outside. "Hey, Devlin, your old man is drunk again," the bigger one antagonized, finishing with a drunken stagger.

The anger that Devlin had subdued exploded in an overhand right that the bully never saw. Although he was a foot shorter and forty pounds lighter, he rocked the twelve-year-old's head back, splitting his lip.

During the next ten minutes, Mike Devlin learned the relative definitions of *discretion* and *valor*. Both twelve-year-olds pounded on Devlin and demanded that he admit that his father was nothing but a drunk. A denial of silence was his only response. They finally quit beating him for fear of seriously injuring him. Devlin watched them hurry away, knowing they would never bother him again. His refusal to concede had gained him victory.

The Greyhound's first stop was Cincinnati. Jack Tarver checked the schedule; it was exactly on time. Their plan was to cover the money at all times. At each terminal, Tarver's car was to set up as far away as possible, and he would use binoculars to watch the luggage compartment, which was on the bus's right side. The two "passengers" would mill around close by to ensure the security of the suitcases and to act as an arrest team if the extortionist presented himself. The two agents from the other car would go into the bus station and look for anyone suspicious, ideally someone from the Dearborn surveillance photos.

Through his binoculars, Tarver examined the faces of the people depositing and extracting baggage from the bus's hold.

"One, this is Five." It was one of the agents inside the terminal.

"Go, Five."

"I've got two possibles." The agent's voice was distorted as he spoke into a hidden radio, trying not to let the other travelers see his lips move.

"Do they resemble any of the photographs?"

"I can't say for sure, but they *are* Mediterranean types."

"You and Three each take one and keep an eye on them. We've got the grey dog covered." Tarver scanned the length of the bus and spotted the two outside agents. Although they were trying not to be, they were painfully obvious. "Two and Four spread out. Stevie Wonder could spot you two." Tarver watched as the two agents complied, but with failed casualness.

"One, this is Three. My guy's coming out."

Tarver swung the glasses over to the terminal door and

watched a swarthy male in mismatched plaid shirt and pants walk outside. He had a gym bag in one hand and a ticket in the other. The agent surveilling him exited ten seconds later. Through the binoculars, Tarver stared at the Middle Eastern face, trying to memorize it, looking for one distinct feature to positively identify it with any of the twenty-three photos he held in his hand.

The Greyhound driver stood next to the open luggage compartment. The Arab walked up and handed him his ticket. Tarver keyed his mike. "Three, Four, and Six, see if he's eyeballing the luggage." The driver appeared to be asking the Arab if he wanted to stow his bag.

"One, this is Six. From where he's standing, he can see our suitcases."

"Okay, everybody stand by. This could be our man. Five, stay with your guy inside." Five keyed his radio twice, giving the nonverbal signal that he had received Tarver's transmission.

Tarver flipped through the photographs, trying to match one of them with the Arab. It was difficult. All of the surveillance shots were black-and-white, grainy, and had been taken at a distance. A few were full-face, but the majority were taken at bad angles. Trying to gauge their heights and weights was impossible.

The driver checked his watch and closed the hatch. The Arab climbed aboard the bus. "Everybody saddle up. We're about ready to roll. Five, you better get out of here if you want to go with us."

"On my way, One."

Because FBI agents are by nature impatient to find the solution to their cases, Jack Tarver was surprised to feel a sense of relief as the bus lumbered out of the terminal lot unassailed by the extortionist. Fatigue had dissolved all the bluster and bravado agents on the hunt like to bathe themselves in, leaving Tarver a clear picture of the weakness of their plan. Their coverage at the bus stop had been amateurish, made obvious by the extortionist's inventiveness. All other extortions Tarver had worked had one drop site. This one had seven—the six intermediate stops and then the bus's final destination. If the suitcases made it all the way to Miami, Tarver and his crew would be physically and psychologically exhausted. Their chances of error grew dramatically with every stop. By the time they reached southern Florida, he figured they would probably be glad to hand over the bags to the first person who asked politely. He now understood that the extortionist's immediate goal was to keep them off-balance. But if this criminal had already made his best moves, Tarver thought the Bureau still had a chance. He thought wrong.

Bill Shanahan sat across from Thomas West. The attorney's desk separated the two men. "How can I help the FBI?"

Shanahan had been around enough defense attorneys to know there would be no help. The only reason West had agreed to see an agent without an appointment was that, if the FBI wanted to talk to him, it had to be about one of his clients, a client who would undoubtedly need West's three-hundred-dollar-an-hour help. The real vultures of the legal trade loved the FBI. Shanahan decided not to waste any time. "Tell me who killed John Lawson."

"Who?"

"John Lawson was one of our agents until two days ago when someone fired two hollowpoints into his face."

A small smile of arrogance pursed the lawyer's upper lip. "Why would I know anything about that?"

"You were at a meeting with Assistant U.S. Attorney Bell and an attorney named Katz who represented Watusi Sims. You were there representing Caesar Capodicci. Do you remember?"

"Yes."

"Do you remember Bell telling you that one of Detroit's best agents was going to go to work double-time on your client if certain agreements weren't reached?"

"I remember the government threatening my client, yes."

"Then you probably remember asking for the agent's name."

"I may have."

"Bell and Katz say you did."

"If I did, I don't remember getting it."

"That agent's name was John Lawson. If Bell didn't give it to you, it was all over the affidavits. The problem is you asking for his name. Why would you want it?"

West hesitated and then answered defiantly. "I thought Mr. Capodicci should have it in case he was harassed by your agency."

Shanahan laughed. "You sure you want to go with that answer?"

"That's the only answer you're going to get."

"Okay, but I'm going to have to give it a D minus on the grand-jury grading scale."

"I ask an agent's name and I'm part of a murder."

"Sometimes it's that easy. America loves conspiracy theories. If Capodicci had Lawson killed, we'll be able to take you on one helluva ride."

"Are you threatening me?"

"Are you stupid? Of course I'm threatening you. What the hell do you think I'm doing here?"

"Get out!"

Shanahan lifted his large frame out of the chair. He leaned over, inches from West's face. "The U.S. Attorney was right: John Lawson was one of our best agents. But when one of our own gets killed, we all become the best FBI agent. So call that scum you overbill and tell him we're coming. *All of us!*"

The squad secretary answered the phone. "C-Four, may I help you?"

"Yes, ma'am. This is Officer Davidson from Detroit. I know it's the lunch hour, but is Agent Blankenship there?"

"Yes, he is. Would you like to talk to him?"

"Please."

The secretary put the caller on hold and transferred him to Brian Blankenship's extension. "Blankenship."

"Yes, sir, this is Officer Davidson from Detroit. I'm working the security detail at the Renaissance Center. One of the officers here gave me your name, said I should call you. The other day I was dropping off some reports at your office and noticed your Ten Most Wanted flyers. I think I just saw one of them."

"Which one?"

"Is there one named Anderson?"

"Yes, there is. Hold on while I pull the file." Blankenship had been on C-4 almost five years and like all fugitive agents had taken dozens of similar calls from well-intentioned individuals eager to report what the agents referred to as "look-alikes." But every millionth call or so, it turned out to be the right person. Blankenship, with the squad copy of the flyer in his hand, returned to the phone. "Okay, describe him to me."

"Ah, white male. I'd say, thirty to thirty-five years old, five foot eight or nine, hair brown, eyes, I think brown."

The policeman's description was close to that of Danny Lee Anderson, one of the FBI's longest-sought-after Top Ten fugitives, but similar descriptions were the reason people called in. "Anything else?"

"Well, he's in Suite 2803 laying carpeting. When I saw him come in with the carpeting and thought it might be him, I found out where they were working."

Blankenship scanned the flyer: Occupation—carpet installer. "Anderson *is* a carpet installer."

"No kidding. Do you think it's him?"

"I don't know. There's a lot of five-foot-nine carpet layers in this city. Can you remember anything else about him, like scars, marks, tattoos?" Blankenship asked the question because the flyer indicated that Anderson had numerous tattoos on his shoulders and arms.

"Yeah, yeah, I forgot. He has a tattoo of a panther on his right—no, left—forearm."

Blankenship stared at the flyer. Anderson had a black panther tattooed on his left lower arm. He felt his heart accelerate. For a fugitive agent, a Top Ten arrest was the ultimate achievement. It was so rare that, in the history of the Bureau, no single agent had ever captured more than one. "Where are you at?"

"I'm next door in 2805 using the phone. I'll watch and make sure he doesn't leave. How long will it take you to get here?"

"Well, we have a rule here that we're supposed to notify the bosses if there's a chance of a Top Ten arrest and take them along."

"Mr. Blankenship, if it is him and *my* bosses find out I called the FBI and not them, I'll be cleaning out stables at the mounted division. Why don't you come over here and take a look at this guy. If you think it's him, we'll both call in the troops for the arrest, and everybody will be happy."

"Good idea. I'll be there in ten minutes—no longer."

The caller hung up the phone and smiled at the stolen flyer of Danny Lee Anderson. Then he opened the cylinder of his revolver and loaded it with six Hydra-Shok hollowpoints.

III CHAPTER 5 III

The phone rang several times before its persistence fought its way into Devlin's sweaty dream. He looked at the clock. He had been asleep for less than four hours. The best he could manage was " 'Lo."

"Mike, you there?" It was Shanahan.

"Yeah. Yeah, Bill. What's up?"

"Brian Blankenship's been murdered."

Detroit's Renaissance Center had been built in the late seventies with some specific political purposes in mind. The architecturally overwhelming structure was designed to make a statement on behalf of the city's administration, a denial that its downtown was withering and its neighborhoods crumbling. There had been a contest to name the bright glass-and-steel complex. "Renaissance Center" was the obvious choice. It was to be the cornerstone of Detroit's revival, an indication of the Motor City's health. But unfortunately for the shrinking city, good health, unlike disease, was not contagious.

Devlin took an elevator to the twenty-eighth floor. He waved his credentials at the uniformed policeman who was guarding the door. Inspector Wicks was standing with a group of detectives and FBI agents. Beyond them, on the floor, was Brian Blankenship's body, his head encircled by a spill of darkening red fluid.

Devlin stood over the body. The DPD evidence techs had not arrived yet, so the body could not be moved or covered.

The young FBI agent had been shot twice in the face, once through the right cheek and once in the middle of the forehead.

Instead of anger, a strange analytical calm overtook Devlin. He wondered if this lack of emotion was a warning, a release of some uncontrollable level of dangerousness. Whatever it was, he decided not to question its authority but to accept its direction.

The wounds appeared to be .38 caliber. Around both bullet holes were blackened circles. The dark rings were the result of close-range shots in which soot from the gun's explosion lodged under the skin immediately around the wound. The circle around the hole in the cheek was larger than that around the forehead wound. The rule was: The smaller the ring, the closer the shot. So the cheek shot had been fired from a greater distance.

The gunpowder stippling provided more information. The cheek wound had extensive gunpowder tattooing, which looked as though someone had hastily painted small black freckles on the right side of the dead agent's face. Conversely, the lack of stippling on the forehead indicated that the gun had been almost touching the skin when the trigger was pulled.

The soot-residue pattern around both holes gave evidence of the bullet's angle of entry. It was evenly distributed around the forehead wound, suggesting the shot had been fired straight into the victim's skull; but most of the stippling around the cheek wound was above the hole, leading Devlin to conclude that the shot had been fired at a downward angle.

Devlin looked at the agent's clothing. Dust from the floor was on his knees. The same dust was visible on the right side of his trousers and suit coat.

Devlin waved Wicks over. The two men solemnly shook hands. "How do you read this, Jerry?"

In a voice burdened by experience, Wicks said, "The shooter gets the drop on Brian. Has him get down on his knees. First shot hits him in the cheek, fired from, I would guess, no farther than eighteen inches. From the soot pattern, it had to be a downward shot. He was dead before he hit the floor, landed on his right side. The killer rolled him over on his back, stood directly above him, and fired the second shot from less than an inch away."

Devlin was nodding his head. "The killer probably put him on his knees right away so he couldn't charge him the way Lawson did."

"That would be my guess," said Wicks.

"How long has this place been vacant?"

"I've got someone checking at the rental office, but the people down the hall said about a year."

"Anyone see anything?"

"Nothing. We've been all over this floor. Three above and three below, plus janitorial and maintenance. Nothing."

"Who found him?"

"A secretary from down the hall. Her boss wouldn't let her smoke in the office, so she would sometimes sneak one in here. I think she's decided to quit."

"Anything make you think it's *not* the same guy?"

"It's the same guy. This time, he took Brian's credentials. Is there a connection between the two agents?"

"I don't know. I'm sure we've got somebody looking into it, but there has to be."

The evidence techs arrived. Wicks walked over to them and started giving orders. Everyone was asked to clear the area.

The hallway was now filled with people. There were at least a dozen agents receiving assignments from the C-4 supervisor, Jim Harrison. Beyond them, being held at bay by two uniformed police officers, was an anxious cluster of reporters and cameramen. Devlin headed for the stairs.

He drove to the office. There was something bothering him about the shot that had been fired into Brian Blankenship after he was dead. Devlin needed to see the crime-scene photos from the first murder. The FBI lobby was full of reporters and camera crews, some of which he did not recognize. He guessed they were from the networks and the nationals. The thought of

Sudder answering endless questions, not only from the media but from Bureau Headquarters as well, restored Devlin's faith in justice's exquisite tyranny.

There were a few agents in the C-4 area who were getting instructions from ASAC Grant Sandler. The agents had nicknamed him "BBs." It was, they felt, an accurate estimate of the size of the Assistant Special Agent in Charge's testicles, especially when he was dealing with the SAC. He stood bewildered, giving everyone the same order: "Go over to room 2805 in the Ren Cen and Jim Harrison will give you your leads."

On the easel at the front of the room was the same large pad of paper that had been there since the first murder. The title of the case had been changed. It had already been given a code name by Bureau headquarters: GENTKILL, which was a shortening, for computer purposes, of Agent Killings.

On a large adjoining table sat various documents pertaining to the murders. They were all duplicates for the investigating agents' reference. The originals were secured in the case file. Devlin searched until he located an envelope containing the photos taken at the Bridgeline glove factory. He shuffled through them until he found a full-face close-up taken of John Lawson at the crime scene.

He looked like a stranger. It was as if a mediocre artist had tried to paint his portrait using the wrong skin tones, not quite capturing the energy that had defined Lawson's face and his character. And there were those two terrible holes that had torn the life out of him. Devlin looked away from the photo for a moment to recapture his objectivity.

Did a common ground exist between the two dead agents? Common ground could provide a motive. Motives led to suspects. If there was no such connection, then the killer had to be some psychopath who was making his time on earth more meaningful by murdering the enemies of his life—in this case, FBI agents. There were always communications from Washington, warning agents that yet another person with a history of mental illness had sworn to kill FBI agents. In recent years, shootouts between agents and these individuals had become increasingly common. From the time they took their oath, agents worried about being blindsided by some "wacko." It wasn't in the recruiting brochure, but it was definitely part of the package.

In both cases, the second shots were blatantly brutal, unnecessary to ensure death. To Devlin, they seemed to be some sort of self-applauding signature. He wondered if he was reading too much into them.

He picked up another document from the table. It was a copy of Brian Blankenship's locator card. It showed him going to the Renaissance Center, Room 2805, at 12:18 P.M. The file number he listed was explained in someone else's handwriting at the bottom of the page: *Top Ten Fugitive Danny Lee Anderson.*

Both men had been lured to their deaths by someone who knew what kind of cases they worked. Devlin decided there had to be a connection. After his casino shift started, he intended to find out. But first, he had an even more difficult task to take care of: He had to call Knox and tell her Brian Blankenship had been murdered.

The extortionist looked at his watch and smiled. The Greyhound bus was now halfway to Miami. At the Detroit terminal, he had immediately recognized the agent who had so clumsily poked around the physics building at the university. By watching him, he was able to identify at least five additional agents. Probably the local FBI's extortion experts. Now any extortion activity would have to be handled by less experienced agents. *Divide and conquer.*

He was parked less than fifty yards from the Seacard Hospital for Children. Fifteen minutes earlier, he had sent another fax to the hospital:

At least six FBI agents (with their two dummy suitcases) were observed at the bus station. Instead of complying with my demands, you chose to place your confidence in the FBI and are now about to witness the results of your mistake. At exactly six P.M., a second bomb will explode to demonstrate the inevitability of this plan. Neither the police nor the FBI can prevent a third bomb which is set to detonate within thirty-six hours. It is intended to kill as many children as possible. It can be prevented only by your perfect compliance with the following instructions: the $5 million is to be divided equally into five sealed cardboard boxes. Each is to be placed on the back floor of five different automobiles at five different locations. Each auto will have an orange circle spraypainted on the rear door for identification. After placing the box inside, you will lock the door. All boxes will be delivered between one and one-thirty P.M. tomorrow. The five locations are being transmitted on a separate page. The clock is ticking!

PFLNA

The extortionist checked his watch again. Two minutes to six. Where were the police? He wanted them there when the bomb exploded, to show that law enforcement was powerless to stop him. He heard a siren and smiled.

Two police cars pulled up to the front of the hospital, and the officers got out and ran inside. With fifteen seconds to go, he looked up through the second-floor window, where the bomb had been planted. It was a utility room, and the device had been hidden behind an ice machine. A young girl in a bathrobe walked in and started filling a glass with ice. The extortionist was momentarily distracted, thinking about how good a glass of iced tea would taste. One final time, he checked his watch. Five . . . four . . . three . . . two . . . one . . . A split second before 6 P.M., he looked up at the girl and pushed the button on the remote-controlled detonator.

Shanahan knew something was bothering Devlin. They were on their way to John Lawson's wake, and Devlin had not said a word since they left the garage. The call to Knox had not gone well. At first, she was devoid of any emotion. She said the killing proved that Devlin should stop involving himself in the case. He said it indicated that he needed to be involved to a greater extent. She hung up. As Shanahan's car drove through the night, Devlin wondered if he wasn't being selfish.

Finally, Shanahan spoke. "Guess we can cross Watusi Sims and the Sicilians off our list."

"I'm sorry, Bill. What?"

"Sims and the Sicilians."

"Yeah, it doesn't seem like they would have any interest in Brian, does it?"

"Right now they've got agents going through every one of John's and Brian's cases to see if any name comes up in both." Devlin did not respond, and Shanahan heightened his voice to a storyteller's tone in hopes of distracting him. "Did I tell you about the last arrest I was on with Brian?"

Devlin looked over at him. "No."

"He had this guy who was wanted out of Lansing, Michigan, for a double homicide. So he comes up with an address in the Herman Gardens projects. You know how bad it is in there. Well, we kick the door in, and while I'm cuffing this puke, Brian's covering him. He looks at Brian and says, 'You think you're pretty bad with that gun in your hand.' Without missing a beat Brian says, 'Seeing how we're arresting you for shooting two unarmed people to death, that seems a little hypocritical.' So then this fool gives Brian the I'd-like-to-kick-your-ass stare. So Brian says to him, 'Listen, stupid, you may be the baddest ass in Lansing, but you ain't even the third toughest motherfucker on this block.' "

Both men laughed honestly, remembering Brian Blankenship's uncompromising approach to life. It was something to envy. Devlin said, "I can't believe we're going to one dead agent's wake and talking about another. Why is this happening?"

"I don't know, Mike. Let's just hope this is the end of it."

Then Devlin thought again about his call to Knox. She was right; but so was he.

Devlin and Shanahan stayed at the wake about half an hour. They had waited to give their condolences to Lawson's widow, Sandy, but once she had seen the casket, she had to be sedated and taken away to one of the funeral home's offices.

As the agents were leaving, they were being watched from what the Behavioral Science Unit would describe as a "conservative" automobile. The driver of the innocuous vehicle was there to follow a certain FBI agent home, the agent he would kill next. He knew they would all be increasingly cautious now, and in case he could not lure this target into his territory, he wanted other options available.

Devlin and Shanahan walked out and, with a bunch of other agents, headed to their cars. The killer started his car; he had spotted his agent.

Lionel Seacard, chairman of the board and grandson of the founder of Seacard Industries, sat at the head of the conference table in the corporate conference room. To his right was James Pendleton. A half-dozen other executives sat around the table awaiting the arrival of the FBI. Since the second bomb had gone off and gravely injured the young girl at the hospital, Pendleton had been rehearsing his speech to the head of the FBI, and although he rarely allowed himself to be emotional he was eager to release the snarling dogs of his anger.

The door opened and three agents walked in. They were led by Ray Miller, a tall, gaunt agent who had been with the Bureau for three years, during which he had worked thefts from interstate shipment. The other two agents were also from the property crime squad. "Sorry we're late," Miller said. Everyone introduced themselves.

Pendleton asked, "Where's your boss?"

Miller's eyes widened and his speech slowed to carefully measure the weight of each word, informing Pendleton that this agent was an inexperienced liar. "He's tied up in Detroit. We had another agent killed this afternoon, so he sent us."

"Where's Agent Tarver?"

"Halfway to Miami. We're having trouble contacting him. As soon as we do, he'll be on the first plane back."

"Agent Miller, how many extortions have you investigated?"

Miller realized the question was intended to challenge not his experience but rather the SAC's judgment. "This is my first one, sir."

Pendleton glanced at the chairman of the board with an incredulous look. Sternly, he handed Miller the two-page demand note. Miller read the note and asked, "We understand one of the children was injured in the explosion. How is she?"

The chairman of the board said, "She's in critical condition."

"I'm sorry. I assume you have increased security at the hospital."

Seacard said, "Neal, tell Agent Miller what we've done."

Neal Ferguson said, "After the first bomb, we doubled and now, on some shifts, tripled the number of guards both inside and outside the facility. During each eight-hour shift, we had four additional men searching areas where a bomb could be hidden. We've hired a private bomb dog to search the hospital twice a day, at nine A.M. and five P.M., which is one hour after the morning and afternoon shifts arrive. It was our reasoning that the bomber would probably come in during the extra activity of a shift change and plant the bomb within an hour."

"That sounds like good coverage. Have you considered the possibility of an employee being involved?"

"We've thought about it," Ferguson said, "but we have close to a thousand employees. Where would we start?"

"Where was this bomb placed?"

"Behind an ice-making machine on the second floor."

"Maybe you should start there. How many employees had access to that area between five and six o'clock today?"

"We thought of that, but the room is adjacent to the stair-well. Probably half of the employees could have come up those stairs and hidden that bomb in a minute or two."

The demand note was passed back to Miller. "Mr. Pendleton, the note is signed by PFLNA. Do you have any idea who that is?"

Pendleton said, "We were hoping you could tell us."

One of the other agents said, "I used to work FCI"—he looked at Pendleton—"Foreign Counter Intelligence—I think it's one of those small Middle Eastern terrorist groups."

"Does Seacard Industries have any interests in the Middle East?" Miller asked.

Pendleton said, "We have interests all over the world, including the Middle East."

The three agents looked at one another and felt the numbing bewilderment that comes from being suddenly overwhelmed. Until then, their days and nights had been spent chasing truck hijackers and cargo thieves. They liked what they did. It was the Bureau's grunt work, very blue-collar but clearly honorable. Property crimes were guided by certain tenets, understood by both sides: Stealing was an opportunity, not unlike the lottery; being a thief had fraternal commitments unless someone got hurt; lying was a necessary tool used by thief and agent alike; plea-bargaining was a celebration of victory by both sides. It was predictable and relatively stress-free. Compared with extortion and terrorism, being lied to by some scumbag boxcar thief had a certain civility to it.

But this was different. Blowing up kids for $5 million was inconceivable for these agents, who, given a choice, would take their country-and-western crimes every time. Miller asked, "What do you want us to do, Mr. Seacard?"

The chairman of the board said, "Seacard Industries is a very successful corporation, worth billions. The hospital's five million dollars is a negligible portion of our total assets. So, if one more child is injured or, God forbid, killed, it would be an inexcusable tragedy. For that reason, I have authorized the payment of the entire five million dollars."

A negligible portion of our assets replayed itself in Pendleton's head. Funny, he thought, $5 million was "negligible" and he used to think that his $250,000 salary was a lot of money. That was until his gorgeous wife succumbed to sexual wanderlust and decided to divorce him. After she cleaned out what little they had in the bank, she ran every one of his credit cards to the limit. Then she hired an attorney, who kept his lawyer so busy the final bill was almost six figures. Child support and both kids in prep school at $20,000 a pop. A $300,000 mortgage, two car payments, country club dues, and an unpaid bill with the IRS.

But there was some light at the end of his suffocating tunnel. He had received an "inside" tip in the futures market—coffee. The world couldn't live without it, and because an investor only needed to show 5 percent equity of what was being risked, neither could James Pendleton. It took only $25,000 to cover his $500,000 investment. This one quick, injury-free killing would make him financially healthy.

It was obvious to Pendleton that old man Seacard's decision to pay off the extortionist had stunned the three agents. The vice president found their confusion interesting. The extortionist, whoever he was, had outmaneuvered the FBI and had dispelled the aura of their invincibility. But actually, he agreed with the agents: The extortionist should not be paid.

However, it was his job to agree with the chairman of the board and, in this case, to strongly represent his position. "We realize there are legalities that the FBI must investigate something like this, but I am warning you, if the FBI screws this up *again*, you and your boss will be begging for a job at the post office." Pendleton looked at each of them closely to emphasize his warning.

Between the strength of the extortionist's position and Pendleton's threat, they appeared to be completely bewildered, and Seacard's executive vice president found that curiously strengthening.

Devlin sat in the apartment above the casino, trying to connect John Lawson and Brian Blankenship. Everything he knew about them, from their ages to their assignments, was different. But something had to be common to both of them. The killer was too organized, too disciplined not to have a specific motive. And Devlin believed that motive was hidden in some unknown common ground the two men shared. Mysteries, once their secrets were known, were not that complicated. He just had to keep trying different answers until one fit. Success would not come from intelligent deduction; rather, it would be a result of outlasting the obstacles.

He glanced at the TV monitors. The only players in the casino were the usual undercover agents and informants. He decided his time could be better spent committing a burglary. He packed up his equipment and drove to the office. As he neared the federal building, he could see television news trucks parked around the garage's exit, ready to follow any car that might be on its way to cover a lead in the murder investigation. Devlin parked a block away and, because of his undercover clothes, was able to walk past the TV crews until he was out of their sight. He ducked into the building's sleepy shadows. Using his key card, he opened the rear door and headed quickly to the elevator.

He rode up to the twenty-fourth floor and then walked up the dark stairwell to the twenty-sixth floor, hoping the night crew had not double-locked the back door yet. He tried his key in the door, and it opened. He walked down the deserted hall to the ASAC's secretary's office. He searched her desk for any keys that might open the personnel file room, which was off-limits to the rank-and-file agents. It had always puzzled Devlin why an organization as security conscious as the Bureau allowed keys for restricted areas to be so casually concealed. Any door in the office could be opened if someone had a general idea where the not-so-well-hidden keys were kept. In the second drawer, he found two oversized keys sitting in a bowl of paper clips.

He walked back down the hall to the file room. The second key opened the door. It took him almost five minutes to figure out the filing system, and then less than a minute to find both Lawson's and Blankenship's files.

Someone was in the hallway. Devlin turned out the lights and listened. Two muffled male voices came toward the room, then passed by. One belonged to ASAC Sandler but the other one he did not recognize. He heard only a few words clearly, something about a bomb. It sounded as though they were headed for the ASAC's office. Had he closed the drawer that held the keys?

Devlin opened the door a crack and looked down the hallway. They had already turned into Sandler's office. Devlin had planned on reviewing the files in the personnel room, but now that would take too much time. There was a small copying machine in the room. He shut the door and turned the machine on. In the darkness, PLEASE WAIT lit up. He stared at the red glowing letters, silently ordering them to go out. Finally, green fluorescent letters, READY TO COPY. He started copying both files, page by page, listening for noise in the hallway.

He threw his tattered casino coat over the machine so its strobing light would not find its way under the door and into the hall like some evil beacon bent on ending his career.

When he finished, he quickly turned off the machine and let his ears adjust to the silence. It was still quiet in the hallway. He flipped on the light, refiled the agents' files, and turned off the light.

Now he had to replace the keys and get out of there without being seen. If he was spotted, his clothes would be an immediate reminder of where he was supposed to be. He found a phone on the table next to the copier. After pressing nine for an outside line, he dialed the number for the FBI switchboard.

"FBI Detroit." A new night clerk answered the phone, and

Devlin was relieved because he would not be familiar with any of the agents' voices yet.

"Is this the FBI?"

"Yes it is."

"Yeah. This is Protective Services downstairs. There's a gray Oldsmobile parked in the slot marked A-S-A-C in the basement garage. There's a fire under the hood. Could you send the owner down here right away so we can get the hood open and put it out?"

"Right away!" The clerk hung up. Devlin moved over to the inside of the door and listened. He heard the phone ring and then both men running down the hall. A minute later he was in the stairwell, his string of unblemished break-ins intact.

Along the Detroit River, Devlin drove through Bricktown. Like the cobbled streets the area was named for, it too had stood the test of time. Ancient taverns, cafés, and jazz joints hid in old warehouses like bootlegger's secrets. He wanted to see if Clementine's was open. He turned up Joseph Campau, and although the bar was two blocks away, he could see its customers. It was a warm night and several men and women sat on benches and car hoods outside the old saloon. Inside, another two dozen sat drinking and talking, some shooting pool. Half-heartedly, they argued, insulted, and laughed, but their hands were always within serious proximity of their drinks.

From their clothing, hair length, beards, and earrings, one might have guessed they were a biker gang. In a way they were. They were all members of the Detroit Police Department's Narcotics Unit. Like a motorcycle gang, they roamed the city anonymously, their group an island, stopping occasionally to splinter a door and to make an arrest.

They were strangers within their own department and they treated other cops as outsiders. For them, the job was dangerously exhilarating, and yet, because of Detroit's epidemic drug trade, so futile. They drank by themselves in a commune of isolated fraternity, not caring if they were judged favorably by a world that could never understand who they were or

what they did. An alarming number of them would eventually
.eave the department because of occupational disability
caused either by gunshot wounds or white-knuckle distress.
They never drank at the same bar two nights in a row. It was
part of their moving-target survival.

Because of the owner's failing health, Clementine's was no
longer open to the public. He lived in an apartment above the
seedy bar, and when Narcotics wanted to drink there, they
would knock on his door and get the key. The officers would
tend bar and not allow outsiders to come in. They would drink
long into the night, after which the key would be returned, always with too much money.

Devlin pulled up in front of a fireplug, got out, and shook
hands with several of the cops. They had used his informants
dozens of times for their search warrants. He had participated
in every phase of their process, from being the affiant to working surveillance to manning the raid to joining them at the al-
ways-alcoholic conclusion to their workday. Although he was
an outsider, he was warmly accepted into their fraternal loneliness.

Inside the bar, he said hello to a few more cops. The back
room was empty, so he went in and sat at a booth.

On the table he placed the two copied stacks of paper. He
read through Blankenship's file first. Thirty-two years old; five
years with the Bureau; hometown—Pittsburgh; residence—
Livonia, Michigan; married, two kids; college—Penn State;
major—Business.

John Lawson's file seemed completely incongruent. Forty-
two years old; fifteen years with the Bureau; hometown—
Seattle; residence—Grosse Pointe, Michigan; married with
three children; college—Washington State; major—Physical
Education. One of the police officer–bartenders walked up to
Devlin and set two beers on his table. Narcotics' first round
was always a double. The cop said, "On us, Mike." Devlin
thanked him and went back to the files.

Devlin flipped past the standard Bureau documents: letters

of commendation, promotion notices, performance appraisals, and others. On a page marked "training," he found that Blankenship had been to Quantico, Virginia, for some in-service training: Firearms Instructor, Police Instructor, Applicant Interviewing, and Fugitive Task Forces. When Devlin read the next page, he felt something click into place. It was an FD-302, the Bureau's form for recording any information the writer felt might eventually become testimony in a court of law. At the bottom, the originator's name was listed: Special Agent Brian A. Blankenship, and it was dated almost a year earlier. As a police firearms instructor, he had been teaching firearms to a number of small police departments in the vicinity of Grand Rapids, Michigan. One of the students, Officer William Blackton from the Grand Haven PD, had become argumentative with Blankenship over the relative merits of revolvers and automatics. When Blankenship attempted to end the argument tactfully, Blackton became more enraged, got into a gunfighter's stance, and challenged Blankenship to draw his automatic to see which was best. Blackton had to be subdued. A cover letter attached to the FD-302 indicated that the document had been sent to the Grand Haven PD at their request. Six months later, a letter was directed to Blankenship's file from the police department, thanking him for his cooperation. His report, along with a number of other incidents, was used as evidence against Blackton to prove his unfitness as a police officer and to terminate his employment.

Quickly, Devlin looked through Lawson's file for his list of in-service training, wondering if he was a firearms instructor. Organized Crime—Civil RICO, whatever that was, Applicant Interviewing, Organized Crime (advanced), Money Laundering, and then finally, Firearms and Police Instructor.

Devlin thumbed through more pages until he found an FD-302 dated the same date as Blankenship's. He had been an instructor with Blankenship and had witnessed the incident involving Blankenship and the police officer.

Devlin searched both files again for any additional information regarding Blackton, but there was none. He got up and walked into the bar. The cops were loosening up; their conversations were louder. Devlin held a nonexistent telephone to his ear, signaling the bartender that he needed to make a call. The cop nodded toward the office.

The tiny cluttered room had the mustiness of a crypt. Dust covered everything, testifying to its disuse. Devlin picked up the phone and got a dial tone. Directory assistance for Grand Haven revealed that William Blackton had an unlisted number.

Devlin dialed Shanahan at home. He answered the phone with a disoriented "Yeah."

"This is the front desk with your wake-up call. You said something about wanting to get the young lady home."

"C'mon, Mike, I just got back to sleep from the office calling."

"Kind of late for the office, isn't it?"

"The drop for that extortion is tomorrow. Very Special Agent in Charge Sudder wants *everyone* at the office at nine A.M. All leave's been canceled. And if you call in sick, he wants to see the videotape of your open-heart surgery."

"Is this extortion that big a deal?"

"I guess you didn't hear. A second bomb went off and injured a little girl. She's critical."

Devlin remembered Sandler mentioning a bomb while he was in the personnel file room. "Why a second bomb?"

"It's this guy's way of letting us know every time we miss a hoop. He made the surveillance on the first drop, so he exploded number two at the hospital. Seacard is pissed. One of the big shots as much as told Sudder if another bomb went off, he'd need an alias just to find volunteer work in Mexico."

"Sounds like a legitimate extortion."

"Yeah, and this guy is good. He's got Sudder scared to death. That's why our leader is going with the overkill method."

"And no one is working the murders?"

"On hold until we rescue our image." Conspiracy crept into

Shanahan's voice. "Speaking of the murders, how are you doing?"

"Do you really want to know, William?"

"I'm so tired, I could use a suspension."

"Well, as soon as you get me some telephone information, I'm driving to Grand Haven."

Shanahan laughed. "*Grand Haven.* What's the matter, did you run out of people to piss off in Detroit?"

"Yeah, your contact at the phone company will be the last one."

"Okay, what's the number?"

"It's a name. I need an address for William Blackton. In Grand Haven."

"You know Grand Haven is at least three hours each way. You'll never be back in time to finish your casino shift."

"With everything that's going on in the office, it doesn't sound like they'll miss me."

"Give me your number there and ten minutes."

When Shanahan called back, he gave Devlin the address in Grand Haven. "You know, I could cut class tomorrow and go with you. If this is the guy, you may need a witness or something."

"If this is the guy, the last thing I'll need is a witness."

III CHAPTER 6 III

Unquestionably, the pastime of choice for FBI agents was rumor. For the investigators, who were forced day by day to meticulously gather and prove facts, using rumor and innuendo was deliciously irresponsible. And since these slanderings were usually about their bosses who sat in the Bureau's ivory towers, the street agents' underground eagerly passed them along. The truth became an unfortunate, but sacrificeable, casualty of the Resistance.

But without exception, these men and women of the Bureau were shrewd handicappers, experienced in life's darker motives. In their hands, the truth, especially if capable of further unmasking management, was published at twice the speed of rumor. Malcolm Sudder's decision to involve himself in the Seacard extortion, when two of his agents had been murdered, was a transparent and unpardonable act. The tactic was quickly recognized as the old I-can't-be-blamed-for-what-happens-at-center-court-if-I'm-in-the-bathroom ploy. And now the Resistance was finding it wonderfully ironic that the SAC's bathroom at Seacard was turning out to be every bit as difficult as the Gentkill case.

Jim Harrison was a supervisor who was trusted by the agents, and he was well aware of their feelings about the SAC. But Harrison had bigger problems. As the C-4 supervisor, not only was he in charge of the Gentkill investigation, but now, because of Sudder's tactics, he was responsible for this damned extortion. As demanding as the double investigation was for him, he feared, as he turned into the SAC's office, that things were about to get worse.

Sudder was talking on the telephone. Although he knew Harrison was standing there, he did not invite him to sit down. Too exhausted for any pretense of protocol, Harrison collapsed into a chair in front of the SAC. Sudder swiveled ninety degrees in his chair and stared out the window to finish his conversation. "Yes, sir. I assure you we are doing everything possible . . . I will, sir . . . Yes, sir . . . We look forward to seeing you . . . Thank you, sir." He hung up. "That was the director again. He wanted another update on the murders. I had to rehash what I told him last night. He's getting here at ten tomorrow morning for the memorial service, so at eight-fifteen I want you to brief the supervisors' conference. What are we doing now?"

"We're still going through both men's cases and interviewing anyone whose name comes up."

"Any progress?"

"Not much. We've diverted too much manpower to the extortion to make much headway."

"I tried to explain to the director how serious this extortion was, but he said he was 'taking a very personal interest' in Gentkill and wanted our efforts doubled."

"I don't know what else we can do as long as we've got all these agents tied up on the extortion."

Sudder did not seem to hear the supervisor. "I think we need a new investigative thrust to show the director that we're being aggressive."

Reluctantly, Harrison asked, "What did you have in mind?"

"I see this guy as a nut."

Trying to be noncommittal, Harrison answered, "Possibly."

"Well, I think he is." Sudder's voice had a counterfeited authority to it. To Harrison, the theory lacked any rational thought. Agents familiar with the process knew the SAC was letting *The Force* take over. "Let's get a list of nuts together and interview them. Search our files first, then call the Secret Service. They've got a file on every nut in America."

"You want this done after we finish interviewing the people from John's and Brian's cases, right?"

"How many people are working on that?"

"Only four until the extortion is over."

"Okay, take two and put them on the nuts." Sudder saw the reluctance in Harrison's face and said, "Immediately."

"But there's a good chance the killer is in those agents' files, especially if we find the same name in both. With only two agents working on them, it'll take forever."

The SAC held up his hand to indicate there would be no further discussion of the matter. "Now bring me up to speed on the extortion."

Harrison realized he had no choice but to follow orders, but because of Sudder's concerns about the extortion, he saw a chance to gain something he knew both investigations needed. "We have called in every available agent to cover the drop. As you know, there are five drop sites, which means not only five times as many agents but five times as much technical gear will be needed, everything from surveillance vans to photography equipment. We've called in favors from Chicago, Cleveland, and Pittsburgh, and I'm still not sure we have enough."

"Jim, the technical stuff is nice, but I want to make sure we have enough agents. I don't want this guy to get away!"

"To be completely safe, we could use eight to ten more agents."

"Who's left?"

"Night and complaint duty. And undercover."

Sudder looked up. "You don't mean Devlin."

"I know you think Devlin deserves to be buried, and maybe he does, but he's a hell of an investigator. I've seen him solve some impossible cases."

"No! Not Devlin. Anyone else."

Harrison looked steadily at Sudder. "I'm going to tell you the truth about this extortionist. First, he faxes the demand note, eliminating all trace evidence and all original paper evidence, because it was printed by the hospital's fax machine. The typewriter evidence isn't nearly as good because of the imperfections of the fax machine. Then he sends our six most experienced extortion agents on a wild-goose chase to Florida and, at the time that they are the most difficult to recall, he explodes a second bomb. If Tarver and the others are back up here in time for the drop, they'll be exhausted, and minus their cars." Harrison hesitated, to ensure that what he was saying was registering with the SAC. "And then splitting the drop was very smart. Instead of us staking out one site because we know he has to come there, we have to cover five. That makes it five times easier for us to be seen or make a mistake. He can take his time and scout any or all of them, looking for surveillance. We know he can spot surveillance, because he made all six agents at the bus station. If he sees something he doesn't like, he can explode another bomb and send Seacard another demand. And keep going until he feels they've got it right. This guy is no wacko or thrill seeker. He's worked very hard at this, a lot harder than we have. In my fifteen years, I've never said this before—this guy is brilliant. We're going to have to be very good *and* very lucky. If we don't go after him with our best, we don't have a chance of stopping him." Sudder had started to nod his head in resignation, because he knew he had no choice but to agree to Harrison's next demand. "I want Devlin."

Devlin watched as former Grand Haven police officer William Blackton backed out of his driveway. He drove through the city's small business district to the west side of town and pulled into the Great Lakes Lumber Company. Blackton parked his old beat-up Dodge in an area that looked like the employees' lot.

He went in the office door carrying a brown-bag lunch. In five minutes he was back out and walking toward the stacks of lumber, pulling on a pair of rough-cut tan leather gloves. Devlin waited until Blackton got busy cutting stock with a radial-arm saw, and used the machine's noise to walk up behind him undetected. He pulled out his credentials. As soon as the ex-cop shut off the saw, he sensed Devlin's presence and spun around. Devlin's credentials were open and six inches from Blackton's face. Devlin did not say a word, but studied the suspect's face carefully. Blackton became angry immediately. "You motherfuckers cost me the best job I ever had. Now you're going to cost me the only one I can get."

"I've interviewed hundreds of people at work, and none of them ever lost their jobs. Not even the guilty ones. You'd think, as many times as you had heard that line when you were a cop, you'd be a little more reluctant to use it."

Devlin stared comfortably back into Blackton's anger like a boxer whose strength was counterpunching, waiting to punish him with his own aggression. Blackton recognized the technique. This agent was not going to be maneuvered by accusatory rhetoric. "What do you want?" he asked, in a voice that was as unemotional as Devlin's gaze.

"Tell me about yesterday."

Blackton answered, "You tell *me* about yesterday." Devlin stared back silently. "Am I a suspect for something?"

"Should you be?"

"Where are you from? I don't remember you from the Grand Rapids office."

"Yesterday," Devlin reiterated.

"I'll give you yesterday when you tell me what the fuck this is all about." Blackton folded his menacing arms across his chest and cocked his head to the side in angry defiance.

"You remember John Lawson and Brian Blankenship."

"Every time I walk in this lousy fucking lumberyard." Curiosity narrowed Blackton's eyes.

Devlin watched Blackton's face closely. "They've both been murdered."

Blackton stood silently, considering everything with a cop's logic. He realized that, because of his problems with both of the dead agents, he must be at the top of the FBI's suspect list. He knew from his time in law enforcement that it was a place that no man, guilty or innocent, wanted to be. "C'mon." Devlin looked at him questioningly. "My boss is going to give you my yesterday."

Devlin knew that, in tough cases, the ratio between dead-end leads and solvers was roughly infinity to one. As he watched the confidence in Blackton's stride, he felt that he was about to be set adrift once more in the sea of infinity.

Fatigue and disappointment made the drive back to Detroit seem endless for Devlin. It was almost 11 A.M. when he pulled up in front of the casino. Although he knew no one from the undercover project would still be there, he felt a strange premonition of abandonment. A sad, pale stillness guarded the building. After walking up to hundreds of unknown doors, it was something an agent could sense.

On the second floor, Devlin's fears were confirmed. A note hung from the door that guarded the video recorders:

Report to the C-4 Supervisor ASAP

When Devlin walked into the squad area, the only person there was the secretary. She told him that Harrison was upstairs in the major-case room.

Jim Harrison stood in front of a large black-and-white map of Washtenaw County. He was talking on the phone with his back to the door. Devlin counted five red pins stuck in the map. Two more agents were talking on telephones. When Harrison hung up, he noticed Devlin and motioned him into a small unoccupied room across the hall.

"Goddamnit, Mike. I had you off the hook. I went out on a limb and actually had Sudder bogarted into changing his mind. All you had to do was come in and work this extortion drop and I could have had you assigned to Gentkill."

"So Sudder knows."

"Oh, he knows. We were all in the conference room when he was told you weren't at your assigned place of duty or, in your case, your assigned place of punishment. There's a big difference. It's one thing to wander away from the job, but when you disregard your punishment, you might as well have walked into the conference room and mooned Sudder. Do you know what he did when he was told you were gone? He smiled! Do you know what that means in the middle of all this chaos?" Harrison was attempting to evoke some reaction, but when he saw none was forthcoming, he finished, hoping Devlin would feel threatened by the answer. "It means that dead agents, exploding hospitals, and even his career is less important to him than hammering you. He no longer wants a piece of your ass, pal; he wants the whole thing."

"When does he want to see me?"

"Just be in the office by eight-fifteen in the morning. He'll get to you when he's decided what to do. Right now, you're supposed to go straight home and stay there. He said he doesn't want you anywhere near that extortion. I think he's afraid you'll do something to redeem yourself and he won't get a clean shot at you. It wouldn't surprise me if he had one of the ASACs call and make sure you're at home. So do your career a favor and stay there."

"I appreciate what you tried to do, Jim."

"Mike, I know you weren't screwing off somewhere but, everything considered, maybe you should think about pulling back on the reins a little."

"I didn't know this thing had reins."

"All right, all right. Just keep it from in front of my eyes, will you? I'm investigating enough felonies. Now go home and get some sleep. You look as bad as I feel."

Neal Ferguson had packed $1 million into each of the five cardboard boxes that sat on the floor of James Pendleton's office. The security chief turned to his boss and said, "That's it,

Mr. Pendleton. I'd feel better if you'd verify the count before I seal them up."

"Yes, I guess I should."

As Pendleton stood up, his secretary buzzed him. "Yes?"

"Mr. Pendleton, your broker is on line one."

"Katherine, I told you I was not taking any calls."

"Yes, sir, I know. But he said it was urgent." When used by a broker, *urgent* was never a friendly word. Pendleton felt fear stampede through his chest. "Neal, I've got to take a call. Can you excuse me?"

Ferguson looked at his watch. "No problem. I've got to meet with the FBI and go over the routes. They're already waiting in the conference room. I'll come back after and seal the boxes."

"Don't worry about it. I'll verify the amounts and seal them." As soon as Ferguson closed the door, Pendleton picked up his phone. "John, how are you?"

"Not good, Jim. Coffee's taking a beating. You've got to get out now."

"What happened?"

"A freeze in Brazil."

"A freeze?"

"Don't forget—it's winter down there."

"I thought this was a lock."

"I know, but this was completely unpredictable. I also told you there were no guarantees."

Pendleton could not believe his lack of emotional control; it had always been one of his proudest possessions. He was actually feeling light-headed with panic. "If we get out now, what's the damage?"

"Everybody's running. It's going to be tough dumping it, but I think it's going to cost you anywhere from three to three hundred and fifty thousand."

"Goddamnit!"

"I know, I know. But I told you these things are not without risk."

"How long do I have to cover it?"

"Twenty-four hours, but I can probably hold them off for a couple of days if you're strapped."

Pendleton did not bother to say good-bye. He just hung up and tried to calm the panic racing through his head. *A couple of days* and his disastrous financial situation would become known. Once old man Seacard found out, Pendleton would be able to add unemployment to his list of problems. He closed his eyes and watched as the rushing chaos slowed, finally dissolving into a silent, black plane.

When he reopened them, they were riveted on the five cardboard boxes. No, he couldn't, he told himself. The way his luck was running, he'd wind up in prison. But his mind would not release the idea. One million dollars!

Even though the extortionist was very good, he was still taking a hell of a chance. What could he do if Pendleton took a million? Complain to the FBI? No, he would take the four million and run.

Pendleton was at the boxes, taking the bundles of money out of one of them. Once it was empty, he started filling it with outdated spreadsheets and reports, occasionally lifting the box and then the full one next to it until he was satisfied they weighed the same.

"Shit!" he said out loud. He had not considered the FBI catching the extortionist and recovering the boxes. He dropped into a chair dejectedly. Then he remembered the last meeting he'd had with the FBI and their confusion at the extortionist's plan. He smiled: It was always easier to take on an unbeatable foe once you had witnessed their defeat. The extortionist had beat them, and so could he.

He sealed all five boxes with twice as much tape as was necessary. Then, with a large marking pen, he scrawled his initials across all five taped seams. From his closet, he took a seldom-used gym bag and emptied its contents onto the closet floor. He put it on his desk, and as he dialed the phone, he started loading the money into it.

"Washtenaw State Bank, Mr. Lafler's office."

"Hi, Donna, it's Jim Pendleton. Is he there?"

"One minute, Mr. Pendleton."

After a few seconds, Pendleton heard, "Hello, Jim. I heard about the hospital. Is everything okay?"

"Not really. It's kind of complicated right now, but I need a favor."

"Of course."

"There's a possibility that we might need you to receive and hold a large sum of money for us. And it might be after-hours, in which case we'd have to call you at home and have you meet us at the bank. We would need you to keep it just overnight."

"How much are we talking about?"

"Five million."

Lafler whistled. "Whatever you need, my friend."

"Thanks, Miles. Maybe when this is over we can get back to the golf course."

"It has been a while."

"Oh, I also need a safety-deposit box. I have to put something in it for a few days."

"Today?"

"Yes, in about an hour."

"I'll have the paperwork waiting."

"Thanks."

Pendleton took the gym bag containing the million dollars and threw it on the floor at the back of the closet as if it were something he did not want. It wasn't as though he was stealing it from the hospital; he was stealing it from the extortionist. Besides, the money was donated by Lionel Seacard's fat-cat friends. Out of the five million, they would waste almost a million on conferences in Hawaii, cars that were leased for board members, expensive dinners, and all the other abuses that were becoming so commonplace within charities. Pendleton had seen the figures. Last year, 42 percent of the hospital's contributions went to managing their disbursement. He, on the other hand, would make full use of the million, paying off everyone from his broker to the IRS.

Quickly, he reviewed his plan again. There was only one thing left to do before he took the money to the safety-deposit box. He headed for the conference room.

Ferguson's meeting with the FBI was just ending when Pendleton walked in, his face a mask of darkening intolerance. The room grew quiet. Without being asked, everyone sat down and waited for him to speak.

He let the silence intimidate them for a few more seconds and then said, "I have only one thing to say to you agents. We put this in your hands once before with tragic results. We do not want you to stop this extortionist, but the law is on your side. If you decide to go against our wishes and try to apprehend this individual, you'd better make damn sure that you do not make any mistakes, because if there is a screwup and another bomb is set off, our lawyers will own each and every one of your homes. And if you *do* apprehend him, the five boxes containing the corporation's five million dollars are to be brought immediately at any time of the night or day to Neal Ferguson. I have personally sealed and encoded each box. If they are opened or tampered with in any way, or if one dollar is missing, I'll be sending my children on vacation with your children's college funds." He glared at the agents. "I hope there aren't any questions." There weren't.

As Pendleton walked back to his office, he congratulated himself on his performance. If the FBI did recover the boxes, they would, after his threats, expeditiously take them to Ferguson. And he would direct Ferguson to take them to the Washtenaw State Bank, where the missing million could be discreetly transferred from his safety-deposit box to the cardboard box. The only thing that could go wrong now was the FBI catching the extortionist. But he had met the head of the FBI; he was betting on the extortionist.

At quarter to one, Neal Ferguson sat uncomfortably in the passenger compartment of one of Seacard's limousines. Stacked on the floor next to him were the five million-dollar boxes. The

FBI had encouraged the corporation to use the limo to give the drop the appearance of being non-law enforcement. The driver was a woman, also from Seacard security. Holding a small FBI radio below the window line, Ferguson said, "We're a quarter of a mile from the first drop."

Jack Tarver's tired voice answered. "Go ahead and deliver your first package. Then, without hurrying, make the others. We're in position on all five. When you get out of the limo, don't eyeball the area. Just make your drops like they're somebody else's problem."

"Will do," Ferguson answered. He had been told that each site was in a strip mall, all within a fifteen-minute drive from one another. And, according to FBI radio traffic, all five cars were in place. He did not know if the locations had been surveilled all night by the FBI, but if they could have seen who was dropping them off, he knew they would have a good start on identifying the extortionist. "Let's go," he told the driver.

When the limousine pulled into the first strip mall, he spotted the car with a drippy orange splotch on the door. He put the first box on the rear floor of the car. Before he locked the door, he did notice that the rear seat had been removed and the floor painted a flat black. The license plate was not visible because the car had been backed into the space. But the FBI was somewhere, watching. As Ferguson climbed back in the limo, he told the driver to head for the second drop.

By one-thirty, all five boxes had found their way onto the back floors of the designated cars. Ferguson was told to drive back to corporate headquarters. The Bureau radios went silent.

At one-forty, one of the FBI units announced, "I've got a tow truck entering the lot. Looks like the same one that dropped the chopper this morning. Break. Any C-Nine unit, are we getting video on this?"

"This is Three-one. I'm making magic as we speak. For your info, all five locations are running tape."

"Copy that, Three-one. Also get some shots of anyone you

see in the area, in case our boy is doing a little pre-pickup surveillance."

"Copy."

"Okay, everybody stand by. The truck is hooking up the car. Looks like we're getting ready to roll."

An agent at one of the other sites spoke into his radio. "This is position four. We have a tow truck approaching our vehicle." Within the next five minutes, the last three locations reported the same activity. When all five cars were moving, everyone seemed to be talking at once. Finally, Tarver's voice took over with a slow, deep, commanding tone. "Break, break, break. This is Four-four. Everyone cease your transmissions. All units assigned to vehicles one and two go to channel blue-three, that's blue-three. Units working vehicles three, four, and five remain on this frequency. Everyone keep your transmissions to a minimum." Tarver realized that the Bureau's forces were again being divided.

In the major-case room, Jim Harrison had agents monitoring both channels being used to cover the extortion. He was able to trace the movements of all five cars on his pin map. He told the agents monitoring the two different frequencies, "Notify all units that all five trucks seem to be heading in the same direction. They may be all going to the same location." The agents broadcasted the information.

"Four-four, this is Five-one. I'm on vehicle three. The truck is taking it down a dirt road. From the undergrowth, it doesn't seem to be well traveled. The surrounding area is heavily wooded. If we follow it and this guy's in there, he'll make us in a heartbeat."

Tarver answered, "Okay, break off. It appears that all these cars are going to wind up together. Just follow us on the radio. Right now, our first priority is not getting burned."

Fifteen minutes later, it appeared that Harrison had guessed accurately. The first two trucks pulled into an isolated Park-and-Ride commuters' lot that had a dozen cars scattered around it.

As the first truck driver was unhooking his car, a second truck entered the lot. Once he spotted the orange splotch on the first car's door, he jockeyed his car as close to it as he could. The last three drivers did the same, arranging the old cars in some sort of prearranged cluster.

Tarver ordered, "I want one of our vans to get into that lot and set up as far from the drop cars as possible, but close enough to videotape the area. And keep me advised."

For two hours the agents waited restlessly. Then, one of the agents in the van said, "Four-four, we've got a white Ford Escort station wagon pulling into the lot." After twenty seconds of silence, he continued. "This guy *is* hinky. He's cruising the lot at about three miles an hour. Looks like it's show time." The radio was quiet again. "Okay, he's sniffing around the target vehicles."

Tarver broke in. "What's he look like?"

"Arab male, late twenties. Hold on, he's exiting the lot. He's away, nine bound on the main."

Another surveillance unit said, "Four-four, he's coming our way, do you want us to get on him?"

"Negative, we're staying on the money. There's a good chance this is our guy. If so, he'll be back." Since the extortionist's favorite tactic was to *divide and weaken*, Tarver decided that he was going to keep everyone right there. Finally, he was in control. The extortionist had to come to *him*.

Another half hour passed before the next transmission. "Four-four, I've got the same white Escort inbound."

The van spoke next. "And . . . he's in the lot. He's dry-cleaning. Now he's heading for the gate again."

"Damn!" Tarver barked at his steering wheel.

"Wait a minute. He's turning around. And . . . he's at the cars. He's out and opening the back of the wagon. He's really wired, looking everywhere. He's going to the closest car and . . . you'll like this . . . he's using a key to open the door."

Tarver made the call. "All units, seal off the entire area. I'm going in." He slammed his car into gear and took off. The driver of the Escort had to be either the extortionist or a pickup man. But no innocent person would have checked the lot twice before going to the cars nor would he have accepted five different keys to pick up boxes from five abandoned cars. No, this was the extortionist.

The agent in the surveillance van said, "Four-four, he's got the first car open."

Tarver accelerated into the lot and could see the cars now. The suspect was bent over in the back door of one of the drop cars picking up the cardboard box. As he stood up Tarver recognized him as one of the men photographed at the Federal Express office. Seeing the FBI car speeding toward him, the man dropped the box back onto the car's floor. He drew a small handgun from behind his back and raised it at Tarver's oncoming windshield. Experience had taught the agent that a windshield, despite what the movies showed, was difficult to shoot through. Some large-caliber, high-velocity bullets had a chance to penetrate it, but this gun was too small. Tarver kept driving toward the suspect and braced himself for the impact, but the extortionist never got the shot off.

All five of the drop cars exploded at once, blowing the suspect through the air directly into Tarver's windshield with enough force to disintegrate the glass.

FBI cars scrambled into the lot. The surveillance van reached Tarver's car first. An agent jumped out, ripped open the car door, and pulled Tarver's unconscious body away from the melting cars.

A couple of other agents probed the edges of the throbbing barrier of heat in an attempt to reach the suspect. Finally, someone yelled, "He's dead, let's get out of here!" The agents, after seeing Tarver, were reminded of their vulnerability and needed no further convincing. They all pulled back except for the Bureau photographer, who at an unsafe distance circled the flaming ring of cars, taping the scene with a child's curiosity. Someone yelled for him to get back, but he did not seem to hear them. He was not an agent; he was a photographer.

Recording things that most people would never see was a rare and precious obligation for him.

He focused his lens on the burning corpse of the extortionist, documenting the end of his life. Later, agents would refer to the event as the Five-Million-Dollar Funeral.

III CHAPTER 7 III

Normally, supervisors met weekly in the SAC's conference room. Since John Lawson's murder, the briefings were held daily at 8:15 A.M. It was not unusual for some supervisors or ASACs to be intentionally late, demonstrating their position in the office aristocracy. The more ruthless climbers thought it was a necessity; they were simply too busy to be *exactly* on time. But the morning after the Five-Million-Dollar Funeral, everyone was in their seat ten minutes early to ensure their arrival before the SAC. None of them wanted to be noticed or singled out for the holocaust that was sure to follow the bungled extortion. At one time or another, they had all witnessed the damage the SAC could do to a career once he got "missile-lock" on the *guilty* person. As eight-fifteen approached, the first-cup-of-coffee jousting was replaced by a Zen-like contemplation. Everyone, fearing missile-lock, hoped to be at least as invisible as Sharon Stone's pantyline.

Finally, Sudder walked in carrying a cup of coffee. "Good morning. Sorry I'm late." Everyone started looking up, chancing eye contact with the SAC.

"Good morning," they answered, straightening in their chairs.

Sudder turned to Jim Harrison. "How's Jack Tarver?"

Under the circumstances, the SAC's concern for one of his agents was unexpected and cast a shadow of confusion across Harrison's face. "Well, because he thought he was going to have to jump out of the car to get to the extortionist, he didn't have his seat belt on. That was the reason for most of his injuries. He ricocheted off of the windshield and then his shoulder took out the driver's door window. He has a concussion and a dislocated left shoulder. Fortunately, the extortionist's body absorbed most of the shrapnel from the blast. Otherwise, it would've blown through the windshield and, in all likelihood, killed Jack."

Sudder said, "Good. Good. Now tell me about the subject."

Harrison opened a folder and read, "His name is Jousef Haidar, twenty-seven years old. He's Egyptian. In this country to go to school at the University of Michigan. A junior, majoring in physics. We checked indices. There was a reference to him in the PFLNA file." Now Harrison read directly from the file. " 'The Popular Front for the Liberation of Northern Africa is a Sunni Muslim terrorist group based in Cairo, Egypt, which calls for the end of Western imperialism in Northern Africa. Specifically, Egypt, Libya, Morocco, Tunisia, and Sudan. The group is composed of several secret cells which operate throughout a region, conducting bombings and selective assassinations of key political figures in an attempt to draw attention to their main goal of returning to Islamic rule in their respective countries.' " Harrison looked up from his notes. "One of the security squad's assets picked up Haidar's license plate at a cell meeting one night. That's how he wound up in the file."

Sudder said, "What else do we have to tie him to the extortion?"

"When Tarver went to the Federal Express office in Dearborn, he had C-Nine photograph anyone hanging around. Haidar was one of the people they got a picture of. Also, the building at U of M that both faxes came from was one of the physics buildings he had classes in." Harrison allowed a small smile to precede his next point. "Last, but not least, he had a part-time job at . . ." He hesitated, to dramatize the indisputability of the last item of evidence. ". . . the Seacard Hospital for Children."

"So that's how he got the bombs in."

"It would appear so."

"What about the cars involved?"

"The car he drove to the drop, the Escort, was a rental under the name of Robert Johnson, the same name he used at Federal Express. The five drop cars had no plates on them. He was real cute: He not only removed all the vehicle identification number plates, but he also cut out the confidential VINs."

"Confidential VINs?"

"They're numbers the manufacturer stamps into the car's frame. They're in a couple of different hidden locations. He did a lot of work, which would explain why he rigged all the cars to blow up. He probably wanted to burn up any trace evidence. He was very thorough."

"Any idea why the bombs detonated prematurely?"

"The only thing we can figure is he must have set the triggering device on the car he was unloading, and when he saw Tarver coming, he dropped the box and set it off accidentally. It probably had a couple of seconds' delay built in, which gave Haidar enough time to draw his weapon. But fortunately, not enough time to get the shot off."

Sudder said, "As far as I'm concerned, this case is solved. Now we can get back to Gentkill." He nodded at Harrison to brief the group on the murder investigation. The C-4 supervisor explained the "nut list" theory and gave full credit to the SAC. "The Secret Service has been very cooperative. So far they've given us only partial lists. This is because their subjects are broken down into different categories, and they are not able to just print out a list of names. Like us, many of them will have to be gleaned from files. Right now, between what we have and what they've given us, there are about one hundred suspects throughout Michigan. By the time Secret Service gets done, it may be another hundred." Eyes, careful not to be seen by the SAC, rolled. Everyone knew how difficult and time-consuming interviewing normal people was. One to two hundred nuts would keep every agent in the division busy for a month.

Sudder said to Harrison, "What do you think the chances are that the killer is on one of those lists?"

Harrison still felt the best lead on the murders was to review the dead agents' files for enemies, but he knew his point would have to be presented subtly. "If there's no connection between the killings and if John and Brian didn't know the guy, there's probably a fair chance this is some nut."

Sudder's eyes flashed a pre-missile-lock warning. "We've discussed this. You have people reviewing their files. If they're not making sufficient progress, you'll have to find a way to get more out of them. The director"—he turned to the others in the room—"has instructed us to conduct a self-initiating investigation. To me, that says he wants numerous investigative thrusts going on simultaneously. Now, what else are we doing?"

Grant Sandler, the number one ASAC, said, "Boss, are you aware that we're getting about fifty tips a day called in?"

Harrison said, "I've been reviewing and prioritizing them, but because of the extortion I haven't had anyone to run them out."

"How many good tips do we have?"

"Good? Less than ten."

"Assign two agents to work them. Anything else?" When no one answered, Sudder said, "Has anyone else considered the possibility that we're dealing with a serial killer? He's taking souvenirs. The only person I know that does this is a serial killer." He turned to Harrison. "Call Behavioral Science and give them this new information. See what they think."

"Bill Hagstrom is flying out with the director. I'll ask him when he gets in."

"Let me know. That brings us to the director's visit today. There's only one word I want to hear describe it after he leaves—*smooth*. Jim and I will brief him on Gentkill, and the extortion if he asks. Other than that, he is only here to speak at the memorial service. He's expected to be out of here by two o'clock. Again, I repeat—SMOOTH! Grant will give you the details, and while he does, Jim, I'd like to see you in my office for a minute."

As they went into the office, Sudder closed the door. Harrison said, "I'm surprised you're not more worried about this extortion. After all, Seacard did lose five million dollars."

"Hey, they said if another bomb went off at the hospital there would be trouble. It didn't. They basically told us to keep our nose out of the decision making. It was their idea to use real money. We did our job. We identified the extortionist and eliminated him as a threat. Damn shame about all that money, but if they would have listened to us, it wouldn't have cost them a cent. What else do we have to do to close the case?"

"Other than a year's worth of paperwork, I haven't got the slightest idea. The evidence, statements, Bureau reports—it'll be a sonofabitch."

"How long is Tarver going to be out?"

"At least a month. When he does come back, I'm sure it will be on limited duty."

"Then who are you going to reassign it to?"

"I don't know." Harrison allowed himself a short laugh. "I don't have anyone I hate that much."

Sudder smiled slowly. "I do." He pushed his secretary's intercom.

"Yes, sir?"

"Get Mike Devlin in here."

Lost in the entrails of the federal building basement was a room so small, so illogical, that most agents were not aware of its existence. Its limited floor space was crowded with a filing cabinet, a table that held a VCR and a television monitor, a chair, a desk, two telephones, a typewriter, three leaning towers of evidence, and Mike Devlin. It was his newest "assignment."

He sat thinking about the SAC's words during the meeting that had taken place an hour earlier. Sudder could not hide his pleasure as he talked to Harrison as if Devlin were not in the room. "I want all the sharp objects taken away from Agent Devlin so he can't further injure himself." Harrison was to keep him on a short leash to deprive him of his freedom. Sudder said he had had enough of "this employee's rule bending" and wanted to be briefed by the errant agent every morning at 9 A.M. without fail. Devlin knew each briefing was designed to be a separate punishment. The SAC would purposely ask grueling questions and then assign trivial tasks for him to perform. Sudder had called it "administrative control," but Devlin realized that as long as the case was open the SAC would use the daily sessions to validate his self-importance. Devlin knew he had to find a way to cut through the usual red tape and get the case closed.

He picked up the green inventory sheets that listed all the evidence. There were seventy-eight items. Anything more than ten was generally considered a level-four headache, two being a migraine, and three a gunshot wound. Each one would have to be processed, packaged, and sent to the lab in Washington. Physical evidence was a blessing, but after a case was solved, it usually became an inexhaustible burden.

Devlin picked up the file and read the summary Teletypes that had been sent to Washington to inform headquarters of the case's progress. The last one reported, in muted terms, that the subject, along with the $5 million that he demanded, had been, in a matter of minutes, incinerated. Devlin read them all and noted some discrepancies in the events leading up to the extortionist's death. He dug through the piles until he found the videotapes taken by the surveillance crews. The last one was labeled SEACARD EXTORTION—FINAL DROP.

After turning on the monitor, Devlin pushed the tape into the VCR. It began as the surveillance-van photographer scanned the Park-and-Ride lot before the arrival of the extortionist's car. All the drop cars were already in the lot.

Devlin watched the sequence as the FBI van circled the cluster of the five towed cars, getting detailed shots of their arrangement. The next sequence was shot from a remote end of the large lot. A white Ford Escort station wagon entered cautiously. It drove around the entire perimeter while its driver scrutinized every vehicle parked there. The photographer had gotten an excellent shot of the driver. Devlin froze the tape and dug through a pile of large envelopes on the desk until he found the one containing all of the Federal Express surveillance photos. The shot of Jousef Haidar was on top. He was the man on the tape. Devlin continued watching the tape until its violent ending. He felt a shudder of admiration as the agents rescued Tarver and then tried to fight their way to an obviously dead Haidar.

The evidence against Haidar was much more than would have been necessary to convince a reasonable jury that he was indeed guilty of the extortion. But a solved case had an unseen harmony to it. It settled comfortably into an investigator's sense of order; Devlin was not feeling that peace. Instead, a small, disruptive fire took hold deep inside of him. He picked up the file again and read it slowly from cover to cover. It left him with one unanswerable question: *How could something so well planned go so wrong?*

There had been three demands sent to Seacard: two faxed and one via Federal Express. Using the fax machine had been very smart, so why was the second letter sent by a delivery service? And why was the extortionist hanging around the location where he could be identified? After having spotted every agent at the bus station, why didn't he make the surveillance van at the Park-and-Ride? Devlin knew that criminals were inconsistent in their crimes, but this one had gone from perfect, untraceable caution to open stupidity.

Devlin pulled out the two faxed demand notes. At the top of each, the fax machine had printed the area code and telephone number where the message was being sent from. The two numbers were different, but notes attached to them revealed that the two phone lines used were both located on the third floor of one of the physics buildings at the University of Michigan. Haidar was a physics student, so that seemed plausible. But something was wrong. Why use the physics building when it could lead back to him? Devlin picked up one of the phones and dialed the head technical agent's extension.

"Jim Peters."

"Jim, Mike Devlin. Do you know anything about fax machines?"

"A little."

"When you receive a fax and the sending number is printed at the top of the page, is that the actual number that the call is coming from—like your machine is tracing the call?"

"No. A lot of people think that, but when you set up your machine, you program in your fax line number."

"So, it could say it was coming from next door but actually be sent from halfway around the world."

"That's right. It's whatever number the sender programs into his machine."

"If he didn't program any number in, will the machine still transmit?"

"Sure."

Devlin thanked him and hung up. The faxes could have come from anywhere; Devlin wondered if they came from the physics building. If the extortionist was moving around with his fax machine, why would he reprogram the number? Why program in any number, unless it was meant to deceive the person receiving the message?

There was a knock at the door. Bill Shanahan walked in. "Is this where they're keeping the political prisoners?"

Devlin smiled. "I didn't think anyone knew where this room was."

"Myself and a certain steno know exactly where it is." Shanahan looked at the mountain of evidence. "But somehow it seems different."

"That's because the lights are on and your pants are up."

"Maybe that's it."

"What's going on up on the surface of the planet?"

"The theory of the day from SAC Sudder is *serial* killer."

"Did he give any reason, other than The Force?"

"Excuse me, did you just mention Sudder and reason in the same sentence?"

"What do you think?"

"Bill Hagstrom's on the way here with the director," said Shanahan. "I'll let him figure it out. I've got enough problems with Sudder's latest 'investigative thrust,' gathering the names of every nut in Michigan and then interviewing them."

"Let me know what Hagstrom has to say."

"Why would an agent so busy with an extortion want to know about a murder investigation? Sounds like Sudder's latest plan to teach you obedience might be falling a little short."

"Somebody should be looking for the Gentkiller. It sounds like you people are going to be too busy."

Shanahan looked at his watch. "That reminds me. I have to go. I got an appointment to interview a guy who shits in the envelope before he mails his threat to the President."

"Sounds like you two were meant for each other."

"Yeah. I've already thought of a way to break the ice. I'm taking him an envelope full of dead flies."

Ten minutes later, Devlin's door opened again. It was BBs Sandler, his hopeless face attempting to be stern. He ripped a taped piece of paper off the outside of the door. "Is this your idea of a joke?" He held up the sign: FREE DEVLIN. It was Shanahan's printing.

"I don't think you want to know what my idea of a joke is."

Sandler tried to glare at Devlin. "You don't have any respect for authority, do you?"

"I'll bet somewhere in your mismanager's handbook it says that authority and competence are interchangeable."

Sandler's anger was finally becoming genuine. "I am your superior!"

Devlin held his tone emotionless. "Is there a purpose to your visit, or is your ego just getting a free hump on Sudder's private whipping boy?"

Sandler now spoke through his teeth. "*Mister* Sudder did not have to send me down here. As an Assistant Special Agent in Charge, it is my duty to ensure that this office runs smoothly. And because you are so disruptive, I'm serving notice that I'm watching you. In fact, you are not to leave this room without informing me or my secretary where you are going."

"Okay, I'm leaving to go to the memorial service."

"No, you're not. After what you did during the director's last visit, I'm ordering you not to go within ten miles of him."

"You're telling me I can't go to the service for two fellow agents?"

"That's right. You can go to the wakes or the funerals, but nowhere near the director. And don't get cute. I'll be there watching for you." Sandler raised his chin and inflated his chest smugly.

Devlin decided he had had enough of the ASAC. "You look positively orgasmic. Should I call your wife and warn her?" Sandler spun around and slammed the door as he left. Somewhere, Devlin thought, a Kmart was missing a security guard.

Again he felt the smallness of the room and the crush of the evidence. He had to find a way out, and much faster than the front office wanted.

Absentmindedly, he rewound the videotape and played it again. He watched the footage of the cars before and after they blew up. Although the tape was grainy, one of the cars seemed to burn more intensely. He realized that he would have to go back and play all the tapes to determine exactly which car it was. The first video was the number one car being taken un-eventfully by the tow truck to the Park-and-Ride. The second was pretty much the same. However, the third tape ended as the towed car disappeared into a wooded dirt road. Devlin checked the surveillance log. The crew following it had broken off because they could have been spotted too easily.

Devlin searched the other videotapes on fast-forward until he found the segment showing car number three being towed into the lot. Something was different about it. He played the tape again in slow motion. The car seemed to be dragging something. Once more, he played the footage of car number three disappearing into the wooded road. He could not see anything under the car before the surveillance team had lost sight of it.

Devlin called Sergeant Tom Michaels. One of Michaels's areas of expertise was bombs. He worked in the Michigan State Police crime lab. Devlin asked the sergeant to meet him in an hour at the Park-and-Ride with his equipment. Devlin dialed the ASAC's secretary and told her that he was going out to the extortion crime scene. As time went on, he knew this accountability to Sandler would become even more strangling. Something would have to be done about it. He packed up the surveillance tapes and left.

Devlin stood at the burnt-out hulks of the five cars and oriented himself as to which cars he had seen on the tape were which. Ten minutes later, Sergeant Michaels rolled up in his crime-scene van.

They shook hands and Devlin asked, "Did you hear about this?"

"Yeah. I did the second bombing scene at the hospital. The locals called us in."

"But MSP hasn't done this scene?"

"This is strictly federal."

"Any difference between the first and second bombs at the hospital?"

"The first was on a timing device, and booby-trapped. The second was command-detonated."

"How close would he have had to be to trigger it?"

"Under two hundred yards, probably within a hundred to make sure."

"That's pretty close."

"Close enough to see the girl getting ice."

"Why didn't he wait until she left?"

"He said it was going off exactly at six. He probably wanted to impress everyone with his punctuality. But in the end, he got what he deserved."

"It would seem so. How do you know it was command-detonated?"

"We found bits and pieces of the receiving device, not enough to trace. I'm afraid the only evidence left is the transmitter."

"What would that look like?"

"They can be just about anything. Anything that will send a signal. They work off a battery. Something like a TV remote control. That's about as specific as I can get."

"Well, all this mess has been reassigned to me."

"As a scientist, Mike, I've always been amazed how you can keep your stock so low."

"Well, just hang on there, Mr. Wizard. I think we're headed for Absolute Zero."

Michaels held his hand up in a no-thank-you gesture and nodded toward the cars. "I assume that's why you called."

"I brought the videotapes of the explosion and fire. When I watched them, one of the cars seemed to burn hotter than the others."

"Bring them in the van. I've got a VCR in there."

"I thought MSP was supposed to be underfunded."

"We are. For the last few years we've been videotaping all major crime scenes. About six months ago we lost a case because the tape was screwed up. No one had ever checked it, so we got the VCRs right in the van so we can view the tape on a full-size monitor and make sure we got a good copy before we release the scene."

Both men sat in the van, watching the monitor. Devlin showed Michaels the object hanging under car number three. When the explosion started the fire, Michaels watched it for a minute and then said, "Yeah, that one definitely had some help. The back end is burning white-hot."

"Any ideas?"

"Yeah. I think I know what boosted the fire, but let me take a look first." He put on a heavy cloth jumpsuit. Both men walked over to the charred cars. "Which one do you think it was, Mike?"

Devlin pointed to the car he had picked out before Michaels's arrival. The sergeant agreed. Carefully, they climbed to the back of the vehicle. "What are we looking for?" Devlin asked.

"See how much more extensive the damage to this car is?" Devlin nodded. "Something additional was used to completely destroy the rear structure of this vehicle. I'm going to need to collect some samples, so give me some room. No need for both of us to get dirty."

Enviously, Devlin watched from outside the ring of cars. People who collected and processed evidence had always amazed him; they never ran out of patience or hope. As if he were a child exploring a series of secret caves, Michaels methodically searched the cars, sometimes disappearing under them. Stopping to search a wheel well with only his hand. Scraping a sample off the ground. Sanding off bubbled paint. He returned to car number three. On the ground underneath the area where the rear seat had previously been, he found semiglossy drippings of hardened metal. He pried up a few of them and placed them in evidence containers.

When he was done, his hands were filthy; his face and jumpsuit were striped with black residue. He went to the back of his van, wriggled out of his jumpsuit, and used a large towel to wipe off his face and hands. Out of a small cooler, he took out a soft drink, cracked it open, and handed it to Devlin. He opened another one and took a large mouthful of the liquid, swished it around, and spit out the taste of the burnt cars. Then he took a sip and swallowed it. "Couple of things, Mike. First, there was one bomb in each car. I think we can safely assume they were intended to eliminate any trace evidence. Second, car number three had at least two secondary devices. From the temperature it would have to reach to cause that kind of melting, I'm going to guess something like a thermite grenade was used. Do you know what that is?"

Devlin remembered the first time he was Officer of the Day in Vietnam. A major was giving him an instructional tour of the command bunker. He stopped in front of a large, dark green metal safe that sat imposingly on the bare plywood floor. On top of it sat a single grenade canister. "That's thermite," the major said. "If we get overrun, just pull the pin and leave it on top of the safe. It burns at about a zillion degrees and will go through that steel plate like tissue paper. All those codes and classified documents will be vaporized."

"Yeah," said Devlin. "We used them in the Marine Corps."

"This guy wanted to get rid of more than trace evidence in the third car. I'm going to guess whatever it was we saw hanging down underneath the car when it came out of the woods is what he wanted the thermite to remove all traces of. And he did a good job. The whole back end is gone. He went to a lot of trouble to cover his tracks; he even removed the vehicle identification number plates *and* the confidential VINs. He knew what he was doing."

"Then how come he blew himself up?"

"Because guys like this don't think well on their feet. They tend to overplan and when something doesn't follow their script, they unravel. From what I saw on the tape, when he saw that car coming at him, he panicked."

Devlin was not convinced. "Maybe."

Michaels stared at the agent for a moment. "I'm beginning to understand why you're in trouble all the time. This case, other than some paper shuffling, is closed. The extortionist is dead, so you can be as sloppy as you want with the evidence. There will be no testimony, no trial, and no appeals. Don't turn this into another pain in the ass."

"There are things that don't make sense." Devlin told Michaels about the Federal Expressed demand, Haidar being photographed, and the fax machine numbers. "And now, the thermite grenades. We're missing something here."

"I don't know. I'm just a physical scientist; you're the social scientist."

"Do you think you can enhance the tape to identify whatever was dragging under the car?"

"I'll take a shot at it, but don't let that Hollywood crap make you think we perform magic."

"You've performed magic for me a couple of times."

"Sleight of hand, Michael. Just sleight of hand."

Among agents, optimism was as rare as an offer to buy the first round, but the new director, Robert August, for the first time in fifty years, was pumping some sunshine down to the street agents. Even the most pathological cynics could see a pinprick of light at the end of their long-darkened tunnels. When he had graduated from law school, August had fulfilled a lifelong dream and joined the FBI. But after three years of being battered by the frustrations of bureaucracy, he resigned. Later, when he took over the Bureau, he did what every hump agent had fantasized about—he started cleaning out the Hooverdome in Washington, D.C. He sent hundreds of managers scurrying from the security of their artificially lit maze into the sunlight of working the street, where the only thing that resulted from kissing ass was bloodied lips.

And August was believed to be the first director of the FBI capable of dialing a telephone. Employees with personal problems were surprised to answer their phone and hear, "Hi, this is Bob August. Have you got a minute?" He would spend as much time on the problem as was necessary. To the men and women of the FBI, he was one of their own.

After the memorial service, the director had asked Malcolm Sudder to ride with him to the airport so he could be updated on the Gentkill investigation. When the SAC finished, August stared at him for a moment. "Malcolm, when I took over last year, I told everyone that I didn't want Headquarters interfering with the SACs running their divisions, and that included me. So I'm not going to involve myself at this point by second-guessing your investigation. But the longer this case remains unsolved, the more likely you are to lose the confidence of your agents."

"My agents are very loyal to me."

"Just remember, loyalty is a two-way street, up *and* down."

"Of course." Sudder tried to sound as though he practiced the director's words regularly, but August detected uncertainty in his tone.

"There are some real downsides to being the director of the FBI, but burying an agent is unquestionably the worst. You've lost two in less than a week, and we still don't have any idea who is responsible. I want to feel confident when I leave here that I won't be back."

"We're doing everything we can."

The director's car pulled up to the airport, and as he got out, he said to Sudder ominously, "Get it solved."

After Tom Michaels had left the extortion drop site, Devlin sat in his car studying a map of the route car number three had taken. He stopped and thought about what he was doing. Completely against his wishes and self-imposed priorities, he was being drawn into this case by its whispering mysteries. But then he reminded himself: If he could find some quick answers, he could get back to the Gentkill investigation.

Reversing the route that tow truck driver number three said he had taken, Devlin drove to the edge of the woods where the truck had exited unsurveilled. From the map, Devlin estimated that the dirt road the truck had traveled was about half a mile long. He parked his car and started walking: From the undergrowth, it was obvious that the road was rarely used anymore. Both sides were thick with trees and bushes. About three quarters of the way through, the track turned at a right angle. Just before the turn, a thin overgrown footpath led away from the road itself.

Devlin continued walking until he reached the point where the tow truck had entered the woods and the surveillance was terminated. The only opening along the entire dirt road was the path by the right-hand turn.

As Devlin walked back up the road, imagining himself as a surveilling vehicle, he pictured the tow truck driving slowly one hundred yards in front of him. The truck made the right-hand turn. It would have been out of sight, he estimated, for fifteen to twenty seconds until the trailing car got to the turn and reestablished visual contact.

After Devlin made the turn, he stopped. He looked down the narrow trail. He followed it until it opened into a small clearing. Old beer cans and fast-food bags were scattered around the opening. On the other side, the path continued, finally ending at a paved parking lot at the back end of a small industrial park. The map revealed that the nearby main roads were easily accessible. Slowly, Devlin walked through the parking lot, not knowing what he was looking for.

All of this was being watched by the *god of all major cases*. Charged with overseeing special investigations, he was responsible for occasionally giving justice a nudge. Unlike the other deities who gave to those begging the loudest, he demanded quality work before providing answers. If investigators were persistent, they were given "hunches" rather than complete solutions; cases could be resolved only through more hard work. All this led investigators to believe that they alone were responsible for their successes. He did not mind. It was part of his plan. He liked them to take pride in their work. Besides, it was part of a god's honor to be anonymous. As was custom, the god searched his book for a proverb to inspirit his instruction. He chose *The Magician's Left Hand*.

IF WE WATCH THE MAGICIAN'S SMOOTH RIGHT HAND, WE HAVE LITTLE CHOICE BUT TO BREATH-LESSLY BELIEVE IN MAGIC. BUT IF WE REBEL-LIOUSLY FOLLOW THE LEFT, HIS DECEPTION, AND OUR FOOLISHNESS, BECOMES OBVIOUS.

Nothing is as it seems. Misdirection has been the extortionist's most valued ally. He has used its psychological shadows to mask his true intentions. All the unsettling questions of this case disappear into the boundaries of these woods. Keep looking.

Devlin walked back up the path, searching the underbrush on both sides. When he reached the clearing, he seemed to sense something, something he could not explain. He probed its perimeter. Ten feet in, he spotted something light in color. He pushed back through the thick brush. He immediately recognized the object from the videotapes. He had seen it on five different tapes. It was one of the million-dollar boxes—*empty.*

||| CHAPTER 8 |||

Not unlike Pandora's box, the empty cardboard container Devlin had found in the woods presented a variety of problems. The greatest of which was that the extortion case was no longer, as the SAC had declared, *solved*. Devlin was afraid that if he told Sudder, he might overreact and have more agents assigned to the extortion. As badly as the Gentkill investigation was going, it at least had a total manpower commitment. Sometimes a case was solved simply because there were so many agents working on it that one of them stumbled over the answer. But they had to be out there to stumble.

If Devlin did not notify the front office about the box, he would not be able to send it to the lab for prints. However, without a suspect, latent fingerprints were of no value. Devlin doubted that the extortionist had touched the box without gloves. Later, if he developed a worthy suspect, he could have it processed for prints. He locked the box in the trunk of his Bureau car, where it would stay until revealing it was advantageous.

The discovery of the container also brought another unsolicited mystery into Devlin's life, which at this point had as much appeal as a second tour in Vietnam. When Pandora briefly but disobediently opened her box, she released all that was evil to mankind, trapping only Hope in the empty receptacle. Devlin would have never guessed how much he and Pandora had in common.

It was almost five o'clock when he returned to the office and found a note taped to his door: *See me immediately—ASAC Sandler.* "The perfect ending to a perfect day," he said out loud and headed for the elevators.

"You wanted to see me?" Devlin knew immediately this was not going to go well. Sandler leaned back in his leather chair and steepled his fingers. A thin veil of superiority drew across his face. "I wanted to remind you to be in the SAC's office in the morning to brief him on the status of the extortion." Devlin stared at him in silence. "Do you understand?"

"I *understood* when the SAC gave me those instructions this morning."

"You have a habit of not always taking your assignments seriously. I thought I would remind you." Uncharacteristically, Sandler was smiling, as if this scene was going exactly the way he had designed it.

Devlin figured he had better exit as quickly as possible. "Is that it?"

Sandler's eyes could not hide their pleasure. "Oh, no. Since you always seem to have your own agenda, it would seem prudent to me that I not only know what you've done for the day, but what you are going to do the next day." Devlin knew what was coming. Sandler paused cruelly, wanting to enjoy it a little longer. "Every day at five o'clock I want two reports on my desk: one detailing your activities for the day and one outlining your plans for the next."

The ASAC leaned back to enjoy Devlin's anger, but Devlin answered calmly, "Sure. No problem. Anything else?"

"Yes, I told the SAC I was keeping an eye on you, and he said he was pleased with my initiative."

"You're going to make a great SAC."

Sandler knew, because of Devlin's well-documented disdain for management, that the statement was intended as the ultimate insult. Sandler hissed through his teeth, "I'll see you at five o'clock tomorrow without fail."

As Devlin left, he knew the ASAC, through his interference, would try to prove to Devlin *and* Sudder that he was in charge, an undertaking infinitely more important than the solution of any case. Devlin needed him out of the way for a while.

He stopped in the break room to get a cup of coffee and sat down with a newspaper that someone had left behind. The headline was one word: GENTKILL. Someone had given the code name to the press. Below were black-and-white credential photos of the two dead agents. Devlin started reading the extensive story until he realized that the majority of it was an interview with Assistant Special Agent in Charge Grant R. Sandler. Halfheartedly, he flipped through the pages as he drank his coffee. They were salted with smaller articles covering the sensational murders. One had an oversimplified diagram of the city that was somehow trying to geographically connect the two murder scenes. Devlin continued to look through the paper, intentionally ignoring the press's circulation-boosting coverage of the crimes. When he found himself looking down at the letters-to-the-editor page, he got an idea.

He took the paper back to his room and read through the local news stories until he located one he could use. He dialed Bill Shanahan's extension. The secretary picked up the call and said he was due in soon.

Devlin reread the story. Mrs. Donna Keating, a black Wayne County resident, had killed her husband. After conferring with her lawyer, she claimed Mr. Keating had physically abused her for years; she had finally had enough and stabbed him to death in self-defense. The medical examiner had counted thirty-two stab wounds, fourteen of which were in the back.

Devlin took out a pad of paper and rough-drafted a letter to the newspaper's editor:

To Whom It May Concern,

As a dedicated law enforcement official in the state of Michigan, I must protest the shameless use of self-defense by women every time they decide to murder some man. Specifically, I am referring to the Donna Keating case.

Thirty-two stab wounds, over a dozen of which were in the back, are difficult to visualize as being defensive. Mrs. Keating and her lawyer are stabbing the American justice system in the back. Future jurors beware: You are being lied to. Stop giving women the license to murder men.

> Grant R. Sandler
> Assistant Special Agent in Charge
> FBI, Detroit

Devlin proofread the ASAC's tirade and put it aside. He checked his watch and tried Shanahan again.

"Bill Shanahan."

"Are you ready?"

"I'm afraid to ask what for."

"To stunt an ASAC's growth."

"BBs?"

"You must be psychic."

"I'll be right down."

When Shanahan walked into the room, he had an I-love-it-here-at-Disney-World exhilaration about him. Devlin asked, "Do you still drink with Art Nestling?"

"Whenever I can drag him away from that damn newspaper."

"Will he do you a favor, lips sealed?"

"Absolutely."

"Then, boys and girls, follow me."

The two agents made sure no one remained working in the five connected offices that belonged to the SAC, two ASACs, and their four secretaries. Shanahan stood guard while Devlin used another poorly hidden key to enter Sandler's private office. It took him less than five minutes to type the letter to the editor on the ASAC's typewriter and to search his desk for something with Sandler's signature on it. Five minutes later, both men were back in Devlin's room and Shanahan was reading the letter.

"How come I never thought of this?" Shanahan asked.

"You do these things for fun. I'm doing this out of desperation."

"I've put one together for tomorrow night that's both," said Shanahan. "I think it will be my best ever but it was missing that crowning touch. This use of the media gives me an idea. I think we're talking *legendary* here."

Shanahan's eyes widened brightly, begging to be asked for details of the impending prank, but the mooning of the director and his wife reminded Devlin not to ask.

It took Shanahan's talented hand only three practice signings before he was able to copy Sandler's signature perfectly. When he was done, Devlin looked at it and said, "Your parents must be very proud."

"When I left home, they told me I should use my powers only for good."

"And now, I believe Art Nestling has a deadline to meet."

"My feet are wings."

After Shanahan had left for the newspaper, Devlin thought he had better get some insurance in case there was not enough reaction to the letter. He called Temper Hanlon.

When Devlin came through the door, Knox had already put dinner on the table and Katie and Pat were just sitting down. During the meal, most of the conversation was between him and the children. After everyone had finished eating, the kids disappeared outside to play while Devlin and Knox remained at the table.

"I got taken off the casino project today."

"And now you are doing . . . ?" Knox asked, as if she were cross-examining a hostile witness.

"You heard about the bombing extortion?"

"The television said the extortionist died in the explosion." Her tone was suspicious.

"That's right. The thing is an administrative nightmare." Carefully, he said, "I'll be stuck in the office for months."

She sensed he was trying too hard to convince her. "Mike, I

know you. You can't leave these murders alone. And that's all I really want."

"Look at Jack Tarver. He was almost killed during an extortion. It had nothing to do with the agent killings."

"That's very comforting."

"Do you want me to leave the Bureau?" The question was gentle, sincere.

"I just want you to be safe."

"If you want me to, I'll resign and never look back. But if I stay, I have to do this."

"I've already told you what I want." She got up and disappeared upstairs.

Devlin found the kids and told them he would not be home until late. They both kissed him good-night.

He drove to the funeral home where Brian Blankenship's wake was being held. It was packed, so he stayed just long enough to give his condolences to Brian's widow. She stared out from behind eyes that saw nothing. Devlin had always hated wakes and funerals; now he remembered why.

Devlin sat in his room and checked the times on the surveillance logs. Using the map, he measured the distance between the Park-and-Ride and the wooded area where he had found the cardboard box. That was another problem he was having: Why cardboard boxes? Usually extortionists wanted the money in containers they could carry, something with a handle—a briefcase or a suitcase. Devlin calculated it would have been possible for Haidar to pick up the million dollars on the dirt road, take it somewhere, and still have plenty of time to drive to the parking lot. But why would he do that, since he was presumably coming to the drop to pick up all of the boxes?

The phone rang. It was Jerome Wicks. "Mike. Can you meet me at the Athens? We've received some tips on the killings I think you should take a look at."

"Fifteen minutes."

Devlin pulled his Bureau car into a parking space marked DPD UNITS ONLY. During the day, the spaces around police headquarters were carefully guarded, but at night, like the rest of the city, fewer rules were enforced. Devlin threw his FBI OF-FICIAL BUSINESS sign on the dashboard and got out.

As he walked the short block to Greektown, he inhaled its taunting smells—garlic being burned into lamb, ovens full of Mediterranean bread, and the singe of flaming cheese.

He turned into a little, everyday bar. The Athens, compared with its brass and Formica cousins across the street in trendy Trapper's Alley, seemed matter-of-fact, even homely. It was always full of cops.

Cops drink in bars that reflect their moods. If Wicks had solved a big case, he would have told Devlin to meet him amid the noise across the street. But the Athens was where they went when the union negotiated a lousy contract, or when a partner was suspended for slapping around some animal. It was also the preferred spot for just getting drunk. Devlin suspected that something more than tips was on the inspector's mind.

Devlin was on his second Bushmills when Wicks walked in. "Sorry I'm late. Here are those call-ins." As Devlin started looking over the sheets of paper, Wicks ordered a beer.

Devlin raised an eyebrow in surprise. "I thought this was going to be a whiskey conversation."

Wicks scanned his friend's face and then gave an almost undetectable sign of resignation. He pushed the beer aside and ordered a Crown Royal.

Devlin went back to the tips. The first one was from a self-ordained psychic stating that the killer was a man named Thomas Last Name Unknown, who was a Sagittarius and lived on Wheeling Street in Detroit. He killed the agents because he was afraid they would find out he had not paid his water bill.

The second was an anonymous tip, naming a Tommy Knight. He had been convicted of bank robbery and recently paroled. The caller said he had heard Knight in a bar bragging that he had killed the agents and that he would kill more. The detective who had taken the call had run a computerized criminal history on Knight and had attached it. It revealed that he had been arrested for bank robbery, but the arresting agency had been the Detroit Police Department. He had never been taken into federal custody. Devlin knew the type. Their courage and their tongues were controlled by the bottle. It was how they became convicts.

The third tip was another anonymous caller, who said the killer was Randall Walton and hung up. Experience had taught Devlin that these callers, whether out of loneliness or desperation, phoned in tips as a candle against the darkness of their dreary lives. They had no real knowledge of the crime. If they had, they would have given the details. In a disturbed way, they felt a certain power: A few words from them and a police agency was sent scurrying to investigate.

Wicks ordered a second drink. "Anything light your fire?"

"Yes, I had a feeling this was the work of a Sagittarius."

"Hey, I'm just passing them along." Devlin looked at the homicide inspector suspiciously. "Okay, okay. I wanted to talk to you about this investigation. You know, you're doing a real lousy job of hiding the fact that you're working on the murders. I heard they gave you that extortion to clean up just to muzzle you."

"Jerry, this is the fourth time I've heard this lecture today. I'm not going to get off of this."

"I know. And you have a history of choosing your friends over your boss's orders."

"A history?" Devlin seemed amused.

"That's how the Puget Sound murders were solved—you were just helping a friend. And how did that turn out? You were responsible for getting Tungworth, and that fool Pilkington used it to get promoted."

"It doesn't matter; he's not killing women anymore."

"I know that. All I'm saying is be a little more discreet. Homicide has open cases on both murders. If you need something done, just call. We can do it *legally*. It still counts as solved, even if you don't cover *every* lead yourself."

Devlin's friendship with Wicks was more than cop camaraderie. They felt a guarantee, an unqualified trust, that left them at ease with each other's problems. Devlin said, "Sometimes it seems like I *do* have to cover all the leads myself."

Wicks stared hypnotically at the ice in his glass. "Did you ever ask yourself why?"

"Knox thinks it's selfishness."

"I guess wives have a right to think that. My first wife did, and when she divorced me I asked myself some hard questions. I realized that I wasn't addicted to my job; I was addicted to doing it better than anyone else. Is that wrong? It was wrong for her, but not for me. It isn't easy. You have to push yourself to go on long after a rational person would have conceded. You do it because no one else will. And it will never be fair, because those who leave at five o'clock get the same paycheck. Right now, there's a hysterical emptiness in this country. People are looking for the purpose in their lives. That's something I'll never have to worry about. In a way it is selfish, but that's who you and I are."

"What does Cassie say about that?"

"Don't forget; she's an ex-cop. I made sure she understood all of this before I asked her to marry me." Wicks ordered another round.

"That's what I can't figure out. Knox knows this is right. If this guy wasn't killing agents, she'd be yelling at me to go find him."

"But he *is* killing agents. Why don't you give Knox, and yourself, a break and pull back on the stick for a while? Let us run out some of the leads for you."

"Thanks, Jerry, but right now I don't have the slightest idea what to do next. And with them burying me with this extortion, it's going to be hard to find any. If I don't do something to cut through the paperwork"—Devlin smiled at Wicks—"something I'm sure you'd call irresponsible, I'll never get back to the murders."

"You'll find a way."

"What makes you so sure?"

"Because you're Irish and that means you're in love with hopeless causes."

"That sounds a little prejudiced. I thought you black guys hated ethnic stereotyping."

"But, Michael, I know you. I'm not prejudiced; I'm convinced."

Devlin did not get to the office until after eight-thirty the next morning. The drinking with Wicks had lasted until after 2 A.M., and when he had arrived home, a small note was taped to the front door. He did not understand its terse message—THE COUCH—until he walked into the living room and found a pillow, sheet, and blanket on the couch. As always, the hell-hounds that rode the wake of Irish whiskey had caused him to sleep fitfully.

In fifteen minutes, he was due to brief the SAC about the extortion. Again, Devlin decided not to tell him about the empty box, because Sudder would undoubtedly charge headlong through the brittleness of secrets already discovered and destroy any hope of a solution. Instead, he would give the SAC some of his own thick-legged bureaucracy: confirming things that were already known, waiting for unrequested lab examinations. Or anything else that would wear down Sudder's desire to feast on him each morning.

But first, he wanted to see if Tom Michaels had determined anything that might help explain the empty box. He called the Michigan State Police lab.

"You know, Michael, scientists are not supposed to be rushed."

"You must have me confused with the Nobel Prize Committee. I'm calling about some melted cars."

"Gee! Let me catch my breath. I'm overcome with self-importance." Devlin laughed. "Okay, I analyzed the metal drippings under the cars. Aside from the melted steel from the frame, I found traces of aluminum powder and magnetic iron flakes under car number three; they're the components of thermite. Also, magnesium and barium peroxide, which are the chemicals of one of the igniters used to set off thermite."

"Did you find it anywhere besides number three?"

"No. It was the only one. I did spend some time looking at the tape of that car being towed. I wasn't able to make it any clearer, but I did enlarge it, and ran it in slow motion several times. Whatever was hanging down underneath moved back and forth, as if it were on a hinge."

"A trapdoor," Devlin said, almost to himself.

"Exactly."

"Anything else?"

"The only other thing was the removal of the VINs and CVINs. Did anybody talk to the tow truck drivers?"

"They were all interviewed. Each one was given instructions and full payment by the guy who burned up with the cars."

"Funny he would go to all the trouble to destroy those numbers on the cars so they couldn't be traced, and then let all five drivers see his face."

"Almost like someone wanted him to be remembered," said Devlin.

"Does that make any sense?"

"It's not supposed to. Do you know any way we can trace those vehicles?"

"I'm no authority on cars; I'm not aware of any."

"Can you get ahold of some of your dicks that work auto theft rings and see what they can do?"

"Sure. Anything else?"

"I'd like to identify the exact makes, models, and years of the cars."

"I should be able to get that done."

"Thanks, Tom. I got to go. I'm due in the SAC's office and I haven't laced up my tap shoes yet."

It was a few minutes before nine when Devlin sat down in the SAC's outer office. "He has someone in there," Sudder's secretary told him.

The door had been left open and Temper Hanlon's uncompromising voice caused Devlin to smile. "Well, I hope you *are* going to do something about this! The female agents are outraged by *your* assistant's insensitivity. The next meeting we have with the director, this will be brought to his attention."

Unpracticed in the technique, Sudder tried to put a patronizing rhythm in his voice. "Believe me, the director is well aware of the letter. Already this morning, he's received calls from not only members of the Black Caucus, but feminist and civil rights groups. He even got a call from the National Trial Lawyers Association. I don't think there's anyone that letter didn't insult."

"And what did Sandler say?"

"He denies writing the letter."

"So you're going to take his word?"

"No, the director and I found a compromise. The ASAC will go back to headquarters for a month or so and receive some sensitivity training."

"Well, I hope we don't see him here, *born again*, in a week."

"I assure you, it will be at least a month. In fact, at the end of a month, the director and I are going to reevaluate the situation to determine whether he can ever be effective in Detroit again."

"You're not telling me this is going to wind up being a promotion."

"Oh, no. If anything, this will have an adverse effect on his career."

"Well, thank you for your time, Mr. Sudder. I'll notify the other female agents." Temper walked out of the office still playing her role; she shot a perfect I-hate-men scowl at Devlin and stomped off. He was going to miss her.

Devlin was kept waiting another ten minutes before being told to go in. The secretary shut the door behind him. Cavalierly, Sudder leaned back at an angle in his chair, his composure apparently recaptured. Temper had made him talk to her as an equal by waving the female flag, so Sudder was obliged to lower himself beneath his station and show concern. But now he had Devlin. Like some sort of sorbet for his self-esteem, Sudder intended to use him to cleanse the taste of crow from his mouth.

Devlin stared at him, confidently avoiding the fellowship of first words. Finally, Sudder chuckled. "Well, here we are again. Me in charge, and you breaking the rules. Why is that?"

"It gives us both something to do?"

"Oh, I'm going to see to it that you have something to do. Do you know why I have you in here alone?"

"I hope this isn't going to be one of those sexual harassment things . . ."

"Because"—Sudder interrupted angrily—"I'm going to say some things I don't want witnessed." He searched Devlin's face for concern, but there was none. "You see, these *details* that I've been assigning you to are not to punish you. They are a progression of evidence to be used against you to have you fired. I knew you wouldn't last at the casino and I know you'll screw up this extortion; and when you do, I'll be there to make sure you never embarrass a man of my position again."

"You would think a *man of your position* would have better things to do."

Sudder took a moment to calm himself. "Oh, I do have better things to do. That's why I won't need a briefing today. You may go." As Devlin got up to leave, the SAC said smugly, "I forgot to tell you, you're due at Seacard in an hour. They want a briefing by the *new* case agent to see if there's some way to recover their loss. If you hurry, you can probably make it." Anger finally flickered in Devlin's eyes. It excited Sudder, and he could not resist one last declaration of his authority. "I will see you again, tomorrow morning."

James Pendleton's secretary stuck her head in his office. "There's an Agent Devlin from the FBI here, and Mr. Hansen from Fidelity Casualty is on line three."

"Tell the agent I'll be with him in a minute." She closed the door, and Pendleton picked up the phone. "Jack, how are you?"

"I think I'm about to have a five-million-dollar headache."

"I know insurance companies would like to think otherwise, but paying claims is part of your contract."

"I had a preliminary discussion with my boss this morning, and he thinks there's some question as to whether we're liable under the circumstances."

"Let me see if I got this right. You are the insurer of the hospital?"

"Of course."

"And, if the hospital had been blown up, *with its patients,* how much do you think that would have cost Fidelity Casualty? Less than five million?"

"I'm sure a great deal more."

"Then, it is our position that you *are* liable. We were paying the five million to protect our patients."

"If we would have been notified before the money was delivered, we would have had firsthand knowledge of its destruction."

"What do you think? That we filled those boxes with old newspapers?" Pendleton allowed himself a small grin.

"I know the money was destroyed, but my boss is voicing these objections."

"Is he there now?"

"Yeah, he's in his office."

"Okay, I'll hold on while you go in there and talk to him."

"About what?"

"I've got some figures in front of me. This year we were insured with you for just over half a billion dollars. We do business with a number of insurance companies, and next year we'll have to decide how much business we want to do with whom. I have a feeling, in your case, it's going to be substantially more—or substantially less. I'll wait one minute for you to find out which." Pendleton heard him put down the phone and hurry away. *Too bad I didn't know all the money was go-*

ing to be burned. If I had any idea how aggravating all this was going to be, I would have taken the entire five million.

Hansen came back on the line. "Okay, he says he'll need some third-party verification of the loss and the circumstances surrounding it."

Pendleton thought about the agent waiting in his outer office. "The FBI was there from start to finish. How about I get them to send you something?"

"I'm sure that would be acceptable."

Sudder had been too eager to send Devlin to Seacard Industries, especially after announcing his plan to methodically fire him. So, although Devlin knew it would make him late for the meeting, he went to Ray Miller to ask him about the Bureau's last meeting with the Seacard officials.

"Damnedest thing I ever saw, Mike. You know how it is when these big shots have problems and we're called in—they treat us like royalty. Well, everybody at Seacard couldn't have been nicer until we're saddling up to cover the drops, and this guy Pendleton comes in and starts threatening us."

"About what?"

"It sounded like he wanted the extortionist to get away with the money, and if by some fluke we did catch him, under no circumstances were we to open the boxes but instead take them directly to the head of security."

As Devlin sat waiting in the executive vice president's outer office, he wondered about Pendleton's illogical behavior. Agents, like everyone else, can mishandle a situation, but the implication that they were capable of theft was not only unreasonable but, under the circumstances, counterproductive.

"Mr. Devlin," the secretary said, "Mr. Pendleton can see you now."

Devlin shook hands as he introduced himself to Pendleton. "I appreciate you coming out here to meet with me. As you know, a great deal of money was destroyed, and we are anxious to recover it from our insurance company as quickly as possible." Pendleton smiled warmly, and Devlin studied his facial expression.

"What exactly is it that you need from the FBI?"

"Unfortunately, after the second bomb went off and critically injured that poor child, we were caught up in the gravity and expedience of the moment and did not take time to consider the administrative problems of reimbursement." Pendleton realized that Devlin was watching him, not attentively, but analytically. Cautiously, he asked, "Do you normally work extortions, Agent Devlin?"

Devlin detected tiny ripples of apprehension in the vice president's speech. His pleasantness also seemed labored. "I've worked a few," Devlin said, turning a cold stare on Pendleton, who refused to break eye contact.

What was bothering Pendleton was, by his count, Devlin should have been the third string on this case. But he did not seem like a person who would be satisfied sitting on any bench. Pendleton was starting to experience a rare, paradoxical euphoria: Devlin seemed both challenging and dangerous. "Specifically, we need a report from the FBI, stating there was an extortion and we did in fact lose five million dollars."

"There's no question there was an extortion attempt, but the money . . ." He gave a short laugh and let the unfinished sentence dangle in the air like a baited hook.

Pendleton took it. "What about the money?" he asked, his voice carrying the slightest vibration of panic. Again, he found himself under Devlin's draining gaze. Although Pendleton did not realize he was doing it, Devlin noticed a slight tightening of his lips. It was the face's way of involuntarily hiding anger, anger fueled by dishonesty.

He looked at Pendleton for a couple of seconds longer before he answered. "Well, there we have a problem." This time, Pendleton did not take the hook. "From what I've read in the file, no one at the FBI saw the contents of those boxes. So we can't report that there was money in them."

Pendleton wondered if Devlin was suspicious or if this was

his normal demeanor. "The FBI knows the money was in the boxes; they were right there when it burned."

"The only thing I know is that we were told by yourself, in no uncertain terms, that those boxes were not to be opened by the FBI under any circumstances. So we don't know what was in them"—Devlin smiled—"theoretically speaking."

"I'm sorry about that. I was under orders from the chairman of the board to do that." Pendleton felt that he was becoming impervious to Devlin's probing eyes and allowed himself a small smile.

Devlin compared it with the smile when he met him and noted it was slightly stronger on one side of his face, another sign of deception. "No problem."

"How can we resolve this discrepancy?" Pendleton asked.

"Who else saw the money in the boxes?"

"Our chief of security, Neal Ferguson."

"Was he in the room when you sealed them?"

"No, he had to get to the meeting with your people."

"So you alone sealed the boxes?"

"Yes."

"Okay, here's what we can do. You give me a signed statement about sealing the money in the boxes, and I'll include it in my report."

"That seems like a reasonable solution."

"Include your full name, address, phone number, date of birth, and Social Security number." He smiled his own crooked smile. "Standard Bureau procedure."

"Anything else?" Pendleton asked.

"I'll need to talk to Neal Ferguson and get a statement from him."

"Certainly."

Devlin stared calmly at Pendleton and said, "He does have a list of the serial numbers, I assume?" Small flickers of fear in Pendleton's eyes answered the question.

With forced nonchalance, Pendleton chuckled and asked,

"I'm sure he does, but if the money's been destroyed, why would you need the numbers?"

"You wouldn't believe the mountain of evidence in this case. I can't find the original list of serial numbers anywhere and they've already been entered into the national computer. I need the list so I can clear them out of the system." Devlin was lying. The bills had never been put into NCIC. His probe about the list of serial numbers had set off a visible concern in Pendleton. He needed to buy some time.

"You mean someone would have actually been looking for the bills?"

"Yes, the Federal Reserve randomly checks any large bills coming through for processing," Devlin lied.

"It must be quite a job taking that number of bills out of the computer."

"It sure is. I'm glad the NCIC clerk does it instead of me. But he can't take them out without a documented reason for their removal. My report, the one you need for the insurance company, will take care of that."

Pendleton stood up dismissively and said, "I know we're putting you in a difficult situation, but we just want what is rightfully ours."

Devlin stood up. "That's what my job is all about—making sure people get what's rightfully coming to them. Besides, I like *difficult*."

‖‖ CHAPTER 9 ‖‖

The extortion was becoming an unyielding maze. Transfixed in concentration, Devlin held his speed at seventy and urged the case's facts through its blind corners and intentional wrong turns. He began to wonder if there really was a passage leading to the solution, or whether the truth would die, unpronounced, in one of the dark tunnels of its designed confusion. Haidar's brilliantly inconsistent plan, the empty box, and now Pendleton hiding something: Were all these things related? He would need some help to find out.

As soon as he arrived at the office, he called Temper Hanlon. When she answered, he said, "I thought you'd be out talking to some of Sudder's people-of-misplaced-reality."

"No. Malcolm the Philanthropic finally got word I was pregnant, and because of that scam we ran on him about male insensitivity, he told my supervisor to keep me busy in the office."

"He's given *me* something else to do too," Devlin said.

"Yeah, I heard about that. The extortionist who will always hold the world record for the shortest time as a millionaire."

"That's the one. I need some help on it, unofficially. Would you be willing to work on something that's a little bizarre?"

"This isn't that thing where I have to wear the rubber underwear filled with butterscotch pudding, is it?"

Devlin laughed and told her where he was.

As she walked in, the intimacy of the tiny room enhanced the things that made her a woman: the gentle, clawing smells;

the smoky brandy of her voice; and a body teeming with new life. She intercepted Devlin's lingering gaze. "I know I look terrible."

Devlin smiled a soft, contradicting smile. "The carpenter is a lucky guy."

For the briefest moment, Temper tinged with embarrassment at Devlin's warmness. For a long moment, they let their eyes settle on each other luxuriously. Finally, she said, "Is this what you had in mind by *bizarre*?"

"Sorry. How do you like my 'office'?"

"Better not let the fire marshal know we're in here. I think we're over capacity."

Devlin looked at her comfortably. "What I'm going to tell you shouldn't leave this room."

"Unless you have some olive oil, I'm not sure *I'll* be leaving this room."

He started with the thermite grenades in the third car and detailed how he had found the empty box. He listed the "mistakes" Haidar had made and then explained the interview he had just had with Pendleton. When he was finished, she asked, "Who's got the million?"

"Right now, the only thing I'm sure of is that Haidar doesn't."

"Is there any tie-in between Haidar and Pendleton?"

"That's what I would like you to try and find out. Working those Medicare-Medicaid cases, you've got the contacts in the medical community. How about seeing if there is any connection between them. Try to find out what Pendleton's involvement with the hospital is. And if you can, run a credit check on him. His personal data is on the signed statements."

"No problem. But at the rate that I'm gaining weight, I think this room's seen the last of me. Anything else?"

Devlin's voice was now soft, personal. "I don't know—is there anything else?"

They were standing close to each other. Temper stared back

hypnotically for a moment and then without a word turned and left abruptly.

He inhaled the last of her dissipating perfume and then forced himself back to work.

Devlin decided to put the extortion aside. Early in his career, when the Bureau measured its agents by production, handling forty or more cases was not unusual. It had taught him that investigations had their own rhythm, their own pattern and speed of resolution. Some phases had to develop before others could be completed. Mistimed interviews or confrontations could delay or even destroy a case's solution. Patience was an old ally of the Bureau, and heeding *the rhythm* helped an agent keep the advantage of surprise. He would let Temper find out what she could and then see how it fit into the mushrooming confusion.

He opened his briefcase and took out the pirated files on Lawson and Blankenship. Painstakingly, for the next two hours, he reviewed them again. The ex–Grand Haven police officer had been the best lead, but he had an irrevocable alibi. Nothing else seemed out of the ordinary. Maybe Devlin was trying to force the rhythm of *this* case too. He needed to get out of that room.

Shanahan sat at his desk and dictated painfully into a handheld tape recorder. When Devlin walked up, he welcomed the opportunity to abandon the bane of his Bureau career—paperwork.

"Are you doing any good with those Secret Service leads?"

"Absolutely zero. I've been up close and personal with more nuts than a vasectomy clinic. It's like we're wandering around in a sandstorm. We have no idea where we are, where we're going, or where we've been."

"Did you talk to Behavioral Science?"

Shanahan gave a short laugh. "You've got to come up out of Cell Block D more often. Hagstrom has been here for the last twenty-four hours. In fact, I just took him to the Ren Cen to show him where Brian was killed, and then to the airport."

"And?"

"He said a good part of his time here he spent with Sudder, listening to his serial-murder theory."

"He's still pushing that?"

"Yeah, because this guy's taking souvenirs."

"What's Hagstrom think?"

"He didn't think a serial killer would focus on a profession. I asked him what about hookers, since they're always being picked off by these guys. He said they're targets because their profession is sex, and serial killers are usually acting out sexual fantasies. Prostitutes are very vulnerable, because it's their job to go off with strangers in cars. He felt the fact that there are still lawyers alive is proof they don't kill by profession."

"Has he got any idea at all about this guy?"

"Best guess, without all the forms filled out? It's someone who's got a hard-on for FBI agents."

"That really narrows it down."

"Yeah, I know. Then I asked him about us interviewing all these crazies. His take on this guy is that he's extremely organized, especially the way he lured Brian over to the Ren Cen. He's not likely to be in any nut file, since those people get their names on paper because of their uncontrollable rantings and ravings and those are the characteristics of a *dis*organized personality."

"Did you ask him about the souvenirs?"

"He said usually serial killers take them to relive the sexual fantasy. In this case, he wasn't sure. He'd have to get back to me. That's what I like about him—he doesn't have all the answers on a Rolodex. He's not afraid to give it some thought and try something new."

"Does he think this guy was specifically after John and Brian?"

Shanahan gave a tired smile. "He asked me not to tell anyone—especially Sudder, since *he's* convinced the killings were random—but he's pretty sure this guy had a reason for picking John and Brian. He's going to do some more work on that too."

"You'll let me know?"

"Of course," said Shanahan. "How's the extortion going?"

"Better, now that Sandler has been rerouted."

"That was exceptional. You've got potential, Michael. As a professional, I'm feeling a little threatened."

"It was just beginner's luck. You're still the Emperor of Poetic Justice."

Shanahan grinned and lowered his voice conspiratorially. "Remember I told you I had one going for tonight?" Devlin nodded. "Even though I always solo, you look like you need a boost. How about it?"

"I've got to run over and see Dr. Zilke and see if he knows anything that can help us. Want to come along?"

"No, thanks. As tired as I am, I'd be afraid of falling asleep. And that's a very unhealthy thing to do in a coroner's office." Devlin laughed. "You think I'm kidding. Did you ever meet that guy that works over there—I don't know his real name but they call him Igor?" He didn't give Devlin a chance to answer. "Big ugly dude. The rumor is he likes *body surfing* with the stiffs, calls it 'stopping for a cold one.' When his wife filed for divorce, one of the problems she cited was his strange sexual habits. He would make her sit in a bathtub full of ice water for a half hour before they had sex. She said it got him 'in the mood.' So, you can go ahead without me. We'll talk about tonight when you get back."

Devlin found Zilke in his second-floor office. As always, the Wayne County medical examiner was glad to see anyone from law enforcement. They shook hands warmly. "Michael, I haven't talked to you since the Tungworth case."

"I guess I haven't needed a favor until now."

Even Zilke's laugh seemed to have a German accent. "Good! No beating about the bushes. What problems do you bring me today?"

"The two agents who were killed. Did you do the autopsies?"

"Yes. Both." Even Zilke's use of words was efficient.

Devlin handed him the crime-scene photos he had pilfered from the office. "I don't know if you have seen these." Zilke studied them intently for thirty seconds and then looked at Devlin. "Because of ballistics, we know it's the same shooter, but what we are unable to determine is the relationship between the killer and the two victims."

"Medically, the only thing I can report is that each of the victims was killed instantly by the first shot. But then, for unknown reasons, the killer used an unnecessary second shot."

"Would the killer know they were both dead after the first shot?"

"As proficient as he seems, I would guess that he knew."

"Then why the second shot?"

"Anger. Hate. You know of no connection between the victims?"

"Not that hasn't been washed out."

"Well, my gut tells me he is not selecting his victims randomly," said Zilke. "The second shots are not your normal coup de grace, like through the heart, base of the skull, or behind the ear. It has been my experience that, when a killer has a choice and shoots someone in the face, it can be a statement against that person or, in the case of law enforcement, what that person stands for."

"Each of them was shot *twice* in the face. Does that mean anything?"

"I think it does. Especially the way Agent Lawson was killed. The physical evidence at the scene indicated he charged his assailant. But the killer took the difficult head shot. That's chancy when the target is stationary, never mind running at him. So, to shoot him in the face was very important to whoever murdered both men. It's like he wanted to disgrace them and to have the last laugh. To dishonor them was an important part of the murderer's scheme. But please remember, these are nonmedical observations that could never be supported during testimony."

Devlin knew that Zilke's observations, supported or unsupported, were usually a safe bet. He thanked the doctor and drove back to the office.

As he flipped through the two dead agents' personnel files on his desk, Devlin recalled Zilke's two-word motive for the killings: *to dishonor*. To intentionally dishonor someone was usually an act of retribution. The murderer may have felt that Lawson and Blankenship had dishonored *him*. But how could two men, so diverse in their professional lives, have dishonored the same man? Devlin's phone rang. It was Tom Michaels from the MSP lab.

"Mike, we got all those cars ID'd. And I got one of the dicks from the Ypsilanti post who works cars to go out and take a look at the scene. He said whoever cleaned up those vehicles was serious about it. Taking the public VINs off is no big deal, but the confidential numbers are placed so they're very hard to eradicate. Most of the time, they're stamped into the frame at structurally critical points, so if you cut or drill them out it can weaken the frame. He said that a good thief will take a cutting torch and remove the entire section, then weld a blank piece of steel into its place. But this guy didn't have to worry about getting many more miles out of any of those cars so he took out the numbers completely. Of course, the fire eliminated everything else."

"Did he have any ideas how we could trace the cars?"

"He said if all of a car's numbers were destroyed, it was unidentifiable and therefore untraceable. It's a dead end, actually five dead ends. Do you still want their descriptions?"

Devlin wrote DEAD ENDS across a sheet of paper and said, "Yeah, go ahead."

After they hung up, Devlin leaned back in his chair and considered *dead ends*. It was a term he did not like; it indicated surrender. Many times, he had found, its use was premature.

All of the cars were twelve to fifteen years old. Other than that, there were no similarities. Some were American, some foreign. Everything from compact to full-size. They had been towed to the five initial drop sites about two hours before the money was placed in them. But Devlin wondered how they had gotten to the original locations before the tow trucks picked them up the first time. He flipped through the file until he found the names and numbers of the five tow truck operators. He called the first three without any luck. He dialed the fourth.

"Yes, sir. I already talked to the FBI."

"I see that. I'm looking at your statement right now. It says you were given money and instructions, which included a map."

"That's right. And I told the other FBI agent, part of the instructions was to leave them and the map in the unit once I unhooked it at the Park-and-Ride."

"And you did that?"

"Well . . . see, I had them under the billing order on my clipboard and when I talked to the other agent I thought I had left them. There was a lot of confusion in that lot with all those trucks coming and going. Last night I was doing the billing and found them."

"Where are they now?"

"I've got them right here."

"I know you've handled the papers, but please don't touch them any more with your hands. If you could put everything in an envelope, I would appreciate it."

"I'm sorry. I thought I left . . ."

"There's no problem. I see you first picked up the car in a vacant lot about a mile away."

"Yeah, it was sitting there all by itself."

"Could you tell how long it had been sitting there?"

"Not very long. The lot was muddy. The mud on the tires was still wet."

"On all four tires?"

"Yeah. Why?"

"That means the car had to be driven there."

"You're right. Does that make a difference?"

"It might. How about plates?"

"None."

"You picked up the car twice, dropped it twice, and all on written instructions. Didn't you think any of that was unusual?"

"Between repo's, practical jokes, and women having their ex-husbands' girlfriends' cars towed into swamps, not much arouses my curiosity anymore. Cops ask questions for a living; I tow cars."

"How did you receive the instructions?"

"A guy gave them to me. The agent showed me a bunch of pictures and I picked him out."

Devlin looked at the statement in his hand. The photo the driver had identified was Jousef Haidar's. Devlin made arrangements to pick up the map and instructions. He called the last towing service, but they could not add anything to their previous statements.

Two things suggested to Devlin that the five cars used by the extortionist were registered with the state of Michigan. First, if they had been driven to their starting points, they would have had, at least for the trip, license plates on them to preclude being pulled over by the police. Second, why obliterate all the numbers if the cars were not traceable through registration?

Devlin looked at the top of the sheet of paper. DEAD ENDS stared back. What had Tom Michaels said, "Five dead ends"? Of the hundreds of thousands of cars registered in Michigan, finding one would be impossible, but finding five specific vehicles all registered to one person might not be.

He called the office contact at the Department of Motor Vehicles in Lansing.

"It's possible, Mike. But it will take an off-line computer search."

"The cars are all at least twelve years old."

"With five cars that old, most of them will be in salvage

yards, which have hundreds of old cars registered to them that would include your five cars."

"No, this will be an individual."

"We'll have to get real lucky."

"How long?"

"I can get it done in a day or two."

"I'll call you. Thanks."

If any of the cars was registered to Pendleton, it would answer a lot of questions.

One other thing had bothered Devlin: Why had the bombs in the cars gone off prematurely? He considered Tom Michaels's theory about the extortionist panicking. The possibility existed, but the bomb maker was obviously experienced. The two bombs at the hospital had been the model of efficiency. The first had been booby-trapped and the second had been set off exactly at the most terrifying moment possible. The bombs in the car were also well designed and had erased all of the physical evidence. No, a man who handled explosives so expertly would not have accidentally set them off. *They had gone off exactly when they were supposed to.*

One ancient, and therefore irrefutable, tale of the Bureau tells of a lone agent who had tracked a fugitive to a mountain cabin and was taken prisoner by the criminal's family. While they pondered the agent's fate, they sought comfort in their clannish music. Before long, the agent was playing the banjo and singing with enough credibility that they decided he was worth trusting and had the fugitive surrender to him.

This parable, all but forgotten in the Bureau's dusty warehouse of history, has been offered periodically as evidence of an FBI agent's diversity of skills. The Bureau has always sought people who, because of their talents and experiences, are able to react successfully to difficult and changing situations. But bureaucracy, by its very nature, has to treat all its employees with equal carelessness, striving toward the faultlessness of mediocrity, leaving the fruited plain of talent within to lie fallow. While some choose to wilt into the paralyzing comfort of this commonness, others find new and gushing rivers for their energies to sail upon.

One such adventurer was William Patrick Shanahan. He was born in Boston's South End, where brawling was considered a primary communicational skill. His father had been a carpenter and cabinetmaker who had passed along to him an acute sensibility of hand and eye. Young Shanahan showed great promise as a sculptor. But none of the art schools that offered him scholarships participated in his life's first and most barbaric love—lacrosse. So he went to a small college in Massachusetts where he majored in lacrosse, beer drinking, and getting by. After graduation, he spent three years in the Marine Corps, finding it a natural extension of college, and then he moved on to the FBI, which was similar to the Corps, except the Marines had "uniforms and adult leadership."

True to the lacrosse players' code, he believed in playing hard and, after the game, playing even harder. The impossible cases that he solved with an almost embarrassed carelessness had a gamelike appeal for him. And Shanahan spent equal time and energy on his hobbies, which he listed as: dining at the steno pool smorgasbord and capering.

Big, good-looking, and confidently charming, he wasted little time on the dating ritual. Always in demand, he inexhaustibly *processed* the women of the office on a first-come-first-served basis. He explained his bachelor's philosophy in a deliberate misquote of General Custer: "Ride to the sound of the party." Once, when someone corrected him, he said, "Riding to the guns *was* Custer's party."

And with the patience and creativity of the sculptor who lay dormant within, Shanahan planned and maddeningly executed his capers. His practical jokes were so complete in their ability to embarrass that they were revered Bureau-wide. Yet their author remained anonymous to all but a few of his closest friends.

Bill Shanahan walked into Devlin's room. "How about it, Mike? Tonight is *the* night."

Devlin knew by his ominous grin that someone had offended Shanahan's delicate sense of justice and was about to be humiliated. "I don't think this is the right time."

"That's exactly why it is the right time. Take a look in the mirror. You need a laugh. Besides, I started setting this up two months ago; I didn't know all this would be going on."

Devlin remained uncommitted. "How about a postponement?"

"Tonight only. Maybe if I tell you who the target is—your best friend in the whole Bureau—Malcolm the Empty Suit Sudder." Shanahan flashed an expression of mock surprise, hoping Devlin would smile his surrender.

"Well, great, Bill. Just in case you lost your notes, the elevator mooning is how I wound up in this room. Today behind closed doors, Sudder promised to run me out of Dodge, and you want to do an anonymous on him? Gee, let's see. Who would he blame for this?"

"He said he was going to fire you?"

"That's why he gave me this extortion. So I could screw it up."

"Then we got to get the sonofabitch. We're not going to take this from him, are we? We've got pride; we've got honor. Hell, we've got *hate* on our side." Shanahan's voice had crescendoed in volume, tone, and drama. Knute Rockne would have been proud.

Devlin laughed. He had always been envious of Shanahan's utter disdain for caution. At that moment, it seemed especially inviting. "This better be good."

"It's not good—it's perfect!"

"Another perfect caper," Devlin said with resigned doubt in his voice.

"We're going to settle a lot of scores with this one. Remember that child pornographer I locked up about three months ago?" Devlin nodded. "While we were searching the house, I found a couple of those classified-ad magazines. Later, I reviewed them to see if this bucket of shit had any ads of his own in there. In one of them I find this full-page advertisement for The Friends of Youth. Do you know what that is?"

"No."

"It's these cruddy old pedophiles who believe it's all right to have sex with young boys. I mean, these assholes are out in the open about it. In fact, this ad was for a fund-raiser—they're going to lobby Congress for legislation! Next thing you know, we'll have a recruiting quota for them in the Bureau. Anyway, the dinner is here, tonight. Hundred dollars a pop. So, I blue-slipped the hundred under some vague expense in the case and sent it with this long letter requesting all these details about their organization. They sent back a ticket for the dinner and a long, rambling response to my questions. But what I really wanted was their stationery. I've got a friend with a color copying machine. He blocked out everything but the letterhead and made me some great duplicates of their stationery. So then I typed this glowing letter to Sudder, telling him that because of his remarkable contribution to law enforcement he has been selected as our Man of the Year. I enclosed his free ticket. Of course, the cheap bastard sees the hundred-dollar price tag and figures he's got a healthy freebie. The letter also instructs him not to tell anyone about his selection, because of all the candidates for the award, he is the only one who knows. He was being told in order to ensure his attendance. And not to worry about news coverage, because members of the national media would be there."

Devlin laughed. "And in the category of Disgracing Thine Enemy, this year's winner of the Grudgee is . . ."

"Wait. That's only half of it. Do you remember when Brian got in trouble in court over that informant he used in the search warrant, and then that asshole Woodson from the newspaper wrote that article frying him the next day?"

Devlin thought about Brian Blankenship again. It had happened a year earlier. Brian had been so eager to do a good job that he *adjusted* some information he had received from one of his better informants. In a search warrant, the affiant not only has to present the probable cause, but he has to qualify the source of that information. Great care has to be taken when presenting the informant's track record; if it is too specific, it can give clues as to his or her identity. Brian's source had a very limited background, so if he had been 100 percent accurate in his description, it would have been tantamount to putting the source's name on the document. The information about the criminal activity was correct, but in order to protect "his man," he restructured some facts. When the search warrant was challenged in court, Brian was not experienced enough to *protect* the truth. The judge, who later apologized, blasted Brian. Woodson, a confirmed Bureau-hater, wrote a frenzied article about the fascism that still exists in today's FBI. For once, Sudder did the right thing as the SAC and demanded an apology from the newspaper. They declined, and after that, every time a chink was exposed in the FBI's armor, the paper assigned the story to Woodson, who gladly used it as a vehicle to justify his hatred of the government. Devlin thought of Brian lying in his own decomposing fluids on the floor of the Renaissance Center, a man who had always given more than he was asked. "I remember."

Shanahan put his finger to his lips to signal Devlin's silence, picked up the phone, and dialed. "Alan Woodson, please," Shanahan said in a deep southern voice. "Is this the Alan Woodson who writes those great articles about the FBI? . . . Good. I've got a story that's going to win you a Pulitzer Prize. Do you know what The Friends of Youth is?"

Devlin had to leave the room because he was afraid he could not control his laughter. When he heard Shanahan hang up, he went back in.

Shanahan was smiling. "He's so excited, his dick is harder than Chinese algebra. He guaranteed me he'd be there without fail, photographer and all."

"You know, whether it's logical or not, Sudder will blame me."

"I don't think so. Art Nestling, being from a rival paper,

gave me Woodson's private post office box number. It's on the envelope as the return address for The Friends of Youth. As soon as Sudder sees Woodson, photographer in tow, at the dinner and matches it with the return address, it'll be nothing but allegations and counterallegations."

Shanahan's inventiveness was inspiring. Not only was the SAC's career about to hit a nasty speed bump, but a large dose of revenge was about to be donated in the name of a fallen comrade. "Let's go."

"I borrowed the surveillance van with photographic equipment in case there's a need for documentation later on."

For Shanahan, a practical joke never ended; it constantly fed the future. At the most inappropriate times and places, photographs of the night's festivities would mysteriously be posted, driving The Suit crazy.

Devlin said, "I suppose you've factored in enough time for me to buy you a few beers first."

"I would think that's what a civilized person would do."

At the bar, Shanahan solemnly held up the first beer and said, "May this evening be rich with humiliation and ever so satisfying for Brian Blankenship, a helluva agent."

||| CHAPTER 10 |||

People who enforce the law for a living are aware that within Stupidity lurks its own punishment. For them, it is a natural justice, unlike the one they so laboriously force on criminals. Once Devlin had been given a case in which an agent had gotten into a traffic altercation that degenerated into a gun being pointed at his face. When Devlin finally identified the assailant, he found him in the hospital; he had been shot in the face. The case was closed without protest because everybody involved had felt justice's warm, healing whirlpool. No court could ever match the sweetness of life's speedy prosecution. But sometimes, Bill Shanahan conceded, justice, even for the terminally stupid, needed a broker. His plan the night before had been everything he had hoped for.

As usual, Sudder, The Friends of Youth's Man of the Year, arrived fifteen minutes late. It was a practiced technique he used to avoid conversation which, for him, always seemed to impress people far less than his title. Shanahan had counted on the SAC's social evasiveness to keep him unaware of the evening's impending events.

Wearing his own tuxedo, Sudder felt a little self-conscious about being overdressed. In fact, he noticed no one else in the small banquet hall had even worn a tie. But then none of them was the Man of the Year.

He found his seat and began eating. Everyone was friendly and wondered who the well-dressed gentleman was. Intermittently, he introduced himself as the FBI Special Agent in

Charge, and one by one, the other diners at his table excused themselves. Expecting a raid, they found their way out of the building.

Not until the dessert came and Sudder was eating his second piece of cake, courtesy of his AWOL dining companions, did he realize that something was amiss. Someone had started a rather graphic speech about First Amendment rights. Then a slide show, which was greeted by cheering, began. There had been a terrible mistake, but how?

That was when Alan Woodson and one of his newspaper's photographers walked in and easily spotted the SAC sitting alone in his tuxedo. The photographer's exploding flash started most of the seventy guests toward the door. Sudder knew that Woodson's presence could not be a coincidence; he had to be the orchestrator of this setup. During the ensuing scuffle, Woodson's nose was bloodied, an arm was ripped off the SAC's tuxedo, and the motor drive of the photographer's camera yipped happily away.

When two of the organizers of the fund-raiser found out who Sudder was, one of them jumped into the fray, while the other, the ACLU's number in hand, headed for the phone.

As the police arrived, Shanahan set his beer down on the floor of the van and, squinting through the van's photographic periscope, started snapping pictures. Although the police had separated the main combatants inside, they were considerate enough to start round two outside the hotel entrance. Shanahan considered the night a personal masterpiece and talked of retirement. But Devlin knew that William Shanahan, Righter of Wrongs, would again strap on Justice's terrible swift sword just as soon as someone else was mistreated.

After Special Agent in Charge Sudder was led off to the First Precinct amid loud denials of homophobia, Devlin and Shanahan drove to the Athens, intent on a long, alcoholic celebration. Without admitting any knowledge of the specifics, Shanahan mischievously told a group of cops sitting at the bar that his boss had just been arrested, charges unknown. When a lieutenant offered to make a call on the SAC's behalf, Shanahan politely threatened his life and then explained how he had heard Sudder was involved with a group of child molesters. The big Bostonian then told them about how the SAC had mooned the director of the FBI in the elevator. The cops, mostly from Armed Robbery and Homicide, were world experts at between-line reading and before long had a pretty good idea of the source of the SAC's problems. As they listened to Shanahan, all of them, including the *endangered* lieutenant, roared with laughter.

Devlin couldn't help but admire Shanahan's reckless disregard for consequences, even when it seemed to border on the cataclysmic. It was an appealing way to go through life. Devlin thought about what had happened that day with Temper; Shanahan would probably not have hesitated to say or do something about what they had both seemed to feel. But there was a difference between him and Devlin, and that difference was Knox. She was everything Devlin wanted in his life: a sense of purpose, excitement, family. Most of all, theirs was an affair that promised to last forever.

Devlin stood up and told Shanahan, "I've got to go."

"Whoa! We've barely got this thing off the ground."

"You'll have to take 'er up without me, Mr. Sulu. I've got a date."

When Devlin arrived home, he found Knox in bed reading. He undressed and turned out the light without asking her. Before she could protest, he put his hand over her mouth and gently held it there.

Instead of struggling, she took a moment to understand what he was doing. He was telling her: No arguments, no explanations, no recriminations, just physical love. Their life with each other existed on two tiers: the one that processed the sweet and sour routines of Everyday, and the Forever level. Tonight they would sneak below the arguments that had become their Everyday and retravel the physical secrets of their marriage.

She bit his hand hard, but not hard enough to hurt him. He

understood that she too was setting limits. By accepting this unspoken retreat, she was in no way compromising her position about his involvement in the Gentkill investigation. He took his hand away and anxiously covered her mouth with his own.

Their lovemaking had an exciting exploration to it, as if they were love-at-first-sight strangers. Eventually, they fell asleep in each other's arms.

Devlin arrived at the office at 9 A.M. and went straight to the SAC's office, trying to gather enough lies to bluff his way through the morning briefing. The secretary informed him that Sudder was not feeling well and would be on sick leave for the next day or two. Devlin noticed the newspaper on her desk; it was opened to an article entitled: FBI CHIEF "WRESTLES WITH" FIRST AMENDMENT ISSUE. Although the paper was upside down, Devlin recognized one of the photographs accompanying the article. It was a one-black-one-white sleeve shot of the SAC.

Devlin sat at his desk and took a moment to warm himself with his temporary freedom. The extortion had taken some unexpected turns that he was not willing to overlook. The first step was getting the list of car owners from the DMV. He looked at the evidence stacked up around him. Most of it, if his theory was correct, was to deceive him, so processing it would be not only foolish but counterproductive. He decided not to do anything until he received the list of registrations from Lansing. He went to see Shanahan.

Shanahan was on the phone and carefully taking notes about what he was being told. Devlin looked over his friend's shoulder to see what he was writing. Shanahan was talking to Bill Hagstrom at the Behavioral Science Unit.

He hung up and looked at Devlin. A hint of a smile reminded Devlin of the events of the night before. Shanahan said, "Aren't you supposed to be in briefing The Suit?"

Devlin smiled. "He's on sick leave."

Shanahan laughed. "Probably at the tuxedo doctor."

"It *was* a grand evening." Both of them laughed for a moment and then Devlin asked, "What did Hagstrom have to say?"

Shanahan picked up his notes. "Again, he said the killer is a male, race unknown but probably white. He's a compulsive person. Thorough to a fault. The second shot for each victim was like dotting the *i* for him, making sure everything was complete. It was also a statement of the *final word*, to show who was finally right, in control. Because of that, he feels we're looking for someone with deep-seated feelings of inadequacy. Someone who will go to any length to prove his position."

"Is he a serial killer?"

"Hagstrom says he thinks he's working too fast to be a serial killer. They like to take their time and carefully choose their victims. Part of their control fetish is picking their victims methodically, to the point that it becomes part of the ritual. It's almost as important as the kill itself. He says this guy is taking too big a chance working so fast; serial murderers don't do that. Everything has to feel *right* for them to hit. Besides, they have an afterglow period where they relive the fantasies, which makes the intervals between kills, especially the initial ones, longer than this guy is taking."

"Then what about the souvenirs?"

"Hagstrom believes that this guy collects one item from each victim so he has a physical object to remind him that he is superior to each of them. The fact that he has taken their forms of identification, their badge and credentials, may be his way of stripping them of their official identities."

"So, not only has he killed them, he's also trying to erase the fact that they are FBI agents."

"I guess so. Hagstrom thinks this guy has a grudge."

"A specific grudge, like I want to kill John Lawson; or in general, like any FBI agent will do?"

"Probably specific."

"Based on . . . ?"

"Victimology. The way they were set up. The double head shots. The short time between murders."

That was one more vote for a connection between the victims and their killer. This time from Bill Hagstrom, one of the wizards of BSU. They were known for their high-profile work on serial murder cases, but what most people did not realize was that they were deluged daily with everything from serial rapists to kidnappings to everyday murders. For the agents in the field who were pragmatic enough to call them, these specialists saved them thousands of miles and hours as they uncannily cut through the smoke screens left by the criminals.

"What do you think, Bill?"

"From the start, I thought this guy wanted John and Brian specifically. Evidently, from what Hagstrom says, something they did pissed him off."

"He must have had some contact with them on the job. He not only knew how to lure them into a trap, but he knew about the hollowpoints. So, he knew more about the Bureau than just who he wanted to kill."

Shanahan said, "I don't know. I've run through it a hundred times. I can't find any connection."

Devlin noticed a green-jacket file on Shanahan's desk. Green was the color coding for an informant file. "What about informants?"

"Informants? They're user-friendly. They tell us lies and, in return, we overpay them."

"But most agents who work informants hard sooner or later wind up in trouble over them."

"True, but then you're back to the same problem: organized crime versus fugitives. Apples and oranges; nothing in common."

"Let's not look for something they had in common. Instead, we'll see if any of their informants were problems and then look for a connection to the other agent."

"I'll have the informant clerk pull all their files. After everybody leaves tonight, I'll bring them down to your room."

"Okay. I've got some leads to cover on the extortion. I'll be back by five."

Devlin drove to Washtenaw County. He wanted to see all of the pickup locations and drop sites for himself. Experience had taught him that many of the mysteries of a case are answered once the investigator has touched the ground where they took place. First, he located the sites where the tow trucks picked up the five cars orginally. They were all relatively secluded, confirming something Devlin had suspected. If the extortionist had driven the cars to those spots, there had to be an accomplice to pick him up and drive him back. There was no public transportation, and hitchhiking, considering what was at risk, was not likely. He marked the five points on his map. Next, he went to the strip malls where the five million-dollar boxes had been placed in the cars, and marked them on his map. After he finished, he drove to the towing company that had accidentally kept a copy of the extortionist's instructions and picked them up. As requested, they were sealed in an envelope. In his car, Devlin put on a pair of plastic gloves and opened the envelope.

The instructions were typewritten in terse, incomplete sentences, one sentence per line, as if a mathematician were solving a complicated problem. He could tell from the type that it was not a copy, so there was a reasonable chance that it could be matched with the machine that had printed it. There was also a possibility of latent fingerprints. Devlin made a note to call the Immigration and Naturalization Service so he could obtain a set of Haidar's prints, but held little hope that anyone's prints but the truck driver's would be found on the document. The map was simply a black-and-white photocopy of a standard road map with heavy red lines drawn on it to mark the locations and routes. He dropped both sheets of paper back into the envelope and placed it in his briefcase.

He drove to the industrial park that was located behind the wooded area where he had found the empty box. After checking his map, he clocked the distance to the physics building at the University of Michigan. It was only four and a half miles. Haidar's off-campus apartment was a half mile away. It had been searched the night he had died, but nothing relating to the extortion or the bombings was found. He had been extremely careful at his own residence not to leave evidence, but so careless everywhere else. It was becoming obvious that these inconsistencies were part of someone's plan.

"Malcolm?" Sudder stiffened at the sound of the FBI director's voice.

"Yes, sir."

"Your secretary told me you were at home on sick leave. I assume you've seen the newspaper coverage of your attendance at the Friends of Youth dinner last night."

"Yes, sir."

"Well, I need to hear your side of it."

"The only thing I can say in my defense is that I was set up by that *Communist*, Alan Woodson."

"We're going to find out about that, but why would you go to something sponsored by a group like that?"

"I didn't know who they were."

"We're the FBI; we're supposed to know."

"I know, sir, but with everything going on around here, it slipped through the cracks."

"With everything that's going on, shouldn't you be at the office?"

"I thought it would do more harm than good today."

"I'm not happy, Malcolm. You've got two unsolved agent murders, five million dollars lost in an extortion, and you're out in a tuxedo socializing with a bunch of child molesters. I'm supposed to leave in a couple of hours for Australia to give a series of speeches at the International Chiefs of Police Convention, but I'm worried about the situation there."

"I assure you everything here is under control. The Gentkill investigation is being given the highest priority, and the extortion is solved, which means there will be no more bombs going off in hospitals. I have just been told that Seacard can probably recover the five million dollars through their insurance company. And as far as this incident last night, once the facts come to light you will see I am completely innocent."

"If these speeches hadn't been scheduled a year ago, I'd cancel. I'll be calling you daily for an update. And to make sure the facts *do* come to light, I'm sending an OPR team out to Detroit. They'll be there day after tomorrow. I don't want to read anything in their reports about your lack of candor."

The Office of Professional Responsibility was the FBI's version of Internal Affairs. Because the director was personally notifying him of their investigation, Sudder realized the importance that was being placed on the incident.

"Don't worry, sir. You won't."

"Malcolm, get these murders solved."

Before Sudder could finish his *Yes, sir*, the director hung up.

When he got back to the office, Devlin went to see Doug Patton on the Foreign Counterintelligence Squad. One of their major responsibilities was to monitor the activities of certain dissident Arab groups located in the Detroit region. As he approached the squad area, he could hear Patton before he could see him. Devlin sat down in a chair next to Patton's desk and watched him curiously. Tall and fair with bright red hair, Patton was a contradiction of stereotypes as he spoke rapid, flawless Arabic into the phone, like a foreign actor whose voice was being dubbed.

Patton hung up. "What's up, Mike?"

"Jousef Haidar. It was your source that got his tag at that PFNLA meeting."

"What exactly do you need to know?"

"I've read the file. I know enough about the PFNLA. I want to know how Haidar fit into that group."

"That's the odd thing about this. He didn't. He was brought to that meeting by a friend who knew his family. The group is very small and very secretive. The only way you can get in is by knowing someone. Haidar only went to the one meeting and didn't seem all that interested in the group's goals."

"I think someone else is involved in the extortion. The logical choice is the PFNLA."

"At the Bureau's direction, my source has become very active in the group. He says there's no way they're involved."

"And you trust him."

"Mike, he's never lied to me." It was the highest compliment a source could be paid. Few agents could say the same.

"Maybe he was just using the group's name to put some teeth into his threats."

"These people would have felt disgraced by their name being used for financial gain. Remember, they want an end to Western imperialism. Anything that has to do with money would be a contradiction to their philosophy. Like I said, someone in the group knew his family, and Haidar would have known they were capable of taking it out on his relatives. He could have used the name of a dozen other similar organizations without endangering his family."

"You don't think it was his idea then?"

"The guy, whatever he was, was no dummy. Using the PFNLA name would have been a basic, non-Arabic mistake."

"Non-Arabic?"

"Anyone who understands the Middle Eastern terrorist mentality, because of retribution, would never have considered it."

"So, if he had help, it wasn't from the PFNLA."

"That'd be my guess."

After leaving Patton, Devlin stopped at Temper Hanlon's desk, but she had already left for the day.

An hour later, Shanahan walked into Devlin's room with a box of green-jacketed informant files.

Devlin said, "I'll take Lawson."

"Anything in particular we're looking for?"

"Let's look at the closed informants first. Start with the ones who were most recently closed and work your way back. See why they were terminated."

Both men started flipping through the pages. Almost immediately, Shanahan said, "Here's one. Closed for providing false information." It was unusual for the operating agent to list "false information" as the reason for closing a source. The informant was usually given the benefit of the doubt. Besides, it was embarrassing for an agent to admit that he had not detected a lie as it was being told, but instead, had found out after the information had been recorded and used. But that was Brian Blankenship, full steam ahead. Maybe that was what got him killed.

Devlin said, "Look through the information the source has given. See if any of it was OC related." As Shanahan read the pages, Devlin continued to review his stack of files.

Shanahan said, "Yeah, here's some."

"Who does it say he disseminated the information to?"

"It doesn't say. It's a gambling case. Lawson worked gambling."

"A lot of sources in the office give gambling information. It's easy money for them. Let's look at the rest of them and see if there's anyone else."

For the next hour they reviewed files, occasionally finding one that had to be read page by page. But in the end only the one had warranted a second look.

The informant was Roger Bach, who was also known as Desiree Chaparral, a headliner at the Emerald City Café in the Six Mile and Woodward area. While searching for a bank robber, Brian Blankenship had met Bach and realized his potential as an informant. Not only was he a well-known member of Detroit's gay community, but he had an uncle who was the biggest supplier of video-poker machines in the Midwest. Although the machines were legally argued to be "just video games," bar owners knew that their installation would bring handsome illegal gambling profits. The most recent page in the file was a memo stating that Bach had lied to Blankenship about some information used in an unsuccessful search warrant.

Devlin said, "Are you in an Emerald City mood?"

Shanahan shook his head with good-natured reluctance. "I swear to God, first thing Monday, I'm going out and finding a real job."

Gentkiller: It was a good name. Not all that different from *Giant Killer*. Very heroic. He liked it. He had collected dozens of newspaper articles about the murders and had reread them endlessly; he *was* a giant killer. But one in today's paper worried him. An unnamed FBI source had said that he felt there was some as-yet-to-be-found tie-in between the two deaths, someone who had a connection to both men, and that theory was being pursued.

Of course there was a connection, but the fools were not supposed to figure that out. If it was ever discovered, his identity could be revealed. It was a flaw he had overlooked. His mind flashed back to the glove factory and he remembered all the agents wasting their time looking in the wrong places. He decided that a little randomness in selecting his next victim was exactly what was needed to distract the FBI.

Like a damp fog, the light seeped out of the club and painted the doorman's face a dusty green. His job was to keep trouble out, and he sensed a different purpose in the two suit-and-ties who stood in front of him. He raised a cynical eyebrow. "Can I help you, gentlemen?" Devlin and Shanahan opened their FBI credentials. Startled, the doorman asked, "Are you two serious?"

Playfully, Shanahan put his arm around Devlin and said, "No, we're just sort of dating."

The doorman smiled appreciatively. "What brings the straightest of the straight to the Emerald City?"

"Roger Bach," Shanahan said.

The doorman cocked his head, puzzled. Devlin answered, "Desiree Chaparral."

"Tell the bartender. He'll get her for you." He opened the inner door for the two agents and they walked into the civilized blare of the bar. As they made their way through the crowd, eager glances turned cautious. Devlin watched the bartender, who looked attentively beyond them, obviously being signaled by the doorman that they were the law. Behind the bar was a small stage. A performer in a long, white-beaded dress lip-synched and danced extravagantly to "Simply Irresistible." Some of the audience stood next to their tables and enthusiastically followed along. Shanahan said, "I don't think we're in Kansas anymore, Toto."

They sat at two stools in the middle of the bar. The bartender's head was shaved, and he had a full black mustache. A large gold cross hung from his right earlobe. He placed his hands, arms straightened, at the back edge of the bar as if holding it between himself and the two agents. In an uncommitted tone he asked, "Can I help you?"

Devlin said, "We're looking for Desiree."

The bartender stared back for a few moments and then said, "Jackson or Chaparral?"

"Chaparral."

Without another word, the bartender walked to the end of the bar and through a door that led backstage.

Devlin asked Shanahan, "What do you think?"

"I don't think the killer is in *this* building."

"Yeah. I'm afraid it's another one of those leads that looks so good on paper but makes you feel so stupid when you run it out."

The bartender reappeared. "She'll be right out. Want a drink?"

Shanahan said, "Not just yet." Devlin noticed his partner was watching the performer onstage and was starting to enjoy the music.

Through another door, Roger Bach, in the guise of Desiree

Chaparral, came in and walked up to the agents. He was dressed in an expensive lavender gown and wore a large black wig. In a husky, feminine voice he said, "I'm Desiree. Can I help you?"

Quietly, Devlin asked, "Roger Bach?"

With the slightest hint of indignation, he said, "Yes."

"Brian Blankenship."

"Oh, that's why you're here." He sat down next to Devlin and waved a drink order at the bartender. "I heard about it on the news. It's too bad. Even though we had some problems, he was a nice guy. You don't think I had anything to do with it?"

"What the FBI does best is cover bases. This is just another base. What kind of problems did you and Brian have?"

Bach lowered his voice. "I was giving him some help on video-poker machines. My uncle's a supplier." When Devlin didn't look surprised by the information, Bach said, "I guess that's all in my file." The bartender brought him his drink. "You guys want something or are you"—Bach deepened his voice humorously—"*on duty?*"

"Not right now, thanks," Devlin answered.

"See, I used to do my uncle's books. In the everyday world, I'm an accountant. So I knew how many machines he had where. I used to pass it along to Brian, but after my uncle's places kept getting hit, he suspected me. So he gave me some false information about a huge shipment, and when I told Brian, the FBI intercepted an empty truck with a search warrant. Since I was the only one my uncle had told about it, he knew it was me."

"Did you tell Brian all that?"

"No. After my uncle caught me, he told me that he was having me watched and if I ever went near the FBI again, he'd have my balls cut off. Now, while that may not seem especially critical given my immediate circumstance, I'm sure the surgical method would not have been AMA-approved. So even though Brian called me several times after that, I avoided him."

He looked into Devlin's investigative stare. "How good a suspect am I?"

"You're fading fast. How about other agents?"

"Brian's the only one I knew by name. The first time I met him there was someone with him, but I don't recall his name."

"John Lawson?"

"Doesn't ring a bell. Is he the other agent that was killed?"

"Yes. Do you remember where you were when Brian was killed?"

"I know exactly where I was. Ironically, all last week I was on jury duty. We heard a burglary case. Wayne County Circuit Court."

"Good. That's easy to check."

"I've got to go change. Is it okay?"

"Sure. Where's a phone I can use?"

"Come on in the back."

As Devlin got up, an announcer's voice loomed from somewhere. "The Emerald City Café is proud to present, all the way from New Orleans, the breathtakingly beautiful *Misty Dawn!*" As the crowd cheered, Devlin disappeared through a door.

Fifteen minutes later he returned; the performer was still onstage. Devlin sat down next to Shanahan, who was drinking beer from a bottle. A second bottle was waiting for Devlin. Shanahan watched Misty with a young boy's fascination. "Bill, Bach is clear. He was on that jury."

"Is this the most beautiful woman you've ever seen, or what?"

Devlin looked at the performer's exquisite, flawless face. "Shanahan, I hate to tell you this . . ."

"Don't say it."

Knowing Shanahan, Devlin just smiled patiently and picked up his beer. "Did you buy this?"

"No, the old gent at the end of the bar."

Devlin looked down the way Shanahan had pointed, and an older man with obviously dyed hair waved at him as though they were old friends. Devlin raised his bottle in thanks.

Misty Dawn, as she finished her last number, seemed to be singing it directly to Shanahan. Another round of beers came. When the act ended, the announcer said, "That concludes our show for this evening, but feel free to stay around and dance." Some slow music came on, and several couples, all men, got up and started dancing.

Devlin asked, "Aren't you the guy who didn't want to come here?"

But Shanahan was looking over his partner's shoulder. Devlin turned around to see Misty Dawn coming at Shanahan under full steam.

Misty held out a hand and said, "Dance?"

Shanahan was taken by surprise, but recovered quickly. "Sorry, I don't slow-dance on the first date."

Misty nodded at the bartender, and immediately the music changed. It was Chubby Checker singing "The Twist." Misty looked at Shanahan. "How's that? Now you can keep me at a distance—for a while."

Shanahan, who Devlin was sure had never been intimidated in his life, turned to him and shrugged his shoulders. "When in Rome."

"Just remember what happened to the Roman Empire."

Devlin could see the fires of reckless abandon in the Bostonian's expression and listened as Shanahan summed up his philosophy of life. "The object of all this is to have fun, isn't it?"

In a voice that tolled the obvious, Devlin said, "I hope there's no need to tell you this, but that's a guy."

Shanahan turned and started out on the dance floor. Over his shoulder he answered, "Not until you get his clothes off."

Devlin laughed and drank his beer. Shanahan and Misty instantly became the center of attention. Devlin watched the crowd and was sure there was hardly a man in the room who wasn't falling in love with his partner.

The song ended and everyone applauded. Shanahan thanked

Misty, walked to the bar, and gulped down what was left of his beer. "Let's get out of here."

Devlin said, "But you looked like you were having such a good time."

Shanahan laughed. "That's why I got to get out of here."

When they got to the door, Shanahan, ever the crowd pleaser, turned and waved to everyone. Most of them waved back. Devlin said, "I guess wherever you go, you're destined to break hearts."

"Just making friends for the Bureau, Michael, just making friends."

It was true. Wherever Shanahan went, people formed a fresh opinion of the FBI. Devlin was sure that if his partner was ever invited to a South American tribal wrist-slitting ceremony, everyone would have the time of their lives. But Bill Shanahan's real magic was that when he left, there would be no scars.

III CHAPTER 11 III

Malcolm Sudder was worried about his sexual patterns. More accurately, he was worried about the Bureau's interpretation of his sexual patterns. In twenty-four hours, a couple of headhunters from OPR would be there investigating the Friends of Youth incident, and they would undoubtedly recommend a session with the Bureau psychologist.

The previous FBI director, whose tenure had been labeled by the agents the If-You-Feel-Crazy-When-You-Put-Your-Hand-in-My-Pocket-Go-a-Little-Lower-Until-You-Feel-Nuts era, had been guided by an assistant director into deciding that the agents needed access to psychological counseling. After all, it was the nineteen whineties. So a search was launched. The same inscrutable logic that had divined the idea dictated that it should be a person who was *aBureau*, someone who was not FBI straitlaced and conservative, but a therapist the agents could go to in confidence, without fear of becoming the subject of a Bureau report.

The search ended with "Looney Tunes" Lassiter, a Ph.D. of psychology and a magna cum laude at the Takes-One-to-Catch-One School of Social Sciences. When FBIHQ sent out their *Eureka!* Teletype announcing the hiring of Lassiter as a consultant, the agent population groaned like an old oak floor that had been trod on too many times. "Not again" was becoming the new Bureau's battle cry.

Looney Tunes's first masterstroke—and because his contract with the FBI was per session, his first financial coup—

was to tour all fifty-nine field offices to teach the agents how to deal with stress. Because this was the "director's baby," and because agents normally had to be threatened into doing the simplest of tasks, they were marched in inescapable formations to the seminars. There too was Looney Tunes's wife, "Daffy," also a Ph.D. One agent described the couple as looking like the illegitimate offspring of a Klingon raid on Sesame Street. Their remedies for stress reduction were equally interplanetary.

Way out in front of whatever was second, Looney and Daffy declared sex was the number one method of stress reduction. It did not matter who, what, where, when, how, or which hand; just get in there and do it. As they spoke, frightening pictures of the two psychologists, knotted in love, formed unavoidably in the agents' minds. At each of the offices where the Lassiters *performed*, there was a marked reduction in sexual activity.

The agents, always seeking to prove the absurdity of the Bureau's leadership, now had incontrovertible evidence that its managers need never be taken seriously again. However, the doctors' suggestions were found to be useful by a number of agents who safaried deep into the confines of the steno pool to obtain stress reduction from some of the more medically sympathetic female employees. But the less gullible women of the FBI used it to tell the agents to "go destress yourself." Other enterprising rule breakers, knowing a freebie when they saw it, immediately started calling the shrink's answering service, claiming stress had caused whatever violation they were currently under investigation for. That was one of the joys of working for the United States government: It was never too late to start a new defense.

But Sudder felt he did not need a defense. His intentions had been in compliance with Bureau guidelines, except for his failure to fully identify the motives of The Friends of Youth. And within twenty-four hours, if he was any kind of manager at all, he would be able to decide exactly whose fault that was.

He looked at the first three of his phone messages. They were from a variety of FBIHQ officials, demanding an explanation of the newspaper story. The photographs that accompanied the article were of the SAC, the reporter, and at least two screaming pedophiles rolling around on the ground in front of the Barrington Hotel. The series of shots had caught the SAC in either some very compromising positions or some very illegal wrestling holds, and Headquarters wanted to know which. Because he had already discussed it with the director, he would not return any of those calls and the rest of his messages could wait.

It was rumored that the new director was going to terminate the Lassiters' contract, but Sudder was afraid that wouldn't happen until Looney Tunes, and probably Daffy, had their way with him. He cringed at the thought of those "hippie" shrinks asking him questions about his personal sex habits. He suddenly realized he had no feeling in his genital region. But he refused to panic, because he had a secret method for getting the blood pumping below the old waterline again. He headed for the morning supervisors' conference, his missile-lock extraordinarily aroused.

Devlin had arrived at the office around 8 A.M. From his room in the basement, he had called the SAC's secretary and was told that Sudder would be tied up all day and would not have time for Devlin's briefing. He took it as a signal from the major-case god: another day untethered, make the most of it.

He called the Department of Motor Vehicles and was informed that four companies had cars identical to the drop cars registered to them. They were all salvage yards and had, over the past two years, registered hundreds of wrecks. However, only one private individual had registered the same five cars with the state of Michigan. Devlin gave a short disgusted laugh when he heard the name—Robert Johnson, with the same fictitious Dearborn address Haidar had used at the Federal Express office. Another dead end. But he did not have time for dead ends, so he asked his contact to determine the previous owner of each of the five vehicles. Maybe they would remember whom they sold their cars to. He was told the information would have to be hand-searched and he should call back in an hour.

He called Temper's extension and asked her to come down to his room. When she walked in, he said, "I looked for you yesterday afternoon."

"I had to take a couple hours of throw-up leave. Only I would get *afternoon* sickness."

"The first pregnancy is usually the toughest."

"The first! After this one, the carpenter's not getting near me unless he has a foolproof birth control device, like a wetsuit."

Devlin smiled. "Did you have any luck with Seacard?"

"I called a guy I worked a case with at Health and Human Services. He said there's been rumors about the children's hospital for a couple of years. Even though it's heavily endowed, they raise money every year they will never be able to spend. Especially this year, they raised over three million. Most of the contributions came from the corporation's fat-cat friends. Other than that, Pendleton and the hospital seem clean as a whistle."

"Any connection between Pendleton and Haidar?"

"Not that I could find."

"How about Pendleton's credit check?"

"Maybe today; if not, tomorrow for sure. What are you hoping to find?"

"There's something that doesn't make sense. He was worried about those serial numbers. If all that money was burned up, the serial numbers would be meaningless. I want to see what kind of financial shape he's in."

"I'll let you know. And I'll check with a few other people I know in the business. Anything else going on?"

Devlin smiled as he thought again about the Friends of Youth dinner. "As soon as the statute of limitations expires, I've got a great story for you."

"Come on, Devlin, or maybe I should let Sudder know who authored the ASAC letter to the newspaper."

"Okay, okay." Devlin held his hands up in surrender. After swearing her to secrecy, he told her how Shanahan had set up the SAC and evened an old score for Brian Blankenship.

Temper laughed uninhibitedly, with a rush of honest, reckless energy. Then she grew uncharacteristically quiet. "That was nice, you guys getting some revenge for Brian." The dead agent's memory welled up in her eyes. "The last time I talked to him, we had just finished one of those god-awful interview boards, and he was running around like a maniac trying to get all the paperwork done by the deadline." She chuckled. "You know how awful his paper was."

"Yeah, but he sure loved the job. Too bad he couldn't have been there last night; it was his kind of brawl."

They both sat quietly, then Temper said hypnotically, "Mike, when you catch up with whoever did it, throw in a little extra for me." Devlin nodded.

After the supervisors' meeting, Sudder returned to his office renewed. He was again in charge. Confidently, he leafed through the remainder of his messages, wasting no time throwing out any from the Bureau, until he found a call from James Pendleton. He buzzed his secretary. "Pendleton called yesterday?"

"Yes, sir. Around ten A.M."

Pendleton was the last person Sudder had expected to hear from. After the second bomb had exploded at the hospital, he had made his feelings about the FBI quite clear. So Sudder had assigned Devlin to the extortion, not only to punish him, but to punish Pendleton with Devlin's resistance to authority. "Did he say what he wanted?"

"No, sir. Just that you should call him at your earliest convenience."

Convenience did not sound very hostile. "Did he call, or was it one of his staff?"

"It was him. He said, 'Have him call *me*.' "

"Can you get him for me?"

After a few seconds, Sudder's secretary had Pendleton on the line.

"Mr. Pendleton?"

"Malcolm, how are you? I saw the paper yesterday and wanted to see if you were all right. Of course, I don't believe a word of it."

"Thank you. I appreciate that. And there is no truth to any of it."

"Good. I also wanted to call and apologize for the way I treated your agents after the last bombing. The chairman of the board was there, and I was under a lot of pressure. But I'm sure a man with your responsibilities understands."

"I certainly do."

"Good, because that's really why I'm calling. The chairman of the board called me in yesterday morning and was worried about the hospital *and* the corporation being targeted by other criminals in the future. With the increase in extortions, executive kidnappings, and corporate terrorism worldwide, he is concerned about Seacard's interests. He asked me if I thought we needed someone on board who has some expertise in heading off these problems. I told him after what we had been through, I thought it was absolutely essential. And then I said I thought if we could get you interested, we should consider approaching you. Would you be interested?"

One of the things Sudder had taught himself to be cautious of was 180-degree reversals. "I don't know what to say. This is completely unexpected."

"I remembered you had told me you were eligible to retire, and I know you have leadership experience in these areas. Mr. Seacard was a little taken aback at my suggestion, because of the money that was lost, but I reminded him that the FBI was actually responsible for—excuse my bluntness—the *elimination* of the extortionist. If we had listened to you and not used real money, there would not have been any loss. The corporation was, at that point, willing to pay the five million just to get the extortionist to stop. But now there is no longer a threat, and we will recover the money, which I told him was being greatly expedited with your help."

"What was his reaction to that?" Sudder asked cautiously.

Pendleton gave a short laugh. "He's a tough negotiator. He said as soon as you help us settle with the insurance company, I could bring you aboard—if you're interested."

Sudder thought about his present situation. The director was hounding him not only about the Gentkill investigation, but also about the less-than-satisfactory ending to the extortion. And now Pendleton was calling him with an inviting solution to his problems. He had his time in; he could simply retire to Washtenaw County, where he was sure they never heard of The Friends of Youth. And the salary, he guessed, would be six figures. "That's very generous of you."

"You'll find I decide quickly and I act quickly. I like my people to do the same. Can you be out here at one o'clock today for lunch?"

"I'll be there."

Devlin called the DMV back and wrote down the names and addresses of the previous owners of the cars used in the extortion. They all lived in Washtenaw County, three in blue-collar Ypsilanti and two in Ann Arbor, where the university was located. He headed for his car.

The first address was a run-down house on a dirt road, outside the city limits of Ypsilanti. Fifty yards off the road, the structure was half hidden by waist-high weeds. Two ancient cars, partially cannibalized, had been laid to rest in the backyard. A fifteen-year-old van covered by more rust than paint, apparently the resident's current transportation, was parked next to the house. Devlin knocked on the door. There was no answer. He knocked harder. After thirty seconds, a man, half-asleep, answered, "Yeah."

"Billy Gray?"

"Who're you?"

Devlin held up his credentials and watched the man struggle to gain full consciousness. "FBI! What'd I do?"

"Absolutely nothing," Devlin said, his voice purposely bored.

Gray smiled loosely. "Well, in that case, c'mon in."

Once inside the living room, Gray offered Devlin a seat on the couch. It was stained and worn and probably served as a bed most of the time. People like Billy Gray had very little to offer visitors except their hospitality. Devlin had seen agents make excuses not to sit on dirty furniture. It was something the owner sensed immediately, and an unproductive interview was invariably the result. Devlin sat down comfortably. "You sold a 1979 Pontiac LeMans about six months ago."

"Ah, yeah. Why do you want to know about that?"

"The vehicle, after you sold it, in fact just a couple of days ago, was used in a crime. Obviously, the crime has nothing to do with you. We're trying to identify the person you sold it to. Nothing more."

"Ohhhh," Gray said cautiously, his mind searching for any possible problems his answer might cause him. "Just some guy."

"Do you remember what he looked like?"

"No."

"White, black?"

"Don't remember." Gray's memory loss was not uncommon. Some people, because of something to hide, distrust of authority, or not wanting to get involved, simply refused to tell what they knew.

Maybe Gray thought the FBI agent was lying about his reasons for being there, so, Devlin concluded, it *was* time to lie himself. He had noticed on a table next to the couch a girl's photograph in a cheap frame. The vintage of the photo, judging by hairstyle and clothing, was a couple of years old. The girl, at the time the picture had been taken, looked to be about eight years old. The living room and the adjoining room had no evidence of anyone other than Gray living there. Devlin guessed he was divorced and the girl lived with her mother. Everything in both rooms was uniformly covered with dust and greasy smudges, except for the spotless glass that covered the photo and its frame. "He molested a couple of ten-year-old girls." Devlin watched the anger rise in Gray. He knew the truth would now be more important to this lonely father than his own self-preservation.

"That dirty sonofabitch. Have you caught him yet?"

"No, we're not exactly sure who he is. Is there anything you can remember about him?"

"Let me think. You know, I just woke up, and my head's still a little foggy." Gray could not look at Devlin. It was a good sign. Practiced liars can look a person in the eye, until they have to tell the truth. "Yeah, I remember now. A white guy, older, dressed nice. He asked me how much. I said four hundred dollars. Paid cash. That's about it."

"Did he take the car right then?"

"No, that's right. Came back that night."

"Alone?"

"No, I saw another guy. He waited outside in a car."

"Did you get a look at him?"

"It was getting dark. Just got a glance at him. He was dark, like an Indian or Arab."

"Old?"

"No, I think he was younger." Devlin took out a photo of Haidar and showed it to Gray. "That could be him. Looks like him."

"Can you say for sure?"

"Like I said, I just got a glimpse. Sorry."

"The older guy. Anything distinctive about him? Limp, tattoo, glasses?"

"I don't really remember."

Satisfied that Gray had told him everything he could recall, Devlin handed him his card and asked that he call if he remembered anything else.

The next two interviews were not as productive. They remembered a well-dressed white male paying them cash for their cars and coming back later to pick them up. Neither had seen a second person. One of them thought that the buyer might have worn glasses.

The fourth owner lived in an upper-middle-class neighborhood in Ann Arbor. No one was home, so Devlin drove over to the campus and found the building that the demand notes were supposed to have been faxed from.

The first two floors were classrooms and labs; the third and fourth were administrative offices. He found a secretary in one of the third-floor offices and identified himself. He told her he was looking for the location of the two phone numbers he had. She took out the Physics Department's telephone directory and thumbed through it. "That's rooms 308 and 311, but they both have been turned into study rooms, so the phones have been taken out."

"May I take a look?" The secretary accompanied him down the hall to room 308. She took out a ring with a dozen keys on it and opened the door. The room contained a two-seat couch, a table, and a couple of chairs. Devlin looked along the baseboard until he found the telephone outlet. "Has this been disconnected?"

"I would think so, but I'm not sure."

"Is there a phone around here we can borrow?"

"Next door. I'll be right back." Devlin searched the rest of the room to see if there was another place to plug in a phone, but he could not find any. The secretary came in with a phone and a long cord. Devlin plugged it in and lifted the receiver. "It's still working. How about 311?"

They walked to the room and again she used a key to open the door. Devlin used the phone to test the outlet. It was also working. Devlin and the secretary walked back to her office. When he asked her for a copy of the phone list, she gave him hers. As he rode the elevator to the first floor, he noticed it also contained the names of all the physics majors, including Jousef Haidar.

* * *

Pendleton made sure the Seacard red carpet had been rolled out for Sudder. When the SAC arrived, the executive vice president was "a little backed up," so one of his sparkling young assistants gave Sudder a tour. His instructions were to show their guest the benefits of being a Seacard executive. The offices where they worked were the first stop. Each was a sanctuary of authority, furnished in rich, thick decor. In such a place, a person could be wise, aloof, compassionate. It was an environment in which the most difficult decisions could be easily made.

The assistant introduced him to an attractive brunette named Chris, who, if he came to work for Seacard, would probably be his personal secretary. Sudder guessed she was about thirty-five years old, and he was surprised that he noticed she was not wearing a wedding ring. "How do you do, Chris?"

"It's an honor to meet you, Mr. Sudder. I'm looking forward to working for you."

"Well, that certainly would be nice."

Next, Sudder found himself in the executive garage. It was as immaculate as the rest of the building. Big haughty cars sat on a shiny tile floor. "Of course, you would be given a new car each year, and you'd park here. They wash and vacuum the cars daily. The corporation likes its managers to look like executives. That's also the reason behind the clothing allowance." Sudder glanced at the assistant's tailored suit and was suddenly self-conscious about his seven-year-old synthetic tie.

They walked along a quiet hallway. The carpet felt as though it were ankle deep. The walls were lined with original paintings, mostly oils and watercolors. At the end, a heavy, hand-carved door opened to a dining room filled with dark oak and white linen. The kind of place where it seemed as though the waiters should speak with arrogant accents. Sudder was seated, and within a minute, Pendleton joined him. The SAC turned around to thank the assistant, but he had simply vanished. The two men shook hands. "Thanks for driving out here on such short notice, Malcolm."

"The tour I just had was worth the trip."

"This *is* a great place to work. Top medical, stock options, vacation. Seacard is very good to its executives. They feel if they can capture your loyalty, everything else will fall into place." A waiter silently appeared at their table. Pendleton looked up at him and said, "Have Julian come out here for a moment."

Thirty seconds later, the chef came out of the kitchen to their table. "Yes, Mr. Pendleton."

"Julian, this is Mr. Sudder. He is presently the head of the FBI in Michigan, but we are trying to convince him to come to work with us. Can you create something that will weaken his resolve?"

"Do you like salmon, Mr. Sudder?"

"Very much."

"Very good. And you, Mr. Pendleton?"

"Salmon sounds great." The chef disappeared into the kitchen, and immediately the waiter was stocking their table with breads, soups, and salads.

Although Sudder was starting to feel very comfortable with the idea of working at such an ideal place, Seacard's apparent indifference to the loss of $5 million still nagged at his sense of survival. "This is all very gracious of you under the circumstances."

"That money is not a problem. Corporations deal with profit and loss. If that money was lost, it would not be anything significant, but it was not lost. I've come to an agreement with the insurance company. As soon as they receive your agency's report, we will be reimbursed in full. And as I told you, Mr. Seacard said the minute that happens, I'm green-lighted to bring you on board."

"Did you tell Agent Devlin you needed that report?"

"Yes, I did."

"Any problem?" Sudder asked.

"Ah, I don't think so."

Sudder noticed some reservation in Pendleton's response. "He can be irritating, but he knows how to get things done." For the first time, Sudder cleared his throat. "I'll make sure he's moving in the right direction, and quickly."

The chef came out carrying two plates and placed them in front of Pendleton and Sudder. He stood back and patiently awaited their opinions. The salmon had been grilled in a raspberry glaze. Sudder tasted his first. He turned to the chef. "That's the best salmon I've ever had."

Pendleton tasted his. "Julian, this is exceptional, even for you." He looked back at Sudder, who was happily putting another forkful of fish into his mouth. "Are we tempting you?"

"I hope there's an executive gym, because with food like this, I know I'm going to need it."

Pendleton smiled warmly. "Well, in that case, I guess we should discuss salary."

Devlin drove back to the home of the owner of the fourth drop car. "I'm looking for Raymond Keller," he said, as he opened his credentials.

"Look no further." Keller smiled and invited Devlin in.

"I'm inquiring about the"—Devlin looked on his list—"the 1982 Chevrolet Caprice you sold about four months ago."

"I ran an ad in the Ann Arbor paper. The first night, I got a call from this man. He was very impatient. He insisted on coming immediately to see the car. Wouldn't be put off. He paid me seven hundred dollars in cash. The car had some body damage and needed a new muffler, but when I told him about it, he said it didn't matter. He gave it a short test drive and came back later to pick it up."

"When he came back, was someone with him?"

"I don't know. I didn't see anyone."

"What else do you remember about him?"

"He was white. Your height and weight. Maybe forty, forty-five. His hair was light brown going to gray."

"Any unusual characteristics?"

"Ah, let's see. Yeah. He had the slightest German accent, like maybe the first ten years of his life he lived in Germany."

"Are you sure the accent was German?"

"With a name like Keller, *Jawohl*! My parents emigrated here when they were in their thirties. I know German when I hear it."

"I guess you would."

"Can I ask you what this is about?"

"The car was used in a crime."

"Was the person who bought it from me involved?"

"Probably." Devlin sensed something was bothering Keller. "Why do you ask?"

Keller hesitated before answering. "You know that a lot of us who live in Ann Arbor are U of M graduates. We love the school and we love the community, so it's awkward for me to tell you."

"Mr. Keller, as a result of this crime, two men have died and a child was critically injured."

Keller nodded. "I understand. When he took the Caprice for a drive, I took a look at his car. It was new, an Audi S4. A beautiful machine . . . it had a U of M faculty sticker on it."

Devlin drove to the Seacard Hospital for Children. He showed an overly cautious guard his credentials and asked to see whoever was in charge of security. Ten minutes later, he was sitting in an office looking at a copy of Haidar's personnel file. He read it three times and could find nothing in it connecting the Egyptian student to Pendleton or anyone else.

When he was finished, he asked to see the areas where the bombs had exploded, and a security guard was called to escort him. They went to the roof, and Devlin surveyed the location of the first explosion. The damage was minimal, and repairs had not been needed. In the second-floor utility room, the repairs had already been made. The window had been replaced, and the cinder-block walls had been patched and painted. Devlin ran his hand over the scarred walls. "How's the girl?"

"The last I heard, she wasn't doing too well. We're going right by the ICU. We can ask."

The Intensive Care Unit was designed in a wheel pattern. The nurse's station was at the hub, enabling whoever was on duty to monitor all six rooms. As the guard asked about the girl's condition, Devlin looked in through her window. Involuntarily, he put the palm of his hand against the glass and was calmed by its cool restraint. He wanted to be kept out, because nowhere within his abilities could he find anything to help her. As confused as a child himself, he could only stare, safely outside.

The top half of her head was covered with bandaging. An IV tube ran down from a clear plastic bag and made a barbaric entry into her lower left arm. Hints of blue traced her veins. Her hand was elegantly fragile, as if sculpted from unflawed alabaster; it was poised in a gesture that seemed to suggest forgiveness. Her mouth was carefully carved; her lips were perfect and held the beginning of a smile, as if she were anticipating the end of a funny story. So close to death, yet so full of life.

Goddamnit, Knox was right! He was too selfish; he couldn't go into that room. He was afraid he wouldn't be able to make a difference, and that would make him just like everyone else. But Knox would never seek the safety of distance. She would be there, touching the girl's hand, in some way transmitting a promise of serenity.

Without a word, Devlin turned away and hurried out of the hospital.

A necessary part of his plan was that he be blamed for the third murder. If the FBI made a mistake and decided it was the act of a copycat killer, they might continue to search for someone connected only to Lawson and Blankenship, which could eventually lead to him. But if they were certain the Gentkiller had committed the third murder, the murder of an agent who had no connection with the first two, they would have no choice but to conclude that he was randomly selecting his victims. The surest way for him to be credited with the third homicide was to use the same gun. And once the ballistics were matched, his anonymity would be ensured.

But finding an accessible target quickly would not be easy. He was certain the agents were now more cautious than ever.

He switched on the television. The news had become an addiction. And why not? They were all talking about him. One of the local channels, because it was across the street from the federal building, was doing a story while their cameras were shooting live from their own windows. The reporter was describing the tactics of one of the national television crews that was positioned at the exit to the FBI's garage. "They sit there and wait for a car to leave. If it looks like the Bureau agents are going to investigate a lead in the case, the crew follows them."

As if on cue, a Bureau car left the garage but the news truck did not follow it. The anchorman came back on the screen. "Bob, why didn't they follow that car?"

"Insiders tell us that agents are under strict orders not to work alone when covering leads in this case. That car you just saw leaving had only one agent in it. And since it's after five, he's probably on his way home."

The Gentkiller turned off the set. He knew how he was going to kill his next victim.

As Devlin drove to the house of the owner of the last car, he sent a silent message to the major-case god: *Let this be the lead that identifies Haidar's accomplice.* But the owner was not home.

Devlin found the nearest gas station and searched the phone book for Audi dealerships. There were three within a reasonable distance.

The first one was fifteen minutes away. After identifying himself, he was directed to the new-car sales manager. "I'm trying to identify a black Audi S4 that was purchased within the last year."

"What makes you think it was purchased here?"

"I know the owner lives in the Ann Arbor area."

"That doesn't mean he bought it here."

"I have to start somewhere."

"Okay, what's the owner's name?"

"That's what I'm trying to determine."

"I don't suppose you have a plate or VIN."

"I didn't want to make it too easy for you."

The manager laughed. "The only way we can do that is to pull all the sales for the last year and go through them one by one to determine which ones are black."

"Okay."

"I'm sorry, but I don't have the personnel to do that."

"Just point me in the right direction. I'll do the rest."

"This way, then."

For the next hour and a half, Devlin looked through the dealership's sales records. When he finished, he had a list of three black Audi S4s. Only one was registered in or around Ann Arbor, and it was registered to a woman. Her name was Sandra Cantor. Devlin dialed her home number.

"Hello."

"Is this Sandra Cantor?"

"Yes, it is."

"This is campus security at the university. Do you drive a black Audi S4?"

"Why, yes, I do."

"Are you on the faculty here?"

"No, I'm not. What is this about?"

"Then you don't have a faculty sticker on your car?"

"No."

"I'm sorry. We have the wrong Audi. Thanks for your help."

Devlin checked the time. The other two dealerships would be closed before he could get to them. Just as well. Agents prided themselves on being able to create leads that immediately solved cases, but pragmatically, even simple crimes were not solved easily. After reviewing a year's worth of sales records, Devlin realized his *single-lead solution* was another one of those that, when investigated, created additional leads. When that happened, the best thing to do was to abandon it, bury it deep in the file, and reconsider it only when all else failed.

The major-case god sent Devlin a message: *Solutions that are elusive when pursued usually surrender themselves to patience.* Devlin turned on the radio and thought about the night before with Knox.

By the time he got to the office, it was almost six o'clock. The office was deserted. He cleared everything off the desk in the cramped room, which added to the surrounding clutter. He took out a large pad of paper and wrote at the top: EXTORTION UNSUB. Below it, he started listing everything he knew about the unidentified subject: White male. Forty to forty-five years old. How did Keller describe him? Devlin checked his notes: He said he was Devlin's height and weight with graying, light brown hair. Devlin put a question mark after the description. Experience had taught him that when a witness describes a suspect as looking like the agent who is conducting the interview, the information should not be accepted as gospel. Keller seemed intelligent, but even smart people were sometimes guilty of this transference.

Devlin continued the list. Drives a new black Audi S4. University of Michigan faculty sticker. *Faculty?* Slight German accent. Access to the physics building. *The physics building.* When the secretary had taken Devlin to the two study rooms, she had used a key to open them. Devlin laughed at himself for missing the obvious. Tomorrow morning he would know who the UNSUB was.

The major-case god smiled.

III CHAPTER 12 III

In light of his revelation regarding the extortionist, Devlin now wondered if he was also being *blinded by the obvious* in the Gentkill investigation. Unwittingly, agents sometimes made cases more complicated by searching for gray shadows in which to hide perceived villains with earthshaking intentions. Invariably, they did this while straining to look through the smoke coming from the gun at their feet. Maybe Devlin was guilty of that, reading too much into personnel files, hollowpoints, and psychological profiles.

He decided to investigate only one of the murders and to quit trying to relate it to the other. Blankenship was the logical choice. Because he had been in the Bureau about a third as long as John Lawson, there would be far less ground to cover. And because Devlin was on the same squad, he was familiar with the type of cases that the young agent worked. Blankenship's cases, Devlin felt, were the most obvious lead.

He called Shanahan at home. "Bill, did anyone ever review Brian's cases for suspects?"

"They were just getting started when The Force took over and guided Sudder to his nut theory. Harrison kept a couple of people working on them, but he eventually had to pull them to interview wackos."

"How many did they look through?"

"I'm going to guess about twenty, just pending cases. I know they didn't touch his closed stuff."

"The way he liked to work, there has to be a couple hundred of those."

"The file clerk ran a printout. I think she came up with close to two-fifty. Why?"

"I'm thinking about reviewing them."

"By yourself? It'd take you a year."

"I think I know a way to do it quicker."

"How?"

"You gave me the idea with that story about Brian locking up that murderer from Lansing."

Shanahan gave a short laugh. "Wasn't even the third toughest mutha on the block. Brian did love to get in their face."

"Exactly. If the killer is somebody he personally locked up, maybe he dug the spurs in a little too deep."

"Enough to kill him?"

"A lot of them are wanted for murder; besides, you know these people kill by urge, not reason."

"But how does that tie to Lawson?" asked Shanahan.

"You play pool. Ever try to make two balls with one shot?"

"Sure."

"What happens?"

"You usually miss them both."

"But if you take them one at a time, you have a much better chance. If we solve Brian's murder first, maybe it will give us position on John's. Right now, we can't find the connection between them. But if we can solve one, the other should follow. I did find some overlap, though: They taught firearms together. You know, when we go after someone that's extra crazy, we like people along we can rely on, and those firearms guys really trust each other. Maybe John went along on some of Brian's arrests. Looking at his arrests seems to be the most logical lead."

"Again, you're back to big numbers. Brian locked up a lot of people."

"We'll run them to see who's still locked up and who recently got out. If you could give me a hand, it might not take that long."

"Believe me, there's nothing I'd rather do, but they're shipping me out tomorrow to Grand Rapids so some of the small-town *unhinged* can scream obscenities at me."

"How long will you be gone?"

"They told us to plan on three to five days."

"There is something I need you to do. You know that computer specialist, Amy, don't you?"

"I've *known* her in the past."

"The only way we can get a list of all of Brian's arrests is a categorical computer run. There's only two people in the office that have that kind of access."

"I suppose, since I'm leaving tomorrow, you're talking about tonight."

"You *are* a clear thinker. Will she keep it quiet?"

"She has so far. I'll call you back."

Less than five minutes later, Shanahan called back and said he was leaving to pick up Amy.

While Devlin waited, he remembered he had not interviewed the owner of the last drop car. After a series of phone calls that took over an hour, he finally reached her. She could not recall anything more than an older white male paying three hundred dollars in cash for a car she described as being "on its last legs." Then Devlin called home and Katie answered. She said Knox had gone next door to help their elderly neighbor move some things, so he told his daughter to let Knox know he would be working late at the office.

Devlin realized that his impatience to get the list of Blankenship's arrests was making the time drag, so he busied himself by processing some of the extortion evidence. He organized it not to prove Haidar's guilt but rather the *German's* involvement.

An hour later, Shanahan walked in carrying a thicker stack of printouts than Devlin had hoped for. Shanahan said, "There are seventy-two names."

"I'll have the night crew run them through NCIC for criminal histories so we can find out who is still in custody. While they're doing that, I'll start looking at the files."

"The night clerks will do that for you?"

"As soon as I order them a couple of large pizzas," said Devlin.

"Be careful. The way they like to eat and sleep, they've been known to slip into three-day food comas. Better get the work done up front."

"Thanks for the help. I'll get it whittled down while you're gone."

"Do you think this is it?"

"Anymore, I don't think I'm much of a judge of what a good lead is."

"I'd better get Amy home. Save a few of the good ones for me."

Devlin made a list of the seventy-two names, along with corresponding dates of birth, and took them up to the night desk. After he made his request, the night supervisor opened the negotiations with a predictable "We're kind of busy tonight."

Anticipating a long night of reviewing files, Devlin did not want to waste time bartering. He countered with one word, "Pizza." Sensing the weakness of Devlin's position, the supervisor deliberately hemmed and hawed until a final bid of "with everything" concluded the transaction.

In the closed-file room, Devlin pulled the first twenty-five cases and took them back to his room. After a half hour, one of the night clerks brought in the corresponding computerized criminal histories Devlin had requested. The clerk assured him that after another hour *and* the safe delivery of the promised pizzas, Devlin would receive the remaining forty-seven printouts.

Devlin reviewed each rap sheet and, out of the twenty-five men, was able to eliminate fourteen, thirteen of whom were still in custody; one was dead.

An hour and a half later, the forty-seven other criminal histories were delivered, along with two runt-of-the-litter slices of pizza and a can of lukewarm beer. Devlin handed the clerk twenty-five dollars and told him to keep the change—a reminder that, like Iran-Contra, the pizza-for-printouts affair had never happened.

Devlin continued to eliminate individuals who were still in custody, but a number of the arrests showed no dispositions. Many police departments, whether because of manpower shortages or lack of administrative responsibility, failed to submit final dispositions to the FBI in Washington. When he was finished, he had lined out eighteen more, leaving him with twenty-nine suspects. Of those, some would be in custody, but their incarceration would have to be verified by calling the individual police departments. He returned to closed files and pulled the cases of the remaining suspects. Sometime during the review of the fourteenth file, Devlin fell asleep.

But his wife had not. He was supposed to be working late at the office, but she was afraid to call him. If he did not answer, her interpretation, whether accurate or not, would be that he was out, alone, looking for a man who would not hesitate to kill if confronted.

She picked up the phone and dialed.

"St. Barnabas."

"Father, it's Knox. I'm sorry to bother you so late."

The priest recognized the emotion in her voice. "I was just sitting here reading. Is anything wrong?"

"No. Mike's working late, and I needed to talk to someone."

"And you're worried about him."

"I know somebody has to catch this person, but when I tell Mike how frightening it is to think about him being out there, he doesn't seem to understand."

"Knox, a man's greatest fear is that he is not capable of accomplishing what he perceives needs to be done. So the bigger the problem, the more he will focus on it. And of course, this in turn will take him away from the other important things in his life. Which brings us to a woman's biggest fear—a lack of commitment from her man. Different things are important to men than women. But don't think that he is any less committed to you because he thinks he has to solve these murders. Just remember, it takes a lot of courage for Mike to do what he's doing."

Knox considered the priest's words for a moment. "I know you're right, Father. It's just that all these *heroics* are taking a toll on me."

"Don't be too hard on him, Knox. More than anything, he wants to be your hero."

"Thanks, Father. I'll see you tomorrow."

"Good. We can talk some more then."

Knox hung up and took from the nightstand the book her husband had so memorably interrupted the night before. She caressed its cover with the palm of her hand. For better *and* worse, she thought. She pressed the book against her chest and, after a few minutes, fell asleep.

Around 6 A.M., another plummeting dream jolted Devlin out of a sweaty sleep. He had just enough time to go home, shower, and drive to Ann Arbor.

He slipped quietly into his bedroom and found Knox asleep. He sat down in a chair next to the bed and watched her. She had angled herself over on his side of the bed and had wrapped her arms around his pillow. He still found her thrilling. He showered, dressed, and wrote her a note:

My mother once read me this story:
The poorest of beggars knocked at the door of a meager forest cottage and asked the man and his wife if they had any food to spare. At their dinner table, they shared equally what little they had. When they had finished, the beggar, in the blink of an eye, transformed himself into the king. He explained he had searched his entire land, and their goodness was without equal. "Shall I grant you riches?" he asked. The

man took his wife's hand and said, "We could not be richer." "Then, everlasting life," the king insisted. "It does not matter how much longer we have," the man explained, "as long as we spend it together, because, for us, each moment apart would be an eternity lost." Years later, the man died and the moment life left him, his wife and their cottage disappeared and in their place stood two great, eternal oak trees, their limbs hopelessly entwined.

When Devlin arrived at the physics building, the parking lot was still empty. He pulled his car into an adjacent student lot that offered an unobstructed view of the entire area. He leaned back in his seat and fought off sleep. The lot filled slowly, and by nine o'clock the black Audi had not appeared.

He knew his hunch had to be right. All of Haidar's self-incriminating blunders were so inconsistent with the overall intelligence of the extortion that they had to be intentional. There had to be a second extortionist, the same man who had bought the five cars. Someone who would have extensive knowledge of the rooms and phones in the physics building. And like the secretary who had shown Devlin the rooms, he would have keys to check if the phone lines were still active. In all likelihood the faxes had not been sent from that building, but if the lines were checked and they were not working, the FBI might realize that a false trail had been laid to point at Haidar. Haidar did not have keys for the locked rooms. But if the German with the faculty sticker was a member of the university's Physics Department, he would.

At five minutes to ten, a sparkling black Audi glided into the faculty lot. Devlin lifted a camera to his eye and, through its telephoto lens, noted the license plate. As the driver got out, Devlin started snapping pictures. He met the description of the individual who had bought the cars. After leaning back into the Audi to get his briefcase, he stood upright and pushed his tie inside the jacket of his gray double-breasted suit. An angry arrogance covered his intelligent face. He turned and walked impatiently into the building.

Devlin raised the radio room and had them run the license plate. It came back to Sebastian Draxler at an Ann Arbor address. Out of his cluttered briefcase, Devlin retrieved the student-faculty directory the secretary had given him the day before. It listed Draxler as a Ph.D. in physics and chemistry. He was also Jousef Haidar's faculty advisor.

At the edge of the parking lot, Devlin found a pay phone. From the departmental directory, he dialed Draxler's office number.

"Hello, Doctor Draxler here."

"Oh, you're a doctor. I'm sorry, sir. This is Bill Wilson from Michigan National Bank. I'm in the fraud department. One of our tellers accepted a bad check for three hundred dollars and the person who passed it used this phone number as his business number. The name the man used was Roger Reardon. Do you know anyone by that name, Doctor?"

"Roger Reardon? No."

"I'm sorry to bother you." Devlin hung up. He had chosen the name Roger Reardon because of all the *r*'s in it. Draxler still had a slight rattle when he pronounced the letter; it was the most difficult sound to eliminate from the German dialect.

When Devlin got back to the office, he dropped the roll of film at the office photo lab and asked that it be developed right away. He took the elevator to the basement and found two notes on his door. One was to see the SAC immediately, and the other was from one of Devlin's old sources. He was in jail and wanted to see Devlin right away.

As he opened his door, the phone rang. Devlin, fearing it was the front office, picked it up and held it to his ear without answering. Finally, the caller said, "Hello?" It was Shanahan.

"Hello, Bill."

"Did you have any luck with Brian's cases?"

"I've eliminated forty-three names. There may be more in

custody, but there's no disposition entered on the criminal histories."

"Anything promising?"

"I just started reviewing them. Nothing yet. How're things in Sleepy Hollow?"

"Even the fruitcakes are nicer out here. They don't raise their voices and they never use the MF word. I think they'll have to unionize if they want to be competitive."

"Who are you working with out there?"

"Nelson Conway. Do you know him?"

"Isn't that the new guy they call The Golf Machine?"

"Not anymore. Can't even get his putter out of the bag."

"What happened?"

"Well, he was sitting down in the Charlotte Division in that nice North Carolina climate, playing a ton of golf. I think he was on the PGA Tour when he was younger. Anyway, the OC squad up here has a project out at the Oak Hollow Golf Club—allegedly it's mob-owned. So they want Conway to come up and beat the brains out of a few of the golf hustlers at the club, after which the undercover agent would rent him out to fleece some fat pigeons. That way we could get inside and maybe eventually seize the club under the RICO statute. It's worth a ton of money. But Conway's wife is from Michigan, so he said he would do it if he could be permanently transferred to Detroit. The Bureau figured that anyone who demanded to be in Detroit belongs there, so up he's sent. The UCA really built him up at the club and gets him a match with a guy they call Short Game, who is very old and very fat. Conway shows up and they play. Short Game takes twelve thousand from him in nine holes. You should see this poor bastard. He doesn't talk. He doesn't eat. He can't even look at a golf course."

"How'd he lose?"

"No one can figure it out. He's a big hitter. Can drive the ball a mile, and accurate too. That's why they call him The Machine. The day before, he practiced on the course and did fine.

But the day of the match, he was all over the place. And he isn't a real flexible guy; he's taking it very personally."

"Well, if anyone can teach him flexibility, it's you."

"Not around here."

"A *little* slow?"

"A little? One of the major recreational activities here is to go down to the fish ladder. Do you know what that is?"

"Sounds a little too Department of Natural Resources for me."

"It's a series of man-made stairs to help the salmon swim upstream. It's bad enough that this country is obsessed with becoming failure-proof, but now they're doing it for the goddamn fish. Where's the natural selection process? Give me Detroit. Dope dealers killing dope dealers. There's natural selection."

"Any chance you'll get out of there sooner than you thought?"

"I doubt it. And me dragging around this cadaver, I'm going to have to put a caper together just to get this guy's heart restarted."

"I'm sure he's in good hands."

"I got to go. I thought I brought enough clothes, but I'm going to have to buy some more underwear."

"Even out there you find someone to wear it out."

"Well, we are a service-oriented organization."

Devlin hung up and headed for Sudder's office. The normal reaction for an agent being summoned so abruptly by the SAC would be to backtrack in an effort to recall what sins he had committed. But Devlin figured that, between the Ghost Rider napalming, pedophile tag-teams, and everyday chickenshit, Malcolm Sudder's motives were harder to identify than Jimmy Hoffa's guardian angel.

When Devlin reached the SAC's office, he was quickly shown into the room; Sudder was ready for him. Strangely, he understood some things about Devlin. All men needed power, but that power took different forms. For Sudder, it was the authority of his position. For Devlin, it was the ability to solve difficult cases. Sudder had used that insight to punish Devlin when he had assigned him the solutionless tedium of the casino project, and then, the extortion. But now he wanted Devlin's cooperation instead of his dissent, so he would dangle the appropriate carrot. "Mike, come on in and sit down." Devlin settled into a chair in front of the SAC's desk. "Jim Harrison has been after me to start using you for something other than the extortion. He thinks it's a waste of ability. And we can use all the help we can get with these murders . . ."

The SAC's secretary stuck her head in the door. "Sorry to interrupt, sir, but the two gentlemen from OPR are here."

Sudder had almost forgotten that his *interview* was scheduled for that morning. "Tell them I'll be with them in one minute." After she left, the SAC turned back to Devlin. "Bottom line—I'm tired of all of this bickering. I think both of us need to act a little more like adults. So, how about a draw?"

"What about the extortion?"

"Other than that report Seacard needs, don't worry about it. We'll let it sit until Jack Tarver gets back. Hell, the extortionist's dead and Seacard will have their money back."

"I wasn't aware that you knew about the report."

Sudder cleared his throat. "Mr. Pendleton called me about it yesterday."

Devlin considered the SAC's proposition for a moment and then said, "No more briefings?"

"Nope."

"And I can work on Gentkill?"

"Yes."

"I'll have that report done ASAP."

"Good." Sudder beamed. "On your way out, tell my secretary to send in those two pricks from OPR. I'm ready for them now." He put his hands behind his head and leaned back in his chair buoyantly.

When Devlin walked out into the waiting area, the secretary was not there, so he leaned over to the grim-faced headhunters and, with a don't-shoot-the-messenger shrug of the shoulders, told them, "He said you two pricks could go in."

Back in his room, Devlin considered what he had promised the SAC—to get him the report "ASAP." It was not really a lie. *As soon as possible.* Devlin knew he could not *possibly* complete the report until he had resolved all of the case's inconsistencies. Hell, who was he kidding? He would never write that report. Both he and the SAC had told lies, only Sudder had announced his by clearing his throat. And the SAC's dishonesty could mean only one thing: His loyalties, for some reason, were shifting to Pendleton. Consequently, Devlin's investigation of the Seacard executive would have to be kept from Sudder.

After picking up the surveillance shots of Sebastian Draxler from the photo lab, Devlin drove back to Washtenaw County. He felt that Raymond Keller, because he was observant enough to detect both the German accent and the faculty sticker on the Audi, would be the best of the drop cars' previous owners to identify the photograph of the man who had bought the vehicles. He tried his home first and, when no one answered, consulted his interview notes. Keller worked for an investment firm in downtown Ann Arbor. "Mr. Keller, do you remember me?"

"Sure. Agent Devlin, right?"

"I've got some photos I'd like you to look at."

Devlin had had the photo lab search their files for shots of white males approximately the same age as the professor. They had come up with six others. Devlin placed Draxler's in the middle of the pack and handed them to Keller.

Slowly, he scanned the faces until he got to Draxler. He looked at it for a few extra seconds and then quickly finished looking at the rest. He shuffled back to Draxler's photo and said, "That's him."

"How sure are you?"

"Positive."

On the way back to the office, Devlin stopped at the Wayne

County Jail to see his old informant. He knew what the source would want, what they all wanted—to get out of jail. Devlin told him he would see what he could do.

When he returned to the office, Devlin found a note on his door. Knox had called and she wanted him to meet her at St. Barnaby's after work. On his desk he found a large envelope from Temper Hanlon. There were a number of pages inside with a note from her:

> Sorry I missed you. Had another doctor's appointment. (Pony Express riders spend less time with their feet in stirrups.) Here's the info you wanted on Pendleton. If you need anything else, let me know.
>
> Temper

The other pages were a credit report. There were notices of late payments and maxed-out credit cards. It also showed inquiries from banks and S & Ls, indicating that Pendleton had tried unsuccessfully to borrow money from a number of different sources.

Devlin called the Ann Arbor Resident Agency. The eight-agent office was responsible for all of Washtenaw County, where Pendleton's banks were located. Riley Smith answered the phone. "Mike Devlin, calling *me*. That reminds me: I'd better make sure my liability insurance is current."

"You don't get into trouble *every* time I call."

"The question is, am I going to this time?"

"If you're going to be defensive, I could take my business elsewhere."

"Is this *official* business?"

"You certainly have lost your spontaneity out there, Riley."

"And you, being a good friend, are probably going to change all that."

"Well, I am working this case of yours."

"If you're referring to the Seacard extortion, no thanks. That was The Suit's decision for Detroit to handle it. You guys were supposed to solve it and make him look good, not use five million in cash to torch a bunch of old cars."

"This entire case happened in your territory, and I am willing to turn it over to you so you can bask in its glorious solution."

"In case you haven't read the manual lately, Mike, it's still against the rules for agents to use drugs."

"Next, you'll be telling me that I was given this case as a punishment."

"You? Being punished?"

"Okay, Riley, I'm going to let you off cheaply."

"Oh, boy. Tell that to the scar tissue on my ass."

"Can you keep this to yourself?"

"There's a surprising request. Why don't I just call up OPR and ask them to read me my rights over the phone?"

"I love old-Bureau camaraderie."

"What did the FBI agent say when he wanted to be suspended for sixty days without pay?"

"What?"

"How can I help you, Mike Devlin?"

Devlin explained in detail his suspicions about Pendleton. "Any ideas?" Devlin asked when he finished.

"It sounds like he has at least some of the money."

"If he's worried about serial numbers, he must."

"How did he get it?"

"He was alone when he sealed the boxes. Must have taken it then. Why else wouldn't he want their head of security to take care of a small detail like that? And who's the extortionist going to complain to if he's short?"

"Yeah, Pendleton probably took as much as he could, but not enough to make the guy set off another bomb. The question is, how much and, more importantly, where is it?"

Devlin said, "I've been thinking about that. If the extortionist was caught at the drop and all five boxes were recovered, what would Pendleton have had to do?"

Smith thought for a second. "Put the money back. That's why he insisted no one else could open the boxes."

"That's right. Do you know the head of security?"

"Neal Ferguson? Yeah, I've dealt with him a few times."

"Well, since he wasn't allowed to close the boxes, we know he isn't involved. How about talking to him? If we're right about all of this, he had to have specific instructions where to take the boxes. I think wherever that was, especially if it was a secure location like Pendleton's office, where he could work in privacy, that's where the money is."

"Sounds logical."

"And you thought I was going to get you in trouble."

"Hey, don't kid yourself. Pendleton's got a lot of juice around here."

"Into every life a little rain must fall."

"There's a considerable difference between 'a little rain' and Tropical Storm Michael."

After Devlin hung up, the major-case god, who was also responsible for case rhythms, sent a message: *Let Riley Smith run the next extortion lap.* So Devlin turned his attention back to Brian Blankenship's closed cases.

He reviewed the last fifteen files. Even though a few of the twenty-nine names on the list sounded familiar, none seemed to be a priority. First, he wanted to verify who was still in custody. He started calling the police departments that had filed the original warrants and asked to talk to the detectives in charge. Because they had to take them to trial, they usually knew where the subjects of their cases were. By 6 P.M., Devlin had verified the status of sixteen of them, six of whom were no longer in custody. The last thirteen could wait until morning; he had to meet Knox at St. Barney's. But because he knew Sudder's *generosity* in settling for a draw would end tomorrow morning, when he did not receive the extortion report, Devlin decided his best course of action would be to stay out of the office as much as possible. Collecting everything he thought necessary to work elsewhere the next day, he wrote a note to the

SAC, advising him that he would not be able to complete his report "for at least one more day." He took the note upstairs and left it on the SAC's desk, hoping Sudder would not immediately recognize its *at least* loophole. He headed for the Cass Corridor.

As always, Father Richter opened the front door of the hospice. "Michael, how are you?" the priest asked as he shook hands. He stared attentively at Devlin and held on to his hand longer than custom would dictate.

Devlin stared back. "I guess Knox has talked to you."

"A little."

Devlin knew *a little* meant that he was supposed to supply his side of the disagreement. "Can we go in your office?"

Just then, a case of evaporated milk came falling through a large metal chute next to the front door. "The Lord shall provide," the priest said. He then raised the cover on the outside of the chute and yelled to the unseen donor, "God bless you." He turned to Devlin. "We get things like this day and night. I like to think of them as miraclettes." He waved Devlin into the study.

Once they sat down, Devlin said, "First of all, Father, I don't think Knox is wrong. I saw a young girl yesterday who had been critically injured, and I felt so helpless because I couldn't do anything for her. But at the same time, I knew Knox would have found some way to help her. It really made me question my priorities."

"And that makes Knox right about you not being involved in the investigation?"

"I don't know anymore."

Richter's voice now took on a religious authority. "You are a man who is defined by your ability to accomplish difficult tasks, and Knox is a woman capable of great compassion and nurturing. Normally, both of you use those abilities to make the world a little bit better, and normally, your abilities comfortably complement one another. But due to the absolute insanity of these murders, your need to catch the killer and Knox's need to protect you have become enemies of one another."

"It's making her so unhappy."

"And her unhappiness makes you feel like you're failing her."

"It's just that she's such a good person."

"You are both good people, but because of this conflict, you're both becoming unsure of yourselves and the boundaries of your relationship. I'll tell you what I told her. It's unfortunate, but you are both right."

"Then how do we resolve this?"

"There's only one solution to both problems: You must find the killer—quickly and carefully."

Devlin smiled. "And what did you tell Knox?"

"To keep on your ass about being careful."

"Did she buy it?"

"Only Jesus was able to change water into wine. She wants you completely off the case. So be careful, because if anything happens to you, she'll be coming after me."

"I guess I'll just have to ride it out."

"Like I told her, just be aware of each other's needs."

Knox walked in and said, "Hi."

Both men stood up, and Devlin answered, "Hi."

Knox looked at Richter. "I hope you've been beating him up, Father."

"He's taking care of that himself. You'll both excuse me."

Devlin asked, "Where are the kids?"

"Staying with friends, overnight."

"Sounds promising."

"I thought we could go out to dinner first."

"First? Sounds *very* promising."

Devlin sat down and pulled Knox onto his lap. "Sometimes, like now, I put the job in front of everything. It's like I'm trapped. Someone has to find the answer, and if I work hard enough, I sometimes can. And since I can only do one thing at a time, you and the kids are temporarily shuffled into second place. But you are all that really counts."

"I know. But why does it always have to be you?"

"That's why I took this job—so it could always be me. You used to be proud of that."

"Do you know how lonely I would be without you?"

"I can give you a long list of bosses who'll tell you I'm not that easy to get rid of."

Knox put her head on his shoulder. It felt electrifying and sexual, like the first time she had ever touched him. "I liked your note."

"Did it work?" She tilted her head up and whispered in his ear. "Hey," he said, "we're in church here. Something like that is a mortal sin."

The thought of using the media as a stalking horse amused the Gentkiller. He sat in his car, watching the television crews a block away. They waited to follow any Bureau agents driving out of the garage who might be investigating the murders. But what they did not know was that they were about to select the Gentkiller's next victim.

He opened the cylinder of his revolver and ceremoniously loaded it with six hollowpoints. He rolled down the window and welcomed the tranquil night air.

A car pulled out of the garage, and he started his engine. The Bureau car made a quick right-hand turn and disappeared. One of the trucks took off after it. The killer leaned back and turned off the ignition.

Twenty minutes later, another TV truck started up; another vehicle was exiting the garage. This time, the truck, after looking into the car and seeing a single agent, shut off its engine. The Gentkiller started his.

Over a rehearsed course that avoided the media vehicles, he drove quickly up two blocks and over one. Just ahead of him, stopped at a red light, was the lone FBI agent. As always at night, the downtown streets were deserted.

He pulled up on the right side of the car, beeped, and rolled down his window. The agent's passenger window was rolled up, so the killer just pointed at the agent's right front tire.

The agent leaned across the seat and rolled down the window.

"Looks like that tire's about to go flat."

"Thanks," the agent said, and put the car in park. He got out and walked around to the right side, within three feet of the killer. When he saw the tire was fully inflated, he looked up.

The Gentkiller shot him once in the face and calmly drove away.

In Devlin's estimation, dinner went well. They ate at The Mediterranean Club, a noisy restaurant at the edge of Greektown. The food was good, and the entertainment, especially the bouzouki player, was pleasantly distracting. Knox had enjoyed herself, and the conversation was mostly about the kids, the two carefully avoiding Devlin's hunt for the agent killer.

Afterward, as they were leaving the downtown area, the Bureau radio sawed through the air, "All available units, an agent needs assistance at Third and Abbott. Repeat: An agent needs assistance, Third and Abbott."

Devlin held his breath and Knox stared at him with terror-stricken eyes. He turned the car around and drove the short distance in silence.

Purposely, he parked a half block away from the intersection that was already crowded with agents, police, and media. Without looking at his wife, Devlin said, "I'll be right back."

He flashed his credentials at one of the cops holding back the media. The dead agent was facedown. No blood was visible, but the uncomfortable position of the body verified its lifelessness. The hips were slightly raised above uselessly positioned arms, so that too much of the agent's weight rested on his face. Without touching it, Devlin looked into the dead agent's car. The only thing he noticed was the driver's window was up but the passenger's was down. Another ruse, he thought. He scanned the neighborhood. Every building was a business and there were no lights on in any of them. He looked up and down the streets, and aside from a few arriving agents, there was no traffic. Then he noticed Knox. She was standing as close to the murder scene as the police would let her.

He walked over to her quickly. She said, "Who is it?"

"Andy Fox. I don't think you knew him."

As her eyes stared vacuously at the body, her head snapped slightly to each side, almost like a twitch, indicating that she didn't. He put his arm around her and led her away.

When they got in the car she said, "Will you leave this alone *now*?"

"Leave it alone! How do you leave something like this alone when you know there might be more?"

Whether she felt the point was arguable or not, Knox did not say another word. When they got home, she went up to their daughter's room and shut the door.

When Devlin finally slipped into an inky ocean of sleep, its time machine sent him back to the day his father had died. His death had proved to be as unceremonious as his life.

Ten years earlier, Devlin had received a call at the office from "a friend" of his father's whom Devlin did not know. His father was in the hospital and not expected to make it through the night. Fifty years of alcohol were demanding final payment. He had left home when Devlin was fifteen, and they had seen each other about once a year since then. It was tough growing up without a father, but for Devlin not as tough as with one. Financially, it was difficult, but at least he was without the daily terror of alcoholism. Devlin started working after school that year, and with each job he had found a new opportunity to reshape the Devlin name.

He reached the hospital a few hours before his father's death. The old man barely recognized his son and, when he did, seemed surprised that he was there. "See Tommy at the bar. He's got a letter for you," his father said, seemingly draining himself of what little life was left. The last few hours Devlin sat and watched his father, who had always been a brawler, finally relinquish his life. No complaints, no regrets, and no fear of whatever was next.

The bar was in an old Polish section of Chicago. Deteriorating neighborhoods surrounded the Hamlet, but the Poles obliviously carried out their daily lives. Devlin's father had, over the years, become the saloon's senior statesman. He was always good for a loan, which the patrons paid back with honorable haste. And he was always available for a story or some advice.

Devlin opened the envelope that Tommy had kept in the safe. Inside were instructions that were not addressed to anyone:

Have me cremated at Orlowski's Funeral Home. They quoted me $1,500. Buy the house a round.

The "will" was not signed. With it were sixteen one-hundred-dollar bills. Devlin called Tommy over and gave him one of the bills and told him the next hundred dollars' worth of drinks were on his father. Most of the men came up to Devlin and offered their condolences, some with a story about his father. One remembered an incident that seemed to sum up his father's life. Thomas Devlin, without bragging, always said that he had never been to a doctor or dentist and would never go. On this particular day, one of his front teeth had a painful abscess. As he sat there trying to drink the pain away, a fellow patron asked him in a kidding tone if he shouldn't see a dentist. Devlin's father asked the bartender for a pair of pliers and a shot of brandy. As he put the pliers to his mouth, he said, "Physician, heal thyself," and extracted the upper front tooth with a quick jerk of his powerful hands. The medical procedure was completed by holding the shot of brandy in his mouth, unswallowed, for five minutes—a task much more difficult for him than the actual extraction. No ceremony, no complaint—just get on with the day's drinking.

As the men started exchanging stories about Thomas Devlin across the bar, Devlin saw that his father had been a friend to all of them. He realized that over the last decade he and his father had also become friends, but Thomas Devlin was incapable of being his father. It was simply a skill that had been excluded from his genes, like tone deafness or color blindness. In his own way, he was a good man; he was just not able to be a father.

Other than the hour Devlin spent at the bar, there was no wake, no announcement in the newspaper, no service. Another barstool was available at Tommy's. Since then, a death so purposeless had been one of Devlin's greatest fears.

||| CHAPTER 13 |||

Deception was becoming a familiar enemy of Mike Devlin's. Sebastian Draxler had brilliantly harnessed its influence and in so doing had taught Devlin to distrust the obvious. Instead, he would let all the tiny inconsistencies that refused to be altered become the compass that pointed to true north. Although, during the analysis of the third Gentkilling, all the discrepancies could be theorized away, Devlin would not allow himself to be distracted from them. The third agent had been shot only once in the face. According to the Behavioral Science Unit and the Wayne County Medical Examiner, the killer's overriding motivation was to humiliate the first two agents, and the second shot was the uncontrollable demonstration of that need. Also, there had been no isolation of the victim, which had been so necessary in the first two murders. A time during which, Devlin suspected, the Gentkiller reveled in his advantage, his *superiority*. And no souvenir had been taken. "He was probably scared off" was the easy explanation to all these variations, but Devlin felt otherwise. The actual killing was only the end product of the humiliation; without it, there was no reason to murder.

He also knew that any good architect of deception builds into his plan the desire of the target to be misled. Everyone wanted to think the killings were random. Agents did not want to believe that their name was on a list somewhere, but rather, if they were careful, they could avoid the disorganized assaults of this madman. And since they were already investigating every nut in Michigan, it was just a matter of time until he was caught.

So the night before at the murder scene, few had shared Devlin's suspicions. The haphazard selection of the third victim had confirmed the theory of the agents and media alike: No connection existed between any of the victims.

Because the Gentkiller had gone to the risk and trouble of committing this murder, Devlin was more convinced than ever that some common ground did exist between John Lawson and Brian Blankenship. And since he had repeatedly failed to discover that link, he was forced to return to his tedious solve-one-solve-them-all approach to Brian Blankenship's murder. He sat at an empty desk in the Detroit Homicide Unit and tried to find some enthusiasm for the list of the dead agent's arrests that he held in his hand. By working at a location other than the FBI office, he avoided not only the SAC and his demand for the extortion report but also the media-driven pandemonium that now flooded the office.

The list was undoubtedly the most logical lead in solving the agent's murder, but Devlin knew the crimes could not be reduced to mathematical equations and then solved by finding a value for x. Navigating through the uncharted waters of a homicide often caused logic to capsize. Cases were never solved by brilliant investigators, just dogged ones. He picked up the phone and called the next police department.

It was almost noon before he got the last callback. Of the original seventy-two individuals Blankenship had arrested, sixty-one were still confined. That left Devlin with eleven suspects who were free at the time of the murders. He packed up his notes and walked over to Jerome Wicks's office. "Oh, you're finally here."

Wicks smiled at Devlin. "That's the funny thing about being the head of Homicide. They expect you to go to these command meetings. How long have you been here?"

"All morning. I had to make some phone calls."

"The FBI's phones aren't working?" Devlin shrugged matter-of-factly, but Wicks detected a slight avoidance in his eyes. "Sounds like you're using this for a hideout."

Devlin feigned indignation. "Me?"

"Who were you calling? That is the question I'm supposed to ask, isn't it? And that will lead to the reason you're here, which will turn into the favor you're about to ask for."

"You know, Jerry, America was built on the pleasures of foreplay. What do you do when you have sex—smoke first?"

"The favor, Michael." Devlin explained what he was doing and Wicks said, "Sounds reasonable. At least, it's where I'd start."

"There are eleven possibles. I don't have to tell you that's a lot when you're trying to find a killer."

"One wrong one is too many."

"Is your offer to help still good?"

"Of course."

"What can you spare?"

"Things are only mildly chaotic right now. Part-time, maybe two teams."

"Can they handle two suspects apiece, for starters?"

"If we don't get real busy." Wicks looked through the criminal-history printouts for the four men. "Should we bring them in and interrogate them, or did you want some foreplay first?"

"Whatever makes your ego hard."

As soon as Devlin started his car, the Bureau radio spoke, "Central to Four-one." He did not answer but waited to see how long it would be before he was called again. If the message was being put out at the SAC's request, it would not be long. "Central to Four-one."

Devlin put the car in gear and picked up the handset. "Central, this is Four-one. Tell the SAC I'll be at the office in fifteen minutes."

When Sudder received the call that Devlin was on his way in, he had just finished his sixth news conference of the day, and it was not one o'clock yet. The death of the third agent had brought out not only every last representative of the national media but correspondents from almost a dozen foreign countries. They all were asking the same question: Why wasn't the world's premier law enforcement agency able to solve the murders of its own agents?

Sudder's secretary buzzed. "The director is on line two."

Between media briefings, the SAC had been on the phone all morning with a steady stream of Bureau officials wanting answers. The first call had been a lowly Headquarters supervisor. Each subsequent call increased in rank and length. Because the director was in Australia, Sudder had hoped he could avoid his call. "Good afternoon, sir."

"It's four A.M. here, Malcolm, and I haven't been to bed yet."

"It's been crazy here too."

"Tell me something I'm going to want to hear, Malcolm. Tell me you have a good suspect. Hell, tell me you have a bad suspect! Lie to me; I don't care. Just give me some hope."

"Well, sir, we do have a number of promising . . ."

"I meant, lie *intelligently*! Do you have anyone to zero in on?"

"Not yet."

The director paused and then said in a voice wilted by second-choice resignation, "I don't like getting involved in the Field's business, but it's time. I'm sending Welles Findley out there. Do you know him?"

Sudder had worked for the assistant director during his last assignment at Bureau Headquarters. "Yes, sir."

"Good, he'll be there in an advisory capacity. He's bringing twenty-five agents from other divisions. I'm also sending Bill Hagstrom from BSU. He'll stay until it's solved. Use him."

"Yes, sir."

"I'm flying back in three days. I can't get out of here any sooner. I'm coming directly to Detroit. That will be Friday. I want a news conference set up for eleven a.m. Do you know what I want to announce?"

"Yes, sir."

"Set it up."

"Yes, sir."

"And, Malcolm, if I can't announce the arrest, I'll have to find something else to talk about. Am I clear?"

"Perfectly."

They hung up. He knew that the director was well aware that Sudder could retire anytime, and if Gentkill was not solved by Friday, the director would, through an unending series of transfers from New York City to Butte, Montana, force that retirement. Fortunately, he had the job offer from Seacard to retreat to.

His secretary buzzed again. "Mike Devlin's here."

"Give me one minute." Sudder wanted a moment to prepare for Devlin. He reminded himself of their meeting the day before. Devlin had accepted the agreement and promised the report ASAP. But then he had found the note this morning saying there would be at least a one-day delay. One day he could handle; the director had given him three. At least he wouldn't be interrupted by those two gunslingers from OPR this time. When they had walked in the day before, they were surprisingly angry. Scalps were their job, but they weren't getting his.

He decided he would give Devlin one more day. "Send him in, please," he told his secretary. Once Devlin was seated, he said, "I got your note. What's causing the delay?"

Devlin was surprised at the patronizing tone. "I'm reviewing evidence and tying up some loose ends."

"I thought you wanted to get to work on Gentkill as soon as possible."

"I do, but the people at Seacard did not give me any time frame. Did they say the insurance company needed it by a certain date?"

"No, but I'm anxious to get this out of the way. Frankly, I need you on the murder investigation."

"You gave me the extortion knowing it would take a long time to finish."

"I know, but that was before. I want that report by ten A.M. tomorrow. Nothing fancy, just that there was a legitimate extortion, and that the subject, along with Seacard's five million, is now ashes. You don't have to worry about evidence or loose ends for that."

"I don't want that report to come back in six months to haunt us."

Sudder smiled. "You're assuming we'll both be here in six months."

Devlin could not tell whether Sudder was threatening to fire him or forecasting his own retirement. Neither option seemed that unattractive.

Devlin sat in his room surrounded by extortion evidence. For a brief moment, he considered the SAC's words and then took out the list of murder suspects.

The first name on the list was Anthony Wayne Nestler, a black male, now thirty-four years old. Blankenship had arrested him four years earlier; the charge was Unlawful Flight to Avoid Prosecution for Armed Robbery. His criminal history indicated that he had pled guilty to Assault with Intent to Commit Armed Robbery and had been sentenced to two to five years. He had served a year and then completed a year of parole. He was not currently "on paper."

Devlin called the radio room and had Nestler checked for a current driver's license; he did not have one. He called his contact at the Department of Social Services. Nestler was not receiving welfare, but his mother was.

The house was a tired gray frame on the near east side. Devlin knocked on the door politely. An old, heavyset black woman with steel-gray hair answered. "Yes?"

"I'm looking for Debra Nestler."

"That's my daughter. Can I help you?"

"Yes, ma'am. Can I come in?" He held up his credentials and watched as her eyes turned cautious. Without a word, she opened the door for him.

They sat down in the kitchen. It was furnished with worn, ageless furniture. An ancient radio sitting on a windowsill wheezed out a sun-faded song. She asked, "What do you want with my daughter?"

"I need to talk to your grandson, Anthony."

There was some relief in her expression. "What's he done now?"

"As far as I know, nothing. I just need to talk to him about a case I'm working on."

She looked at him with narrowed eyes, informing him that she knew about the police and their hidden agendas. Devlin understood her reaction. It was always the same. "If Anthony had a problem, do you think I would be here alone?"

Because she understood how the police operated, she could not doubt Devlin's explanation. "He don't live here."

A woman her age, given the chance, preferred not to lie, but Anthony was family, and she would lie whether he needed protection or not. For Devlin, it was the same game of tic-tac-toe he had played a thousand times. The same moves would be played in the same order, and it would end in a draw, which is all Devlin really wanted. "Do you know where he lives?"

"Sure don't."

"Do you know how to get ahold of him?"

"Not really."

"How about your daughter?"

"She don't live here."

"Do you know where she lives?"

"Sure don't."

"Does she work?"

"Yeah, but I'm not sure where."

Devlin had allowed her to lie her way into a problem. "Mrs. Nestler, why don't I make this easy on both of us. I want Anthony to call me today. If he doesn't, your daughter, who you tell me not only works but doesn't live here, can talk to the welfare fraud investigators. I don't want that, and I know you don't, so have him call me. The sooner the better." Devlin knew he would get the call. The grandmother would see to it, not because of the threat, but because it was the only way she could ease the guilt she felt for lying so poorly.

Less than an hour after Devlin returned to the office, his phone rang. "This is Anthony Nestler. You were to my grandmother's today."

"I just need to talk to you."

"What's this about?"

"What have you been doing?"

"Nothing, man!"

"Then you shouldn't have any problem talking to me."

"When?"

"Now."

"I'm at the Popeye's Chicken, on Woodward just below Grand."

"You working there?"

"Yeah, but that's no problem. You can come on."

"Twenty minutes."

As soon as Devlin walked in the restaurant, Nestler spotted him, so Devlin sat at an isolated booth. Nestler finished removing some chicken from the fryer and then walked over to the booth. He carefully wiped his right hand on his long white apron and offered it to Devlin. "You really shook up my grandmother."

"Would you have called if I hadn't?"

Nestler smiled. "No."

"Do you know why I'm here, Anthony?"

"No."

"I'm eliminating suspects."

"Suspects for what?"

"If you'll cooperate, I can cross you off." Devlin smiled confidently. "Unless you're the one."

Nestler gazed back evenly. "Since I went to the joint, I ain't done nothing. So why should I help you?"

"Think of it as helping yourself, unless you like the FBI poking around your personal life."

Nestler laughed. "Nobody's that innocent."

"Before I tell you exactly what it's about, let me ask you a few questions. Did you ever work at the Bridgeline glove factory?"

"Where's that?"

"On Fenkell, west side."

"No."

"Have you ever been inside it?"

"No. I don't even know where it's at. I'm an east sider."

"Okay, here's an easier one. When was the last time you were in the Ren Cen?"

Nestler thought for a second. "At least a year ago."

"Where'd you go there?"

"In that Italian restaurant on the first floor."

"A date?"

"Yeah."

"Ever been on the twenty-eighth floor? In some offices there?"

"Never."

Devlin was not picking up any signals of deception, but ex-cons were usually well-disciplined liars, so he decided to try a bluff. "What would you say if I told you we had your fingerprints in those places that you have never been?"

Nestler smiled comfortably. "I'd say, you should save that hum for the tourists."

Devlin laughed, admitting he had underestimated Nestler. "I'd say you're right." They both laughed. "Okay, Anthony, I'm going to be straight up with you. Remember when you were arrested by the FBI on the armed robbery?"

"The FBI? I thought I was arrested by Detroit. They took me down to their headquarters in Beaubien."

"It was a joint arrest. With DPD."

"I don't remember any FBI."

"Do you know any FBI agents?"

"Just you."

"How about Brian Blankenship?" Nestler shook his head. "He was with Detroit when they arrested you."

"I don't recall the name."

"John Lawson?"

"Nope."

"Both those agents were shot to death."

"And you're looking at me because the one arrested me?"

"It's as simple as that."

"So, are you crossing me off your list?"

Devlin's instincts told him that Nestler was not a good suspect. He had been out of prison and off parole for over two years. Why would he wait that long before seeking revenge? Besides, as soon as Devlin had contacted his grandmother, someone as familiar with the justice system as Nestler, if he were guilty, would have been on the phone with his lawyer. His arrest had been uneventful and would not warrant any degree of revenge. He took out his list, and after positioning it so Nestler could see his name, Devlin drew a line through it.

Sebastian Draxler was just finishing his second class of the day. He had decided to teach both summer-session courses to give him a reason to be around the physics building day and night. The success of the extortion had depended on it. The faxes had appeared to have been sent from the third floor, which had drawn the FBI agent there, and that in turn enabled Draxler to identify the six agents at the bus station, all necessary parts of his plan to further intimidate Seacard *and* to bewilder the FBI. And now that the case had been resolved and the "extortionist" killed, he would continue to spend the majority of his time in the building guarding his million dollars.

After class he went to his office, where he was scheduled, by university mandate, to be available for student conferences. He hated office hours, a time when the intellectually unwashed could, without pretense or ceremony, waste his time in agonizing half-hour increments. Fortunately, no one had made an appointment, so he started packing up his briefcase, preparing to leave.

One of his students, Eric Henderson, stuck his head in the door. "Doctor Draxler, do you have a minute?"

Henderson was an engineering student. Draxler thought of him as hardworking but not bright enough to be a physics major. The conflict was as old as the two disciplines: Physicists discovered how things worked, and then engineers got paid for bastardizing the results. Henderson's academic pursuits were, therefore, inconsequential.

"If it will not take any longer than a minute, yes."

They both sat down. Henderson said, "You're probably not aware of it, but I'm on a scholarship here. And I need a B in your class to maintain it."

Draxler hated it when a student tried to negotiate a grade. He took out his class book and, after reading down a column, said, "Looks like you'll need a ninety on the final."

"I know. I was wondering if there was anything I could do."

"How about studying harder?" Draxler's voice was emotionless.

"I'm having trouble with some of the thermodynamics."

Draxler could see desperation in his student's eyes. "It's all in the text."

"I know, I know. But I've had trouble with that book all session."

Draxler looked at his watch. "I'm sorry. I have a small personal crisis I have to get to." He motioned to a large, well-organized bookshelf. "Take whatever you like. Just leave me a list and lock up after yourself. I've got to go."

Draxler walked to the elevator and pushed the down button. He thought about Henderson, alone in his office finding the questions and answers for the final exam.

They were all so easy to seduce, and all so expendable. It had been that way with Haidar. As with so many of the gifted foreign students, he was immature. Unlike Draxler, Haidar, as a youth, had been pampered by a family and a country hungry for intellectual successes. Once Draxler had explained to him the injustices his father had suffered at Seacard's hands, there was no holding back the young Egyptian. Maybe because he was an Arab, he had revolution in his blood. He saw all of it as some intellectual game, and because his great American professor thought enough of Haidar to include him, he gladly charged ahead. Of course, the promised $2 million cut had probably helped.

Sebastian Draxler prided himself on settling all scores. He had taken care of Seacard, and just for the exercise, tonight he would come back to his office and rid the world of one more small-minded engineering student. It would not take him long to make up a new final exam.

It was three o'clock when he reached the parking lot. He started his Audi and took a few seconds to listen to the baritone surges of the German-built machine. Although he had no reason to believe he was being followed, he drove with apprehension, rapidly turning down one-way streets and then cutting his speed in half, spending more time looking in the rearview mirror than through the windshield. Finally, he drove down a long dead-end street and pulled over, waiting for surveillance that never materialized. When he was satisfied that he was not being followed, he drove home.

After parking in the garage, he stood on his front porch and took one last look at the street behind him. To the right of the front door was the keypad for the alarm system. Carefully, he pressed in the five-digit code. As soon as the "armed" light went out, he stabbed his key into the front door lock and went in.

Across the street and up two houses sat an old station wagon whose original color could no longer be distinguished. On top, roof racks held worn aluminum extension ladders that were tied at both ends to the car's bumpers. A small red flag hung from the back end alerting drivers to the ladders' excessive length. The rear windows were all darkened glass.

Lying in the back of the wagon, on a carefully positioned series of cushions, was Tommy Hollings. A rifle-range spotting scope sat on a small tripod, perfectly positioned between the back window and Hollings's right eye. The device was aimed at the center of Sebastian Draxler's alarm keypad. Hollings copied the alarm code into a small black pocket notebook and then took a sip from a glass filled with Jack Daniel's and ice.

He set the glass in an anchored holder and picked up his cellular phone. He dialed Draxler's house. After two rings, Draxler answered. "Hello. Doctor Draxler."

"Is Sam there?"

"You have the wrong number." The professor hung up abruptly.

"That's what you think, Doc," Hollings said into the dead phone. He had called the number three hours earlier, when he had set up his surveillance. There was no answer then, so he went to a nearby gas station and paid the attendant five dollars to watch his ladders. He took out magnetic signs and hung them on both front doors of the car: ED'S ELECTRONIC REPAIR. He drove back to Draxler's house and boldly parked in his driveway. With a large TV repairman's toolbox in hand, he went to the front door and patiently rang the bell several times. Between rings, his practiced hands slid a key blank, which he had roughed up with a file, into the door lock. As he attempted to turn it, he marked the blank with smooth spots caused by the lock's pins. After a few more doorbell rings, Hollings took his toolbox and left. At the gas station he reoutfitted the station wagon for surveillance. While he awaited Draxler's arrival, he lay in the back of the station wagon and took out his Curtis Clipper. With the plierslike instrument, he meticulously snapped notches into the key blank at the pin-marked points. Patiently, he smoothed the cuts with a small file.

He had finished the key an hour before Draxler came home. Now everything was ready. The next time the professor left, Hollings would go to work.

He finished his drink and rolled over on his back. He would sleep until nightfall, when he would wake up automatically. He always had; it was one of the reasons he believed he was a born burglar.

Devlin's next suspect was the first of two white males on the list. He had tried to ignore Bill Hagstrom's theory of "probably a white male," but the interview of Anthony Nestler reminded him that the surest way to recognize a bad lead was to become the servant of its futility. Pursuing Blankenship's arrests no longer seemed as promising as it originally had, so Devlin was using Hagstrom's profile to find the best of the bad leads before his interest in the list completely disappeared.

Ronald Jacobs was a bank robber. In the late seventies, he had robbed twenty-three banks in Michigan before a lone sheriff's deputy apprehended him and three accomplices. During their three-year spree, they had taken over half a million dollars in cash. Once released on bond, they found that their financial obligations were growing. Fees for bondsmen and lawyers caused them to return to robbing banks. In a span of ten days, they hit three Ohio banks for over $100,000. Jacobs spent fifteen years in Marion, the federal system's toughest prison. While there, he became obsessed with weight lifting, working out eight hours a day, until he won the Mr. Strongest-White-Guy-in-the-Joint title. When he was released from prison, he had gotten into a barroom brawl. Wanting to test his twenty-one-inch arms, he beat a biker half to death. Assault and battery charges were filed and, because of Jacobs's propensity to rob banks during stressful times, an unlawful flight warrant was issued for the usually ignored crime.

Blankenship, through an informant, arrested Jacobs at an old prison associate's apartment. Once the jury got a look at the complainant, whose ill-fitting suit refused to hide the fact that the biker was more repulsive than a master bank robber, they believed Jacobs's self-defense testimony and acquitted him after twenty minutes of deliberation.

Devlin guessed the interview was going to be difficult. Because Jacobs had served time in Marion, it was not likely that he would be very obliging. Jacobs's driver's license showed a Rockville, Michigan, address. Devlin doubted if he would be that easy to locate. It was probably the residence of a friend or family member.

Rockville was a small town located in Macomb County. The chief of police, Tom Henessey, was a retired Detroit PD lieutenant. Devlin had known him when he was in charge of the Holdup Bureau. Because Henessey was an old bank-robbery detective, Devlin thought he might have kept an eye on Jacobs's activities.

He pulled into the Rockville PD lot and parked in a space marked VISITOR. After showing his credentials and asking to see the chief, Devlin was told to take a seat. A minute later, Henessey came through the door and shook Devlin's hand warmly. Devlin had seen it before: Cops after twenty-five or thirty years of frustration in Detroit get a "cushy" job in small-town white suburbia and find, between the politics and the chickenshit, a new level of frustration. Henessey was obviously glad to see someone who spoke his language. "Mike, how are ya?"

"I'm good. How's life after Detroit?"

"It's okay. Better for the family. Better schools. You know."

"You're not missing a thing downtown."

"That's what I hear. What can I do for you?"

"Ronnie Jacobs." Henessey led Devlin into his office and closed the door.

"Has he been hitting banks again?"

"I hope not. He'll never talk to me if he has. It's about the agents who were killed."

"You think he's good for those?"

"He's just a name on a list. One of the agents that was killed popped him once. I also have ten other guys I'm looking at. Wicks is running some of them for me."

"Anything promising?"

"To tell you the truth, I think I'm heading south, leading a large flock of wild geese."

Henessey's phone rang. "Yes . . . put him on . . . yes, Mayor . . . we're going to hit it at seven-thirty tonight, just before the Tigers start. If they're booking, they should be busy at that time . . . yes, sir, I'll let you know." He hung up. "Fucking politicians."

"Sounds like he thinks he's a cop."

"He's got some friend who contributed a couple of grand to his campaign. The guy fancies himself a gambler. He's been betting with a sports bookie up on Gratiot. He's into him for almost ten grand, so he wants us to take him off so he doesn't have to pay. He goes to the mayor, who orders me to take care of it."

"I would think you would welcome the action."

"We've taken two other bookies to trial since I've been up here. The people in this county love sports and feel gambling is a legitimate extension of it. Both were found not guilty. Besides, my boy's pitching tonight. There's a scout from Michigan State coming to the game, and Bobby always seems to throw a little better when I'm there."

"Bobby's graduating from high school?"

"I know. It's hard for me to believe too. He's developed into a hell of a pitcher. He's got a nice curveball and his fastball's in the low nineties. And he's an honor student too. With my daughter already in college, it sure would help if he could get a scholarship."

"Do you have to go on the raid? Can't you just send your dicks?"

"I've only got two detectives. All that gambling paraphernalia—it'll take the three of us half the night."

"Who's the bookie?"

"Nick Trampelli. Ever heard of him?"

"I think I have heard his name."

"When I get my hands on him, he's going to wish *I* never heard his name."

"Maybe he won't be there."

"Don't get my hopes up. Anyway, Ronnie Jacobs. If you

want to talk to him, you got to call his mother, Helen. She's in the book."

"The usual."

"Right. If he wants to talk to you, he'll call."

Devlin stood up to leave. "When you talk to Bobby, tell him I said good luck tonight."

"He'll appreciate it, Mike."

Devlin drove back to the office. He found Helen Jacobs's phone number in the southern Macomb County phone book and called her. He told her who he was, his phone number, and that he wanted to talk to her son. Anything more would have been a waste of time.

While he waited, he called Nick Trampelli. "Yeah," Trampelli answered.

"Nick. Do you know who this is?"

Although bookies have to do business on the phone, they are always wary of being recorded. Trampelli immediately understood the caution in Devlin's question and knew not to use the FBI agent's name. "Yeah."

"Have you got a cellular?"

"Yeah."

"Call me on it."

The phone rang almost immediately. "Mikey, what's up?"

"You're going to get hit tonight, around seven-thirty."

"You sure?"

"Yep. Now do me a favor."

"Sure."

"I want you to clean that place out. Take everything including the phones and the garbage."

"Hey, we're used to moving. By six o'clock there won't even be fingerprints left here. But why?"

"I don't want the cops to find one piece of evidence that they'll have to bother with."

"You got it. I really appreciate this, Mike."

"You know how to repay me."

"I know, I know. In fact, I got something for you, but let me call you back. I want to get the truck started on the way over here. Seven minutes."

Devlin hung up and looked at his watch. Most bookies had two uncanny abilities, one for numbers, the other for time. Inside their heads were some surprisingly accurate clocks. They were the products of too many years of horse races and game clocks running out. Seven and a half minutes later, the phone rang. "Yeah, Mike, I was going to call you with this. Have you guys got a man undercover at the Oak Hollow Golf Course?" Devlin remembered his conversation with Shanahan, but did not answer. "Oh, yeah, what's wrong with me? You can't tell me. Let me put it this way. I hear a story that there's an undercover fed out there. Somebody recognized him. He brings up some golf hustler, who also may be with the G, to play some of the pigeons. Anyway, a guy named Short Game scams him and takes twelve grand from him."

"Short Game must be a hell of a golfer."

"Naw. He can play but he ain't that good. This guy he beat was good. Real good. They see him practicing the day before, and this guy can hit the ball a mile. But they know how to take advantage of that. Good golfers who can drive the ball almost always hook it so it curls to the left. Guys who aren't that good, like Short Game, fade the ball left to right. Well, you probably know that some of the boys are involved in running that club, so Short Game gets the groundskeeper to move all the pins to the far right side of the green so your guy's ball will always be running away from the hole while Short Game's is curling at it."

"It seems like a good golfer should be able to overcome a lot of that."

"Yeah, you're right, but they also used phony scorecards. Every third hole, the yardage was listed fifty yards too long, so this guy is driving the ball fifty yards over the green. The next hole, he figures he's strong that day so, even though the yardage is correct on the card, he leaves it fifty short. Once he gets it corrected, it's mismarked fifty yards too *short* on the next hole. Fucking Jack Nicklaus couldn't beat Short Game under those conditions."

Devlin's other phone rang. "Thanks, Nick."

"I'm the one that's thankful. I know cops stick together. Why'd you call me?"

"I guess because cops stick together."

Devlin answered the other phone. It was Ronnie Jacobs. He agreed to meet Devlin at a bar near the Hazel Park racetrack.

When Devlin walked in, he spotted Jacobs. His short sleeves exposed his brutal arms. They were difficult not to stare at.

Devlin introduced himself and said, "I wasn't sure you'd call me."

"That's all behind me now."

Devlin noticed a deep scar at the point of Jacobs's chin that seemed to be about .38 caliber in diameter. It then changed to an incision scar that ran four inches up the right side of his jaw. "Interesting scar."

Jacobs understood Devlin's appraising glance. "Yes, it's a bullet wound."

"Doesn't look that old."

"About a year. A ways back I had to clean up this biker. When a jury let me off, some of his buddies felt justice had not been served."

"They still looking for you?"

"I don't think their memories are that good, but if they are, they'd better be wearing something real bulletproof."

"I would think with the way you're built, you'd only have to fight guys who are blind or insane."

"I never look for a fight."

"Get in many fights in the joint?"

"There are no fistfights in prison. You either walk away or you kill someone. No defending your honor. There's just living and dying. You don't have the luxury of anything in between."

"Ever kill anyone inside?"

Jacobs looked at Devlin carefully, taking the time to read his eyes, his face, and his hands. He saw that calmness that all cops eventually surrender to. A patience. One thing at a time. The question was not meant to entrap Jacobs, merely to define him. "Yeah."

"Remember when the FBI picked you up on that assault?"

"I guess so."

"Tell me about the agent."

"Young. Kind of excited, but decent enough. When we got back to your office, he gave me a cigarette and let me make all the calls I needed to. Why?"

"Someone killed him."

Both men stared into each other's eyes. Finally Jacobs said, "I think you know it wasn't me."

After a long analytical silence, Devlin said, "I think you're right."

At a little after 9 P.M., Sebastian Draxler left his house and drove off. Tommy Hollings waited ten minutes before exiting his car and walking to the front door. After entering the alarm code, he used the key he had made to gain access to the house. Once inside, he found the phone and dialed Draxler's office. "Hello. Doctor Draxler." Hollings hung up. He had timed the drive to his office. It would take him almost fifteen minutes to get back. Draxler had left the lights on, so Hollings moved through the house quickly, using his experience to determine which rooms needed no further exploration and which rooms contained secrets.

The single bedroom was masculine and contained no indication of anyone else living there. He also checked the bathroom for the number of toothbrushes and feminine products. He did not want to be surprised by a second resident. He came back to the bedroom and searched for anything that was locked, but he could find nothing. The house was a single story, but it did have a basement. Out of his "TV repair" box, he took a small black flashlight and turned its beam into the darkened basement.

The main room of the basement contained an enormous

workbench. Although it was covered with dozens of items, it was orderly. One section had chemicals in marked jars, glass tubes, flasks, and a triple-beam scale. Another area contained a couple of small electrical motors and some hand tools, including an expensive soldering gun. On top of an old blond school desk in the corner sat a telephone, a fax machine, and a portable typewriter. Hollings searched the drawers and found nothing. The rest of the basement, aside from some woodworking equipment, was empty. Hollings had committed over a thousand burglaries and now sensed that there was something else in the basement. All of the equipment and material there did not seem to have a final purpose. There was no end product to Draxler's efforts.

He adjusted the focus on his flashlight beam and searched the paneled walls for anything hidden, but structurally there was no room for any type of secreted storage space. The only thing left was the ceiling. It was the drop type with removable white panels. "Come on, Professor, you're not going to be that obvious," Hollings whispered. He scanned the entire ceiling with the beam of his flashlight until he found himself in the corner where the desk was. On the corner tile, he spotted the slightest traces of gray smudges left by fingers. Standing on the desk chair, he pushed up the panel and stuck his head and flashlight up above the suspended ceiling. On a solidly constructed wooden shelf sat a dark-colored vinyl briefcase. He put it on the desk and placed another call to Draxler's office. Draxler answered, and again, Hollings hung up without a word.

He took out a set of lock picks and inserted the tension bar into the right-hand lock. Then, working a stubby pick deeper inside, he was able to line up the pins; the tension bar started to rotate the lock's cam. Thirty seconds later, he had the other lock open. Inside were two pounds of C-4 explosive, electrical blasting caps, and some booby-trap devices. Also in the briefcase were several pages of drawings and maps, one of which was a diagram of a car's rear-seat area with a remote-controlled trapdoor built in.

Hollings picked up the phone and hit the redial button. There was no answer. He had to assume Draxler was on his way home. He took the drawings and maps from the briefcase, snapped it shut, and replaced it along with the ceiling tile. He picked up the phone and put it to his ear and then placed the handset on the fax machine to his other ear. Two dial tones. The fax machine was on its own phone line. Quickly, he unplugged it and then replugged it. A short slip of paper hummed out of the machine reporting a power failure, but Hollings's purpose was to use the printout to obtain the number of the fax line. There was none. Draxler evidently had not reprogrammed it in. Hollings needed that number. He checked his watch. It was going to be tight.

He hung up the phone and dialed the operator on the fax machine. "Operator."

"This is telephone repair. I need a drop-wire ID."

As the operator read him the number off her computer screen, he copied it into his pocket notebook.

He went out through the front door and made it to his car just as the black Audi turned the corner.

Hollings was amused as he watched Draxler look at his alarm keypad questioningly. The light was out. He pushed in the code to arm it, and the light went on. He punched in the entry code and stared at the panel as the light went out.

Inside his car, Hollings smiled and said to himself, "Don't worry, Professor. Soon all your questions will be answered—by your new partner."

The only other white male suspect on Devlin's list was William Thomas. Although it was a common name, Devlin had thought it sounded familiar. When he opened the file, he knew why. The arrest 302 not only had Blankenship's name on it, it had Devlin's.

Billy "The Kid" Thomas had been first sent to prison at the

age of sixteen. He was given two life sentences for a double murder, committed during the armed robbery of a suburban Detroit bar. After he had obtained all the money, he killed the owner and his wife for no apparent reason. Twenty-two years later he was paroled. Within six months, he was wanted for another armed robbery, and Blankenship obtained a federal flight warrant. Two months later, they got a call that Thomas was at one of his hangouts, a west-side bar. Blankenship grabbed Devlin and a third agent, who had since been transferred to Dallas.

The ensuing arrest turned into a brawl. Because Thomas's friends were at the bar, he decided to demonstrate his hatred for the law. It took the three agents more than twenty minutes to subdue him. Subsequently, the armed-robbery charges were dropped due to a lack of evidence. But because of the fight in the bar, he was charged with Assaulting a Federal Officer and did a year at the federal prison in Milan, Michigan.

Devlin remembered Billy the Kid's eyes; they were unquestionably psychotic. But Devlin suspected that because Thomas had survived twenty-two years in prison at such a young age, he knew how to control and direct his rage. He continued to flip through the file looking for anything that might lead to Thomas's whereabouts; he saw something that sent a jolt of adrenaline through his chest.

After the arrest, Thomas was interviewed by two agents: Brian Blankenship and John Lawson.

Lawson had asked to sit in on the interview because, for three years of his murder sentence, Thomas had been the cellmate of an organized-crime figure Lawson was interested in. Predictably, Thomas had not said a word—nothing; he had not even asked for a lawyer. He just sat there, focusing a homicidal gaze on the two agents.

Devlin checked his release date from Milan. It was less than two months earlier. For the first time since he had started checking Blankenship's arrests, he felt uneasy.

Taking the elevator to the twenty-sixth floor, Devlin asked

the night clerk to run Thomas through DMV in hopes of finding a current address for him.

While he waited, he walked over to the west side of the building and pulled a chair up to the window. Half of the fluorescent orange sun had lowered itself irretrievably below the horizon. He wanted to take a moment to enjoy its serenity, because he knew he was the last of the Detroit agents who had arrested or interviewed Thomas. And if Billy the Kid was the Gentkiller, he was already looking for Devlin.

The Gentkiller sat in his car a block away from the house of his next victim. He had followed the agent, whom he liked to refer to as the *real* Number Three, from John Lawson's funeral. He had been watching the house for hours, but did not think Three was home. But that was all right; he liked the chase. It had a warm rush to it, not unlike the murder itself. He closed his eyes and revisited the glove factory and the Renaissance Center, remembering the helpless look on their faces when he told them who he was and why they were going to die. As helpless as they had left him. And now there was only one left.

He started his car and put it in gear. *Tomorrow night, Number Three. Tomorrow night.*

||| CHAPTER 14 |||

Although it was only 8 A.M., the six paramedics sat drinking the house speciality, Bloody Marys. The bartender had a special spigoted crock in which he let a dozen large jalapeño peppers soak for days in two gallons of Russian vodka. He served the stinging drinks in large glasses that were Ball jars with handles. He made them extra strong for the EMS technicians, because they were his regulars. And because he had heard their stories about working the midnight-to-eight shift in Detroit, a city with a seemingly insatiable need to mutilate the human body.

From a corner booth, Mike Devlin sat and watched them. It was the same as with cops or firemen; their day ended with some sort of postcombat ceremony. They had joined up to make a difference, but now were happy to celebrate survival. They drank the biting drinks in large gulps and waited for the vodka's warm, flooding hypnosis.

Jerome Wicks walked in and sat down across from Devlin.

"Any luck?" Devlin asked. Fatigue was minimizing his need for conversation.

"We talked to two of them. Nothing. Did you do any good?"

Devlin looked at the fatigue covering Wicks's face and decided not to tell him about Billy Thomas. Not only was he in command of one of the most overworked homicide units in the country, but he was already running out leads on four suspects for Devlin. It was an unwritten law of criminal investigation, when leads are divided up, that you handle your own, no com-

plaints. Of course, if Thomas became a clear-cut suspect, he
would bring Wicks in. Furthermore, Devlin had no real evidence that Thomas was the murderer. He wasn't the first good
suspect in the case, and after spending half the night looking
for him, Devlin was not even sure he was in Michigan. "I
found two of them," Devlin answered. "Both spectacularly un-
spectacular."

Wicks looked into Devlin's sluggish eyes. "Did you get any
sleep?"

When Devlin had gotten home, his kids were asleep and
Knox was waiting for him. "Mike, I suppose if I could stand
off at a distance, I would love you for what you're doing. But
being this close, I'm scared. While you're out there, all I can
do is wait and hope the phone doesn't ring. I don't want to
argue about this anymore. I know it won't do any good. But
I will not pretend everything is okay. It can't be until this
maniac is caught." She would not allow herself to cry,
because emotion would have diluted the litigation of
her words. She turned off the light and curled up in bed.
Although he was tired, Devlin slept only intermittently,
thinking about the woman who lay next to him, so determined, so vulnerable.

"Some" was Devlin's cloudy answer to Wicks. "I can't figure out this guy's motive."

"Twenty-five years ago when I came on the job, if there was
a murder, the first thing you did was find out who had a motive.
Now they kill each other with such indifference, anything can
qualify. I had one last week. Two guys sitting next to each
other in a restaurant. One asks the other for the ketchup. 'Fuck
you!' was the answer he got, so he shoots the guy six times,
steps over the gurgling body, and gets the ketchup. He's sitting
there eating a hamburger when the scout car shows up. During
his statement, he tells us he thinks he was justified. People no
longer have any concept of right or wrong. If it feels good, do
it. Now we'll be serving this animal three meals a day for the
next fifty years. The funny thing is, if we had released him, he

would have been dead in six months. Detroit can be one large, self-cleaning oven."

They each had a second cup of coffee and left.

Devlin arrived at the SAC's office at 10 A.M., and after the secretary announced him, she said, "Mr. Sudder wants to know if you have the report ready."

"No."

"No, sir," she reported into her phone. She listened for a moment and then hung up. "The SAC will be with you as soon as possible."

A few minutes later, Charles Wiggens, one of Sudder's more loyal supervisors, arrived and was admitted to the SAC's office. A minute later, Devlin was told he could go in.

Sudder sat sternly behind his desk; Wiggens was behind his boss's right shoulder with a notebook on his lap and his pen at the ready. "The report?" the SAC said.

"I haven't finished my investigation," Devlin answered flatly.

"Didn't we have this conversation yesterday?" Devlin stared back silently. Sudder looked back at Wiggens as a signal to start recording. "On today's date at"—the SAC looked at his watch to dramatize the accuracy and fairness of his instructions—"ten-ten A.M., I, Special Agent in Charge Malcolm A. Sudder, Detroit Division, ordered Special Agent Michael Devlin, for the *second* time in as many days, to prepare a preliminary report regarding the Seacard extortion. Agent Devlin, do you acknowledge receipt of that order?"

"Yes."

Sudder stared into the agent's level gaze as long as he could. Devlin's refusal to be intimidated by the threat angered him. "Oh, that's right, you're one of those veterans. You think because you have a separate appeal process, you can't be fired. But even a veteran cannot ignore a direct order twice and expect to keep his job. You *will* have that report on my desk, without fail, by ten A.M. tomorrow morning. Do you understand?"

"Yes," Devlin answered simply, knowing any further conversation would be a waste of time and ink.

When Devlin walked out of the SAC's office, the secretary
handed him a message. Wicks needed a call right away. Devlin
ducked into an empty interview room and closed the door.

"Jerry, it's Mike."

"We got one of your suspects here. They just brought him
in. You want to sit in on the interview?"

"I'm on my way."

Devlin walked into Wicks's office. "Who is it?"

"Reginald Hatton." Hatton had been arrested by Blankenship ten months earlier for an attempted murder. A Detroit
Recorders Court jury had found him not guilty, despite the testimony of three eyewitnesses. Wicks asked, "Did you know we
had a fresh warrant for him?"

"For what?"

"Shot another woman." Devlin shook his head. Wicks said,
"Hey, the jury let him off the first time. In his mind, it's no
longer a crime."

"Who got him?"

"Major Crimes." Major Crimes Mobile Unit was the fugitive section of the department. On the street they were known
as The Big Four. It was a nickname that came from the fifties
and sixties when four officers, all required to be at least six
feet tall, rode in ominous black Buicks. On the car's rear window ledge sat a black box carrying a Thompson submachine
gun, a visible warning to anyone considering going the distance with them. When The Big Four had lumbered out of the
huge old Buicks and asked questions, they got answers. In the
late seventies, when someone noticed the escalating number
of unserved warrants, the unit was reestablished. There were
still four officers to the car, but the Thompson had been replaced by an onboard computer. "Let me get the sergeant in
charge of the crew in here." Wicks walked to the door and
waved the policeman into the room. Devlin introduced himself and asked, "How did you get him?" If an informant had

been used, maybe Hatton, if he was the killer, had confessed something to him.

The sergeant was one of those cops who tried to be completely cynical, but every once in a while it slipped out that he still liked his job. "We've been looking for him for a couple of weeks, but then the inspector here says he wants to talk to him, so we made him a priority. We stopped by his mama's last night and got in her face. Left a card and told her to have him call us. Well, he calls back to give us some shit, but because he didn't have any change, the genius calls collect. The phone is outside this rooming house. We set up on it this morning. He comes out, makes us, and runs back in. This house is big, and we know this guy's a shooter, so we figure fuck it, and call for a dog. So we're searching this place. Can't find him. At the same time, the dog and his handler are working their way through the rooms. In a third-floor closet the dog hits. There's enough clothes on the floor to dress everyone in Somalia. Piled from the floor to the ceiling. The dog dives right in. He's in so far all we can see is the tip of his tail, but we can still hear this muffled barking. Finally, we hear this fuck screaming that the dog has his leg. Slowly, the dog moonwalks out of the closet with Junior's calf in his jaws. When we get him dislodged, do you know what he says?"

Devlin looked over at Wicks, who was smiling. Obviously he had already heard the story. "No."

The cop smiled. "Real serious, he turns to me and says, 'How'd that dog know I was in there? Did you show him my picture?' "

All three men laughed, and then Wicks said, "Great suspect, Mike. He'd probably still be trying to find his way out of the closet if it wasn't for the dog."

"You don't think he's the diabolical mind behind the agent murders?"

Wicks grinned. "Of the thousands of murders I've worked, this is the first time a suspect has been eliminated because of his IQ."

* * *

Devlin sat at his desk trying to concentrate on the remaining suspects. None of them seemed as promising as the elusive Billy "The Kid" Thomas. He put in a call to a friend at federal probation. Maybe Thomas was still on parole.

While he waited for a callback, he called the C-4 secretary. "Sue, when I was upstairs this morning, I heard Bill Hagstrom being paged. Do you know if he's still in the office?"

"I'm looking at him. He's using Shanahan's desk while he's gone."

When Devlin got to the squad area, Hagstrom was just hanging up the phone. "Bill, I'm Mike Devlin. I work with Shanahan."

"You're the guy in the basement."

"Finally, some recognition."

Hagstrom laughed. "Where is that big Irish maniac?"

"The last I heard, he was in Grand Rapids interviewing enemies of the Bureau."

"Part of Sudder's nut theory?"

"You sound skeptical."

"I tried to explain it to Sudder, but it's extremely difficult to penetrate cement. I tried to tell him the third homicide was committed to mask any relationship between the first two. What he should be concentrating on is finding that relationship. He told me that he had already investigated that possibility and could find no connection."

"And?"

"And, I get paid to handicap people. I don't think your boss was being entirely truthful."

"Be thankful you're just passing through."

"Do you know who Welles Findley is?"

"The assistant director?"

"That's right. The director has ordered him in here to watchdog this case. I'll talk to him about it but, like Sudder, he wasn't promoted because of his ability to work a case. Was there anything I can help you with?"

"I just wanted to see if there was anyone who thought this last murder was a smoke screen."

"So far, I think we're the only two who do."

Fifteen minutes later, there was a soft knock at Devlin's door. It was Peggy Wilson, the typing supervisor. "Hi, Mike. Got a minute?"

"Sure. Come on in and sit down, if you can find room."

"I need you to initial off on these 302s. They're from the undercover project at the casino. The supervisor says all the logs have to be accounted for before he can close the case."

"Sounds like one of those fibs management tells so they can get their stuff to the front of the line."

"Tell *me* about it. We've been buried with the paper on the murders. Nothing else has been getting out of the pool. This s.o.b. makes up this nonsense so we'll do his dictation first. He must think I'm a virgin."

Devlin finished initialing the forms. "Thanks for walking these down, Peggy."

She looked at the clutter. "How are *you* doing?"

He did not answer. He was thinking about what she had said: *Nothing else had been getting out of the pool.* "Dictation is really backed up."

"Some of the stuff is a month and a half old," she said.

"Has anyone asked you to pull out all of John's and Brian's work?"

She thought for a second, as though she was wondering why no one had. "No."

"Well, they have now."

After forty-five minutes of searching assignment sheets, filing cabinets, and typists' drawers, Peggy piled eleven cassette tapes and seven rough-drafted letters on the desk in front of Devlin. He said, "I'm going to take these to my room."

"No problem. We wouldn't have gotten to them for another month."

On the way downstairs, Devlin picked up a tape player in

the technical equipment room. He drew a line down the middle
of a sheet of paper and started separating the items of dictation
by agent. Lawson had six and Blankenship twelve. First, Devlin scanned the rough-drafted pages. Most belonged to Brian.
They were terse and in the Bureau-ese that fugitive agents routinely used. Lawson's were a little longer and factually more
creative. None of them implied any circumstance that would
have resulted in murder.

Devlin dropped the first tape in the player. It was John Lawson. Eerily, the dead agent's voice filled the tiny room. "Please
help. I'm desperate." Devlin's heart beat four quick, hard
strokes. "This report is thirty days late at the Bureau. If you can
get it out right away, I'll have your baby." With his appeal
over, Lawson let his voice slip into a dictational drone. The report covered the very routine daily activities of one of Detroit's
LCN members for the preceding six months. The other tapes
were equally generic, until Devlin played one of Brian
Blankenship's.

"Steno, this is Brian R. Blankenship on C-Four dictating the
results of an agent-application interview board. Also present
were Special Agents R. William Dixon and John Thomas
Lawson . . ."

Devlin hit the stop button. Could that be the connection?
Applicant work was generally considered to be the most tedious and therefore the least sexy type of investigation in the
Bureau's rather deep quiver of challenging violations of federal law. But could it evolve into murder?

Applicants took written and psychological tests and, if
passed, were afforded an interview board. Agents trained in
evaluating them would ask a series of carefully designed questions to determine the applicants' suitability for the position of
Special Agent. Everything from first impression to current
events to work ethic was scrutinized. But for a considerable
number of candidates, the board was the end of the road. Under the oral assault of experienced street agents, lesser applicants were isolated and then sent to the employment gallows.

Every year, thousands of men and women were turned away, their hopes of becoming an FBI agent gone. But could that disappointment be great enough to cause someone to commit murder?

Some of the applicants did seem to have a long-distance relationship with reality. Devlin remembered one application that had been circulated in the office for its amusement value. Its author, who had listed his hobbies as weight lifting and firearms, had attached, as was required, a photograph of himself that turned out to be much more informative than the entire application. A bandanna held back his long dark hair and two bandoliers of ammunition crisscrossed his bare chest. A note was sent back telling him that the U.S. Marshal Service was looking for a few good men.

Since anyone could apply, maybe a rejection had been the final indignation for some delusional person who, like a thousand others in the country, stood daily on the brink of homicidal frustration.

Devlin called the radio room and asked them to put out a message in the Grand Rapids area for Shanahan to contact him immediately. Twenty minutes later he called, and Devlin explained what he had discovered.

"Christ, it's hard to picture an applicant committing murder, but it *is* a connection."

"Can you get Amy to run a list of all the applicants rejected by interview boards that John and Brian sat on?"

"Switch me up to her extension and I'll see if her computer can do that."

Devlin transferred Shanahan's call and within seconds Devlin's phone rang again. "Mike, she's on another line. She said to give her a couple of minutes and then switch me up there again."

"What's going on out there?"

"Slow motion. Especially having this poor bastard Conway moping around."

"That reminds me," Devlin said, and then told Shanahan

what Nick Trampelli had told him about how Conway had been hustled at the Oak Hollow Golf Course.

"That'll make his day when I tell him. And I will consider myself totally inept if I can't convert this to a long night of free drinking."

Devlin's other phone rang. It was Amy. Devlin again sent Shanahan's call to her. Five minutes later he called back.

"Nothing's ever easy. She can do the search, but the way the computer is set up, they don't distinguish between accepted and rejected. She can give you all the boards the two of them sat on together. Then you'll have to pull files and find out which applicants were turned down."

"When can she do it?"

"Hey, I owe you for this free night of drinking I'm about to enjoy. She's running them now."

After Devlin hung up, he called Wicks at Homicide. "Jerry, if your people haven't talked to the last suspect, have them hold off. We're checking on another possibility."

"Don't worry. We wouldn't have gotten to it for a while. We just got a fresh scene—a four bagger, and one of them is a minister. I've got the mayor's office on hold. Let me know." Wicks disconnected him.

Suddenly Devlin remembered Shanahan's conversation with Bill Hagstrom. What had he said about the taking of the badge and credentials? He called Hagstrom's extension, but there was no answer. Then he remembered Shanahan's notes.

Devlin found Shanahan's desk in its usual state. He always bragged that its disorder was part of an elaborate security system: If he could not find anything on it, how would some Russian spy? His filing system, once realized, was quite simple. Everything, whether worthless or priceless, was stacked in one precarious pile. Each item, like a glacier forced to give up its secrets every millennium or so, would be handled when it rotated to the top. Devlin took it as an extremely good omen when he found the notes of the conversation with Hagstrom after only ten minutes. Shanahan had written:

The fact that he has taken their forms of identification, their badge and credentials, may be his way of stripping them of their official identities. Not only has he killed them, he's also trying to erase the fact that they are FBI agents. He has a grudge.

Devlin considered the profiler's analysis. If the killer was a person who was told he was not good enough to be an FBI agent, he might react exactly as Hagstrom had said.

But was he creating a solution of convenience, reading nonspecifics into the evidence to support his theory? He had to keep in mind that this was just another possibility, not unlike the *obviousness* of the Grand Haven police officer or the *logic* of the list generated from the Blankenship arrests, which reminded him that Billy the Kid was still a good suspect.

An hour later, Amy brought a stack of printouts to his room. She said, "There's about ninety-four names. I can't tell exactly. Some are duplicates and some have been reinterviewed and passed. You'll have to pull the files to find out which." Devlin thanked her and she left.

Each sheet contained the information for an applicant: name, address, phone numbers, test scores, and file number. As Shanahan had said, the printout did not state whether the board had passed them or not, so Devlin headed for Closed Files.

Surprisingly, it was a simple matter to determine which applicants had failed their interviews. A Summary Status sheet was the top page in each file. One of its categories was *Interview Board*, after which a score was typed in, or the words *Not Acceptable* appeared.

Out of the ninety-four applicants, forty-eight had been permanently rejected. Recalling Hagstrom's "probably a white male," Devlin turned each of the forty-eight files upside down and opened the back cover to the last page of the first document filed, which was always the application itself. On the back of the last page was the applicant's photo. Devlin used these to divide the files into two stacks: white males and all others. There were thirty-two white males. He took them back to his room.

Something else occurred to Devlin. The last phase of an interview board was to allow the candidate to ask any questions he or she wanted. Many times the applicant, out of genuine interest, asked the board members about their individual assignments. It was, after all, their first chance to have a street agent's insight into the realities of the job. And the killer had possessed *specific* knowledge about his first two victims.

Then he considered the hollowpoints. Another piece of information the killer could have picked up during the interview. To murder them with standard Bureau ammunition could have been, at least in his mind, a further stripping of their dignity.

Devlin wanted to read each of the reports detailing the applicant's interview. They usually did not enumerate the candidate's questions, opting instead for a simple "showed interest in the operations of the Bureau"; but if he could find a question about hollowpoints or the agents' specific duties, he might have a starting point.

When he opened the first file to the interviewing board's report, an alarm went off in his head. On the cover sheet, the first item listed was the names of the interviewing agents—the *three* interviewing agents. There were always three agents on the board. If he was right and a rejected applicant was the Gentkiller, another agent could be in danger—*if* he was right. He checked the time. It was just after 8 P.M. Agents were at home, less vulnerable, but Devlin decided they should be notified as soon as possible. Quickly, he scanned the files making a list of *third* agents. The first two files had the same three agents' names. But when he opened the third file, he was stunned. The third agent's name was *Temper Hanlon*.

Something she had said during their last conversation replayed itself involuntarily: *We had just finished one of those god-awful interview boards.* Devlin grabbed the phone and called her house. After three long rings her husband answered.

"Tom. This is Mike Devlin. Is Temper there?"

"Hi, Mike. No, she got called out to work."

"How long ago?"

"About a half hour."

"Who called?"

"Clerk at the office. She said he was calling for her supervisor."

"Was she coming to the office?"

"No, he wanted to meet her at the Ferndale Train Station."

"The one that's a restaurant now?"

"Yeah. Why, is anything wrong?"

Devlin considered the popular restaurant, not the most likely place for a murder. "Not that I know of. Did she say which clerk called?"

"No, in fact she said it must have been a new one because she didn't recognize his voice."

"If you hear from her, have her call me at the office."

"Sure will, Mike."

Devlin hung up and headed for the night desk. The supervisor was typing up a complaint he had just received. Devlin asked, "Did one of the clerks call Temper Hanlon at home within the last hour?"

"I don't think so. John's the only one working right now. He's picking up trash. Let me page him." After the clerk called back, the supervisor said, "No, he said he hasn't phoned anyone tonight."

Devlin started toward the door. "Call the Ferndale Train Station. See if they can page Temper. I'm going out there. She may be in trouble."

As soon as Devlin's car cleared the garage, his radio spoke, "Central to Four-one."

"Go, Central."

"I tried calling the restaurant. All I got was a recording saying they were temporarily closed."

Devlin felt fear's insistent nausea. "Call the Ferndale PD. Tell them we think an agent is in trouble at that location. I'll meet them there. I'm about fifteen away."

A steady, muting rain had started to fall. Although Devlin drove recklessly through it, sometimes passing on the shoulder at eighty miles an hour, an imprisoning calm settled over him. He tried to ignore its cold, reasonable message: *It was too late*.

As he turned the last corner, a block from the restaurant, he jerked his foot off the gas pedal. He did not want to go any further. He could see the stationary blue lights twisting slowly in the slick, black parking lot, surrounding Temper Hanlon's pickup truck.

Devlin parked next to a police car that was blocking off the lot and identified himself. He walked over to her truck. The driver's door was open. Her body was on the ground next to it, covered with a blue plastic tarp. It was the last thing he wanted to do, but he looked under it. She had been shot twice in the forehead. Her mouth sagged crookedly toward the ground, but her eyes, still open, seemed to have found one last thing to smile at. Unexpectedly, Devlin thought about the fetus inside of her that would journey no further. Two lives had been taken. He put the palm of his hand against her still-warm cheek.

A uniformed sergeant walked over. "I'm sorry. We're trying to preserve the area for the evidence tech."

Devlin gently lowered the tarp over Temper's face. He stood back and let the cool rain distract him. As he looked around the confusing scene, he noticed for the first time that the restaurant was closed. He asked the sergeant why.

"Weird thing. We got a call today during lunch. Someone took a hornets' nest in the bathroom and rigged it to fall the next time the door opened. When it broke open, a couple of the customers got stung pretty bad, so they closed for the day. They thought they got all the hornets out but they wanted to give it overnight to make sure."

"Have you canvassed the neighborhood?"

"We're doing it now. But you can see, because this used to be an active train station, that there aren't many residences around here."

"Was anything taken from her?"

"The only thing we know for sure was her gun. The holster on her belt is empty."

"How about her badge and identification?"

"They're in her purse along with her wallet."

Without a badge, credentials, or a gun, an agent had no way to prove his or her official identity. Accumulatively, the killer had taken all these items from his victims. If he was not going to be allowed to be an agent, neither were they.

Devlin went to his car and picked up the mike. "Central, can you go to Papa?" He wanted to talk to them on the private, scrambled channel that could not be intercepted.

"Switching to Papa."

When they came up on the coded frequency, Devlin asked, "Are you aware of the situation here?"

"That's Ten-Four. Ferndale PD called back and notified us about ten minutes ago."

"Is the C-Four supervisor on his way out here?"

"We just got off the phone with him; he's en route."

Ten minutes later, Jim Harrison pulled into the parking lot. He identified himself to the officer in charge of the scene. He was given a brief rundown by the sergeant and inspected the body and the truck. He and Devlin got in his car.

"How'd you get here?" Harrison asked.

"Temper was running some stuff for me on the extortion through her medical contacts. I called her at home, and her husband told me she was out here. Said the new clerk called her. It didn't sound right, so I came out."

Harrison looked at Devlin suspiciously. "And that's all you know?"

"That's it," Devlin lied. If his applicant theory was wrong, Harrison did not need to be burdened with it. If he was correct, there would be no more murders, because all three board members were dead. He looked over at the rain running off of the blue tarp. If he was right, he wouldn't need anyone else.

Harrison said, "The office told me that the killer called Temper and said he was the new clerk. I wonder how he knew that there was a new clerk. And how did he get Temper's phone number?"

Devlin smiled sadly. "You know her. Take-no-prisoners. Her number was in the book."

"What about the clerk?"

"New clerks or even new agents never know when to hang up on someone asking too many questions. And if someone asks enough questions, they are eventually going to defend their ignorance by saying 'I'm new here.' This guy is no dummy."

Harrison gave him a hard look. "You sure you don't know anything more about this?"

"I'm working your goddamn extortion, remember?"

In a tone filled with doubt, Harrison said, "Sure." As Devlin looked off into the peaceful rain, a couple of television trucks arrived. "You'd better get out of here. Sudder's on his way, and I don't think he would be happy to see you hanging around."

More than anything, Devlin wanted to drive a hundred miles an hour back to the office and find out which applicants had been rejected by John, Brian, and Temper, but if he was right, there was no hurry—the Gentkiller's revenge was complete. Right now, he had to tell Knox about Temper. With the media at the scene, she would soon know.

As he walked in the house, the program Knox was watching was being interrupted with a news bulletin. Devlin switched off the set. She looked up at his face. "What's wrong?"

"I'm sorry. There's been another killing."

She stiffened. "Who was it?"

"Temper Hanlon."

She had met Temper at a wives' club party. "Temper. Wasn't she pregnant?"

"Yes."

"Why?"

"I have an idea it was a grudge killing. All of them were. If I'm right, there will be no more killings."

Devlin started to say something else, but Knox interrupted

him. "No, I don't want to hear anything else tonight. Just come to bed."

Upstairs, she looked in on both of the children as they serenely slept. She thought about Temper's unborn child and started crying.

In their bedroom, she settled into her husband's arms. She feared the morning, because she had recognized the look in her husband's eyes—the murderer had to be found, at any cost.

In the darkness, Devlin could feel her silently crying. Hours later she dropped off to sleep, but Devlin remained awake. Endlessly, Temper wandered in front of him, laughing, smiling, entertaining him with her irrepressible energy. Just before falling asleep, he remembered her last request of him: *When you catch up with whoever did it, throw in a little extra for me.*

III CHAPTER 15 III

By 5 A.M., with his promise to Temper burning inside of him, Devlin could no longer accept sleep's sanctuary. He dressed quickly. Knox, he suspected, was feigning sleep. He kissed her hard enough to wake her, but she did not stir. He left quietly.

The expressway was not crowded yet, so Devlin was able to reach the office in twenty minutes. On his desk sat the files of the thirty-two white males. He reviewed them and found nine applicants who had been rejected by interview boards made up of the three dead agents.

One by one, he went through the files and made notes on a pad of paper. He placed them in chronological order, the most recent rejections first. His experience had taught him that violent people were usually unable to wait for revenge to cool before serving it. The most recent were the most likely.

Considering the limited amount of time he had before Sudder permanently grounded him, Devlin decided the only investigative avenue open was to confront each person on the list.

Unexpected interviews were usually more productive because the guilty had less time to construct defenses. Devlin would have preferred to surprise each of the nine men, but *ambushes* took planning, which took time. Also, because of the nature of the person he was looking for, arriving unannounced was much safer. But these were advantages he could not afford.

He would use a ruse, telling the individuals they were being contacted for an entirely different reason. Then, at the most strategic point, he would surprise them with questions about the murder. It was not perfect, but the device would provide some advantage and safety for Devlin.

He would tell them, because of new federal legislation caused by the national increase in street crime, the Bureau had been mandated to hire a thousand new agents within the next year. The field offices had been instructed to reconsider all applicants previously turned down. And since these nine men had passed everything but the interview board, which was subjective at best, they would be first to be reevaluated.

Devlin wrote down a list of questions to be asked. He would tell the "applicants" that the questions had a variety of purposes. The first question was designed to test their recall: How many of the interview board members' names can you recall? Some would be able to remember the lead interviewer's name because of personal contacts setting up the appointment, but anyone who was able to recall all three would move to the top of Devlin's list.

The second question was: Why do you think you failed the interview? The killer, Devlin hoped, would lean toward blaming the three agents.

Then, under the guise of current events, he would ask the applicant to discuss any news stories involving the FBI. The local as well as the national news had been filled with the coverage of Gentkill. If any of them failed to mention it, Devlin would assume they were trying to avoid the topic and he would look at them a little closer. If they did bring it up, he would ask for as many details as they could remember, hoping the killer would reveal something only he knew.

Finally, under the heading *Investigative Skill*, the suspects would be asked how they would, given the opportunity, go about solving the murders. Devlin reasoned the murderer would have a one-of-a-kind insight. Hagstrom had defined the Gentkiller as compulsive, with extreme feelings of inadequacy, and willing to go to any length to defend his position.

Once the applicant presented his investigative strategy, Devlin would attack it, hoping to provoke him into exposing himself. He knew that anyone who was that fragile would be obsessed with demonstrating his authority, whatever the cost. Like the second shot fired into each of the victims, nothing was too excessive if it proved his point.

Of course, only the killer's interview, if he was in the stack of nine, would get that far. Then, depending on the situation, Devlin would determine whether he would become accusatory, inviting the suspect to take a polygraph, or withdraw quietly and seek a clandestine search warrant for his residence.

Devlin reread the questions. He was ready. He dialed the work number for the first name on his list. "Nicholas Draper, please."

"Speaking."

Devlin explained the reason for his call and the urgency of the interview; today would be best.

"Today would be great. Do you want me to come down there?"

Devlin knew he could not have people showing up at the reception desk and asking for him, especially people who obviously had nothing to do with the extortion, which was supposed to be his only concern. "No, I'm going to be out your way this morning. Is there someplace we could meet? I assume you don't want your employer to know you are considering employment elsewhere."

"Right, right. How long will this take?"

"Less than an hour."

Draper named a restaurant near his office. Devlin told him he would meet him there at eleven-thirty.

Devlin's other phone rang. It was Shanahan. "What the hell happened with Temper?"

Devlin explained how she had been lured to the restaurant and killed.

Shanahan asked, "Was she on any interview boards with John and Brian?"

"Yes."

"Then that's got to be it."

"Right now, it's just a coincidence. And not the first one I've run into in this case. Remember, I was so sure it was that Grand Haven cop that I drove over there to stack him up."

"What are you going to do, then?"

"There are nine white males who were rejected by the three of them. I'm going to do some pretext interviews. If he's one of them, maybe I can identify him."

"By yourself?" Devlin explained the phony-hiring story he was going to use. "Sounds safe enough, but if you get the slightest vibration you're on to someone, you call me."

"Of course. When will you be back?"

"Actually, we're less than an hour away. We got a call about six-thirty this morning. Sudder's calling everyone back. We just stopped for gas, so I thought I'd call you."

"What's Sudder want?"

"It's that Welles Findley the director sent in to look over Sudder's shoulder. I guess he feels he has to solve the case. He's taken a look at a bunch of the suspects and likes a couple of the nuts that we've interviewed and wants a concentrated effort on them. He has to show that he's made an investigative impact before the director gets here tomorrow. If you think they've had us jumping through some strange hoops up until now, just stand by. You *ain't seen nothin'* yet. You're one lucky sonofabitch, Devlin."

"It's been a while since anyone called me that. Lucky, I mean."

"You'll be running out logical leads while the rest of us will be fighting off nausea brought on by chasing our own tails."

"I'll see you after you get in."

Devlin called the second name on his list. The woman answering said he no longer worked there, and when Devlin asked where he might be contacted, she told him that the man had been transferred to Georgia three months earlier. After hanging up, Devlin checked his file. He had been interviewed almost six months earlier. Devlin drew a line through his name. *Eight to go.*

"Mr. Sudder, please hold for Mr. Pendleton."

Sudder cursed Devlin. He knew exactly what the purpose of Pendleton's call was: that damn report. And because of Devlin's foot-dragging, he was about to appear inept. "Malcolm, how are you?"

"Just fine, Jim."

"Good. I thought I would have heard from you or Agent Devlin by now."

"I know. I've been on him daily about the report, but he says there's a few loose ends to tie up. Did you see the article in the newspaper this morning?"

"Yes, I did. It quoted you as saying the case is closed."

"I did that intentionally so Devlin couldn't say it was his responsibility and delay this any longer."

"That's very smart, Malcolm. But if you come to work for us, you'll have to understand that, unlike the government, we are not concerned with who is at fault or what's being tried. We are interested only in results. Results, or profits, is how a corporation is measured. Results are always our goal."

"I see your point."

"Excellent. Allow me to make one more. Goals are meaningless without deadlines. Yours is tomorrow by the close of business. It's quite simple, really: If I have that report by five o'clock tomorrow afternoon, you have a job. We are interested in people who can get things accomplished."

"I understand, sir."

"What kind of loose ends does Devlin have?"

"He didn't say."

"I see. Devlin *does* work for you, doesn't he?"

"Of course, but . . ."

"*But* is an excuse word."

"You'll have the report without fail."

Pendleton hung up the phone. Theft was always a chance,

but that's why it was profitable. But the difference between those who profit and those who go to prison is the minimization of that chance. Once Devlin completed that report, and the serial numbers were taken out of the computer, there would be no risk. The insurance company will have paid off the five million, and Agent Devlin, along with the rest of the FBI, will have moved on to other priorities. And as far as everyone but Pendleton was concerned, the million dollars sitting tax-free in the safety-deposit box would no longer exist.

Sudder gave Charles Wiggens a direct order. "Don't come back here without Devlin." After a frantic fifteen-minute search, the supervisor found him in his basement room.

When Devlin was escorted into the SAC's office, Sudder looked at him. "Let me say this again: You were ordered to bring me that report *today*."

Devlin noticed Wiggens writing furiously. "I told you. If I'm going to be responsible for its content, I have to be satisfied with its accuracy."

"Have you seen the morning paper?"

"No."

Sudder handed him one from the pile on his desk. "Open it to page three." There was a long article about the extortion. Included were a number of photographs, everything from Jousef Haidar with his immigration number held in front of him to the final scene of burned-out cars. One large photo, with surprising clarity, reproduced all three demand notes. A number of drawings traced the routes of the tow trucks, and a timetable tracked Haidar's short life in the land of opportunity. "Did you see where I'm quoted as saying the case is closed?" Devlin did not answer. Sudder's tone became emphatic. "*I'm* taking the responsibility for the content of your report. It's all there in black and white, in a major newspaper." Devlin continued his silence. "I have called back to the Bureau. They told me if I don't have that report by tomorrow, I can go ahead and fire you. So I'm going to say it officially, for the record: This *is* your last chance. By eleven A.M. tomorrow morning. On my desk. The Seacard extortion report or your credentials. And if you decide not to submit that report, I want you here by eleven anyhow. This time I want to know exactly where you are prior to the director's arrival so you can't embarrass me again."

Standing up, Devlin put his hands on Sudder's desk and leaned within inches of his face. "It'll always be a mystery to me how people like you are put in charge when your only priority is to screw up people's lives so you can hate yourself a little bit less. You're nothing but a pain in a decent agent's ass." Devlin pushed off the desk violently and, in a threatening voice, said, "I'll see you tomorrow morning!"

As Devlin exited the SAC's office, he noticed Shanahan next to the doorway talking to the secretary. He followed Devlin down the hall and, at a safe distance from the ears of the front office, asked, "Are you going to do the report?"

"I'm going to bring this case to its logical conclusion."

Shanahan stopped and raised his voice as Devlin continued to walk away. "You're not going to do it, are you? You hardheaded . . ."

Devlin turned back to him. "I would think with the director coming to town a creative guy like you would have plenty to do."

Shanahan smiled, and little candles of mischief lit up his eyes.

Back in the SAC's office, Sudder turned to Wiggens. "Charles, I want you to take care of something for me. It's very important."

"Yes, sir."

"By no later than ten tomorrow morning, I want you to have that extortion report done for me. I am sure Devlin won't do it and with the director coming I want everything in order."

"That should be no problem. Whose name do you want on it?"

"Use mine. Pendleton will like that."

Tomorrow, Sudder thought, was going to be a great day. The director was coming in to remove him as SAC, but instead, Sudder could beat him to the punch and announce he was quitting this thankless job. And then he would personally drive the extortion report out to Pendleton in time for lunch. But as satisfying as all that would be, the thing he looked forward to the most was firing Mike Devlin.

As Sebastian Draxler was about to leave his office, the phone rang. "Hello."

"Doctor Draxler, as someone who has been involved in breaking the law most of my life, I've got to tell you, your plan was the most brilliant thing I've ever seen."

"Who is this?"

"You really don't need to know who I am for what we are about to do."

"What are we about to do?"

"We're about to become *associates*."

"Associates? In what?"

"That million dollars you got from Seacard."

"What are you . . ."

"Doctor, I've complimented your intelligence. Please don't insult mine. Let me explain my position. I think you are a man who appreciates efficiency, so let's save all that time we would have spent trying to bullshit each other. I am, by profession, a burglar. I've done a considerable amount of time in prison. At present, I occasionally do some work for a private investigator who will also remain nameless. He was recently hired by Mister X, who felt his wife was being unfaithful. So my employer had me put a recorder on her phone line. Well, it turns out she was hot and very heavy with a young man named Jousef Haidar. He told her everything. How he would soon have enough money so she could leave her husband and be with him. And then he told her about you and Seacard and five million dollars. When he was killed, and all that money was burned up, I thought my golden goose had up and died. But when I read the first story about it in the paper, it dawned on me that you had no exposure at all. They had all this evidence link-ing Haidar to the extortion, even that crap about the terrorist group, but nowhere did Doctor Draxler's name appear. So I started wondering about things like, why were there five different cars, which meant five times as many chances for something to go wrong? And five different routes? But what bothered me the most was putting the money in the car with the explosives. I've been a thief and in prison most of my life. Anyone who has ever used explosives will tell you, never put them with the money. See, if I wanted to blow up the cars to get rid of evidence, although I doubt if you left any in those cars, I would have made five little bombs and set them in those wrecks *after* I took the money out. The only thing I could think of was that the money was supposed to burn, but I couldn't figure out why. That's why when you went to your office the other night, I broke into your house."

"That's impossible!" Draxler said angrily.

"One seven nine seven one." Hollings recited Draxler's alarm combination, his voice composed. Draxler was silent. His mind raced through his house searching for evidence of the extortion. "Yes, Doctor, I found the hidden shelf downstairs in the ceiling. If you need further convincing, go downstairs and check your fax machine."

Draxler set the phone down and hurried to the basement. For the first time since he was a child, what he saw panicked him. In the receiving cradle of the fax machine were a number of pages. The last one was being received as Draxler watched. The top sheet contained all three demand notes, freshly typed, as they appeared in the newspaper. At the bottom, the brand name, model, and serial number of the typewriter was also listed. Draxler realized that the typewriter was missing. The caller had used it to type the demand notes. His message was obvious. The FBI's laboratory, if the burglar gave it to them, could match Draxler's typewriter to the demand notes.

The other pages were wiring and mechanical diagrams for the cars. There were no specifics on the sheets to connect Draxler to them, but he was sure he could be identified through his handwriting or the latent fingerprints he had undoubtedly left on them. He cursed the vanity that convinced him to keep mementos of his "perfect" crime.

Now, for the first time, he understood the terror that Seacard had felt, unable to defend itself against an unseen enemy. He laughed loudly. Their suffering was as rewarding as their money.

He picked up the basement phone and, in a voice that was efficient but slightly unsure, said, "Continue."

"Even after I had all your notes I couldn't figure it out until I read the paper this morning. One of the things you had drawn was what looked like a map, but there were no streets marked on it, just this right-angle turn with a line leading away to a parking lot. But the paper had all the routes the tow trucks had taken. The one through the woods is your little map. Then I figured out the remote-control trapdoor diagram and why all the boxes had to be placed on the rear floors that were painted black so you couldn't see the one false bottom. The money was put in the cardboard boxes so it would completely burn. It all fit together. As the truck went up that road you dropped the box, took the money, and had your car in the parking lot. Absolutely ingenious."

Draxler knew he, like Seacard, had no choice. "How much?"

"Just two hundred and fifty thousand. Now, I know you think that's a lot, but you know if I asked for half, you'd have to give it to me. But this was your score. You put a lot of effort into it."

"That's very generous of you."

Hollings felt Draxler's sarcasm. "Sorry, I've got obligations."

"And what obligations will you have to *me*?"

"What I *have* is good news for you but bad news for me." Hollings paused. "I've got cancer."

"Cancer?"

"My lungs. Three to four months at the outside. That's why

I need the money. For my family. The only thing I've ever given them in the past is grief. That's why it's important that I leave them something now. So I'll trade your property for the two hundred and fifty K, and in a couple of months I'll just be a bad memory."

"Does the private detective know anything about this?"

"No."

"What about Haidar's girlfriend?"

"I'll have a talk with her. A bonus. It won't cost you anything extra."

"I would like that resolved before we go any further."

"Since we're going *further* today, I'll talk to her right away."

"Today?"

"Right now, time is very precious to me. I'll call you at four and we'll plan on getting together tonight."

"And then I won't hear from you again?"

"Doctor, I feel bad taking any part of your payday. This is a onetime shot for my family so I can die in peace. And, Doctor . . ."

"Yes?"

"It *was* brilliant."

Draxler was reluctant to accept the compliment, but one of the best parts of brilliance was recognition. "Thank you."

The third name on Devlin's list was Joseph Bouton. He worked as an assistant manager for Sears in Livonia, a western suburb of Detroit. The woman answering the phone paged him. Thirty seconds later, he picked up the phone. "May I help you?"

Devlin introduced himself and explained the purpose of the call. If Bouton was still interested, he should be interviewed immediately. Bouton agreed and chose a nearby park for one o'clock that afternoon.

Devlin had listened carefully to not only Bouton, but Nicholas Draper, whom he was to meet in fifteen minutes. Neither man had seemed apprehensive or reluctant.

Of the eight remaining suspects, Devlin had appointments to see two of them. If he could set up two more for that night, with a little luck he could schedule the last four for the next day. He had decided not to let Sudder's threat of "tomorrow" deter him.

Nicholas Draper had chosen a Mexican restaurant. He was working feverishly on his second basket of chips when Devlin arrived. The salsa bowl was nearly empty and a good portion of it speckled the white paper place mat in front of him. Devlin estimated that he was at least fifty pounds over the Bureau weight standard.

Draper wiped his hand on an already exhausted paper napkin and shook hands eagerly. "Nice to meet you." Before Devlin sat down, Draper's fingers were back in the basket of chips. Spotting the wounded place mat, he checked his tie for similar trauma.

"What's good here?" Devlin asked.

"Everything! Ever had nopalitos?"

"What are they?"

"Cactus. Without the needles, of course. The Mexicans consider it a delicacy."

"Is that what you're having?"

"No. The Mexican sandwich. It's a little more for your money."

When the waiter took their order, Draper ordered the Mexican sandwich with extra cheese and Devlin ordered a cup of coffee. Devlin asked, "Do you mind if we do this while you eat?"

"Not at all. I've only got an hour for lunch."

Draper finished off the second basket of chips and signaled for another. If he was the Gentkiller, it was not affecting his appetite. Devlin enjoyed watching the passion and efficiency with which Draper eliminated his food. He could not imagine this man, who was so preoccupied with maintaining his blood sugar level, having killed anyone unless that person happened to wander into the path of his knife and fork. "I think an hour will be much more than we'll need."

After Devlin left the restaurant, he headed toward Livonia and his second interview. Draper was still working on his meal. The sandwich, layered with tortillas, meat, gravy, and an occasional vegetable, was as big around as a sombrero. If his life insurance company had seen the amount of cheese covering it, they would have been forced to cancel the "natural causes" portion of his policy. Fortunately, by the time Draper started to sweat, Devlin had completed his questions. Draper could not remember any of the agents' names who had interviewed him, but they had made him somewhat uncomfortable about his weight, telling him he was expected to maintain a certain level of fitness not only during training but later in the field. He knew his weight would be a problem, but thought he would "give it a shot anyhow." All in all, he was fairly happy with his life. Devlin did not bring up the agent murders. Mentally, he lined him off of the list. *Seven to go.*

Joseph Bouton was more like what Devlin was looking for. He had a chronically dissatisfied look about him. His eyes seemed almost black and had a distrusting intensity about them. They were unsettling, never looking away from Devlin as they talked.

Devlin started with the usual disarming small talk, which had no effect on Bouton. He wanted to talk about becoming an FBI agent and little else.

"Okay, Joe . . ."

"Joseph."

Devlin figured it was never too soon to start pressing buttons. "What's wrong with *Joe*?"

" 'S'not my name." Bouton's clipped speech was offensive, signaling that he had better things to do.

"Okay, Joseph. I've got some questions I need to ask you . . ."

"If I get them right, will I get hired?"

"I'm sorry. There are no right answers . . ."

"Oh, so this is to be subjective, like that goddamn interview panel that flunked me. Do you know how well I did on the written test?"

"I know you did quite well." Devlin had no idea of Bouton's test score. "That's why I'm here talking to you. We can't understand how the board could have rejected you when, up until that point, you had been such an outstanding candidate. This happens sometimes with inexperienced interviewers. Did you have any type of confrontation with them?"

"No."

"Let me see if we're talking about the same people. Do you remember any of their names?"

"Agent John Lawson, another guy, and a girl named Temper something. She said she was an agent."

"Yes. They were all agents. Why do you think they gave you the grades they did?"

"Does this question count?"

"Only your honesty counts."

Although Bouton's eyes were locked on Devlin, they seemed to be snapping back and forth. Something was straining behind them. "I think they were afraid of me." He leaned back and folded his arms, as if no further explanation was necessary.

"Afraid of what, Joseph?"

"Same thing that has plagued me my entire life—competition. Afraid I'd be better than them."

"How do you deal with that? It has to be awfully frustrating, knowing you're better and not getting a chance to prove it."

"Damn right it is."

"Well, how do you deal with it?"

"I just work harder, become better."

"Ever think about letting those agents know how you feel?"

"Waste of time. If I told them, they'd ignore me. That's what always happens. They ignore me."

"When that happens, what do you do to get someone's attention?"

Bouton's eyes finally shifted downward; his words softened. "That's something I've been asking myself my whole life, but I can't seem to find an answer."

"If someone had done to me what they did"—Devlin hesitated, to underscore his candor—"I'd find some way to get even."

Bouton looked up, confused. "How could you get even with an FBI agent?"

The answer took Devlin by surprise. The thing that had attracted Bouton to the FBI was what now absolved him of any involvement in the murders—the myth that the FBI was unconquerable. A place that, once reached, would calm the obsessive-compulsive Roman candles that ruled his mind. For such people, becoming an FBI agent was a level of achievement that could not be challenged and would finally silence their critics. But unfortunately, when the Bureau rejected those people, they felt it was a confirmation of their inadequacy. Devlin suspected that the killer, if a refused applicant, suffered from a similar misjudgment.

But Bouton, in his own disoriented way, had too much reverence for the FBI and its agents to be the Gentkiller. Additionally, he was not able to remember all three agents' names. Devlin was now sure if he could find someone who did, he would have the killer.

Six to go.

||| CHAPTER 16 |||

Time's incorruptible persistence was now becoming another of Devlin's enemies. He had six suspects to go, and by eleven the next morning, Sudder would, at the very least, further obstruct his efforts to eliminate them.

When he returned to the office, he found the mail clerk knocking on his door. "What brings you down to the disenchanted forest?"

The clerk smiled. "I wasn't sure this is where you were. I've been trying to catch you for a couple of days to give you your mail."

Devlin took the stack of envelopes and thanked him. He sat down at his desk and laid them aside. The next suspect was Stanley Sadowski, a CPA who worked at a downtown Detroit accounting firm. Devlin called him.

"Gee, that sounds really great, Mr. Devlin, but I have a class tonight. I'm working on my MBA so I'll be a little more attractive to the Bureau the next time around. I would be available after nine o'clock."

Devlin was looking for shortcuts now. "At your home?" He did not like the idea of meeting a suspected killer on his own ground for a number of reasons, but he had no choice.

"That would be fine. Nine-thirty?"

"I've got the address."

Absentmindedly, Devlin picked up his mail and started flipping through the envelopes. He stopped suddenly when he got to a large brown envelope addressed to him. He recognized the green, slashing handwriting. It was Temper Hanlon's.

Inside was a smaller envelope with a note from her, dated two days earlier.

Devlin,

Enclosed are some more of the employee records from Bridgeline Glove. Mr. Codswallor mailed them to me, and when I called him to thank him, he said they were some he had found around the house, but the bulk of them were still up north. He was leaving that night to go up there and would bring them back in a couple of days. Since I've been out sick so much, I gave him your number. My truancy is also the reason I have put this in the mail.

Once again, us white-collar pukes have made you violent-crime cowboys look good. The next time I see you, I expect to be worshiped.

Temper

For a moment, Devlin could hear her laughing and he could smell her perfume lingering on the pages.

He opened the enclosed envelope from Codswallor and halfheartedly scanned the records, stopping occasionally to make notes. He called Riley Smith in Ann Arbor and updated him.

"This is getting interesting, Mike. I called Seacard's head of security like you suggested. He said Pendleton had given him explicit instructions that if the five boxes were recovered, he was to make sure he was present and then take them unopened to the Grayton State Bank and personally stand guard until Pendleton got there. So I called my contact at the bank. He said that the president is a golfing buddy of Pendleton's and not to contact him unless you want Pendleton to know about it." Smith stopped talking and Devlin could hear him shuffling through papers. "Here's something you're going to like.

Pendleton rented a safety-deposit box the day of the drop and, later the same day, paid it a visit."

"I guess we know what's in the box."

"Yeah. Just waiting for the serial numbers to cool off. The only question is how much is in there."

"Do you think we've got enough for a search warrant?"

"I've been giving it some thought. The probable cause is borderline. This all started with some suspicions you had about Pendleton. I'm sure you're right, but they are still only observations. An even bigger problem is we can't prove there was a theft. Officially, all the money was burned. We have some evidence, but it's very circumstantial. The judge signing search warrants this week is tough. He wants action when something's wrong, but you better be damn sure you can prove something's wrong."

"What you said about the bank president gave me an idea. Here's what we can do . . ."

When Devlin was done explaining, he said, "Sudder's been all over me about this report. If I don't have it to him by eleven tomorrow morning he's threatened to fire me."

"Neal Ferguson told me Pendleton has offered Sudder a nice, fat job. I'm sure it's contingent upon the report being submitted."

"Now it all makes sense. I lied to Pendleton and told him the report was necessary to remove the serial numbers from NCIC. He's using the job offer to ensure its delivery."

"Didn't anyone ever teach you that lies can come back and bite you in the ass?"

"I think we're about to find out if that's true."

A great reluctance entered Smith's voice. "Mike, I don't know if you heard. The little girl from the second bombing died this morning."

Devlin let the phone slip out of his hand, onto the cradle. He slowly closed his eyes and again was looking into the hospital room window. He remembered a pair of perfect lips and a kind, fragile hand.

* * *

"Doctor Draxler?"

Draxler recognized the caller's voice immediately. "Yes," he answered with uncharacteristic resignation in his voice.

"Are we ready?"

Draxler looked at his suitcases. "I think so. What about the girl? You were going to talk to her."

"I just hung up with her. I explained how she was an accessory to the murders, because she knew about everything beforehand, and because she had planned to enjoy the fruits of the crime with her boyfriend." Hollings chuckled. "She's scared shitless. In fact, she agreed to also make a contribution to my retirement fund. Don't worry—she'll never be heard from again."

"Good. Now, how do you suggest I get this money to you?"

"Well, it won't be quite as ingenious as the way Seacard got it to you, but I think you can understand my wanting to remain anonymous."

"Perfectly."

"In Detroit, there's a bar, Doc's, on the corner of Fort and Green. There's a police station across the street, so don't get nervous. It comforts me to know there's a cop around if I need one. There's a phone outside the bar. Be there as soon as it gets dark and wait for my call."

"What about the items you have of mine? When will I get them back?"

"After I have the money, I'll return them within twenty-four hours. I'll drop them off someplace where no one will be able to find them but you."

"Are they in a secure location where someone won't stumble across them until then?"

"Where I have them, no one could find them."

"I'll await your call." A MISTAKE.

Devlin called the fifth suspect, David Jackledge. He worked at Dynetech, an international computer corporation. "Corporate security. Dave Jackledge. Can I help you?" Devlin gave his applicant pretext again. "I see. When would you need to talk to me?"

"Tonight would be best for me. Wherever is convenient for you. Dave, can you hold on a minute? I've got another call . . . Thanks." Devlin set the receiver down and picked up the ringing telephone. "Mike Devlin . . . Oh, yes, Mr. Codswallor . . . I appreciate it. How about the list of fired and disgruntled employees? . . . Great. I'm working on this alone, so I'll have to pick them up myself. Will I need some boxes or will they fit in my briefcase? . . . Good. Right now a list can't be too short. I'll copy it tomorrow and mail it back. Is seven o'clock good? . . . See you then." Devlin hung up and picked up the other phone. "Dave, I'm sorry. They've got me buried down in this dungeon, which features some of the finest telephone equipment manufactured in the seventeenth century."

Jackledge laughed. "I understand. You would think with a name like Dynetech we would be on the cutting edge, but sometimes it seems like the seventeenth century is light-years into the future."

Devlin laughed. "Are you available for an interview tonight?"

"Definitely."

"I've got one stop to make first, then I would need less than an hour of your time. Where's good for you?"

Jackledge lowered his voice. "I moonlight at night. The company discourages it, but it's ten dollars an hour. It's helping me pay off my college loans."

"Would it be okay to meet you there?"

"Oh, yeah. I work as a security guard. It's usually just me and a couple of other guys. No bosses. They move us around a lot. Let me put you on hold. I'll call and see where I'm at tonight."

Devlin's other phone rang. "Mike. How are you?" It was Knox.

"I'm fine."

"I'm at St. Barney's with the kids. I'd like to go to Temper's wake tonight. Can you stop by and pick me up? Father said he'd watch the kids."

"Sure. I've got a couple of phone calls to take care of. I'll see you in about an hour."

"Thanks."

Devlin went back to the other phone and waited for Jackledge to come back on the line.

"Mr. Devlin . . . Tonight we will be at the old Cadillac plant on Jefferson."

"The one they're tearing down?"

"That's the one. That's why they need us there. Thieves come in to steal plumbing or anything else that's metal, which isn't that big a deal. But if they injure themselves then they want to sue General Motors."

"Thieves have rights too."

Jackledge laughed. "As a native Detroiter, I'm well aware of that."

"Dave, I should be out there between eight and eight-fifteen. I have to pick something up in Oakland County. But I'll be coming straight out from there. So if I'm a little late, that's why."

"No problem. I'm there until midnight."

As he drove up Cass Avenue, Devlin replayed Knox's words, looking not for any sort of armistice but rather for a return to that toughness he had always admired in her. That she wanted to accompany him to Temper's wake was a good sign, a rejoining of their purposes. But he knew Knox well enough to realize that the skirmish was not over.

Father Richter greeted Devlin with a handshake. "I'm sorry about Temper Hanlon."

"Thanks, Father. I'm supposed to pick Knox up."

Richter looked at the clock on the wall. "You're a little early. She'll be done in a minute."

"Has she said any more to you about all of this?"

Richter smiled playfully at Devlin. "And what, violate the sanctity of the confessional?"

"Father, I know there's no confessional here." Devlin held up a ten-dollar bill.

"I think you've found a loophole in the tenets of the Church." The priest grabbed the money from Devlin's hand and pushed it into a locked donation box near the front door.

"Mike, it's simple. She feels threatened. Not for herself, for you. She's one of the most empathetic creatures the good Lord ever designed. She not only cares about other people, she somehow becomes them when they are in crisis. It is truly a rare quality. If the Church could bottle it, there would be no more problems in this world."

"I know Knox. I've tested her Christianity more times than God tested Job, but she's never reacted like this before."

"The murders of the agents have caused her to identify with their spouses, and she has gained a terrifying insight into your being killed, especially after seeing that dead agent the other night. She's experiencing pure, intense panic. That's why she's spending more and more time here. If she's not home, she can't get that phone call. I've seen this before. As police chaplain, I have dealt with a lot of cops and their families. You build a wall between yourselves and the rest of the world, including your family. You think if you rid the world of evil, your family will automatically be safe. But Knox resents that. She knows you live dangerously. Hell, that's probably why she married you. But because you make it seem so secret, she feels as threatened as if it were another woman. Believe me, she just wants to be let inside. To be, in her words, involved in your conspiracies to ensure the survival of the world."

"She said that?"

"Just talk to her, Michael."

Devlin walked back to the kitchen and found his children washing and drying dishes. "Hi, Daddy," Kathleen said energetically.

"Hi, Katie." He looked at his son, whose head was down in an obvious display of dissatisfaction. "Hi, Pat."

"Dad, men don't have to do dishes, do they?"

"Men have to do dishes and boys have to do dishes. The difference is that men don't complain about it." The boy's face did not seem reassured by his father's words; he just knew he could no longer complain. Devlin asked him, "Where's Mom?"

Without raising his head, he thumbed over his shoulder at a small living room. With one last attempt at clemency, he said, "Then how come I never see you doing them?"

Devlin left the question unanswered. He went to the doorway of the living room and found Knox with an eight- or nine-year-old girl in her lap. The child's cap lay upside down on the floor next to the chair. Small blue gems dotted her earlobes. As Knox read to her, she stroked the fuzzy blond scalp of the girl's head with her cheek. The girl was drifting off and had a serene smile. Devlin had seen his wife like this before. She would read and caress long after the child was deeply asleep, as if making the girl's dreams happier. She did not notice Devlin.

He walked back into the kitchen and said, "Katie, why don't you take a break. Us men will finish here." Careful not to let her brother see her, she nodded knowingly to her father. He watched her leave, thankful that she took after her mother. She tiptoed into the living room and silently studied her mother's gentleness.

As Devlin and Patrick were finishing, Knox came into the kitchen and told Patrick he could go and quietly watch television with his sister. With a trace of a sardonic smile, she said, "Are you just helping out or are you considering a career change?"

"A change wouldn't be bad. Maybe it's time for me to take one of those nice desky coordinator's jobs. Mike Devlin, drug-reduction coordinator or Mike Devlin, media representative."

Knox laughed deeply. Devlin realized he had not heard her

laugh since John Lawson's murder. "You? Media rep? That should enhance the Bureau's image."

David Jackledge sat in front of the computer at his desk and queried: MIKE DEVLIN. The on-line informational service his company used accessed the full text of more than sixty newspapers. The only article with Devlin's name in it had been in the *Detroit News*:

Today Marion Lee Tungworth was identified by Special Agent in Charge Royal K. Pilkington as the Puget Sound Murderer. Tungworth, according to Pilkington, was responsible for the death of more than forty women in the Seattle, Washington, area.

Tungworth, a Detroit native, had kidnapped the sixteen-year-old daughter of FBI agent Thomas Anderson. Ms. Anderson was returned to her family unharmed after a shootout that left Tungworth and Agent Edgar Livingston dead and another agent, Mike Devlin, wounded.

An unnamed source at the Detroit Police Department stated that Agent Devlin, contrary to claims by the FBI hierarchy, was in fact responsible for identifying Tungworth as the killer and the girl's safe release. When asked about the statement, FBI officials declined comment.

Jackledge did not finish the article. He closed his eyes and remembered Devlin's back outside the glove factory. What the report had said was evidently true: Devlin was someone to be reckoned with. Somehow, he had figured out the connection between the Gentkill victims.

Jackledge had overheard the conversation with Codswallor. Amos Codswallor. How could he forget that name? The day Codswallor had fired him, Jackledge had called him "cock swallower." And now he was causing problems again, giving Devlin a list of fired employees. Right now, Devlin had to be fishing—otherwise he would not be using that clumsy applicant ruse. But once he had time to sit down with those Bridge-line records and find Jackledge's name, he would know exactly who the killer was. He cursed himself for using the factory, but it was an area he was familiar with. He was not going to make that mistake this time. The old Cadillac factory had no connection to him. He knew it was unguarded, because he had scouted it when he was planning Lawson's murder.

What else did that reporter say? Devlin works alone and usually against orders. And that's what he told Codswallor on the phone: He was working alone, "in a dungeon." Reading between the lines of the newspaper article, that seemed to be the way he preferred it.

Jackledge had only one choice: He had to kill Devlin and get that list in his briefcase. That briefcase, with Jackledge's name in it, would be the most ironic souvenir of all.

Devlin sat with Knox in the back of the chapel. A steady stream of people were shaking hands with Temper Hanlon's husband. He smiled weakly and thanked them for coming; the confusion never left his eyes. Knox leaned silently against Devlin, both of her hands around his arm.

An exhausted woman in a dark dress walked over to them and said, "Excuse me, I'm Sandy Lawson."

Devlin stood up. "I'm Mike Devlin. This is my wife, Knox."

"Yes, I know who you are. I'm sorry I missed you at John's wake but it . . . it was a very difficult time . . ."

Knox was up and had her arm around Lawson's widow. "We're so sorry. Please, sit with us." Everyone sat down and Knox asked, "Is there anything we can do to help?"

"Oh, no, thank you. We're doing better. At least the girls and I are. But my son, Sean, he's twelve, and I think he's feeling the pressure of being the only male in the family now. I brought him with me tonight to show him this happens to other families, but he refused to come in."

Devlin asked, "Would you like me to go and see if he's all right?"

"I think it would be good for him to talk to another man, especially an agent."

"I'd be glad to."

"He's outside. You'll know him when you see him—looks like his dad. And if you don't mind, could you talk to him about baseball?"

"Baseball?"

"Yes. He's quite a baseball player. Just finished the Little League season and made all-stars. But he quit. He and his dad used to practice all the time. Now that John is gone, he says he hates baseball. If you ever saw him play, you'd know he loves it."

"I'll take care of it."

As Devlin stood up to leave, Sandy Lawson grabbed his hand and squeezed it. "Thank you so much." Knox could see that she was grateful for more than him talking to her son. After Devlin left, she looked at Knox. "I'm sorry. About the only reason I haven't completely lost my mind is because of what your husband is doing. I know as someone who believes in God I should not want revenge, but I just can't get rid of my anger. I remember John telling me about when Mike saved Tom Anderson's daughter. He was a great admirer of your husband. So when I heard that he was looking for John's killer on his own . . . Well, I'm very thankful."

During the drive back to St. Barney's, Devlin thought about Father Richter's advice, and even though it still seemed illogical, he started telling Knox what he was doing to find the killer. As he spoke, he could see relief flood her eyes. When he finished, she told him what Sandy Lawson had said, and then said, "Father Richter says as long as there are murderers on this earth, God will provide someone to stop them. Just promise me you won't do anything dangerous; I have a bad feeling about this."

"Don't worry. From here on, it's on automatic pilot. I won't go anywhere near the edge."

Devlin parked in front of the hospice and they went in. He

asked, "How much longer are you going to be here? You know I don't like you driving through this neighborhood late at night."

"I know, but Father asked me to do some mailings for him."

"For contributions?"

"What else? I saw the latest projections. By the end of the year, he'll be six hundred thousand dollars in the red. He's afraid the Church will close him down."

Devlin whistled.

"I know. And they do so much for these kids here. The problem is, there's so many organizations asking for help."

"But they don't have you and Father Arm-Wrestle threatening them."

Knox laughed. "That's why I want to get those letters out. There are too many to finish tonight, so if it's all right, the kids and I are going to stay over tonight. Once Father locks up, it's a real fortress. The precinct cars check on us regularly. That way, I can finish in the morning."

"Okay. I've got a couple of interviews tonight, so I'll be working late. I'll call you in the morning." Devlin went into the living room and kissed his children good-night. He stopped by the library to thank Father Richter for his help. The priest was scowling at the accounting ledgers that were spread out on his desk like maps of enemy positions. "Too bad bank robbery is still a sin," Devlin said.

The priest smiled a calm, tired smile. "How did it go with Knox?"

"Exactly as you said it would. I think you bought me some breathing room. She and the kids are staying the night."

"I know you're concerned about them being down here; they'll be fine."

"I know."

The priest's voice changed its rhythm. "Have you ever wondered why Knox comes down here?"

"I guess because she loves helping these kids."

"That's the obvious answer. But there's another reason. Do you remember when she first started coming here?"

"Right after she met you, a year or so ago."

"Well, it wasn't right after she met me; it was a couple of months later. But it *was* right after you were shot."

Devlin thought for a moment. "I don't understand what one has to do with the other."

"She is a woman of strong religious belief. I think she sees her time here as storing up some sort of currency, which she can spend to protect you. As long as you're out there traveling the roads you do, she'll be coming here to provide for your safe passage. And the more danger she perceives, like now, the more time she'll spend here. Fortunately for me, she needs St. Barney's as much as the kids who come here."

Devlin wondered how he had not seen what the priest had. "I guess I take too much for granted."

"Don't be too hard on yourself. This is what I do for a living."

"Thanks, Father. I'll get out of here and let you get back to keeping this place afloat."

Father Richter smiled warmly. "You've seen the children here. Do you think God would allow this place to be taken from them? Or Knox?"

"I don't think God's worried about it. He knows a tough gatekeeper when he sees one."

III CHAPTER 17 III

Sebastian Draxler considered the murder he was about to commit and dismissed it as meaningless. It was as inconsequential as the deaths of the others. This blackmailer, an admitted lifelong thief and convict, would be missed even less.

Foolishly, he had told Draxler that all the evidence he had stolen was in a place where no one could find it. But if someone did, it lacked anything specific to identify Draxler. Without the blackmailer's finger-pointing, it was just some drawings and a typewriter.

And within twenty-four hours, none of this would matter. He would be living in the place of his birth, Germany. He remembered the longing in his father's eyes for the "old country" after Seacard had dismissed him. His spirit had been broken, and he was capable of only the most menial work. Ironically, he was employed irregularly as a gas-station attendant, pumping the fluid for which he had developed a number of chemical processes when he was a chemist for Seacard Industries. He was responsible for research that had enabled the corporation to receive over two dozen patents. The resulting profits were incalculable. When he filed suit, claiming that he had developed one of the procedures on his own time in a home laboratory, Seacard's attorneys mowed him down in court, and he was fired without being given a penny. Draxler wished he had burned a hundred million of their dollars.

When terminated, his father was fifty-five years old and emotionally unable to recover. He would sit and dreamily recall the grandeur, the precision, and the immaculate order of the Germany of his youth. Now, with the country reunited and its economy straining, Draxler's million dollars could be judiciously invested. Separately, East and West Germany were world powers in the chemical industry. United, they would someday dwarf the United States, and Draxler's fortune would be made. But first, this common thief had to be dealt with. By night's end, he would be dead.

From among his luggage, Draxler picked up an attaché case and set it carefully on a table. He opened it and made the final electrical connections. He had booby-trapped the case in the event that its lid was forced open. He closed the top and carefully locked it. Then he turned the case upright and dripped several drops of Super Glue into each lock opening, permanently freezing the pins. Should the blackmailer ask for the key, Draxler would simply tell him he did not bring it, because if he had been stopped by the police he did not want them to be able to unlock it. He knew they could not force it open without a search warrant, for which they would have no probable cause. Besides, the blackmailer had opened a similar case without a key when he had broken into Draxler's house. And why would Draxler try to cheat him? The blackmailer still had all the evidence. Then, as the blackmailer drove off, Draxler would detonate the bomb. For safety, he took the battery out of the transmitter and put the deadly items in opposite pockets of his suit jacket.

He would watch this man die as he had Haidar. With Haidar, he had simply driven by as the young Arab was about to fire his gun, and pushed the button on the transmitter. The command detonation was a symphony of sorts, the combination and culmination of every aspect of his plan, the thunderous and fiery final chord of destruction. Seacard's $5 million—or, more accurately, $4 million—were gone forever. And Haidar's death sealed, with finality, the student's sole responsibility for the costly but failed extortion.

Draxler loaded his luggage into the car. He had one stop to make before heading to Detroit—to pick up the million dollars.

Again, he drove erratically to ensure that he was not being followed. By the time he reached the campus, he was satisfied he was alone. Using a series of keys, he made his way to a forgotten storage room in the basement of the physics building. He squeezed through a maze of dusty old filing cabinets and desks. At the far end, partially turned toward the wall, was an old standing bank safe. When Draxler had originally discovered it, there had been no combination for it. He called half a dozen locksmiths before he found one experienced enough to open it and then to change the combination. Draxler watched him carefully and later reprogrammed it himself.

He opened the safe and took out a traveling bag containing the money. He checked its contents and then put it in the trunk of his car with the rest of his luggage.

An hour later, Draxler stood uncomfortably next to a phone outside Doc's bar. The prostitutes kept approaching him, reasoning that a white dude in a suit must be looking for a date. Even though he was mesmerized by how they used their tongues to demonstrate why they should be financially courted, he politely but firmly declined their offers. In his left hand, he held the attaché case containing the blackmailer's payoff. Draxler knew from his own crime that the burglar was probably watching him to make sure he was alone and that he had the money.

A half a block away, a dark-colored station wagon with ladders lashed to the roof sat unnoticed. Hollings lay in the back, watching Draxler through his scope. He dialed his cellular phone.

Draxler answered cautiously. "Hello."

"Got the cash, Doc?"

Knowing the blackmailer was watching, he answered yes and, as if his subconscious was verifying it, held the case up to the phone. Draxler smiled to himself. If there was justice in

America, it took Sebastian Draxler to arrange it. "Where do you want it?"

Jackledge arrived at the old Cadillac plant a half hour before Devlin was supposed to meet him. He parked his car strategically so as to invite Devlin to park next to him and to enter through the nearby door.

Jackledge positioned himself in the building's deeper shadows so that when Devlin came through the door he could quickly shoot him. He could not take any more chances. Someone as resourceful as Devlin must not be given a chance to react to the situation. He could not allow himself the time to enjoy this agent's impending death, as he had with the others. Devlin was different; his dying was simply a matter of survival for Jackledge.

The others had been strictly revenge. They had ended his dream. When he had told his parents that he was having his final interview before becoming an FBI agent, they could not find any fault. At last, he was going to achieve something even they had to respect. But when he was rejected, his parents' criticisms became even more enraging, endlessly questioning the direction of his life.

But he had made the FBI pay for it. He had won three separate victories, maybe more glorious than actually becoming an agent. Even the fourth agent he had killed to cover his tracks was a victory of sorts. He wished he could scream his achievement into his mother's and father's faces, forever quieting the inadequacies of their own lives. But now Mike Devlin was trying to ruin everything. He had to be killed and the list of names from the Bridgeline glove factory destroyed. It would be chalked up as just another random killing by the Gentkiller. He loaded six hollowpoints into his gun and waited.

Mike Devlin cruised along Jefferson Avenue. He could see the dying outline of the dinosauric Cadillac plant. He felt no urgency but rather an unusual contentment now that he had settled his differences with Knox. As far as his problems with

Sudder were concerned, he had done what he thought was right. Now he could only sit back and accept what the Big Dealer handed him.

Jackledge heard a car's tires crunching stones in the parking lot. They slowed to a stop. Then the metallic disengaging of a car door from its frame and one final, slamming thud. Jackledge held his breath involuntarily, until the throbbing pulse in his neck made him noiselessly release the air in his lungs. The worn steel door nearest the parked cars groaned as it opened. Jackledge held his breath again as the half-opened door cast a khaki light immediately in front of it. He pushed himself an inch deeper into the lifeless shadows.

All at once, he was there in front of Jackledge, his back a perfect target.

Jackledge fired once, then again and again until he had one bullet left. From the floor, only the slightest sounds of life could be heard. Jackledge rolled him over and saw that he was still alive. "You are one tough motherfucker, Devlin. But you lose." With protracted enjoyment, he raised his gun and fired his last shot through the heart of his fifth victim. "I'll take that list of names you got from Codswallor too." He picked up the briefcase that lay next to the body and walked quickly out of the building. He was overdue at his parents'.

He was in control of his life again. It was funny, he thought, how murder was the only thing that could now offset the misery that his mother and father stirred daily within him. He wondered if he could stop.

⫴ EPILOGUE ⫴

Even death could not remove Sebastian Draxler's mask of angry arrogance. Devlin stood over him and took a moment to study his discontented face. There was no fear, no surrender, just a confirmation that life was maddeningly arbitrary.

Devlin had watched Draxler enter, heard the shots, and then saw Jackledge leave with the professor's briefcase. Devlin assumed he thought it contained the names of the Bridgeline employees. As soon as he recovered the money, he would deal with Jackledge.

Draxler's keys were in his suit coat, and as soon as Devlin took them he noticed one of them was unexplainably hot. He searched the pocket they had been in and found a square nine-volt battery and the small black plastic cap that normally protected its terminals. It probably had been knocked off during the shooting and the key had completed the circuit, causing the battery to heat up the key. What had Tom Michaels said when Devlin asked him about detonating transmitters? *They work off batteries.*

Then he remembered the one day of bomb training he had received in the Marine Corps. The technician, when priming the bomb, always kept the hell box with him. That way, someone couldn't accidently hook it up and set off the bomb while he was standing next to it. Devlin searched Draxler's other pockets and found what looked like an ordinary garage-door opener, except a section had been cut out of the bottom. Devlin jammed the battery into it as though he were speed-loading a magazine into an automatic pistol. For his own safety, he took the battery out and put it in an empty pocket.

He walked out to the Audi, opened the trunk, and searched the luggage. The money sat unassumingly in a plain, unlocked case. After a quick count, he realized that the entire million dollars was there, and he transferred it to the trunk of his Bureau car. Then he searched Draxler's car for a bomb. When he could not find one, he got in his car and drove fifty yards and got out. Using the hood of the Bureau car as a shield, he loaded the battery into the transmitter, aimed it at Draxler's car, and pressed the button. When he heard nothing but the device's sending tone, he knew where the bomb was.

He drove to Doc's bar and parked behind the station wagon. Hollings got out and slid into the passenger seat of Devlin's car. He handed Devlin the cellular telephone he had been using. "Thanks. It came in handy," he said. "Did you get the money?"

"Yes."

"Do you think he was going to pay me?"

Devlin thumbed the transmitter in his pocket. "I don't think so."

"How'd you know he'd have the money with him?"

"The day you broke into his house, I called our airline contact and had a stop put on their computers. After your first call to him, he made reservations for Germany. A one-way ticket. His flight leaves in an hour."

"Where's he at now?"

Devlin looked at the gray, withering face of his informant. It had been only four days since he had gotten him out of jail, but the cancer's accelerating greed was obvious. Although he appeared weakened, a recent nobility had found its way into his eyes. Devlin owed him the truth. "He's dead."

"You?"

"Someone else . . ."

Gracefully, Hollings held up his hand. "Mike, I don't want to know."

"Do you need anything?"

"The only thing I needed was not to be in jail when I died. And you letting me help you with this allows me to exit with a little dignity."

"If your family ever needs anything . . ."

"I appreciate it, but they're mostly gone." Hollings held out his hand, and Devlin gripped it sincerely.

After he watched Hollings's car drive off, Devlin got on the expressway and headed west. Fifteen minutes later, he drove slowly by the small frame house that Jackledge rented on Detroit's northwest side. There was no garage, and Jackledge's car was not in the driveway.

Devlin parked half a block away and dialed Shanahan on the cellular phone. "Bill, are you awake?"

"Yeah. Sort of."

"Write down this name and address." He gave Shanahan Jackledge's full name and address.

"Who's he?"

"He's an applicant who was rejected by John, Brian, and Temper. He was also fired from Bridgeline."

"Do you think it's him?"

"It's him," Devlin answered with simple, unemotional authority.

"Do we have enough for a search warrant?"

"Just get out there; something will come up. And, Bill, you didn't get this from me." Devlin hung up and called Jerome Wicks, giving him the same information.

Out of his briefcase, he took the envelope he had received that morning from Temper. He looked again at the list of fired employees from the glove factory she had enclosed. He had written Jackledge's home and work numbers next to his name. He dialed his home phone. There was no answer. When he had called Jackledge at work to set up the interview, he pretended to get a call from the factory's owner, knowing that Jackledge would then want to eliminate Devlin. He had Hollings send Draxler to the Cadillac plant for the payoff, and Jackledge had assumed he was Devlin. Ironic, Devlin thought; Temper Hanlon had solved her own murder. And now Devlin had to keep his promise to "throw in a little extra" for her.

Jackledge, returning from his parents', pulled his car into the driveway. He got out carrying Draxler's briefcase and disappeared into the house. Moments later, Shanahan's car pulled to the curb a couple of houses from Jackledge's. A few minutes later, Wicks parked behind Shanahan. Neither of them saw Devlin. He drove around the block and hit the redial on the cellular phone. After rolling down his window, he jammed the nine-volt battery back into the transmitter. As the phone started to ring, he drove down Jackledge's street, coming up behind Shanahan and Wicks.

"Hello."

Devlin recognized Jackledge's voice, and as he passed in front of his house, he said, "Welcome to hell!" He aimed the detonator out of the window and pushed the button.

Abruptly, a crushing explosion launched screaming light from every window on the first floor of Jackledge's house. Stoically, Devlin watched in his rearview mirror as Shanahan and Wicks ran toward the house.

He drove along the surface streets heading toward the Cass Corridor. Suddenly, he felt exhausted, but he had one more stop to make.

Wicks had said it best. Detroit was one big, self-cleaning oven. Draxler had been seen trolling around Doc's. The police would guess that he was the victim of a hooker-robbery gone bad. And Jackledge, soon to be exposed as the Gentkiller, was killed playing with explosives.

It was almost 1 A.M. when Devlin parked his car up the street from St. Barnabas. He had carefully avoided telling Riley Smith about the million dollars Draxler had taken from Seacard, so there were only four people who had known of its existence: Devlin, Draxler, Temper, and Hollings. Soon Devlin would be the only one left. He took Draxler's case out of the trunk and got back into the car. Seacard security had prepared five separate lists of serial numbers, one for each box. Devlin checked the bills and identified the corresponding list. He walked up on the front porch of the hospice. There were no lights on the first floor. Quietly, he lifted the large metal cover on the chute next to the door and shoved the case through it. He walked quickly down the stairs and was surprised to be caught by Father Richter's voice delivering its nonspecific "God bless you."

Devlin got back in his car and tore up the list of serial numbers corresponding to box number three. As he drove away, he slowly let the pieces float from his window, joining all the other meaningless litter that had been abandoned in the streets of Detroit.

At eleven the next morning, the SAC's conference room was filled to capacity with managers. It was back to business as usual: The "busy" supervisors were again arriving demonstratively late and the really insignificant decisions were growing in importance.

The briefings had all been good news. The director was arriving within the hour to give a press conference announcing the solution to the Gentkill investigation. Also, Sudder had hinted that he was retiring. And although he would only say he had been offered a job with a major corporation, everyone in the office by then had guessed he was bound for Seacard Industries. He said it was with a great deal of pride that he was able to do so, after solving both the extortion and Gentkill.

The two supervisors coordinating the director's visit had just finished their briefing. Sudder said, "Sounds like everything is under control, but as I have previously ordered, I want to be notified immediately when his limo enters the garage, so I can personally ride down in the elevator to prevent a recurrence of what happened during his last visit to the office." Both the supervisors noted Sudder's instructions.

Sudder turned to Jim Harrison. "How about updating everyone on Gentkill?"

"Late last night, Bill Shanahan received an anonymous tip that David Nelson Jackledge was in fact responsible for the deaths of our four agents. Shanahan immediately went to Jackledge's home in Detroit and, as he arrived, witnessed an explosion inside that killed the subject. Shanahan searched the house, and under Jackledge's bed he found a metal lockbox. When he got it open, he found Lawson's badge, Blankenship's credentials, and Hanlon's Bureau issue. Shanahan also found another gun in the same room as the body and he thinks it's in good enough condition to be test-fired. It's being flown back to the lab right now and we should have an answer in an hour or so. Probably while the director is still here."

Sudder smiled. "Good."

"We checked his name in indices. No connection to Agent Fox could be found. But Jackledge was an applicant, rejected by an interview board made up of Lawson, Blankenship, and Hanlon. Evidently, failure is becoming more and more unacceptable in our society."

Sudder said, "Good work. Now I'd like the ASAC, Supervisors Harrison and Wiggens, and the principal legal advisor to come to my office."

When everyone was in Sudder's office, he buzzed his secretary. "Send Devlin in."

Harrison said, "I don't think we need everyone in here for this."

The SAC smiled. "The people in this room have to give agents orders every day. I think it's important they see what happens to someone who thrives on disobedience."

Devlin walked in and a smirk of impending vengeance overtook Sudder's face when he saw that the agent was not carrying any paperwork. The SAC looked around the room. "You're all witnesses. This man has repeatedly ignored my orders. It is now past eleven A.M. and, contrary to my instructions, he has not submitted a preliminary report in the Seacard extortion matter." The managers in the room squirmed at the obvious display of Sudder's conflict of interests. Impervious to their reaction, Sudder continued. "Do you have any defense to offer?"

Unexpectedly, Devlin laughed. "The reason I didn't prepare that report is that *I* did not want to be an accomplice to a multi-million-dollar insurance fraud."

Sudder sat in his chair, stunned. "What the hell are you talking about? You're not going to bullshit your way out of this."

Devlin walked around the huge table to the SAC, which caused him to recoil slightly. He dialed the switchboard and said, "Would you put that call on this line, please?" The phone rang, and Devlin hit the speaker switch. Riley Smith came on the line. "Riley, I'm in the SAC's office. Can you give us a run-down of what's happened out there this morning?"

"We have arrested James Pendleton"—Sudder's face became knotted with confusion—"and he has already confessed. When the extortionist started setting off bombs and the chairman of the board ordered him to pay the demand, Pendleton loaded up one of the boxes with paper and took the million. He hid it in a safety-deposit box at the Grayton State Bank because Mike had convinced him that all the bills had been entered into NCIC, although they hadn't. Pendleton was demanding that the FBI give an official report to their insurance company so that the case would be closed and the money's serial numbers could be removed from the computer."

Sudder sat paralyzed, now understanding why and how Pendleton had manipulated him as part of the scheme. The office's principal legal advisor asked, "Riley, why did you arrest him in the first place?"

"He rented a safety-deposit box at the bank, and the day of the drop, he visited it. After interviewing him, Mike became suspicious, and we tried to get a search warrant. But the judge was not satisfied with the probable cause. He thinks safety-deposit boxes are kind of a sacred cow." Devlin glanced at Sudder, who seemed to have stopped breathing. "My contact at the bank told me that the president was a close friend of Pendleton's and that anything he heard he would immediately pass on to him. So after the judge turned us down for the search warrant, Mike came up with the idea that we go back to the judge and get a search warrant for Pendleton's person or carrying bag. It would be based on my going to the president of the bank and asking him what was necessary to get a search warrant for the box, hopefully causing him to notify Pendleton. The judge ruled that if this resulted in Pendleton visiting his box within twenty-four hours, we could search him for currency with the extortion serial numbers as he left the bank. That's exactly what we did, and now I'm sitting here with a million dollars of Seacard's money."

"Thanks, Riley," Devlin said, and turned off the speakerphone. He sat down in front of Sudder and stared at him, while addressing everyone else in the room. "You're going to have to excuse us." The group of careerists, knowing when distance was politically advantageous, quickly filed out of the room. "Malcolm, it's time."

"For what?"

"To find another job."

"Go to hell."

"You really don't see the damage you've done here, do you?"

Sudder smiled sadistically. "Damage? The director is about to arrive here, and as soon as he's briefed about how the leadership in this division is responsible for solving the murders *and* for luring Pendleton into giving up the million dollars, I'll probably be promoted on the spot."

Devlin got up to leave and smiled resignedly. "I wouldn't be surprised."

Fifteen minutes later, Sudder received a call that the director's limousine was about to enter the federal building garage. He buzzed his secretary to have her find someone to operate the intraoffice elevator and take him to the basement to meet the director. When she did not answer, he dialed a series of supervisors, who also did not answer. He concluded that they were all busy preparing for the director. From his desk, he took the override key and hurried to the elevator. It stood waiting, doors open.

He stepped in and put the key in the override lock. He turned it to the right, and the doors closed. But the car started rising. Sudder was startled, because the FBI office was on the top floor. He did not know that reprogramming the elevator's computer would cause it to rise one additional floor, a floor normally used only by maintenance employees and repairmen.

The doors opened onto the dark and dusty twenty-seventh floor. Two tall men wearing ski masks got in; the thinner one pointed a putter threateningly at Sudder as the doors closed.

With Assistant Director Welles Findley close at his heels, Bob August entered the McNamara Building through the garage door in the basement. Already waiting at the elevator were a number of television crews. With a series of clicks, their cameras' bright lights came on, and one of the reporters, microphone in hand, stepped up to the FBI boss. "Director August, is it true you're here to relieve the Special Agent in Charge?"

Surprised by the question, the director looked straight ahead at the elevator doors. The arrival light lit up, and as the doors opened, the intrusive cameras swung around and shot into the car.

On the walls were several poster-size black and white photos chronicling Sudder's unflattering exit from the Friends of Youth fund-raiser. Standing with his back to the doors, each wrist handcuffed to the side handrail, was Malcolm Sudder. He was clad only in boxer shorts, and a large cardboard sign hung on his back:

WE HAD HIM KEEP HIS SHORTS ON THIS TIME
BECAUSE ONE ASSHOLE IS ENOUGH TO LOOK AT
—The Agents of Detroit

Ignoring the light rain, twelve-year-old Sean Lawson stood in the batter's box and waited intently. The pitcher wound up, and as he released the ball, the boy saw it exit his hand between the thumb and forefinger—*curveball*! Patiently, he kept his weight on his back foot waiting for the slowly arcing sphere. At the perfect moment, his body uncoiled in an explosion. The ball seemed to accelerate as it disappeared deep over the centerfield fence. He had never hit a ball that far, and he allowed himself a small smile.

From the pitcher's mound, Mike Devlin smiled back.

**Mike Devlin's got some more problems.
And Detroit's just the beginning of them.**

**WITNESS TO THE TRUTH
by Paul Lindsay**

For a glimpse of this explosive novel, please read on. . . .

As Devlin slowed his dark blue Chevrolet to a stop, he searched the house's driveway. He was looking for a new black Mercedes-Benz with Alabama plates. At the end of the driveway, a car was angled around the back of the house barely visible from the street. A black Mercedes—but with a Michigan plate. Even in the dense light the car's silky newness humbled its surroundings. A curly telephone antenna rose from the top of the rear window. Devlin pulled an old pair of artillery binoculars from under the seat. They cut through the dimness between the two cars, allowing him to read not only the license plate but more important, the plate holder: "Dixie Motors, Birmingham, Alabama." He smiled. The plate had been changed, but not the holder.

He took his foot from the brake and silently coasted until he was out of sight of the house. Adjusting his side mirror to watch the house behind him, he opened a pulpy tan folder. He took out a blue three-page document. The color demanded expeditious handling, but Devlin judged urgency by content, not color. This one was hot. The Birmingham, Alabama, office of the FBI had sent it to the Detroit office. The subject of the communication was Leroy Osgood Taylor, also known as Leroy Thomas, also known as "Lee." Wanted by the Birmingham Police Department, Taylor, a large-scale cocaine trafficker, was charged with a double homicide. Two of his dealers had

307

"fucked up his money," so he summarily terminated their employment by shooting them each three times in the back of the head. Both victims were sixteen-year-old black males. One of Taylor's accomplices later confessed, naming Lee as the shooter. He also told the Birmingham police that immediately after the murders, Lee had fled to Detroit, leaving a telephone number where he could be contacted. Taylor had reasoned that he could easily hide in Detroit's lush forest of dope dealers and murderers. Also included in the communication was a detailed description of Taylor and his car. A mug shot was enclosed.

The last paragraph was captioned "Leads." It read, "Detroit will attempt to locate and apprehend the subject through telephone (313) 555-7113."

The last line on the page was underlined, warning, "*Consider the subject armed and dangerous.*"

The telephone number came back to the house where the Mercedes was parked.

He made a decision. A decision he knew would later be challenged.

"DE Four-one to Central," Devlin said into his radio handset.

"This is Central; go ahead, Four-one."

"In ten minutes call the Fifth Precinct and advise them that an agent needs assistance arresting an individual wanted for murder in Alabama. The address is 7778 Ashland."

"7778 Ashland. That's ten-four, Four-one."

Quietly he got out of the car. Without shutting the door completely, he closed it far enough to extinguish the interior lights.

Devlin went back to his trunk and took out a screwdriver and two other items known to car thieves as a slim-jim and a slammer. With these three tools a thief could steal a car in less than sixty seconds. The slim-jim, made from a strip of flexible metal twenty-five inches long with a square notch cut at the side of one end, was a tool requiring patience and a certain touch. Conversely, the slammer, originally used for auto body repair, was a two-and-a-half-foot-long rod with a self-tapping screw device at one end and a heavy handle at the other. A five-pound free-floating metal weight slid along the rod. It was a tool requiring only strength.

Cautiously, Devlin walked to the house. He was relieved to see that all the windows were closed and dark. As he turned up the driveway, he reached inside his suit jacket and unsnapped his holster, raising his stainless-steel magnum an inch, then letting it drop loosely back into its leather casing. He lightened his footsteps, but they still seemed too loud. As he reached the driver's door of Taylor's car, he looked back toward the street protectively. He inserted the slim-jim between the window and door frame, pushing it down until he could feel the locking mechanism. In short, upsweeping arcs, he worked the metal strip until the notch caught the release arm of the lock. A quick pull, and the door was open. The interior had the smothering odor of dead cigarette smoke made more irritating by the residue of some syrupy cologne.

Devlin felt under the seat. No gun. If Taylor had one, it was in the house with him. The telephone was appended to the dashboard and appeared to be functional once the engine was started. He inserted the screw end of the slammer into the ignition, turning it stiffly until half of the case-hardened screw was anchored in the ignition lock. Holding the handle with his right hand, he threw the sliding weight hard into the handle. Twice more he slammed the weight away from the ignition, which popped out still attached to the tool. Working by feel only, he guided the screwdriver into the electrical circuits that had previously been protected by the ignition lock and turned the starting mechanism clockwise. The engine started inaudibly, and the phone lit up.

Quickly he dialed the number he had received from Birmingham. After six rings a drowsy black male answered with an irritated "Yeah."

In a black voice Devlin said, "Lee, day axed me ta call en tell ya dat da po-lice is comin. Day be der in fit-teen minute." He hung up.

* * *

The side door of the house exploded as Taylor came running out wearing pants, no shoes, and pulling on a shirt. His car keys in his teeth. He unlocked the car door and quickly got in, attempting to put the key in the ignition. When he could not find the keyhole with the usual thrust of the key, he realized the lock was gone.

"What the—?" he wondered out loud, but his unfinished question was answered when he felt the unmistakable hardness of Devlin's magnum pressed against the back of his head.

"Guess I'm a little early, Lee."

Witness to the Truth
by Paul Lindsay

Published by Fawcett Books.
Available wherever books are sold.